Also by Jack M. Bickham
published by Tor Books

Ariel
Day Seven
Miracleworker
The Regensburg Legacy

TIEBREAKER

JACK M. BICKHAM

TOR

A TOM DOHERTY ASSOCIATES BOOK
NEW YORK

TIEBREAKER

A TOR BOOK
Published by Tom Doherty Associates, Inc.
49 West 24 Street
New York, NY 10010

ISBN: 0-312-93144-1

First edition: June 1989
0 9 8 7 6 5 4 3 2 1

one

The last thing I had on my mind was somebody breaking into my condominium and dragging me into the past.

What I was worried about right now was a heart attack.

I could imagine the headlines in the papers the next day: *Former Wimbledon Champ Dies on Court*. And the sub-head, *Heart Attack Fells Smith in Charity Tourney Match*. What they wouldn't add was the obvious: *40-Year-Old Idiots Should Not Try to Beat Hotshot Kids*.

It was early July in Richardson, Texas, my home, just north of Dallas. Which means hot. Ten-thirty at night, when old folks should be home with their feet propped up, ready for Johnny Carson. I had been on the court with the hotshot TCU varsity player for three and a half hours, which was at least two hours too long, and we were both getting pretty sick of it.

Hotshot, whose real name was Randy Ferrell, looked like he wanted to kill me.

My legs felt dead already.

It was just a little community tournament, the first annual Richardson Charity Open, ostensibly held for the sole purpose of raising money for the Heart Fund but in reality a promotion for the tennis club, which badly needed an infusion of new-member money. The men's field, open to anyone with a racket and the fifty-dollar fee, had started with forty-one hackers, five good junior players, a half-dozen solid seniors, seven intermediate club players, the club pro, Hotshot, and me.

Hotshot, TCU's number one, took out our best paying member in the quarters, 6–0, 6–0, and then humiliated Jack Stephensen, our club pro/manager, 6–1, 6–3 in the semis. Hotshot had toyed with Jack in the second set, hitting cute dink shots and netting some serves unnecessarily to prolong the fun, which Jack had too much pride to end by giving up or purposely hitting out on crucial points. It hurt to watch it.

I had come up through the easier half of the bracket, resisting the temptation to go dumpers and get the hell out of the thing, with the result that I had walked onto the club's lighted center court a little before seven this evening for my turn facing the lion who had eaten everybody else.

The Southwest had been having one of its normal July heatwaves, and it was still 90 degrees despite the hour. The green paint on the concrete was splattered with dark spots, probably my sweat although I secretly felt like it might be my blood. Almost everyone had gone from the four-row bleachers and my legs were just about gone, too. I had long since pushed myself well beyond the limits of sanity for no good reason except my dislike for Hotshot and the way he had humiliated a friend of mine.

Across the net, he bounced a ball at the line, getting ready to serve with that artificial, practiced-a-million-times, machinelike motion that most of them were taught now. His white shorts and shirt were as sweat-soaked as mine, and his blond hair looked pasted to his forehead. But he was still only twenty, a beautiful athlete, and I wasn't getting any younger.

He almost surely had me at last. He was up 8–10, 6–4, 11–10 and 40–love, triple set point, and we might have been safely home an hour ago if I hadn't had the brilliant

2

idea of making this tournament follow the old-time scoring rules as in the Davis Cup, no tiebreakers, to give the players their money's worth. Or if I had had the sense to go in the can two hours ago when my legs started to give out.

Too late for any of that. He served.

Somehow I got my Prince composite on the yellow blur and bounced it down the line, hitting the back corner, close. He glided over to get it and I thought I saw the angle and guessed, chuffing up toward the net. This is ridiculous, I thought, and then: *Come on, legs! You can do it!* Here was the ball, just where I had guessed. How nice. Putaway.

Hotshot slammed his racket onto the pavement and turned and yelled at the middle-aged woman calling the back line. She looked scared but stubborn. He wheeled and strode across the court to glare up at Dr. Hugh Olafson, our volunteer in the chair.

"That ball was out a foot!" Hotshot screamed.

Dr. Olafson, a lean, gray-haired man of sixty with bottle-bottom eyeglasses, leaned forward solicitously. "The ball was called good."

"It was out! Couldn't you see it was out?" Hotshot's face was very red. "Can you see *anything* through those glasses?"

"The call was good," Dr. Olafson told him, "and I agree with the call."

"You're idiots! You're the worst stupid so-called officials I've ever seen! What's the matter with you people around here? You're blind!"

Dr. Olafson leaned back in his parasol chair and shifted into High Phlegmatic. "Continue play."

"What are you? Homers? Is that what this is? A homer job for the old guy over there? I've never seen so many bad calls! Don't you people realize who the star of this tournament is? You don't screw the player who brought in the crowds! That stupid goddamn woman back there couldn't call a line if we were playing with volleyballs! This is the worst thing I've ever seen!"

He kept raving and hurling insults, his voice getting louder and shriller. Dr. Olafson listened with an eerie calm.

I had had an interesting conversation with Dr. Olafson in the club bar a few weeks earlier after an especially gross bit of bad acting by one of our spoiled millionaire tennis teenagers in a match shown on ESPN. Dr. Olafson had pronounced tennis referees who allowed such behavior to be significantly lacking in guts. He, he had told me at that time, knew the solution.

Now he leaned forward to peer down at Hotshot through those thick glasses, and applied the solution. "Play. Now."

"*No! I'm not playing until you change that call! I—*"

"Undue delay," the good doctor said. "Forfeit one point."

"*What?*"

"The score is now forty–thirty," Dr. Olafson told him. He added, "Play."

I thought the kid might explode.

"Play," the doctor repeated with significant emphasis.

Ferrell stormed back to his racket, picked it up, bashed it against the pavement, wiped his forehead on his arm, gave the good doctor a killing look, and signaled for the ballboy to toss him balls. Which the kid, pale, did.

I waited, doing a little shuffle to prove to myself that I wasn't comatose. *Come on, legs.*

The ball went up over there and the racket came down and the yellow blur went wide to my forehand. I stabbed and got it back down the line. Hotshot blasted a backhand to the other far corner, a clear winner. Nobody in his right mind, especially a forty-year-old magazine writer not in the very best of shape, would have gone after it.

So naturally I went over there and scooped up a lob that looked like it was going nice and deep. Hotshot scurried back from the net he had just taken. I staggered up there behind my lob. Which was a mistake.

There was a puff of wind. The ball fell shorter than I

4

had expected. I saw Hotshot cock his arm for an overhead. He could pass me on either side for the winner, but his glance betrayed where he planned to hit it. Right between my eyes.

Self-defense is a wonderful thing. I got my racket in front of my face just in time. The ball hit it, turning the handle in my hand. By a freak of fate, the resulting dropshot volley plinked over, a netcord, and fell for a winner.

The kid, with dead eyes, walked halfway in to the net. "Goddamn you, old man," he said softly. "Why don't you just give up?"

I grinned at him.

So now we were at deuce.

It would be just wonderful to report that I pulled it out after that. God knows I tried, punishing myself a lot more. We went to deuce another eleven times, and I had two break points. But finally I had to make a passing shot with him coming to net, and I guessed crosscourt, which he guessed too, and he put away the final winner.

At the net he gave me a wet fish, waved insolently at Dr. Olafson, gathered his gear, and headed for the lockers. I sat on the courtside player bench and started setting a new world's record for Gatorade while the last dozen onlookers filed out of the stands. I removed my knee brace.

Jack Stephensen came over and sat beside me. "You okay?"

"Sure."

"You're white."

"Always have been."

He ignored the feeble humor. "I thought you had the prick."

"Me, too."

He studied me for a long moment. "Hey. I know you didn't even want to play in this thing. I didn't think the committee was going to be able to talk you into it. You didn't have to half kill yourself out here tonight."

"It was fun."

"Balls. I know why you did it, and I just want you to know I appreciate it, Brad."

"Okay."

Jack walked away. A skinny young man with pale pink glasses strolled over to take his place. His name was Jess Beurline and he had been covering the tourney, more or less, for the newspaper in Plano. He was a recent graduate of North Texas State at Denton.

"Good match," Beurline told me with the solemn authority of the young.

"Lot of fun," I agreed, draining another Gatorade.

"I guess he was better than you expected."

I looked up at him. "What do you mean?"

"Well, it was pretty obvious that you could have put him away early."

"Oh?"

"Sure, everyone could see that. He was tight and you were moving well. I guess you wanted to extend the match for the crowd."

I wondered what match he had been watching, but didn't reply.

"Then," Beurline went on, "he got loose and you saw your tactical mistake, but the momentum had changed."

"Oh, right. Momentum."

"I guess that's why you went in the tank there at the end."

"In the tank?"

"Sure. You went crosscourt three times in a row. Anybody could see you were throwing in the towel."

I gathered up my equipment.

Beurline persisted. "Not to worry. The untrained observer would never notice, and I won't mention it in my story."

"Thank you, Jess. I deeply appreciate it."

He wouldn't quit. "Tell me, Brad: I guess Randy was really on tonight in the latter stages. Did he surprise you? Is he, at his best, as good as any you've ever played?"

I thought fleetingly of Connors in LA and Borg at Wimbledon. Then decided explanations were too hard. I said, "He's pretty wonderful."

He jotted a final note and closed his book. "I'd like to do a feature on you some time. Think we could set up a time?"

"Call me when you're ready."

"Great. What I'm thinking about is a real in-depth look at the life of a former tennis great who writes freelance tennis coverage for the magazines, and plays a little at a local club. Sort of a Where-Are-They-Now piece. How does a man handle his advancing years, and so on."

"Maybe we should wait until I move into a senior citizens' village for that one, Jess."

He stared. Then he said, "Oh. You're joking."

"Good for you."

He left, puzzled. I limped to the clubhouse, where the muscle spasms started. I was feeling sorry for myself when I heard the ugly sounds coming from the toilets and realized that my worthy opponent was in the end stall, casting his bread upon the water. That made me feel a little better.

A little over an hour later I drove home. As I approached my condominium, I saw a faint, moving light against the slatted curtains of the living room. I hadn't left any lights on, and I lived alone, so no one was supposed to be inside.

I slowed the Bronco and looked more sharply from the street. From this angle I couldn't see any light. Maybe I had been mistaken. I didn't think so.

Rather than pulling in the front driveway, I went on to the next corner, turned right, found the alley entrance, turned right again, and poked up the narrow concrete alley with my lights turned off. Behind my condo I parked on the garage ramp out of sight from inside.

Going soundlessly to the side door of my garage, I unlocked it and slipped inside. I didn't need a light to find the shelving that held the camping gear, or the .38 revolver tucked inside a sleepingbag cover.

My key opened the back door to the kitchen without noise. Everything black in there, but a thin bead of gray under the closed door that led to the dining room, and the living room beyond. Rather than going that way, I used the side hallway to reach the front of the house. The front door to the living room was closed too, but I could hear the faintest sounds beyond it.

It was one of those sliding pocket doors. Made a racket when I slid it hard into the wall and went inside, hitting the wall light switch in the same motion.

The faint light I had spotted earlier was from the television set, which had a western on it. That had been the source of the sound, too.

He was sitting comfortably in my recliner chair, his sock feet stretched out and one of my beers in his hand. My Smith & Wesson didn't seem to startle him at all.

"Brad," he said, unmoving. "Good morning."

two

"You asshole!" I said.

He grinned at me and my weapon. "This is great. This is really dramatic."

He was tall but not as lanky as I remembered him from our last meeting almost five years previously, wearing jeans and a madras shirt and camp loafers. In those days he had looked like a kid, but now he had lost a little of his sandy hair, and his face had been roughened by unacceptable losses. Under some circumstances I might have been happy to see him again.

"Where did you park?" he asked improbably.

I put the revolver on the TV set with an angry thunk. "You were really stupid to come in here this way, you know."

"If you had parked in front, or opened your garage door, I would have heard you and turned on more lights so you wouldn't get all paranoid."

"I might have shot your head off."

"Are you kidding me? I've seen you shoot."

"What do you want, Collie?"

He uncoiled from my chair. "You look a little strung out."

"What do you *want*, Collie?"

9

Collie Davis turned the TV off and sat down again, but this time on the couch, leaving me my chair. "It was really pretty important to see you as soon as possible, but not in the public eye."

So he had driven into the fringes of the neighborhood, walked up the alley, picked the lock on one of my doors, and come in like a second-rate burglar. It didn't strike me as all that smart. But there had always been things about the Company that didn't make a lot of sense to me, so I chose not to argue about it.

I repeated, "What do you want, Collie?"

"We've got a little contract job."

"I'm not interested in going to Norman or someplace and interviewing college candidates."

"How would you feel about Belgrade?"

"What state is that in?"

"Funny. Shall I start at the beginning?"

"You can start," I told him, "by getting out of here."

"We need a tennis player. Tennis journalist."

"What for?"

"Go to Belgrade for their new tournament, do some journalism, play in the celebrity matches, handle something routine for us on the side."

"The Belgrade International is in less than two weeks."

"Right."

"That doesn't give me or anyone else a lot of time."

"It gives enough."

"Why me?"

"You fit the job description. There aren't many who do."

"Get Ted Sherman," I said, naming another former tennis pro who, like me, had done some scut work for them in earlier years while earning his real money on the players' circuit.

"We prefer you. You're more reliable and you've had more training." He paused to light a cigarette. "Besides, he's in the hospital with back trouble."

"So I'm the best man for the job because I'm the only man?"

He ignored that. "Do you know Danisa Lechova?"

"The Yugoslav singles player? Sure. I know who she is. We've never met."

"She's twenty-one now," Collie told me unnecessarily, "and most people think she'll be the number one women's player in the world by next year this time. They've brought her along very slowly, evidently guarding against the kind of burnout that seems to hit a lot of the potentially great female players just as they start to win big. But many people think she'll be better than Navratilova, Mandlikova, or Graf inside another year. May already be."

I had seen Lechova play on television, and had been impressed. She was tall, slender, blond, beautiful, and absolutely unflappable, combining the cool of a Chrissie with the dynamite attack of a Martina. "She's great," I conceded. "So what?"

"So she didn't play in the Wimbledon that just finished."

"Strained knee, I heard."

"Wrong."

"What's right, then?"

"The Yugoslav government kept her out. Now they've set up this whole invitational tourney in Belgrade to showcase her and her sister."

"Are you telling me she wasn't injured—that they kept her from traveling to England for the biggest tournament in the world?"

"Precisely. They pulled her passport. Her sister Hannah's, too. They can't leave Yugoslavia."

"Jesus Christ. Why?"

"Who knows for sure?"

"You do."

"No. Really."

"I think you're lying."

11

He shrugged. "The point is, she's had enough of it. She wants to defect to the U.S."

"Why doesn't she just wait until the U.S. Open in September and walk out of the locker room and ask for asylum? Surely her passport thing will be cleared up by then."

"Don't bet on it."

I thought about it. "Collie, what are you not telling me?"

"Nothing," he said, lying smoothly enough.

"There may be a lot of people over there who would like to come to the West," I pressed. "Why is she of such interest to us? She may be great, but she's still just a tennis player."

Collie's jaw set. "There are good reasons."

"Want to name one?"

"There's no need for you to know."

I sighed. Somehow I had known he would say that. They were very dramatic sometimes, these guys. "All right, then," I said. "Danisa Lechova wants out, you think you can get her out during the tournament over there, and I can help. How?"

"All you have to do is go over there, play in the celebrity, write some copy, interview her a couple of times, and facilitate communication between her and the people who will do the work."

"A go-between."

"Yes."

"Is it that hard for her to talk to people?"

"We can't risk their seeing her talking direct to our people on the scene."

"They watch her that closely?"

"They keep a pretty close eye on her, yes."

" 'They' being the UDBA?"

He looked a lot more uncomfortable. "And possibly the KGB."

12

"The Jugs have never let the Russians meddle in their internal affairs. And you're telling me the UDBA and the KGB are *cooperating* in watching Danisa Lechova?"

"It's an unusual case, Brad," he said lamely.

"I think you better tell me what's so special about this girl."

"I've told you as much as I need to. Besides, your part is relatively straightforward."

"Right. The last time one of you gave me that line, I almost got my kneecaps crushed."

"This is different. This is easy."

"Just dodge the UDBA and the KGB. Right."

"Well, there's also a minor problem with her coach."

"Fjbk? Is Fjbk still coaching her?"

"Yes. Miloslav Fjbk. Serb. Not a bad player once. Great coach. You know, I'm sure, about the work he did with Lendl a few years back; Lendl went to him. Fjbk sees Lechova as his greatest production as a coach. Also, although he's an old fart—over forty—it appears he's interested in a lot more than the lovely Danisa's backhand."

I let the old fart comment pass. "So the man who makes contact with her will have a jealous lover glowering nearby."

"He's not her lover. We're told she isn't even aware of his crush. He's . . . circumspect. But our informants say he watches her like a sheepdog, and goes crazy if she so much as smiles at a young man her own age."

"Well, that's good, then," I said. "Fjbk shouldn't worry about me. I'm almost as old a fart as he is."

Collie missed my irony. "You'll go, then." He stabbed his cigarette into the ashtray.

"I don't know. This all sounds fishy as hell to me."

He gave me his sincere, let's-be-honest look, which he did rather well. "Brad, would we lie to you?"

"Yes."

"It's routine."

13

"I may not be very smart, Collie, but I've done enough for you guys to know that these last-minute assignments are never quite routine."

"Well, we realize that it's inconvenient for you. So I'm authorized to offer more than the usual one hundred sixty dollars per diem."

My suspicions deepened, but only enough to resemble the Grand Canyon. "How much more?"

"Whatever you think is fair," he told me with opaque eyes.

"And it's routine," I said sarcastically. "Right."

"The highest authority wants her out of there as soon as possible, and the Belgrade International gives us our chance. You're the only man who can get close enough to her to work well as our go-between. You can name your own contract price on this one. You can make a small fortune."

I walked to the door. "Okay. That's it. Out."

He looked startled. "What did I say?"

"You son of a bitch. I never did *anything* for you people for the money."

"I didn't mean to imply—"

"I'm not rich," I cut in, really steamed, "but I'm getting along. If you want a mercenary, go find one of your turncoats, out making a mint of taxpayer money on the college lecture circuit, telling the kids how awful the CIA is. Tell one of *them* to name their own price. They'll probably be willing to sell you their loyalty again for a week or ten days, if the price is high enough."

"Calm down, Brad. My God."

"You calm down, Collie. On your way out of here."

"I was just trying to show you that it's a vital assignment."

I looked at him and took a few deep breaths. The fatigue and disappointment of the match had frayed my temper. I had been too sensitive, perhaps.

I said, "If I do it, it won't be for the money."

"Fine."

"I'll take per diem. Nothing more."

His lips quirked. "How noble. You and Ollie North, right?"

"Screw you."

Collie yawned.

I told him, "And I might not do it anyway."

He grinned, irritatingly confident again. "We'll provide you with a printout of background information on these people and precisely what we want done, and how we want you to do it."

"When do I get that?"

"You can get it tomorrow, but you'll have to go down to the Federal Building in downtown Dallas and meet me there to read it. The orders say none of it leaves the office."

"You break in here in the middle of the night to avoid our being seen together, and then I'm supposed to waltz into the Federal Building? In broad daylight?"

He looked blank. "Who would recognize you?"

"Thanks!"

"So what do you say? Are you on board for this one?"

"I just have a few thousand questions to clear up first. How do I get an invitation to play in the celebrity over there?"

"We can take care of that."

"I don't have an assignment. It's not believable that a freelance tennis writer flies clear the hell and gone to Belgrade to cover a new tournament on speculation."

"Assignments from one or two of the big tennis magazines can be arranged."

"And I'm supposed to go over there, contact Danisa Lechova, then pass messages back and forth between her and the people who will actually get her out."

"Right. Simple."

I knew *that* was a lie. I asked him more questions. He was evasive. The printouts, he said, would tell me all I needed to know.

There was far too much here that I didn't know. That

was one of the reasons I was interested. It was clear that the Company really wanted this girl . . . was ready to mount an extraordinary effort to get her out promptly. I was very curious why. And I had helped before on no more basis than realization that *somebody* thought it was important.

Still, I kept probing and he kept dodging. We maneuvered for quite a long time. Finally it became clear that I was going to accept or reject this job on the basis of vastly incomplete information. I gave up trying.

"Okay," I said wearily.

"So you're on board," Collie said with satisfaction, trying to close like an insurance salesman.

"I'll read the printouts."

"Which means you're on board."

"Which means I'll read the printouts."

"Close enough."

"When and where in the Federal Building?"

"Tomorrow. Two o'clock. I'll meet you at the testing office." He got up to leave. It was almost 1 A.M.

"Incidentally," I told him at the back door, "about our Ted Sherman. Who can't take this assignment because he's in the hospital?"

"Right. Back trouble."

"I heard," I told him, "that he went someplace for you people a few months ago, and got his cover blown by some people who weren't as gentlemanly as we try to be. I heard they stuck an anode up his penis and talked to him a long time with the high voltage on. I heard he's in the hospital because he now lacks a lot of physical equipment that most men value very highly, and it's going to take the shrinks a long time with him after the urologists and plastic surgeons get done."

"God!" Collie said. "Where did you ever hear crap like that? That's ridiculous! Totally untrue. *Totally.*"

"Really?"

"Absolutely!" He looked sincerely shocked.

Good liar, Collie.

three

Elsewhere

Browning, Montana

It was morning but already hot in Browning. A stiff wind out of the south blew yellow clouds of grit across the intersection of U.S. Highways 89 and 2. Dominic Partek had not expected this kind of discomfort when he chose Montana as a place to hide.

A big RV lumbered off U.S. 89 and into the Shell station, kicking up a tiny cloud of dust of its own. It pulled up to the full-service pumps and the driver touched his horn.

Partek, the lone attendant on duty, detached himself from his penny-pitch game with three raggedy Indian boys on the front ramp. "Work to do. I will be right back."

"You better!" one of the kids cracked. "You owe me thirteen cents!"

"I always pay, my friend." Partek went out to greet the people in the RV.

They were from Ohio and they wanted a fillup, both tanks. The woman went off in search of the restroom, and the chubby, middle-aged driver rhapsodized about the Black Hills while Partek was pumping in the gas.

"We've never been in the Rockies. I guess we've got a treat, huh?"

Partek smiled as he finished the fuel and started on the windshield. "They are very beautiful."

"You a native?"

"Yes," Partek lied.

"You must get to the mountains often."

"Every chance I get." He had never been in them.

The man paid him. The woman came back. Both of them stared at the bluish bulk of the mountains on the horizon. "Not much farther to Glacier, is it?"

"Thirty-one miles to St. Mary Campground at this end of the park."

"Good spot?"

"Yes. All the campgrounds fill up early."

"That's what we heard. We figure on checking in before noon, getting us a spot, then looking around."

"Good luck."

The camper pulled away, nosing west onto the highway. Partek watched it blend into the ragged line of cars and RVs headed in the same direction, passing a low, WPA-style brick building behind a yellowed grass lawn on the north side of the road. People often went past the Museum of the Plains Indians without realizing what they were missing. Too bad.

Partek walked back to the kids. They made a spot for him. The one named Billy had just won three cents.

"Your turn, Johnny," a kid named Jerry told him. "If you feel like living dangerously."

Partek wiped his hands on a red towel. He wondered how many people in the world really understood what it felt like to live dangerously.

He had done it almost all his life, but never as dangerously as now. He wondered if ordinary people ever experienced the ache in the midsection, the constant dread of discovery. If the Ohio tourist failed to find a good campground, would he experience this painful constriction of breathing that Partek lived with daily?

Partek knew he wasn't really sick. The breathing problem was merely his body's protest against his iron control of the fear and anxiety battering at the doors of his mind.

Poor Buckeye, he thought, never experienced things like that.

Lucky Buckeye.

He pitched his penny, making a bad toss and purposely losing again. The kids loved beating a grownup. He liked kids. And they were the only companionship he could risk right now.

"Ouch. I'd better drop out a while, guys."

"Yeah, just when we were getting to you!"

He went into the glass building and sat behind a greasy table and watched camper traffic churn back and forth along the highway, adding to the grit clouds that swept across the wide pavement, partially obscuring the other gas stations, cafes, beer joints.

It's safe here, he told himself.

He knew better. Nowhere was entirely safe.

They might come any time.

Dominic Partek was thirty-nine, but he felt much older. A slender man, dark-haired, with a pug nose and square chin, he had the short, stubby legs of his peasant ancestors and the long, slender torso he had gotten from his mother. He was five feet, ten inches tall, 160 pounds, in moderately good physical condition. He spoke flawless idiomatic English and wore his jeans and blue denim shirt and Adidas like a native, and his driver's license said he was from Missouri.

The truth was something different.

Partek was not from Missouri. He had never been there. That was just the license stock that the counterfeiter had had on hand when Partek needed a new ID fast.

Partek was not even an American.

I'm not any nationality now, he thought with sudden anguish. And then he thought about his sister, whom he had never known. *And I will never see you now, either. Never know my family.*

Unless they can do as they promised they could do . . .

His eyes felt hot: tears. Again he felt almost overwhelmed by his dilemma. Whatever he did, he seemed sure to lose. His pursuers might be anywhere, ready to run him to ground like a scared little rabbit. He, who had been so often the instigator, the unafraid one.

The little boys drifted away, waving goodbyes. They would be back. Partek was always good to them. They cut the loneliness a little. He was grateful for that.

A few more customers came. Partek glanced now and then at his watch. One of the other attendants arrived at a few minutes before noon, freeing him to go to lunch.

Partek limped to his 1984 Chevrolet pickup and drove up the street to where he always had his sandwich. There were some other workers in the small, low-ceilinged room, and he nodded to some of them, the ones he had come to recognize during his month in Browning.

He sat at the end of the counter alone, his position not inviting company.

Molly Walkingstick, the owner, came out from the back and put a glass of ice water and his silverware in front of him. "Afternoon, Johnny. Usual?"

"Yes. That would be fine."

"I'm kind of surprised to see you in here right now."

Partek looked at her. "Why?"

"Didn't your two friends find you at the station?"

"Friends?" The chill in his gut deepened. "I guess not. When were they in?"

"Oh, golly, two or three hours ago. David and Steve, they said their names were."

"Oh, yes. David and Steve." Partek had never known any David and Steve.

Molly Walkingstick shrugged. "Maybe they're waiting

at the motel. Shucks! Me and my big mouth! They said they wanted to surprise you."

The chill was overpowering. "They're great jokers."

"Durn! And I spoilt it!"

"Molly, it's okay. Believe me."

Molly sighed and returned to the kitchen in back.

Partek slipped off the stool and went into the side hall as if going toward the men's room. Instead, he let himself out the side door, hurried around the windowless wall of the building to his truck, and got inside.

He did not go to his room in the Warbonnet Motel. What was lost was lost. He drove straight out of town, heading for Cutbank and points beyond. It was more than a hundred miles before he so much as stopped for gasoline at a small station and convenience store. His stomach was killing him. He did not think he could put up with this for a long time.

But until he learned whether the Americans could deliver on their promises in Belgrade, he had no options whatsoever.

This time, he thought, he would hide deeper. And wait.

four

It had been four years since I had done any kind of assignment for them and I had figured I was off the hook. Collie's visit was an unpleasant reminder that maybe you're never off the hook, unless you choose to resign from living.

As tired as I was, I lost a little sleep about it the rest of the night. By morning I still wasn't sure. But then my curiosity, and an archaic sense of duty, overcame my doubts.

This much I knew: they wouldn't be this interested in Danisa Lechova just for her abilities as a tennis player. The stakes had to be a lot higher and more complicated than I could guess. Which fascinated me.

And also told me that they must really need me, or they wouldn't have asked.

And—I told myself—it would be a good working vacation, returning to bigtime tennis for a week, seeing some old friends, getting a change of scenery.

That people sometimes got killed on little junkets like this did enter my mind, but perhaps it really would be a routine job. I devoutly hoped so. I was concentrating hard on that hope when I walked into the old Federal Building and met Collie.

He took me on a byzantine stroll through narrow

corridors and finally into a room behind a sign that said it was an office of something called the Agricultural Stabilization Service. The front office was devoid of furniture, and a bulky man in a summer suit was standing there. He and Collie knew each other and he nodded, went behind us to lock the hall door, and resumed his stance against the bare metal wall. Collie took me next door.

This room contained a lot of computer equipment, another bulky character, and a tall woman with a gorgeous figure and a face like a hatchet. There were two desks and an elaborate communications console with both radio and telephone equipment in place. The computer stuff was arranged along two walls, interconnected by dense black cables strung across a bare tile floor.

Collie sat me down at a keyboard console facing a fourteen-inch computer screen. The woman pulled a little folding room divider halfway around my back so even they couldn't read over my shoulder. Then she powered up some gadgets while Collie unlocked the combination on a thin metal attaché case and removed a single slim cartridge which he inserted into a Bernoulli box. The woman sat at a nearby keyboard and did some security commands that allowed the cartridge to boot up. The first page of text appeared on my screen.

"You know how to page down?" Collie asked.

I looked at my keyboard. "I hit the 'page down' key, maybe?"

"I knew you were a genius." He patted me on the shoulder and withdrew beyond the screen somewhere.

What came up first on the screen was condensed data about *LECHOVA, DANISA, DOB 11 NOV 65.*

The place of birth was listed as Belgrade, Yugoslavia, and the parents were listed as Leon and Geneta Lechova, POB and exact DOB unknown, both citizens of Yugoslavia, both now instructors in what we would call physical education in the Tito School, Belgrade. The parents were today both in their forties.

Danisa, the computer report said, attended state schools and was unknown until a small article about her appeared in a state newspaper in 1975, when at age ten she won her first small tournament against girls ranging in age up to sixteen.

The article said her athletic parents had introduced her and her sister, Hannah, to numerous sports at a very early age. Danisa, it said, was given a cut-off tennis racket at age three, and quickly showed a precocious talent for the game.

Reading between the lines, I decided her parents drove her like hell. There was a long list of academic awards she had won, starting in the earliest grades. Hannah, her older sister, excelled, too.

In 1981, Danisa got to the quarterfinals of the German Open. There was a story from the time in which tennis journalists rhapsodized about her talents and courage, but quotes from her father berated her for "quitting" in the third set against Mandlikova. The score in the deciding set had been 6–7 (11–13), which made the father's excoriations sound rather strange.

In 1981 also, the Lechovas first used Miloslav Fjbk to coach their daughters, a relationship that would later become his full-time occupation. Fjbk, once a pretty good player—he was on their Davis Cup team twice—came with a reputation as a dour slave driver and perfectionist who had driven a couple of mid-class European male players far higher than anyone would have predicted their talent could go. His coaching relationship with Lendl had been brief and stormy, and hadn't ended well.

After 1981, the Lechova girls dropped out of the sports news for three years except for an occasional news note about some local tournament appearance. Fjbk and their father were bringing them along slowly, keeping them in school, guarding against burnout.

In 1983, both Lechova sisters graduated in the same class. Hannah went into a women's unit of the army, but with a public relations type of job assignment that kept her near home and free to continue work on her tennis. Danisa won a scholarship to the academy where she started major work in history.

In 1984, after Danisa lost to Chris Evert-Lloyd in three sets in Rome—all three sets going into tiebreakers—tournament appearances became more regular for both young women. Danisa won the Monte Carlo that April, playing on clay, her favorite surface. The sisters lost in the finals of the women's doubles in the same tournament, and were cruising in the French Open the following month when Hannah twisted an ankle and forced a default in the semis.

There were some personality profiles on the disk, plus some other psychological stuff of the type they like to make up in Virginia sometimes when they have nothing better to do. A little of it was interesting. The general impression on Danisa was of a bright, energetic, frighteningly talented young athlete who was trying to build herself some kind of balanced life. Her sister, Hannah, was also very good, but by no means a potential star like Danisa.

There was no evidence of serious stress between the girls or in the family because of Danisa's stardom. Hannah, however, was into state politics, and had apparently turned in a friend for "disloyal speeches against the government" in 1985. If Danisa really wanted to defect, she was probably at odds with a sister who seemed well on the road to becoming a superpatriot.

The girls' father, Leon Lechova, the computer screen told me, was a former middle-distance runner who once won a bronze at the Olympics. This was during his tour in the Yugoslav army. Later he played a lot of soccer and tennis, and began teaching in 1965, the year of Danisa's birth.

Danisa's mother, the former Geneta Trencek, had been on state gymnastics teams but never attained any major successes. She had been teaching a year longer than her husband, and also taught physical culture classes at the Tito

School. She sounded like a formidable woman, demanding of her students and herself, and fiercely protective of her daughters.

The remaining screens of routine data on the family were not very helpful. Like just about everyone outside of the corrupt ruling class in Yugoslavia, they lived in a crammed three-room apartment and had been trying forever to get better quarters.

When the Communists took over the country after World War II, they brought all the peasants out of the countryside and into the cities to industrialize the economy and centralize the power. But housing wasn't planned and it had never caught up. You still found eminent doctors living in little more than broom closets, renowned professors jammed with their large families into spaces smaller than we use for garages in our country. If there was any bitterness about any of this among the Lechovas, however, it was buried far beneath the surface. These people were loyal.

Except that Danisa wanted out . . . for no reason the files explained.

The screen files on Fjbk were interesting, but I yearned for more. His DOB was 1934, which made him considerably more decrepit than I, and the information cheered me a little. Beyond that, the sparse data did not encourage me.

Fjbk was a Serb, peasant stock, with an obscure background that included a few years in the Yugoslav army and a career as a minor tennis player who never went down easily but seldom won the big ones. His reputation came as a coach. At one time or another he had worked with such luminaries as Borg, Lendl, Graf, and Miricic. None of the relationships had been of long standing, probably because Fjbk was never satisfied; he wanted every player he worked with to become the world's greatest, and if the player achieved that, Fjbk drove him harder, evidently shooting for All Galaxy.

There were a couple of screens in the Fjbk file detailing

a love affair he had had with a woman named Monselle back in the early seventies. It seemed she was a French ballerina of considerable promise, and the picture formed by the ethereal dancer and the squat, glowering Serb peasant had amused all the gossip sheets. The thing ended badly: she took up with a moneyed count, and Fjbk took the train back to Yugoslavia.

I was wondering as I read this stuff on the Fjbk-Monselle romance why the researcher had chosen to include it in the material, but then I got to the end of the section and found out. Mme. Monselle, it seemed, had deep and proven connections with the KGB apparatus in Western Europe.

The researcher went on to point out the obvious: the Monselle-Fjbk connection, even turning out badly on the personal side, strongly indicated that Fjbk also probably had espionage links, either to the KGB or the UDBA.

The hint made me more sure than ever that there was much more beneath the surface of this pleasant little jaunt than anyone was about to tell me. But the rest of the file didn't help any in that regard.

It did tell me a little more about Fjbk. The Lechova girls had won quite a bit of money in the last few years and Fjbk had gotten a share. With his tangled black hair, Fu Manchu goatee, and squat physique, he had become a recognizable figure on TV tennis coverage and the beaches at Saint-Tropez. He had parlayed his newfound visibility into promotion contracts with Adidas, Slazenger, and Hertz. He seemed to be working on making himself more visible yet: some of his latest acquisitions included a Mercedes, a big red Harley with a sidecar, and a sailboat.

All of which was interesting, but not very helpful.

The last section summarized a few things, then blocked out the facts I already knew about the Belgrade International, and finally outlined my particular mission profile: go to Belgrade, cover the tournament, establish interview contact with Danisa Lechova, and facilitate communication between her and our local people, who actually would do all the hard part.

All very neat.

And most of what I wanted to know . . . left out. It looked very simple and I hoped it would be, but somehow I didn't expect that. I wished again that I had a hint of what might really be at stake.

I finished reading the file, closed it, called Collie, and watched him lock the Bernoulli cartridge away again.

"No problem," he said, turning to me. "Right?"

I took a slow breath, aware that this was my last chance to back out gracefully. Then I said, "Okay, Collie. Fine."

That same night there came the inevitable problem with June.

I should have foreseen it. But sometimes I think I have an infinite capacity for deceiving myself about how people will react to situations involving their self-interest. When I picked her up for dinner, it was with pleasant anticipation and a real joy in simply being with her. I didn't think the job in Belgrade would create A Problem.

The first part of the evening was fine. She looked wonderful, of course, as she always did: bright, slim, buoyant, filled with energy and gladness despite what had been a long day on behalf of a client in district court in Fort Worth. She had won. June liked winning.

She bubbled about it all during drinks and dinner, jangling her gold bracelets, making her pendant earrings bobble as she turned her auburn head this way and that, mimicking her opposing attorney's arguments, her responses, and the judge's grumpy rejoinders. To be truthful I didn't pay much attention to what she said, but I didn't miss anything about the way she said it. She had a way of making her wonderful eyes sparkle that I had never gotten used to. Her facial expressions ran the gamut from acted-out horror to sneaky delight, but even making faces she was beautiful, a joy. I liked to watch her hands, too: large, strong, long-fingered, graceful. She gestured a lot, which accounted for some of the bangle-jangling.

"And how was your day?" she asked finally, over cognac. "Recovered from that match with that awful little shit last night?"

"My body, almost. My pride, maybe not quite yet."

"I really wanted to hear you had whipped the socks off him."

"I almost did, June."

Those big, expressive eyes studied me. "I really wanted to be there, too. But that damned hearing in Oklahoma City—"

"I was creaky at the end. Best you didn't watch."

She mugged. "I'm feeling a little creaky, too."

"Wait till you're as old as I am."

"Thirty-three is no spring chicken, Mr. Smith."

"Seems like it to a man of forty, Miss McCandless."

She lit one of the cigarettes I wished she didn't smoke. It smelled good. "So. Anything else new or different?"

It was then I realized I didn't feel very good about broaching the subject. I made my voice casual. "Actually, yes. I had a nice call from New York today. Interesting freelance assignment coming up next week."

Her gaze sharpened, and I thought her antennae went up. "Oh?"

"Yeah. *International Tennis* wants special coverage on a couple of events in Europe. Nice piece of change and some really good exposure for my byline in both their magazines. I'll have all expenses paid, of course, and go first-class. Looks like I'll get to play in a couple of celebrity doubles events and have a lot of fun."

I stopped. Her eyes were sharper. I seldom made long speeches. I had just made one. I had blown it.

"So where are you going?" she asked.

"Europe. Three or four places."

Her lips thinned. "I hope your itinerary gets more specific before you climb on the first airplane, Brad."

I tried lamely to salvage it. "I'm sure my editor will have a plan drawn up to run me ragged interviewing everybody in sight."

She just looked at me and didn't say anything, and the waiter came and refilled the coffee cups. But the bloom was off the evening, and when she said she wanted to get home early, I drove her there.

At curbside she turned in the front seat to nail me with those eyes, which were now bright with anger. "I thought you weren't going to do any more work for them."

There was no sense pretending. "It's just a little routine job, June."

"Then why are you doing it?"

"I'm uniquely qualified."

"Your tennis?"

"Yes."

"Then *that* part wasn't a lie?"

"I'm going to cover some tennis."

"And do something else."

"Okay. Yes. But it isn't dangerous and it's no big deal."

"Where?"

I paused, forming my response.

She supplied it for me, her tone flat with bitterness: "No need for me to know, right?"

"Well, June—" I began, cajoling.

"*No*, goddamn it!" she cut in hotly. "No need for me to know, right? Isn't that right?"

"It's no big deal."

There was a silence as she stared ahead through the windshield at nothing more interesting than a parked 1986 Camaro. Finally she said in a different tone, "You know I don't want you to go."

"I won't be gone long."

"I'm very serious, Brad."

I met her angry eyes. "So am I."

"So what I want doesn't matter?"

"Of course it matters. But you can't expect to control my life."

"Meaning that you're going whether I like it or not."

"Do you have to put it that way, June?"

"That's the way it is!"

I breathed. "All right, then. If that's the way you want to see it."

"How else could I see it?"

"What's the big deal?" I countered.

She made a little groaning sound of frustration. "You were in Vietnam in 1967. More than twenty years ago. *Twenty years ago*, Brad. Then you came back in 1968 and Elizabeth divorced you. When was it that you started working for the CIA part-time, playing *I Spy* while you were on the tennis circuit? Nineteen seventy?"

"What are you getting at, June?"

"You've never entirely gotten over Vietnam, Brad. And you've certainly never entirely gotten through your divorce, what Elizabeth did to you. I can live with all that. But you're still playing *I Spy*, too. And I don't think I can abide that anymore."

"June."

She faced me, her eyes bright with angry tears. "I can live with the Vietnam ghosts. I can sleep beside you sometimes . . . on the nights when your horniness over-comes your terror of loving a woman again and risking another betrayal . . . and know Elizabeth's damned whor-ish ghost is in there with us between the sheets. You can't help those things. And I've been patient. Three years I've been patient, haven't pushed. You can't help the ghosts. But I can't accept the CIA thing too, Brad. It's too much."

"June, don't do this. Please."

Her earrings swayed as she angrily shook her head. "I know you did things for them before. You say things, and then you never explain, and I'm not supposed to ask. Something in Vienna once. And in London. And Paraguay. And other places. You go and do these things and I'm supposed to know nothing, *be* nothing."

"It's my country, dammit. If I can help with some little deal—"

"It's not just that I don't know what you're doing, or why. I think a lot of the time *you* don't know either. Someone issues an order, and you go and do something—mail a letter or pick up a package or meet somebody—and you never know what it's all about, whether it's worthwhile, whether whatever you do has any results, or whether it was even necessary, or just some damned bureaucrat's idea of cops and robbers."

Suddenly I felt tired and a little defeated. We had been over this ground many times before. "You trust. You do what they ask, if you can, because it's your country and you owe it. You *owe* it. If it works out or doesn't, it's not your concern. You have to accept the ambiguity. You have to learn that. You do what you can and hope it makes sense to somebody somewhere—does some good."

"That's all?"

"What the hell is there for *anybody* besides doing your best?"

With a little moan of frustration, she cracked the car door to get out. I started to open my door to walk her in.

"No," she said.

"I'll call you tomorrow."

"No."

"In a day or two, then."

"No."

I looked at her and didn't know what to say. I knew I should say I loved her, and I wanted to say that. I wanted her and I hurt. But I couldn't quite say it because—on her terms—saying it meant calling Collie back and telling him I had changed my mind.

Instead I tried to make a joke: "Hey. I'll send you a postcard."

She got out of the car. "Don't bother." She walked, pretty heels clicking sharply, up to her apartment entrance and went inside.

I resisted the impulse to cave in and call her. The next day I told the people at the tennis club about my fine writing assignment, and they swallowed it whole, said they could fill in for me while I was gone, and would promote my trip in the club newsletter.

"Good pub," Jack Stephensen said.

The day after that, I got my letter from the tennis magazine, giving me the assignment. Sometimes the Company worked fast.

In the days remaining before it was time to drive out to DFW and board the plane, I mentally reviewed the things I had learned about the Lechova family and Miloslav Fjbk, and did some additional magazine research at the library on Danisa. I wanted badly to call June. Didn't. Collie came by again and talked for about an hour, telling me who I was to meet, and how, and what I was supposed to do. I memorized names and photographs of faces, procedures and bona fides.

I wondered a lot more about why we were so fired up over helping one pretty girl—even a potential tennis star— flee her country. But I didn't ask because I knew Collie would either tell me nothing, or lie. It was none of my business, really. More ambiguity.

The night before I was to leave, I dreamt about a patrol in the Mekong Delta, and then about Elizabeth. The Vietnam dream was bad enough, but in the dream about Elizabeth, she stood facing me, she was naked and beautiful,

33

and she had semen on her thighs, but it wasn't mine. I woke up soaked with sweat and went out into my den and found a pack of Merits that had been in the bottom drawer since I finally quit a year before, and smoked three of them. They tasted stale but pretty good. I didn't sleep any more. I sat up and watched daylight come and waited for it to be time to go.

five

Elsewhere

Langley, Virginia

The meeting started very early. Three men sat around a small conference table: Kinkaid, Exerblein, and Dwight.

"So we've lost him again," Dwight said glumly. "We knew that when we blew the job in Browning. Do we have to rake over it again?"

"Maybe we overlooked something," Kinkaid said, dogged. "Some clue to where he might have headed next."

"Our guys out there say no such luck."

"Maybe they've missed something."

"They're good."

"They fucked up the intercept! What leads you to believe they couldn't fuck up searching his motel room, too?"

"Aw, give them a break."

"It was a mistake to wait at his motel," Kinkaid retorted. "They should have gone straight to the gas station and taken him right then and there."

"Take him for what?" Dwight's eyes were flat and cold.

"Phony ID, if nothing else!"

"No, no," Exerblein put in. In calendar years, he was

35

the youngest of the three men, but in other ways infinitely older: his colorless skin matched his faint blue eyes, which matched his career-man personality. He was going to go far in this organization because he was caution personified. He always had the answers because he never worked in the field, where "answers" so seldom were clear-cut. "He came to us," Exerblein went on. "We're supposed to be his *friends.* Your friends don't arrest you."

Kinkaid looked at Exerblein a moment, clearly struggling with an impulse to tell him he was full of shit. Instead Kinkaid said, "Protective custody."

"Not," Exerblein retorted with that maddening cool, "if he didn't request same."

"So now he's lost again and the other side may be right on his tail and the next time we find him, we may find fishfood in the bottom of a lake, wearing concrete boots."

"Let's review just a minute," Dwight said.

Kinkaid and Exerblein fell silent, one fuming, one waxen.

Dwight, a career man of forty with pale hair and a pale summer suit, ticked off the points on blunt fingertips. "He came to us talking defection and asylum. We checked everything we could check, and it looked legitimate—a real change of loyalty, and not a trick by the other side to put him in where he can get information from us for them, or to feed us bullshit."

Dwight glanced at Exerblein, who had argued as recently as last week that Partek's desire to defect was a KGB trick. Exerblein, perhaps remembering who was responsible for his next effectiveness report, said nothing.

Dwight resumed. "We can't know what happened after our initial contacts. We can only assume that they made further threats on his family. Hearing that—seeing the implications—he could hardly stay with the Soviet delegation in New York, but he couldn't come over to our side either, or they might institute reprisals. So he bugged out to think about it."

"And wait," Exerblein intoned, "to see if we could make good on our promises."

"Or," Dwight countered, "just to think about it—deal with the shock. Up until a few days ago he didn't know he *had* a family anymore, remember?"

Kinkaid said, "None of that is going to help us if the KGB finds him before we do. They'll kill his ass."

"Or kidnap him and fly him back to Russia," Exerblein added.

"In either of which case," Kinkaid said, so frustrated his grammar came apart, "we lose. We should have taken him at once up there in Montana, and figured out the rationale later."

"Well, we didn't," Dwight pointed out. "And now we've lost him again."

"I suppose we can only hope the Russians have lost him, too," Exerblein said, calm as always.

"If they haven't," Kinkaid said, "we've lost one of the most valuable people we've ever had a chance at in this country. Christ, when you think of the places he's worked, the KGB operations he probably took part in, the other agents he could finger—!"

"I've talked to Daniels, at the FBI," Dwight told the others.

"What did he say?"

"He's pissed that we didn't share information earlier. He thinks we're still holding out part of the story on him."

"Are we?"

"Sure. But he says this is his area of authority, et cetera."

"Right," Kinkaid retorted. "Let *them* screw it up."

"Anyway, with chances good that Partek might have gone over the border into Canada, I thought it wise to share info."

"And what now?"

Dwight leaned back in his chair. "Brad Smith is all set up?"

"Yes."

"Well, once he gets over there, we'll be able to get things moving. Once that part is accomplished—assuming Partek is still alive—we've got a chance to salvage this whole business."

Exerblein stirred. "Does Smith know what's at stake here?"

"No," Dwight said.

"Should he?"

"No. His part shouldn't be all that complicated. Let him think it's a simple defection. He's okay, but he'll function better if he doesn't know all the angles . . . feel that much pressure."

Kinkaid said, "Or know how he's being used."

"He's a big boy. He'll get over it."

"Sure. Unless he gets killed over there."

Browning, Montana

Shortly after dawn, a man who looked like a tourist placed a call from a telephone booth at a truck stop. Trucks and campers thudded by on the highway just beyond the man's glass cubicle, and the ground trembled slightly beneath his feet.

"Yes?" a voice answered.

"Sir, I have a collect call for anyone from Sylvester, will you accept the charge?"

"Yes . . . Hello, Sylvester?"

Sylvester—as good a name as any—plugged one ear with his fingertip. "Our information was correct."

"They were about to take the merchandise?"

"Yes. Clearly they wanted it and had it ready to be picked up. However, they delayed. This was an error. The merchandise has since been shipped elsewhere."

"I have new instructions. You are to remain in place. When we have new information, we will contact you."

"I hope," Sylvester said, "our information can be

improved. It is unpleasant to travel so far for a product that has been removed from the shelf."

"Every effort is being made." The connection was broken.

Sylvester left the telephone booth. The day was already warm and he was sweating. He thought about Dominic Partek. He had always liked the man; brilliant, a professional, loyal. Now this.

Sylvester was a killing machine. He did not often use his skills in America. He had never carried out an assignment against a countryman, much less a man he had worked beside, and had liked.

None of that mattered much now, of course. When Partek was found—and he would be spotted again, sooner or later—Sylvester would move with all deliberate speed to reach him before the Americans clumsily tried once more to take him captive.

If Sylvester reached Partek first, there would be nothing left for the Yankees to take into custody.

Sylvester thought of having to kill a friend and former colleague like Dominic Partek. It was very unfortunate.

Sylvester decided he would use a gun if at all possible. A gun was less personal. Using a gun would be less painful for him because he would not have to touch his former friend.

Belgrade, Yugoslavia

Late-day sun gilded the nylon-composite underside of the huge dome that covered the People's Sports Arena in New Belgrade. Seated in the first row of the vast and nearly empty stands behind one end of the center court, Coach Miloslav Fjbk watched with total concentration as Danisa Lechova tossed a ball high, then came through it with a sharp, powerful motion that put every ounce of her strength and timing into the serve. For just an instant, there was nothing in the world for the dour Serb except Danisa's body, her movement, the meeting of racket against ball at the very peak of the toss.

For Fjbk, it was a moment of timeless love.

Danisa Lechova's serve, overstruck very slightly, sizzled over the net toward another young woman, as tall as Danisa, nearly as blond, and nearly as pretty. Hannah Lechova was ready, but sidestepped the ball.

"Back!" Hannah's sharp feminine cry echoed through the vastness.

Fjbk raised his eyes in irritation. Across the dusty expanse of the arena, in a middle row on the far side, a lone, squat figure sat unmoving. Fjbk had noticed him earlier: Maleeva, perhaps the most powerful UDBA officer in Belgrade. He had been here yesterday for a long time, too. *Why? What did he want?*

Danisa served another ball. It went long, like the one before it. Fjbk felt a pulse of puzzled irritation. Danisa's concentration and timing were terrible today. He watched her closely and saw her glance up toward him—*over his head*—to some point behind him in the stands.

As she prepared to serve again, Fjbk turned abruptly and tried to find the spot her eyes had sought.

Near the topmost row of seating, the slender boy was sitting with his lanky legs over the row of seats in front of him. Fjbk had seen him around before. His name was Kerneck and he attended the academy and he had become a persistent hanger-on. He sent Danisa notes, pleading for dates. She laughed and ignored him.

Or had ignored him in the past.

But now her eyes had sought the trim boy when she should have been concentrating on her practice. The angry discomfort that stabbed through Fjbk was only partly professional concern about her tennis concentration.

Below him Danisa had served another fault, and now dug another ball out of the pocket of her blousy practice tunic. She bounced it. Her eyes wandered briefly over her shoulder, again picking out the boy in the top row.

Fjbk decided. "Time!"

Danisa stopped her service preparation as Fjbk vaulted the front-row railing and strode across the gritty black clay toward her. She was sweat-soaked, the material of the dress clinging wetly to every line and sinew and curve of her, the overhead lights making her sleek arms and legs glisten with wetness. Her hair, tied in a single long braid in back, gleamed wet. The fatigue was clear in her eyes.

"You are not paying attention," Fjbk snapped at her.

"I'm tired, Milo—"

"God damn 'tired'! You are not giving a good effort!"

Danisa's beautiful eyes narrowed under his attack. "I'm trying—"

"You are too far in front," Fjbk told her.

"The toss?" Danisa asked in her husky alto. "It felt—"

"Don't argue. It was too far in front. You have been sliding your right hip early, and now the toss is too far forward and it feels fine, perhaps. But it is not. You cannot reach the ball to turn the racket over the top. The spin becomes too flat."

Danisa's light gray eyes looked dubious, but she turned to the service line center, carefully bounced the ball four times, tensed, tossed. The *thwack!* of gut against ball hammered Fjbk's eardrums.

Net.

And again her eyes swept for an instant toward the top row.

"No, no, no!" In a frenzy of anger, Fjbk twisted the racket out of her hand. "You throw the ball up like a cow! You turn the racket—so—to overcompensate—so—and your hip comes around too early! Do you get nothing right? Look!" He demonstrated, exaggerating every movement, blasting a sharp, flat serve over the waiting Hannah's head.

"You see?" he demanded. "You see?"

Danisa's fatigue vanished as her face curled and she erupted into gales of girlish laughter.

41

"What is it?" Fjbk yelled, torn between rage and astonishment. "What is so *funny?*"

"Oh, Milo," Danisa gasped, holding her sides. "If you could only see yourself, your exaggeration!" Quicksilver, she grabbed the racket back from him and tossed an imagined ball. She jerked her head to one side, cocked her elbow wrong, swung her hip like a gypsy girl in a carnival show, and jerked her pelvis like a bellydancer, all the while swinging the racket like a spastic.

Across the net, Hannah's laughter pealed.

Fjbk's rage vanished. How could any man be angry at this girl? She was the most beautiful and talented and unpredictable woman in the world and he adored her.

His lip curled in a smile he could not control.

"You see how funny you looked?" Danisa cried with glee. "Oh, Milo, we have worked so long today, and we are so in need of rest!"

Fjbk fought to control himself. He had to be cruel now. "Then perhaps you should sleep," he snarled.

Danisa's grin started to fade. "What?"

"Perhaps you should sleep. Sleep for a month, right through the tournament. Fail me, fail your parents, fail Yugoslavia's honor."

The grin was gone. "But Milo, I only—"

"Go into this tournament and play like a cow," Fjbk bit off. "Let Navratilova destroy you. Or Karyn Wechsting, eh? Play like a whore."

The calculated insult did the trick. Danisa's face went ivory. "You have no right—"

"No right? You tell me I have no right?" This was good, this was very good. Now all he had to do was anchor her rage, make it work for him. "I have given you years of the best coaching. And God. God has given you this body, this talent. You play games out here with your talent and you are no better than a whore on the street. You are worse! At least a whore uses her talent the best way she knows how—"

42

Tears sprang to Danisa's expressive eyes. "Get out of my way."

"To serve carelessly, like a cow whore? Maybe you are right, you should take a long nap. Sleep right through the tournament."

Danisa grabbed a ball, faced the line, tossed it, and brought her racket through with vicious, controlled accuracy. The toss was perfect and the ball hammered across the net and deep to the back corner of the deuce service area. A startled Hannah lunged but missed the clean ace.

Danisa turned and glared at Fjbk. He shrugged, spat, walked back to the stands, climbed over the railing to his chair.

Danisa Lechova, her nervous system reenergized by the anger he had injected, began serving like a demon . . . or an angel.

Fjbk watched, as fascinated as the ancients who had been lured to their death by the siren song. She was his creation. She was his song. She would make him famous forever, and secure in his mother country despite his obscure peasant origins.

He adored her.

Across the broad floor of the sportsdome, in the darkened seating area far beyond the lighted gray of the center clay court, there was a slight movement in the stands. Fjbk saw that Maleeva, the UDBA man, was leaving, his back to the courts as he slowly climbed the steps toward the exit.

Fjbk momentarily forgot the practice match between the Lechova sisters. He watched Maleeva vanish from the arena, and he thought, *Why do you watch us, swine? I thought for a while that it was I, Miloslav Fjbk, you had come to spy on. But it is not. It is Danisa. Why? You did not let her play at Wimbledon. You have made her a prisoner in her native land? Why is this?*

You will not do harm to her, swine. Whatever you want of

her, I will die before you or anyone else harms her. She is the best. I love her. I would endure anything for her. I would go back to Naked Island for a thousand years for her.

I will watch you, swine Maleeva. Whatever it is, if it is harm for Danisa, I will not allow it even if you have the hordes of hell on your side.

Below, on the court, Danisa moved to her left and slid into a backhand. Her timing was fractionally off and the ball went wide. She turned, tossing her hair in irritation, and once more her eyes flashed upward, toward the seats behind Fjbk.

It was the last straw. Fjbk signaled for another point. As Danisa served and Hannah returned, Fjbk left his chair and trotted up the steps toward the back.

Kerneck, the boy, saw him coming and awkwardly untangled himself from the chair. He must have read something in Fjbk's eyes because he looked startled and climbed over the back railing to the screened-off mezzanine beyond.

Boiling, Fjbk rushed around the gateposts and caught the boy by the arm, spinning him painfully back against the concrete wall. The boy's sunglasses flew off his forehead and broke on the pavement.

"What do you want?"

"Goddamn you! You leave her alone, you got me?"

"I'll—!"

Whatever Kerneck was going to say, he never said it. Fjbk's jealous rage was fully out. His right fist slammed into the boy's face, knocking him backward, red appearing in a gush on his chin.

"You're crazy!" the boy gasped, scrambling in his attempt to escape. "I haven't—"

Fjbk pounced on him, using a weight advantage of at least one hundred pounds to pin him to the gritty pavement. Fjbk slammed his right fist into the boy's face again, feeling bones shatter. He used his left and his right again, and there was blood everywhere and it felt good.

44

Still straddling the slender boy, he dug a blood-slippery hand into his pants pocket and came out with his prized pocket knife, an American Buck knife with a five-inch blade. He saw the boy's shocked, pain-dazed eyes widen in terror as he snicked the blade open and locked.

Fjbk jammed the tip of the blade under Kerneck's chin, drawing a new bright droplet. "You ever come near her again," he grated. "You *ever!* Goddamn you, boy, I will cut your balls off with my knife, eh?"

Sobbing and choking on his own blood, the boy lay half unconscious, terrified.

Fjbk poked the keen tip of the blade into the tender flesh of his underjaw perhaps a quarter of an inch. *"You hear me, swine?"*

Someone grabbed Fjbk's long hair. Something cold and hard pressed painfully against the back of his own neck.

"Idiot!" the voice said with soft fury. "Move and your brains will decorate the wall."

Fjbk went cold, did not move. His let his knife drop from his hands. It made a little clattering sound on the bloody cement.

The gun muzzle in his neck jabbed harder. "Get up."

Fjbk climbed to his feet. The boy scuttered out of his reach, sitting up and mopping at his broken face with his sleeve. Maleeva moved around to confront Fjbk, his .380 automatic still leveled on the coach's chest.

Maleeva was glacier-white with rage. "You are a madman. You should be institutionalized. Ever again another trick like this, and you will never see the outside world again."

Still dazed by surprise, Fjbk tried to counterattack. "This swine boy is molesting Danisa and Hannah! He—"

"Idiot," Maleeva cut in.

Fjbk stared. The boy got unsteadily to his feet. Maleeva glanced at him. "Can you walk to the car?"

"Yes, sir," Kerneck said thickly.

"Go. Report for medical aid at once."

"What is this?" Fjbk blustered. "You help malingerers who—"

"He is part of our security detail, pig-brain," Maleeva bit off.

"I thought—"

"You thought nothing. You never think. You boast, you posture, you go crazy all the time, you make our work twice as hard, Fjbk. I swear to you, this evil, jealous temper of yours will be your death! And I may be the one who makes this prediction come true!"

Fjbk wiped his face, bent down to retrieve his knife, folded it, pocketed it, suddenly raised up with a radiant grin. In an instant he seemed a totally different personality. "Hey, it was only a joke, right?"

"You would have killed my man!"

"Hey, no! I just wanted to scare him! Hey, I will take the kid for a ride on my Harley, and make up for everything, okay?"

As familiar as he was with Fjbk's mercurial changes of mood, Maleeva was stunned into silence.

Fjbk, giggling and grinning as if nothing at all had happened, rushed around the seatback screening and descended into the arena again.

Still standing with his pistol in hand, Maleeva heard the crazy Serb calling, *Ten more serves, Danisa! Ten more serves for each of you, my pets! Then we will call it a day, eh?*

Maleeva pocketed his weapon and looked down with chagrin and disgust at all the blood on the pavement. It was not hard enough, with all the pressure from national headquarters and Moscow. He had to be saddled also with the world's biggest fool . . . and potentially one of its most dangerous madmen.

For he had no doubt that Fjbk was fiendishly clever, as tricky as a mad child, calculating . . . incendiary . . . wholly unpredictable and capable of anything. If Fjbk had not become a minor eccentric celebrity—he had even been pictured in the U.S. *People* magazine a few months ago on his Harley—if it were not for his celebrity, and the fact that he was the Lechova girls' coach, Maleeva would have arrested him.

But he could not do that. At least not yet. He could only hope that Fjbk held on to his thin thread of sanity and control until this tournament was history.

It was going to be a long tournament.

Outside the arena, and all over the sprawl of Belgrade on both sides of the Sava, streetsweepers and pavement washers were at work. Flags were being hung, parks picked up, benches painted, fountains cleaned, buildings spruced up, trees trimmed, even some of the buses and taxis painted. There were tennis banners everywhere, promoting the first Belgrade International.

Promotion banners on walls carried pictures of Danisa Lechova. She would be the star. Everyone loved her.

Evening shadows sprawled across the wide boulevard surrounding the sports complex when Danisa emerged from her workout, striding with long-legged grace to the Fiat waiting in the wire-fenced lot. Her sister and their coach accompanied her.

A handful of fans clustered outside the fence. They called and waved to her as she neared the car furnished by the state to facilitate her pretournament workouts downtown. Danisa hesitated, took a step as if she might go to the fence to talk to the people there, then stopped as Fjbk said something sharply. She listened, frowned, recovered, sent the fans a sunny smile and a wave, and climbed into the Fiat behind her sister.

Fjbk, nursing a sore hand, drove. The arena guard opened the gate and let the little car through. As it turned north on the boulevard in the direction of Sava Center, another car, a Citroën, pulled away from the curb and followed it at a discreet distance.

Danisa and her companions did not notice the other car, and the fans now disbanding at the fence didn't, either. No one would have dreamed Danisa Lechova was being watched day and night. After all, everyone loved her; no one imagined she was a prisoner.

six

The JAT 747 descended bumpily out of the rain-swollen clouds and began its approach into Belgrade-Surčin Airport. Tired as hell, I looked out from my window seat, getting my first view of Yugoslavia.

I saw tree-stubbled hills, the gray expanse of the Sava River, and briefly, out ahead, city sprawl and the tight cluster of the old city at the place where the Sava conjoined with the Danube. As the 747 glided lower, banking, there was a hazy view of ancient twisting streets and orange tile roofs and church steeples, and beyond them the monolithic concrete blocks of New Belgrade sticking up like tombstones for giants. *So it begins*, I thought.

Local time was 5 P.M. My biological clock said 10 in the morning after an all-night flight. We had passed time zones like Borg used to pass Connors at the net. I hadn't slept much, and was having difficulty tracking mentally.

I needed to be alert. Without knowledge of the native language I had an inkling of how tourists must feel. My country- and customs-briefing had been kept sketchy to make sure I would not blow my own cover by inadvertently revealing knowledge that a traveling tennis journalist shouldn't have.

I had read a little on my own, as any visitor might.

Nominally, Yugoslavia remained a Communist country. But even its buses and taxis were privately owned, and there were few countries in Europe with more freelance small entrepreneurs scrambling after the local equivalent of the buck. Education, health care, and housing, however, were under the total control of a presumably benevolent but often hopelessly corrupt state, and the press and television only appeared to be uncontrolled.

In some ways, the country proved to the world that Tito had been dead right when he fought Soviet domination after World War II. Superficially it was more prosperous than its Iron Curtain neighbors, and its people less volatile. Independence allowed it to trade with both the East and the West, and the standard of living was on the rise.

Inflation, however, was out of control, doubling prices annually for three straight years. And housing in the metro areas like Belgrade had been a disaster for decades. The big projects in New Belgrade had eased the pressure, but not enough. One of the brochures I read had told me that divorced couples in cities like Belgrade sometimes continued to live together because there was nowhere else for either partner to go.

There was slight but growing political dissent. Time was when the pro-Tito majority fought tooth and nail with pro-Russian elements. That continued a long tradition; about half of Yugoslavia's male population died in World War II, and the majority were killed by countrymen who had a different political philosophy.

After the war, Tito's people knew how to deal with Communists who wanted closer ties with Moscow: Prison. The main place—and most feared—was called Naked Island. When people were sent there, they usually didn't come back. If they did, they had learned their lesson.

The UDBA—local equivalent of the KGB—was nowhere near as efficient as its Russian counterpart. But it had plainclothes members everywhere, and informing to the secret police out of patriotism, fear, or hope of returned favors was a way of life. I did not delude myself: anyone might betray me if they guessed my real mission.

My 747 swept in over power lines and the airport fence. I wondered how the local case officer imagined he was going to get someone as visible as Danisa Lechova out of the country. I told myself it was not my problem. I was a messenger boy: get close to Danisa Lechova under the guise of my assignment to write a major feature story on her, wait for contact from the local guy, and pass information between them. And when things started to happen, get the hell out of the way, feigning astonishment.

Very simple. If these things ever were.

I still couldn't help wondering what it was really all about. Maybe I would never know. I thought of June, and how she couldn't handle the ambiguity. But thoughts of June threatened to let all kinds of bad feelings out, so I concentrated again on the view from my window.

The big jet hammered onto the concrete runway and rolled, braking, past patches of engine-seared grass, waiting airliners, a lone French Mirage fighter, a grimy engine factory and several hangars, and then taxiways and grass less scorched and greener, studded with blue and white lights.

Parking at the white marble terminal, the pilot cut the engines. Everybody on board left their seats at once, hurrying to get out and wait. I retrieved my attaché case and Toshiba portable computer from the overhead. It took almost ten minutes to get off the plane and into the terminal.

I followed the crowd down a broad, barren hallway and into a large and equally barren room for issuance of visas. Stood in line.

Finally it was my turn. The sour woman behind the wicket stared at my passport, then briefly at me. "This information is correct, sir?" she asked in heavily accented English.

"Yes."

She touched pen to a form. "Occupation?"

"Writer of sports news. I'm here for the tennis—"

"Nature of business in Yugoslavia?"

"I'm here to cover the tennis tournament for a magazine."

"Duration of stay?"

"Nine days."

"Local address?"

"Hotel Metropol."

She took my passport into a back room, where presumably she checked my name against lists of suspect people. When she came back, she had stamped the visa into my passport. She handed the papers back through the wicket. "Enjoy your stay in our country, sir." She said it like someone who had seldom enjoyed anything in her life. Maybe I was just sour with exhaustion.

In Baggage, I picked up my Lark, then went through customs. That took almost an hour. Several big planes had come in close together and the terminal was packed with tourists lured by the summer season or the tournament. Waiting in line to be checked, I heard English, French, Spanish, German, Swahili, and Portuguese.

I was careful to declare my tape recorder and camera gear.

I was feeling tight inside. Militia, in their blue uniforms, with the five-pointed star on the cap, seemed to be everywhere. Most of them were busy looking friendly for the unaccustomed throngs in for the tournament.

The Belgrade International had been promoted heavily, and these crowds made the promotion look good. A music festival and medieval arts exhibition running simultaneously with it couldn't hurt.

The tourney format was going to be a little weird. Sandwiched in between Wimbledon and Davis Cup zone matches, it was to have a limited invitational field to fit the available time. Elimination play for a handful of qualifying slots would be restricted to two days at a killing pace. Even the headliners—the top pros—would have to play two matches a day in the first two rounds. Nobody would have put up with it if the government hadn't anted up such an ungodly amount of prize money. As it was, everybody would be here, and the whole thing would be run off in eight days.

Nobody was to meet me at the airport, so I needed to exchange some money at once. I found that shop and didn't have to wait long. As I walked back out into the main lobby with a fistful of dinars, someone touched my elbow. "Mr. Smith? Mr. Brad Smith?"

Surprised, I turned to face a little man with the expression of a friendly puppy. He was not more than twenty-five years old, pink and cherubic, with blond hair already getting dangerously thin. Thick eyeglasses gave him a Mr. Peepers look. (Anybody out there old enough to remember Mr. Peepers?) He was wearing a rumpled summer suit and stiffly starched white shirt and a red tie about three inches wide.

"Hello!" he said in almost faultless English, sticking out a moist, soft hand. "I am Michael Nariv. With the tournament committee. Welcome to Belgrade. I shall help you to your hotel and answer any questions you may have."

"I wasn't expecting anyone."

Nariv grabbed the heavy Lark bag, staggering slightly under its weight. "We were pleased to know of your arrival, Mr. Smith. I know you do not cover all the tournaments. Having a journalist with your own past tennis triumphs— winner of the U.S. Open, Wimbledon, doubles champion in the French, and so on—is feathers in our hat. Please follow me. I have a car."

It didn't feel quite right to me. The unexpected never set well on a job. But I went along.

Outside the terminal, dense humidity greeted us. The sun was well into the west, and there was impatient traffic everywhere. Nariv struggled the Lark and the Toshiba into the back seat of a Fiat sedan, awkwardly held the door for me, then drove into the terminal area traffic like a mad stockcar driver.

"The air trip was okay?" he asked, shifting gears with a great clatter. "We have storms to the north, but your plane skirted these, right? These big airplanes, they have wonderful equipment for the avoiding of the storms. We have many extra flights coming in now for the tournament. It will be a great success."

"I hope so," I said.

"The tournament starts next Monday as you know, of course," he chattered on, cutting off a Volkswagen and almost sideswiping a Mercedes truck. "But tomorrow morning, Friday, the qualifying playing begins, and on Saturday also is the celebrity playing. Many notables have already arrived. Becker is here. Connors and McEnroe from your own country, and of course Wilander, Lendl, Mecir, Garcia —many others. The city is very excited. The *country* is excited. This is wonderful. I heard Martina Navratilova arrives later today. Steffi Graf and Chris Evert and your wonderful young player Karyn Wechsting are already here, practicing. And many, many other great tennis journalists such as yourself. The tournament is a big success. Tomorrow night there is the giant reception and party for all participants. The excitement has standed the city on its skull, the awesomeness is total!"

Feeling exhaustion tug at my mind again, I said something noncommittal and he launched into another enthusiastic monologue. We screamed into the city at a rate of speed that would not have been safe in twice the car. The Balkan Mountains to the south were invisible because of haze, and the highway ran through the river flat with only power lines and scattered industrial buildings to break the view. Up ahead I could dimly see the seventeen-story "Black Widow" and the Palace Albania against the clutter of lower structures. As we swept into the old city, I got only fleeting impressions: an ancient Coptic church beside a garage with a yard full of junker automobiles, and a ruin that had to date back to the days when the city was occupied by the Turks.

Michael Nariv chattered happily on. He said he would be my official guide and assistant through the tournament, and it was a great honor, et cetera, et cetera. Sleepy, I half listened. He seemed wonderfully incompetent and harmless.

Which kept a small alarm ticking in part of my mind.

Nariv might be too good to be true.

Also, I realized, this seemingly inept young PR man had spotted me unerringly in an airport teeming with visitors. *How?* And why would the tournament committee assign an employee to a relatively minor magazine writer— which is what I was, regardless of my playing background and wishful thinking?

I paid closer attention to my babbling companion. It was an awfully good act. But suddenly I felt pretty sure it was an act.

Nariv might work for the committee, but he had another employer, too. I would have bet on that. And perhaps every foreign journalist or commentator coming in for the tournament had someone just like him assigned "to help"—and watch. But I didn't think so. Even the UDBA didn't have unlimited manpower.

Which meant that someone had decided I was special.

Which meant—maybe—that I had already been blown, and I hadn't even started yet.

My suspicions meant I had to deviate from the plan at once in order to make a contact. But I had to await an opportunity.

When we walked into the hotel lobby, we found it crowded with other sportswriters and TV people. To my surprise, George Plimpton was there, talking with Dick

Enberg and three people I didn't immediately recognize, and he came over to the desk while I was registering.

"Brad," he said, his long face wrinkling in that smile that combined warmth and ennui. "It's fine to see you again."

We shook hands. "Looking for a book?" I asked.

His grin became crooked. "An article, possibly, on how a Communist nation plays host to the jet-set tennis crowd." He noticed my racket case strapped to the side of the Lark. "Playing in the celebrity, are you?"

"I'm here to write."

"But surely they'll ask you to play. I remember that hot day on center court at Wimbledon. And the match with Connors in Los Angeles. Those were grand times . . . wonderful matches."

"I'm just a freelance writer now, George."

"But a man of your credentials. I'm sure you'll be asked to play."

"Maybe." With the gadfly Michael Nariv obviously hanging on every word, I felt uncomfortable. "I haven't seen a schedule yet."

"Oh, I am sure Mr. Smith will be asked to play," Nariv broke in enthusiastically. "And I am sure the committee hopes you will take part also, Mr. Plimpton."

George looked him up and down. "And you are . . . ?"

"Allow me the introduction of myself. Michael Nariv. I am with the tournament committee." Nariv actually clicked his heels and bowed from the waist.

Plimpton stared at him a moment, then gave up trying to figure him out and turned back to me. "Some of us are going out for *ražnjici*. Wonderful stuff. Would you care to join us?"

I begged off, citing the lack of sleep, and he went back to his waiting friends. I suddenly recognized another of them behind his bushy beard: Bud Collins. He grinned and waved.

Nariv insisted on accompanying me to the door of my room. As we crossed the lobby toward the lift, a tall, well-built man of about fifty detached himself from another man and a striking blonde and intercepted us casually.

"My good friend Michael," he said with a smile that had no warmth in it.

Nariv suddenly looked slightly pale, and very nervous. "Major Maleeva! Good afternoon, sir!"

Maleeva's smile became a grin. He had a beefy face with a blue five o'clock shadow and wide eyes in deep, tired sockets. The smile had a gold front tooth in it. His hair was dense, black, wavy, long. The lobby lights glistened on his oily complexion. In his black summerweight suit and white shirt and gray tie, he looked heavy, muscular, conditioned, military.

He told me, "Please take no notice of Michael's use of a title." His ball-bearing eyes swiveled back to Nariv. "I am off duty, Michael, merely familiarizing myself with some of those for whom we will provide the maximum in personal security and safety."

"Yes." Nariv choked, still uptight. "I—"

Maleeva turned back to me, extending a big paw. "Allow me the honor. I am Ladislav Maleeva."

He reeked of UDBA, the secret police. I shook his hand and gave him my name.

"Oh, yes, of course, Mr. Brad Smith," he said. "Another American journalist. I hope you are one of the truthful ones."

"I try to be."

"It is unfortunate that more of your colleagues in your press do not share your interest in writing the truth."

"Well, they're at a disadvantage, Major. They don't have a totalitarian government telling them what the truth is, the way you do."

For a fraction of a second the startled anger heated his eyes. But he was good; the neat, meaningless smile never faltered. He replied smoothly, "I hope your stay in Belgrade is a pleasant one."

"I am sure it will be."

I had the impression that his eyes were X-raying me. I didn't mind a bit when he excused himself with a vague pleasantry, and poor Nariv and I finally got into the lift.

After we had gotten out on my floor above and were walking to the room, I said, "Maleeva is UDBA, of course?"

Nariv patted his face with a handkerchief. "Yes. He is a very important man."

I didn't reply. Was Nariv acting? I couldn't tell. Maybe the meeting with Maleeva hadn't been accidental at all, but set up so Nariv's boss could look me over for himself. I badly needed to make a contact right away.

"You will wish to have a tour of the inner city later tonight?" Nariv chirped as I unlocked the door to my room. "Dinner, perhaps?" He smirked. "We have lovely female guides. It could be arranged for a very beautiful young lady to accompany you, assist you in finding good food and wine, provide . . . answers to all your questions, and friendship away from home."

I didn't know what the hell to make of the speech. It crossed my mind that he was trying to fix me up so they could blackmail me. But that sounded crazy: I simply was not that important . . . unless I really had been blown already. I realized that I was far too tired to make sense, even to myself.

"I just want some sleep right now, Michael," I told him. "And maybe later a snack."

"In the morning you wish to visit friends? See the tennis facility? Perhaps if it can be arranged to meet Danisa Lechova and her sister Hannah?"

"I would like very much to meet Danisa Lechova as early tomorrow as possible. Yes."

"Good. Excellent. Many journalists wish the scoop of meeting Danisa, of course. But the committee recognizes the importance of your magazine, and an article written in same by a personage of your illustriousness. I will see what can be arranged."

"Fine." I put my bag into the room and turned quickly, or he would have followed me on inside. "See you later, Michael. Thanks."

He handed me a card. "Please call if you have any needs whatsoever. *Any* needs."

"Yes." He was getting on my nerves. I started to close the door.

"I will call you from the lobby in the morning at nine hundred hours, sharply, unless I hear from you in the meantime, my good Mr. Smith. Please remember, we are honored by your presence and the presence of the many other fine journalist who have come to our country to coverage this tournament. You will find our hospitality beyond recall. Anything! Ask anything!"

"Good night, Michael." He was still talking when I closed the door.

It was a nice room, small by American standards, contemporary, almost austere, with white painted walls, chocolate-colored carpet, a modern contemporary table flanked by a lightly upholstered chair, a draped window looking out over a useless, six-inch decorative balcony. Beyond was a wooded park, the Tašmajdan.

I got into my bag and found the bright red T-shirt. I put it on a hanger and stuck it between the draperies and the windowglass as if put there to dry. I checked my watch and then I finished unpacking.

I gave them an hour.

Then I wrote my note: *Trouble? Met at airport by Michael Nariv. Says he is part official welcoming committee. True?????*

Pocketing that, I went down to the vast contemporary lobby and found some postcards in the shop. I sat in the lobby and filled out two of them, one to the club in Richardson and one to June.

It was starting to get dark when I left the hotel and walked down the street toward the main post office. It wasn't far. There was still a lot of traffic on the Boulevard of the Revolution, and many tourists with their cameras and guidebooks.

My man, Mitchell, was standing on the corner studying a street map. The photos of him had been excellent. He was young, dark-haired, casually dressed, blending nicely with the other visitors.

Our eyes met for an instant as I approached. Then he folded his map and stepped up to the curb, ready to cross. As I moved beside him in the crowd, he dropped the map. I bent to retrieve it for him and slid my palmed note inside as I picked it up and handed it back. He thanked me. The light changed. We crossed. He turned right and I walked on toward the imposing gray stone bulk of the post office.

I mailed my cards and returned to the Metropol.

Fatigue was really crashing in on me. I showered, set my travel alarm for an early wakeup, and climbed into bed. Almost instantly I was asleep. Then came the telephone call.

Some European telephones chirp, some buzz, and some ring. Then there was the telephone in my hotel room. Which *braaap*'d.

It brought me up out of deep, exhausted sleep at straight-up 9 P.M.

For a second or two I had no idea where I was. Then I got my eyes open and found the telephone, a chunk of white plastic with a blue light flashing on the front. *What the hell*—?

I picked it up. "Brad Smith speaking."

"Brad?" It was a woman's voice, husky and warm with friendship.

"This is Brad Smith," I said, puzzled.

"Do you remember me? I think we met in London two years ago. It was an okay experience for us—"

I slammed the instrument into its modernistic cradle.

Sleep was scalded out of me now, and in its place was incredulous anger. How clumsy could someone be? It was incredibly stupid to call me on the hotel phone! And then she had—without any masking preamble—simply started to dump the first of her verbal bona fides.

Almost certainly the hotel lines were bugged. Even the dullest Jug militia bureaucrat, wearily reviewing hundreds of routine calls off the tapes every day, would notice *this* weird opening.

I had hoped for a prompt return contact in response to my query about Michael Nariv. But Jesus Christ. This violated every principle as well as every aspect of the set plan for contacts. *This* kind of stupidity was like hanging a "spy" sign around my neck and lighting it with neon.

What kind of a moron was I dealing with here?

Going to the windows, I shot the draperies open. Night was almost upon the city, the sun now a red ball behind lavender and blue clouds on the western horizon. Cars made Christmas-like lights on the street below, and the city glowed in the last sunlight. I could see the vast green sprawl of another park in the distance, and last sunlight on the domes and roofs of huge public buildings, monuments. I thought I could even see a glitter of light on a river, the Sava, far off. Beyond glowed the lights of New Belgrade.

I wished I had someone to call and curse. The woman obviously had been another contact. But she couldn't have been more stupid and obvious. She had almost surely compromised me, plain and simple.

How in *hell* had the people at the embassy picked someone like that? If this first gambit was any indication of how well the operation was laid out, we were dead.

Correction: we might not be dead; we might merely be helpless. It was Danisa Lechova who might be dead.

Looking out at the big, darkening foreign city, I wondered again what in hell made a pretty young tennis star so important to my government. We made stupid mistakes sometimes—God knew I had just had a field demonstration of that—but we didn't mount operations like this without good reason. But what could the reasons be?

I might never know.

Ambiguity again.

Which made me think of June again.

I didn't delude myself about June. I might have sent her a postcard for cover, but we were finished. I felt really sad and really alone.

A pale moon began to show through the city haze. I looked up at it and wished I had given in to myself and brought my alloted 200 cigarettes in through customs. First Nariv, then Maleeva, then my general feeling of galloping paranoia, and now this. Sleep was not going to come back easily.

seven

By morning—after a total of five hours' sleep—I had made a few decisions.

Until someone gave me definite word that my cover had already been blown—that Michael Nariv was UDBA—I would assume I was still operational, and press on.

And I would not seek out further contact with the local guys because obviously at least some of them were morons who might do me more harm than good by attempting clumsy, transparent contacts.

I hadn't gotten any further than that when I went down to the hotel coffee shop early and ordered my continental breakfast. On the Continent, that means beautiful hard rolls, real butter, and coffee so dense you can almost chew it, with a pitcher of the thickest, sweetest cream in the world.

There were only a handful of others in the room and I was just beginning to enjoy my first roll and cup of coffee in solitary splendor when the man marched—I use the word advisedly—up to my table.

"Mr. Smith?" he said, bristling cold hostility. "Mr. Brad Smith?"

I looked up.

He stood a gaunt six feet tall: a gray-haired man nearing fifty, wearing tan slacks and a white summer shirt open at the collar. His deeply tanned face was lighted by vivid blue eyes that crackled with impatience and hostility.

"I'm Smith," I told him.

"I understand, sir," he said tightly, with a heavy accent, "you wish to spend time with Danisa Lechova."

"And who might you be?"

A pulse bulged in his forehead. "I am Leon Lechova."

I stood and offered my hand. He looked at it like it might be contaminated by something, then shook it. His grip was steely.

"Sit down," I suggested.

"No, thank you."

I sat down and resumed my attack on my hard roll and butter.

Leon Lechova's voice rose, more angry: "You are ignoring me?"

"Not at all, sir."

"I wish to speak with you."

"I want to talk to you, too."

"Yet you ignore me!"

I looked up at him, wondering how his thin frame could bear the weight of all the hostility that seemed to be an integral part of his personality. Snap decisions about people are wrong as often as they are right, and I don't like to make them. But I didn't like Leon Lechova, either.

"No, sir," I told him. "I invited you to sit down. I hope we can have many pleasant conversations together in the next few days. But I'm not going to let my coffee get cold."

He pointed a thumb at his chest. "If I say you do not interview Danisa, you do not interview Danisa!"

I put the roll down. This guy could make George Bush lose his temper. "Mr. Lechova, what the hell is it you want?"

His face worked. He grabbed the chair opposite me. "I will sit down."

"Great. Now we're making progress." I signaled the waiter.

"No," Lechova snapped. "No coffee. Never. Heart."

"You have a bad heart?"

"No. Good heart." He scowled at me. "My heart is perfect because I never drink coffee."

"Good for you."

"Neither do I smoke or drink alcohol."

"That's very admirable."

His voice rose an octave. "You mock me."

"No sir, I certainly do not. I know your background in athletics—"

"We are not here to talk about Leon Lechova. We are here to talk about you and Danisa."

"Yes. My assignment is to interview her."

"So I have been informed." His scowl deepened.

"I gather you don't like the idea of my interviewing her?"

"Everybody wishes to interview Danisa."

"Then what's the problem?"

He glared. "Tracy Austin."

"Pardon?"

"Andrea Jaeger."

"What?"

"Too many young players, especially women, are brought into the searchlight too early . . . too fast. Success. It can spoil a young player. We have developed Danisa and Hannah slowly. With care. Now soon Danisa will take her place. She will be queen of women's tennis. I am determined!"

"I hope it happens, Mr. Lechova."

"It *will* happen!"

"I hope so. But there's only one number one. *One.* In the whole world. Do you know what that makes the odds?"

"Danisa will do it. I will make her do it. I will drive her until she does."

"I've known young players who self-destructed because they pushed hard after that dream . . . or were pushed that hard by someone else who needed it even more than they did. If you love your daughters—"

"Of course I love my daughters! That is why I will make them the best, or destroy them trying! I will not allow *anything* to interfere with my goal."

His ambition was as hot as the radiation from a roaring wood stove. Unlike the heat from a fire, it felt sick. *Careful!* I thought. *A wrong word and he really could make it impossible for you to see the girl.*

So I changed tack. "Danisa and her family are already in the spotlight, Mr. Lechova. Stories will be written. This tournament is expected to highlight Danisa, win or lose. Just like Miricic on the men's side."

His jaw set, making the pulse jump again. "Yes. But not everyone can interview Danisa and Hannah. Too much attention wears them out, turns their heads. Distraction. We intend to protect Danisa and Hannah, I do not care what the state says, what anybody says. Do you understand that?"

I bought a few seconds to think by sipping the fine, dense black coffee. I had known he was a fanatic, a slave driver, unforgiving, consumed by his ambition for the girls. Now I saw another dimension.

He was afraid.

The fear was based on an altogether too accurate assessment of what sudden fame could do to young players. One day: obscurity and dreams; the next: the endless spotlight and pressure of trying to stay on top of the world. It had hit Jaeger and Austin hard, although Tracy had had the back problem, too. It had even shaken Boris Becker for a while, and who could say whether a John McEnroe had ever been a happy man, since his phenomenal early talent bought him the supposed right to act like an undisciplined maniac oncourt every time a call went against him?

"You're afraid too much attention will hurt Danisa's career," I said.

"Yes—"

"But that kind of attention has to come if you're at the top, Mr. Lechova, doesn't it?"

"Yes," he repeated. Then he surprised me: "That is why I have come here this morning to see you for myself."

I stared at him. I didn't get the connection or the point.

"You have been at top of tennis," he said.

"Well, the top ten for a year or so, maybe—"

"The *top*," he insisted in a tone that allowed no argument. "I have also read some of your stories in magazines. You respect the game. You respect your work. You tell truth. You are fair. You are not like some. Some know little about the game, and try be funny."

"Thank you."

He glowered again. "You wish to spend time with Danisa?"

I wondered what kind of inquisition her boyfriends must go through. "Yes."

"You want tell what makes her be ticking, right?"

If I corrected his slang, he would blow up. "I'll be covering the tournament. In addition, I want to spend several hours with your daughters—both of them—although Danisa is the focus. The magazine wants a piece that tells how she really is offcourt, what kind of a young woman she is. To get that insight, I need time with her."

He cocked his head suspiciously. "Assassin job?"

"No, goddamn it."

He studied me.

Steamed, I added, "You said you had read my copy. If you have, you know I'm fair."

His teeth clacked together. "All right."

Whatever that meant.

He got to his feet. "You will get your chance to meet Danisa, rally with her and Hannah if you want, talk. You will write your story before you leave Yugoslavia. I will read and approve every word."

"No," I said instantly.

His eyebrows shot up. "No?"

"No! This may sound strange to you, but where I come

67

from, newsmen don't let their sources censor their copy. I may just be a tennis writer, but I'm not about to let you muck around with my copy."

He raised himself haughtily. "Then you will not interview."

"Fine." I had lost it. "Then somebody else will do the feature story—you can't keep her in a bottle the rest of her life—and the other writer might get things all screwed up and cause *exactly* the kind of wrong impressions you want to avoid."

"You don't want to interview?"

"Of course I do! But not on your goddamn terms!"

His expression changed. He said thoughtfully, "You are tough sonofabitch, right?"

I gave him back the same expression. "Just like you."

He nodded sharply. "Okay. Fine. You will see her." He turned and strode out of the restaurant.

I retrieved my napkin off my lap and wiped my forehead with it.

Michael Nariv arrived an hour later. He was ten minutes early, as I had known he would be. We headed for the new sports arena where the tournament would be held. It was a fine day, the sun warm as it moved between puffy white cumulous clouds, and when we got to the sports complex we found players of all rankings working out on the outdoor courts.

Danisa and a few others, Nariv informed me, were on the courts inside where all the major matches would be played. The arena, he said, seated 22,000, and Danisa would play all her matches inside to assure capacity sales.

Sunlight on a vast translucent dome gave a golden color to the interior of the big arena, which still smelled of fresh paint and plaster. All the black clay courts were occupied by players at practice. I spotted Martina rallying with Chrissie under the watchful eye of Renee Richards. On an adjacent court Lisa Bonder was working out with the elegant Karyn

Wechsting. At the far end, Miricic was warming up with Czech Davis Cupper Pavel Slozil. A few other members of the press were scattered around the dark, gleaming stands.

All of that, however, was a fleeting impression. My attention went at once to the number 3 court, where two beautiful young blond women were hitting it back and forth with silent, ferocious intensity. Beside the court stood a squat, powerfully built man with a mane of gray-black hair, a wild beard, and a towel thrown over his thick shoulder: Miloslav Fjbk.

Michael Nariv and I walked across bleacher sections to get closer.

The two Lechova women looked almost like twins at a distance, and their carbon-copy style of play enhanced the eerie impression that Danisa Lechova was shadowboxing with a mirror. Both of them moved with a steady, powerful grace, hitting sizzlers on the lines. Their identical long golden hair, slender tanned arms and legs, and brief tennis dresses furthered the confusion between them. I knew that Danisa was prettier up close, with finer features, and of course her trademark pigtail identified her further; but at any distance they might have been confused for one another. Danisa wore blue, Hannah a pale lavender.

As Nariv and I settled down in the lowest row to watch, however, it quickly became apparent that similarities between the young women stopped short of their games. Danisa Lechova had it all over on her sister, Hannah.

Just as we sat down, Hannah, in the near court, hit a backhand down the line that spat chalk. Danisa was far out of position. She started after the shot as it was struck, and my instant reaction was: *Good. Running it out for the practice.* But somehow or other as the ball skidded off the chalked line she was *just there,* sliding far into the shot and extending her slim body to its maximum length. Her racket preparation, especially under the circumstances, was marvelous. She not only reached the ball, but blasted back a fireball forehand that seared the crosscourt corner markings.

69

"Holy shit," I murmured involuntarily.

Nariv giggled. "She is wondrous, our Danisa, eh?"

I didn't answer him. Fascinated, I watched as Danisa Lechova hit phenomenal shot after phenomenal shot. Her sister, Hannah, was game. She was also grimly competitive, hanging in on every point and winning a lot of them. In other company, I think all eyes would have been on her. That she was hanging on by her fingernails was not a disparagement of her play; it was just that Danisa was fabulous.

After a while, Fjbk stopped play and conferred with the sisters at the net. They resumed their places and Hannah drilled low liners and slices to Danisa's backhand, running her and changing pace. Danisa's returns looked perfect to me, but Fjbk stopped them again and lectured her with a scowl and wagging finger. Her shoulders sloped a little this time as play resumed again. She was being pushed too hard.

Another twenty minutes, and Fjbk called a halt to it. As the sisters toweled their faces and started gathering equipment, Nariv opened the stadium-type gate that separated the seats from the arena floor, motioning to me. "Come! We will meet them now!"

"Don't you think they want to shower and cool down first?"

"It is arranged! Come!"

I followed him. He greeted Fjbk with his usual enthusiasm, and the Serb gave me a glower that would have frozen a bonfire. The Lechova sisters saw what was going on and came over. I had an overwhelming impression of pretty bare arms and long, wonderful legs, and sweat-coiled blond hair and beautiful eyes—Danisa's blue, Hannah's brown—and gleaming, palpitating girl.

"Danisa," Nariv gushed, "Hannah! Allow me to present the former United States Open champion, Wimbledon champion, doubles champion of the French, three-time Davis Cup member—"

"Tennis writer and six-time quitter of smoking," I cut in, extending my right hand. "Brad Smith. Hello."

Danisa shook my hand. Her vivid, happy smile blew me away. Up close she was simply stunning. No small girl, she, and her features were not delicate or weak. Her mouth was wide and what they used to describe as generous, her eyes large for her face, and vivid. And despite her slenderness, the lady had breasts.

"I am happy to meet you, Mr. Brad Smith," she told me. "My father has said we are to have interviews."

Hannah cut in almost violently, "Hey, I hope we have interviews, too!" She seized my hand and pumped it. "Gosh, Brad Smith, you are . . . let me think of the right word . . . you are a *hunk*, eh?" She wriggled from head to foot, with interesting results. "Ooh! You are gorgeous! You want to play?" She rolled roguish eyes. "Tennis? Anything else?"

"Hannah," Fjbk rumbled reprovingly.

"But look at him!" Hannah cried. "Oh, God! All the beautiful men around this place, and Brad Smith here to do interviews! I can't stand it!"

Danisa's calm eyes watched my reactions. She was amused. It was the first of many times I would get the impression she was far older and wiser than her years. Perhaps after this single moment I would never again think of her as a girl.

She said, "It has been arranged we will have time for talk tomorrow, and we play together in the celebrity mixed doubles."

Someone had moved fast. "I look forward to that."

Hannah broke in enthusiastically. "You still like to play, right?"

"Of course." The question surprised me. "Don't you?"

Hannah did more wriggling. "I love it! I love all of it! Sometimes I get so excited I want to play without my clothes on! I would love to play naked, on television!"

Jack M. Bickham

Danisa giggled. "When you do that, be playing someone else, not me. I like people to notice that *I* am oncourt."

"Time for showers," Fjbk interrupted. He was not
amused.

Hannah made eyes. "I have shocked poor Milo." She
put a long hand on his muscular shoulder. "You have to
forgive me." She spun back to me. "You have to forgive me
too, darling. I am Yugoslav, and we are all very emotional."

Danisa studied her sister for a moment with cool,
amused eyes, then turned to me. "You will be at the
reception and ball tonight?"

I told her I planned to be there.

"We might even have time to start our talks then," she
told me.

"That would be fine."

Our eyes met. Hers questioned me. She knew, I
thought, that I was here to help her get out. I wondered—

Hannah broke into any wondering. "We will dance
tonight!" she said, stroking my arm. "You will see I dance as
beautifully as I play this game! Are you a wonderful
dancer?"

"Of course he is," Danisa murmured. "Look at him."

"Ah! I have been looking at him, my sister! I think I
want him for my very own!"

Danisa's smile became a radiant grin. "Hannah, you
will not be allowed to monopolize Mr. Smith."

It was a cute thing to say. But she was not the only one I
watched as she said it; Fjbk was there in my peripheral
vision, and it was his expression that registered most
strongly. His mouth tightened almost imperceptibly, and
there was a faint, powerful narrowing of his big dark eyes. It
was like a galvanic current had surged through him from
head to foot, and only by the quick application of tremen-
dous control had he been able to mask its effect.

Miloslav Fjbk was crazy in love with Danisa.

Then, as quickly as that look appeared, it was gone.
"Come," he rumbled. He put a hand on Danisa's

72

shoulder . . . hairy paw, swollen with power, gentle and tentative on her moist skin. "Shower now," he ordered.

They hurried off, two laughing girls and the squat middle-aged man between them, lumbering on bowed legs, scowling out at the world.

Michael Nariv sighed. "Interesting, no?"

I didn't answer him.

"So," he went on cheerfully, "with them gone, this is perhaps the time for asking you: Did we not meet in London two years ago?"

Looking at Nariv's crooked little grin and the sudden crafty slant to his eyes, I felt new surprise, like icy sludge, creep through my bloodstream. Getting blown away by surprises was starting to get old.

Like a good boy I went ahead with it: "It must have been three years ago if it was London."

Nariv said, "On the bridge?"

"Under the clock."

His shoulders slumped slightly. "So."

"Who the fuck," I asked, "called my hotel room last night?"

"Paula Bansky." His smile widened. "She wished to assure you that I am trustworthy."

So he knew I had been suspicious of him. I pointed out, "She was reckless. I don't like that a damned bit."

He shrugged. "It is all right."

"It is not all right, you *govno*. She started the verbal bona fides right on the damned telephone."

"But the telephones are not monitored regularly."

"How do you know they weren't monitoring for me?"

"It seems highly unlikely."

" 'Highly unlikely,' my ass."

"Why are you so angry?" he asked plaintively. "Nothing was harmed."

"You don't *know* that. You—oh, to hell with it. She shouldn't have called me that way. Just make sure there are no repetitions."

"If you had allowed me to supply you with a female companion, my friend, Paula would have been the one who came to you."

"And how would that have looked, you jerk?"

He couldn't be flapped. "Normal. Paula is very beautiful, and she works for one of the city's busiest escort services. She will, as a matter of fact, be your companion at the reception and ball tonight."

"What are you going to do, Michael? Take pictures?"

He looked around. We were alone in an acre of empty blue seats. "I will be making arrangements for a car. There are to be two cars. You are to tell Danisa Lechova that the thing will be done at the earliest next Tuesday night after play of the second-round singles, and at the latest next Thursday, the day of finals in all doubles."

"What is she supposed to do?"

"I have been told there will be more instructions. She must understand that she cannot make any preparations that might draw notice. When the time comes it will be quick. She will not be able to take anything with her."

"Is that all?"

"I have been told you will have a role in getting her out of the arena area and to a point where she will be met."

"That isn't what I was told. I was told I would be a go-between, and nothing more."

"The plan has been modified, I assume."

"Don't you know?"

He shrugged. "Hey, my friend. I do not know a lot. I carry messages. I am . . . little potato."

"Christ," I said, sighing. "So what are my revised instructions?"

"Your instructions are to come later. There are many details. I have been told it is imperative that you spend a lot of time with Danisa. You will interview her in width. This is not only to establish your right to be close to her at the proper time, but to allow you to form a judgment . . . to make sure you can assure our superiors that her resolve is not going down the tubing as the time nears."

"*I'm* supposed to make that kind of judgment?" I asked.

"Yes."

"Damn it, I'm not qualified!"

He ignored my protest. "There is one more thing."

"There always is."

"You are to do your maximum to win the confidence and friendship of Miloslav Fjbk and the family."

"How am I supposed to do that?"

"Fjbk," he went on as if I hadn't spoken, "watches the young women with the eyes of a falcon. I am authorized to be sure to tell you that Fjbk is a jealous man and can cause grave difficulties for us because of his watchfulness of them."

"I noticed."

"The parents keep close watch on the daughters. Especially the father. There is tenseness between the family over the girls' careers, and the future especially of Danisa. The father and mother. The father will do anything to advance Danisa's career."

I nodded. I would report later about the confrontation with Poppa at the hotel, but right now I wanted to hear all of this.

"You are to be aware," Nariv went on, watching the tennis on a distant court, "that Hannah Lechova has strong ties to the army and to the militia. She is known to have in the past informed on friends she suspected of political deviation. She is maybe the bug in the oint, huh? She is to be handled with kid shoes."

Something told me Hannah might be my biggest immediate problem. The look in her eyes when she smiled at me had not had anything to do with political deviationism.

Nariv took my silence for conclusion of discussion. "You wish now to watch other warming ups?" he asked.

At the far end of the arena I could see Pat Cash, Paul Annacone, Yannick Noah, and several other familiar faces getting ready to work out. Bettina Fulco and Gabriela Sabatini were down there, too. "I'd better go do some journalist work, yes."

"Good." Nariv beamed. "Then I will take you to your hotel, and you will be joined by Paula for a late lunch. It is all arranged."

"What's Paula's role in all this?"

"I do not know, my good friend Brad Smith."

"Seems to me there's a hell of a lot we don't know, especially when we're as little as four days away from carrying the operation to its conclusion."

"Yes," Nariv said, and nervously giggled. "Suspense. Intrigue. Is wonderful, right? Come! Let us go watch the arriving jockstraps."

eight

Elsewhere

Ministry of Culture, Belgrade

In the office building just off Marshal Tito Street, Major Ladislav Maleeva fought for control of his anger as he faced M. Y. Altunyan, ostensibly an attaché for cultural affairs at the Soviet embassy but in reality the KGB's chief Resident in Belgrade.

"This is an internal matter of my country," Maleeva insisted.

"There is no intent to interfere in Yugoslavia's internal affairs." Altunyan, a big man, with mountains of fat rumpling his expensive suit, reached inside his jacket and took out one of the long black cigars that Maleeva despised. Altunyan's fingers looked to Maleeva like Slovenian sausages. "We wish only to cooperate," the Russian added heavily.

Maleeva did not miss the sarcastic condescension. He was trapped, and the KGB Resident knew it. Maleeva hated all Russians and he hated Altunyan more because of his power.

Ordinarily the KGB was only tolerated in Belgrade.

Since the historic schism between Marshal Tito and Stalin, and Khrushchev's self-abasing speech of 1955, Yugoslavia had fiercely defended its right to self-determination. It was by far the most Western of the nations under the umbrella of Soviet power, a point that Maleeva, like all Yugoslavs, was defiantly proud of. But a month ago, for reasons Maleeva could not fathom, the orders had come from the highest authority: the UDBA would cooperate with the KGB on this case.

Maleeva bitterly resented it. But he was a good soldier and he would obey.

He told Altunyan, "We will keep you informed of our surveillance."

"Insufficient," Altunyan responded, fingering the cigar.

Maleeva's voice cracked under his effort to control his anger. "Then what is it you want?"

"I need not remind you that cooperation in this matter has been decreed at the highest levels of government." Altunyan paused, struck a light from a stainless steel Dunhill lighter that cost more than Maleeva made in a week, and touched fire to the cigar. "Routine reports will not satisfy our needs."

"Then what," Maleeva repeated, "do you *want?*"

"This man Nariv."

"He is being watched day and night."

"Insufficient."

"Insufficient?" Maleeva repeated, his eyes watering from the acrid cigar smoke that clogged the office. "*Insufficient?* What more do you expect us to do?"

"We must know his role and mission. Now."

"I told you! We are watching—"

"And I told *you.* That is insufficient!"

"What more can we possibly do?"

Altunyan leaned forward through the smoke. "I will tell you."

* * *

Swift Current, Saskatchewan

The prairie of Saskatchewan looked like it extended a thousand miles.

In some directions it did.

Standing in front of his motel unit, Dominic Partek looked out over the low sprawl of the town of Swift Current, and watched faint cloud-shadows drift across the face of the naked grass hillocks. It was afternoon, hot.

Partek had to decide where next he would flee.

He delayed the decision by staring at the prairie, letting the sadness move through him.

The sadness was unrelated to the danger that choked him. He searched for a reason for it and found one: this barren country reminded him of the flatlands of Serbia around Surčin and Beograd.

He had imagined that nostalgia for his homeland was long since behind him. But in his current predicament the landscape had brought it back.

Partek lit one Players off another and turned his gaze to the bug-encrusted front of his truck. He had driven hard and slept a long time. Now he had to decide his next step.

He faced the cruelest kind of dilemma. If he went back, the punishment would be severe, possibly death. But if he reverted to his agonizing decision to defect to the West, he might be found and killed anyway; and certainly his family —so long thought lost—would pay.

Whatever I do, he thought, *there will be suffering.*

He was sick of it—sick of suffering, of dilemmas, of uncertainty and loss . . . sick of himself.

He remembered his childhood in Surčin. His father had always been ill, had sometimes been drunk and violent. In those times he had beaten Dominic with a cold, terrifying fury. The boy had grown up with terror. Usually his mother had been able to intervene before the beating went too far.

Sometimes Alexi Partek beat her too, for intervening.

Dominic's mother, gaunt and haggard, had always held a full-time job at a bearing factory. But she had always loved him, had held him and smiled at him when he did well, protected him as best she could. And sometimes in the evenings when his father was gone she had sung the old songs. Dominic had adored her, would have done anything for her.

So in school he worked very hard, and was a fine student. His father sneered at his accomplishments, saying they would not improve his chances in life.

Dominic was good in athletics too, which his mother told him should be no surprise: his father, long ago, before his tragic injuries at Stalingrad, had been an athlete. His father, Dominic was told, had been a great hero at Stalingrad, and this was why he limped so, experienced such constant pain, was sometimes violently ill, did not have adequate lungs.

Alexi Partek was from the Ukraine, she told Dominic, and should have been compensated by the Russians for his heroism in the war against Hitler. That the Russians had discarded and ignored him after his great service was only another proof that the Russians were evil men.

Dominic's father had had only one serious conversation with him during his growing-up. On that occasion, Alexi Partek told his son that he should not believe his mother's railings against the Soviet Union. It had been an honor to give up his health for the USSR, Alexi told his son, and if there was a reason now why he drank sometimes, and fell into fits of the blackest and most violent melancholy, it was because circumstances forced him to live here in Yugoslavia, Martina Partek's homeland, rather than in his beloved Ukraine. His wife, Alexi Partek said bitterly, understood nothing. She was *govno*. Everything about Yugoslavia was *govno*.

Disagreements of this sort were part of the fabric of

Dominic's childhood. He worked hard to please his mother and to avoid his father's fists. He led his class through school.

In 1966, Dominic had graduated from high school and entered the Yugoslav army by conscription. It should have been a happy development with hope for the future, but at almost the same time something wonderful and something disastrous happened in the family. His mother, astonishingly, told him that she was pregnant. And his father, after a ghastly scene, ran away.

Sending her son off to the army, Martina Partek was pale but resolute.

"I will manage," she told him.

"Father will come back," Dominic told her.

"No." She was like ice-covered stone. He could sense her inner trembling, but God, she was strong. He had always known she was strong, but in this moment her strength awed him. "He will not come back. But if he tried, he can never stay here again."

"Mother!"

"You are a man now," she told him with an eerie calm. "I will tell you this. Alexi has gone away because of this child in my belly. You heard the shouting, the threats and insults. We cannot feed another child, he says. We are too old, he says. But I tell you this, my son: one time, long ago, there was another child in my belly; Alexi shouted and raved, and I . . . had an end put to that pregnancy. Still sometimes at night, in my chair, I look up from my sewing, and there at the dark-night window I see the face of that child of mine I did not allow to be born. I will not lose this child. I will have this child and raise this child. I will do that. Alexi is gone because he could not confront another child. He will not come back to me because I have chosen this child over him."

Martina Partek's eyes looked far away, and her jaw set. "I do not think I will see Alexi's face at the window in the dark of night."

It had been a grim home-leaving, but once in the army training camp Dominic had put it behind him as best he could, and did what he always had done: fight to excel. Almost all of his pitiful monthly check was mailed back to Surčin. Months passed and he finished basic training and was selected for special code and cipher school near Sarajevo.

While he was in that school, word came that his father had died in Moscow. Dominic was granted five days' leave to attend to final arrangements. By the time he arrived in Moscow, he learned that his father's body had already been cremated, and the "estate" amounted to a cheap watch, a handful of unidentified pills, a few items of clothing, and unpaid rent in a cheap rooming house. Under "Identity" on the certificate of death, the inspectors had written *"Veteran. Unemployed."*

His leave time running out, Dominic returned to his new post. He wrote a long letter to his mother in Surčin, and enclosed a small extra amount of money, borrowed from another trainee. Two weeks later, this envelope was returned to him with the stamp on it: *UNKNOWN.*

Dominic remailed the letter, telling himself the return had been a bureaucratic mistake. It came back again. Badly alarmed, he sought emergency leave. He was told he had just had an emergency leave.

For three more weeks he stewed and waited for the leave that would come automatically at the conclusion of the first phase of his intelligence training. He considered going to Surčin without official leave, but such disobedience of orders would have been contrary to every fiber of his morality. So he waited, scared.

When he finally got to Surčin, he went at once to the tiny wood shack where he had grown up. He found another family there. Their name was Rishtek. They knew nothing about his mother. He talked to neighbors. They said Martina Partek had simply vanished, evidently taking her few possessions with her.

Frantic now, Dominic called on the militia. But they pointed out that his mother had taken her things with her, so foul play seemed highly unlikely. They agreed at last to file a report. Dominic, although young, was experienced enough to know what happened to reports when they were tossed into the maw of the bureaucracy.

His leave ran out. He used every moment available to search, but he didn't know where to search, or how. He spent his last day of leave walking up and down streets in Belgrade, thinking that somehow he would just look up, and by magic there she would be. He realized that he might as well be looking in some other city; he had chosen Belgrade for his blind wanderings only because it was nearest Surčin.

All through 1966, as he finished one school and was immediately sent to another, a haunted Dominic Partek wrote letters, filled out inquiry forms, bombarded the mail with questions. He was convinced that his mother would not have deserted him if she had been in control; he was sure something dreadful had happened to her.

What had happened to her? And to the child she had been carrying?

His letters and tracer forms came back stamped or scribbled on with the stupid monosyllables of drones and functionaries: *NOTED. NAME ON FILE. NO RECORD. FORWARDED. RETURNED. NO ACTION. UNKNOWN. HELD PEND FORM 860. NO DOCUMENTS.* Twice he got short leaves and rushed to Surčin or Belgrade again, but no one knew anything. Old friends shook their heads sadly and turned away. These things happened.

By the summer of 1968, Dominic's hopes had gone. He completed the last phase of intelligence school and was assigned as an attaché in the Yugoslav embassy in Moscow. There he met a man named Kudirka, a Lithuanian who worked in the Soviet government. Their friendship became close, and on a brisk October evening, walking near the walls of the Kremlin, Kudirka bluntly asked Dominic if he had ever considered a career "with a major organization in the field."

"You must know I am attached to the UDBA," Dominic told him.

"I have in mind our own organization," Kudirka replied.

"You mean the KGB?"

His friend smiled.

"You are a member of the KGB?" Dominic pressed, astonished.

"Please do not misunderstand me," Kudirka said. "I do not suggest that you should represent my organization against your own. Your loyalty is unquestioned and of great interest to us. No. What I suggest is an arrangement under which your files could be transferred to our offices on a permanent basis. You would become one of us. We have a great need for men of your loyalty, intelligence, and integrity. We would provide additional training. Within two years' time, you would in all likelihood be an attaché like myself at a Soviet embassy in another part of the world."

"But my government would never agree to such an arrangement!"

"It is not impossible," Kudirka told him.

"My tour of duty extends another two and one half years."

"It is not a major impediment."

Then Kudirka told Partek what he would be paid, and how he would be trained. He spoke of advancement, world opportunities.

They were magic words. Partek had already begun to see the parochialism of the UDBA, and its limited role in the world. He was a good Communist, and despite his suspicion of things Russian, considered the KGB a valiant and praiseworthy operation—the best on the planet.

And here was his chance to become part of it. He had no family to hold him back.

The decision was made. With amazing alacrity, the

Yugoslav bureacracy spat out the reams of necessary paper-work. Before Christmas, Partek reported to an officer in the great old stone headquarters building on Moscow's Dzerzhinsky Square.

How far I have come! he thought in mute wonderment. Then, thinking of his lost mother and the baby, he added, *And how far will I go, in honor of your memory!*

His real life's work began on that day . . .

So long ago, Partek thought now, still standing on the breezy, sunny pavement outside his motel in Canada. He was filled with sadness. He wondered what he would have done on that day so long ago if he could have foreseen what he knew now, if he could have guessed the disillusionment and treachery.

He had thought he was being clever enough in the way he cautiously contacted one of his counterparts in the CIA. He only needed to know at that point how a transfer of loyalties might be handled, how he might turn himself over, be hidden, get an eventual new identity and occupation so he could live out his life in the West.

At that time he had not even been sure he could take such a horrendous step, despite the years of disillusionment with his Soviet masters. He was, in contacting the CIA acquaintance, only gathering information for a contingency.

And he was so careful . . . so circumspect.

But not careful enough. The American FBI knew of it almost at once, and made a contact with him. That was not so bad, but somehow his KGB masters also got wind of his change of perspective . . . possibly a difference in his dispo-sition at work, possibly something of more substance—not enough to justify stern action on their part, but a subtle warning.

That was when they had allowed him to learn about his family, after all these years. So he would know what he had to lose if his loyalty ever faltered.

They must have thought they were being very clever, letting him uncover the old archival information "by mistake." But in reality their ploy had backfired. Rather than frightening Partek, the ruse had disillusioned and enraged him. *They knew this for years, and never told me. And it was my right to know!* His shock was profound.

His American contacts pressed him for a final decision. He agonized and delayed.

"They suspect you, Dominic. Better to come over now."

"I cannot defect now! They will retaliate in Belgrade!"

"What if we could fix that?"

"Fix? Fix what? How? You cannot control the Soviets!"

"What if we could get her out, so there could never be any reprisals?"

"You could do that?"

"We can try . . ."

So Partek had fled, buying time. But that had been a mistake, because now, by his actions, he stood convicted by his KGB masters. He knew they were looking for him. To make matters worse, both the CIA and FBI were also chasing him "for his own protection."

So that now all he could do was keep hiding . . . see if the CIA's promises were fulfilled. If they were, there was hope. If the CIA failed him, he was doomed, like his family.

A truck horn sounded on the highway beyond the motel entrance. The sound jarred Partek out of his reverie, reminding him of the danger and the need to move. He closed his motel unit door, tossed his cigarette into a puddle on the pavement, and climbed into his truck.

He had to keep moving—do the unexpected.

It was the only thing he was sure about right now.

Moscow

In an office of the KGB's First Chief Directorate, hidden off the circumferential highway, two men held a brief meeting.

"Steps are being taken in Beograd?" asked the superior.

"Yes, sir," said the other. "It is being done as we discussed."

The superior made a note. "Good. The report will be brought to my desk at once."

"That has been ordered, sir."

"Now as to Partek . . . ?"

The junior officer concealed his anxiety. "Everything is being done. Of course his picture and description are already in the hands of all our people in both the U.S. and Canada. A special alert has been issued to all operatives in Canada, with details of previous movement."

"And what of the CIA?"

"We are following the progress of the case officers assigned to pursue the matter across the Canadian border. If they locate him, we will know it."

"We must get to him first," the superior said, clenching a fist on the desktop. "You know that this is a potential disaster for us!"

"All efforts are being made, sir."

"And what of Sylvester?"

"He is still in Montana, as ordered. When word comes, he is prepared to move at once."

The superior officer digested the information, worriedly shaking his head. "Partek," he muttered. "Of all our men, Partek! If this does not go well, it could hardly be a greater calamity."

New Belgrade

Late afternoon sun baked Michael Nariv's face as he strolled through the grounds of the Sava Center, waiting for the meeting with his contact. It was nice, strolling the vast green lawns with the truncated pyramid of glass nearby, cars purring along the wide streets, tourists walking idly. Nariv was feeling perfectly fine.

Then, however, he realized he was being followed.

He was not deeply trained, but the surveillance would have been obvious to almost anyone. The two men behind him were not making any real attempt to be subtle.

Nariv immediately panicked.

Hurrying to the curbside taxi stand, he hopped into the first car available, slamming the door behind him.

The driver turned, raising an eyebrow in inquiry.

Nariv blurted the first thing that came into his mind. "United States Embassy! Hurry!"

The driver nodded and put the car in gear. Outside the taxi, Nariv's two pursuers hurried into the cab behind him. Nariv felt sweat burst from every pore on his body.

This is terrible. This is the worst thing that could happen. They are after me, there can be no doubt, and they must be UDBA. I have been discovered. I will be killed.

How could it have happened? He had never done anything so wrong. All he had wanted was the glamour, the excitement . . . the extra dinars. Now what could he do? How could he escape?

His driver turned out of the Sava Center roadway and approached the Gazela Bridge over the Sava. Nariv twisted around to peer through the rear window of the car and saw his pursuers' Mercedes nosing out behind him. Nariv turned back to the front. His panic intensified. He had to be calm. He had to *think!*

The taxi moved up to speed and swept through the tiered intersection leading to the bridge. Then they were on the bridge in multilane traffic, speeding. The other car was still close behind.

Nariv thought about the embassy.

He realized that he could not go there. An attempt to get inside would convict him. He did not think he could get inside before the UDBA operatives seized him.

His only hope was to escape them somehow, then slip around to the embassy and seek asylum . . . protection.

How to escape such pursuers?

Frantically he looked up and down the river as the taxi thrummed over the bridge. He saw his answer off to his left—the trees, ancient buildings, walls, and monuments of the Kalemegdan.

Nariv poked the driver's shoulder. "I have changed my destination. The Kalemegdan—the Stambol Gate—and please hurry!"

The driver nodded his bushy head and changed lanes for an exit. Nariv leaned back on the plastic seat and held his fists over his eyes, fighting to concentrate. When he reached Kalemegdan, he had to have a *plan*.

Kalemegdan—the ancient fortifications and parkland dominating the conjunction of the Sava and the Danube—had been a fortress before history began. Old Roman ruins were there, and fortress walls and towers dating to the Middle Ages. In addition to the maze of streets, walkways, woods, old walls, and monuments, there were the elements of the modern park. It was an area Nariv had played in and explored in his childhood.

Surely, if he could get inside Stambol Gate and past the military museum he could hide himself. Perhaps in the maze of the lower town near Nebojša Tower, perhaps in the Ruzica Church. There were a thousand places.

The following car had dropped back almost a block. Nariv's driver was pressing along, doing well in the traffic. Nariv began to get his hopes up. *I can do this, and they said I could go to America one day. What a story I will tell my children, the ones I have with a beautiful blond American girl!*

The traffic became worse. The bulk of the land rise appeared on the right side of the taxi, and here the sidewalks were choked with people strolling alongside a great gray medieval wall.

The taxi came to a complete halt.

"Hurry!" Nariv pleaded. "Move on! Move on!"

"The way is blocked," the driver said, pointing to a solid jam of cars ahead.

Behind him, the Mercedes was relentlessly closing in. Nariv pulled money from his pocket and tossed it onto the front seat. He slammed the back door open and vaulted onto the sidewalk.

Startled tourists got out of his way as he ran from the street, heading for a great black maw of a gateway in the ancient stone battlements. Behind him he heard car brakes squeal, and knew it was the car that contained the men who were after him.

Through the blackness of the gate Nariv ran, and came out in blinding sunlight on the far side. Ahead was the garden area around the old Roman baths, and off to his right the glitter of the Ferris wheel in the amusement park. Beyond the baths were trees, walks, heavy shrubbery.

Nariv ran in that direction. Within a minute or two he came to crumbling stone steps leading down into a deeply shaded, moss-green grotto where stood a statue to war dead. A squirrel ran, frightened, as Nariv rushed around the statue and plunged through a man-width slot in another ancient fortification. He could hear water running not far away, the Amber Fountain.

There was no sign of pursuit. He began to believe he had made it.

Slightly slowing his pace, he proceeded along a small creek, around the back of another medieval fortification, and down stone steps toward the lower town. Soon he emerged onto an outcropping which looked down upon the gleaming roof of a greenhouse, with walls and willows and Nebojša Tower well beyond, against the blue haze of the confluence of the rivers.

Nariv started down the stone steps.

A bulky man stepped out of a niche in the wall, confronting him.

One of the men who had been chasing him.

Nariv made an involuntary gagging sound and turned, every nerve screaming with fear.

The other man stepped out behind him.

Sobbing, Nariv tried to rush past him. The man caught him and spun him around like a doll. *My God, he is so strong!* Then the other man also had Nariv, pinioning him against the old rocks of the wall, and the second man took something out of his coat pocket and removed it from its cloth container. *A needle. A syringe.*

"No!"

The needle plunged into Nariv's left shoulder, high, and he felt the hot squirt go in. Then reality melted.

nine

That evening, waiting for Paula Bansky to pick me up in the lobby of the Metropol for the ride to the tournament ball, I expected to meet a dull-eyed idiot. What appeared was Miss World.

"Mr. Smith?" she said, looking me up and down with frank, dark-eyed interest. "I'm Paula."

She was diminutive, curvy, and dark, with smashing emerald eyes and a vivacious smile. She was wearing a wine-colored cocktail dress that bared her arms and shoulders, and nicely displayed great legs. She spoke Brit English.

"I think you'll enjoy the reception ball," she said, silvery heels clicking as we left the lobby and crossed the tile entryway to her waiting Cortina. "The music for dancing should be grand."

"You're a dancer?"

"Yes. My husband thinks I'm very good."

Okay, Paula, fine. Now we know you're married, and the old gent realizes his place here.

She drove briskly and well. On the way, she said the tournament committee was posting pairings and times for celebrity play. She said she hoped my posting would put me with Danisa Lechova. She talked about the crowds coming into the city for the tournament.

"You're very quiet," she observed after a while.

"Sorry," I said.

"You aren't ill, are you?"

"No. If your stupid telephone call, with the bona fides right out in the open, doesn't result in my getting killed, I think I'll be just fine."

She flushed. "I'm sorry. That was a stupid mistake."

"Yes, it was," I agreed, and dropped it. The harm was done, and I felt sure she had already had her ass chewed enough elsewhere. I was intent on following my decision to keep going until or unless it became apparent that I had been hopelessly compromised.

At the old hotel that was the site of the ball, cars were snarled in the narrow streets and the local officials had even cranked out a couple of old searchlights to send pale shafts of white across the city skyline and into the low-lying mist. We turned the Cortina over to an attendant and went inside.

The huge ballroom was already crowded. Toward one side, under flag-festooned arches, a big dance orchestra played. A lot of people were already dancing on the large, gleaming hardwood floor. Tables several layers deep surrounded the dance area, and the entire room opened through an elaborate archway into an adjacent room almost as large, where crystal chandeliers blazed with the light of what looked like a million candles. I saw people of all ages and all manners of dress. Many were considerably older than I, the men wearing black or a few pale blue tuxedos, and their ladies in elaborate ball gowns that swept the floor. Most of the younger couples were also formal, although many of the women had opted for the kind of cocktail dress that Paula had chosen. You could pick out the tennis people in the throng: they were younger, leaner, generally taller, and wearing light summer shifts or slacks, with some of the men in open-necked T-shirts. The more formally attired didn't seem to mind; they had come here to look at the athletes, and the casual clothing made the athletes easier to pick out.

I spotted a few friends and waved to them as Paula and I made for a tiny table not impossibly far from the dance floor. Martina told me I looked spiffy, and Karyn Wechsting said she didn't know Texas people ever wore anything but cowboy boots. I told them both they were sweet, but my comment was lost in Martina's hoot of derision, given her own Texas connections.

Paula and I sat down. One tuxedoed waiter brought champagne, and another plied us with about twenty kinds of hors d'oeuvres. A man from the tournament committee came over, dragged up a chair, and talked endlessly about how wonderful the tournament was going to be. I tried to discourage him by obviously not making notes, and when that didn't work I started on a world's record for stuffed mushrooms. He left after a long time when he spied Bryant Gumbel, in town to do three reports for next week's *Today* show. Bryant didn't take any notes either, I noticed.

Paula, her pretty mouth curved in a smile, was tapping feline fingertips on her thigh in time with the music. It was good dance music, mostly of the kind that vanished in America when the big bands declined long ago.

"Dance?" I asked.

"Yes," she said eagerly.

Her husband was right. She was a great dancer. This was fun.

"How long," I wondered aloud, "before Michael shows up and spoils this?"

"He isn't to come tonight," she replied. "It was thought he shouldn't be seen with you except at times when presumably he is showing you around, or discharging other official tournament duties on your behalf."

"So you're my contact."

"For the moment." She followed neatly through a grapevine with a twinkle tacked on at the end, and got slightly rosy with pleasure and excitement. I decided I liked her.

94

"So do you have any news for me?" I asked.

"As I understand it, the celebrity postings are to place you with Danisa Lechova in the mixed doubles against Ted Treacher and Karyn Wechsting. Those are tomorrow, of course. It is suggested that you use much of the remainder of tomorrow and Sunday to interview Danisa extensively, including time with her family at their home if possible, to cement the impression of a major, in-depth article in preparation."

She paused to follow me through a promenade, then added, slightly out of breath, "And on Monday there will be further instructions."

"It's about time."

"The closer you can get to the Lechova family, the better it will be."

"Fine. Anything else?"

She leaned back in my arms to meet my eyes. "I have no idea what's going on. I'm only a messenger girl."

"And a fantastic dancer."

"You agree with my husband, then!"

I didn't answer the reminder.

We danced a few more and then started back to our table when the orchestra took a break and a four-man combo of hairy kids who couldn't read music started making contemporary noise.

"I think," I told Paula, "it's time to try to run into the Lechovas."

"Yes," she said, and we veered off from our table and began a slow, aimless circuit of the rooms.

Five minutes later it worked. We ran straight into Hannah Lechova.

"Oh, no!" Hannah cried, a vision in far too much lace and interestingly too little bodice. "It is the man of my dreams!" She seized my arm and pleaded with Paula. "Oh, let me steal your man for just a few minutes, darling, will you? He is *so* good-looking and I am *so* hungry for conversation with a real man!"

Paula smiled. "I'll be around, Brad." She moved off in the crowd.

Hannah leaned conspiratorily close to me, confirming the existence of her breasts. "She's *gorgeous*, darling! Do you mind I took you away? Is she new for you? Have you fucked her yet?"

"Jesus Christ, Hannah, do you just say anything that comes into your mind?"

"Of course! That is the way I am! Come! I want champagne!" She dragged me through the crowd to the nearest serving tables. "But you have not answered my question," she whispered loudly after we were served. *"Have you . . . ?"*

"Hannah—!"

"Oh! I see! How glorious! You are a true gentleman! If you said you have, you are kiss and tell! If you say you have not, you reveal her tragedy! I love you more every instant!"

Linda Spařlock walked nearby. Hannah's eyes turned just for an instant into cold marble. "She returns weak from the backhand on the move. Everybody says she is wonderful but I hope I get her in tournament. I will kill her."

I didn't respond, but it was an interesting moment. Hannah was not entirely joking, or if she had intended to be, the subtle change in her tone and the marble eyes gave her away. The lady had two personalities. One of them was as hard and competitive—and possibly as mean—as an NFL linebacker.

We drifted through the crowd, stopping to talk for a moment with a tournament official who reddened with pleasure at Hannah's compulsive, automatic flirting, then to hear Zina Garrison's story of a rough flight in from Frankfurt. A young man in an army uniform came over to say hello to Hannah. He seemed drawn and tense, but eager to please her. She went cold, unapproachable as a cemetery statue. It took him a couple of minutes for the chill to sink in. Then he went away.

"Seemed like a nice guy," I said, puzzled.

"He is an enemy of the state," she snapped.

"What? In an army uniform?"

"I have heard him speak openly against the state."

"Like how?"

"He boasted that he could operate assignment of housing better than the government. He said—openly!—there is corruption at all levels, and this has ruined the honesty of the Yugoslav peasant class."

I tried a lame joke: "Sounds like at least a death penalty offense to me."

Hannah's teeth clicked like a trap. "No. But he is now in the army, where he can be watched."

A small chill went down my back. "Sad."

"No!"

"You can hardly be happy to see a friend in that kind of mess."

She turned to me, her eyes flaring hotly with vindictive pride. "Of course I am happy. I did my duty as a citizen."

I finally figured out what she was saying. "You turned him in."

"My duty."

I had been warned about her chameleon personality—the fanatic-patriot side of her. But we had been having fun—I thought—with the repartee. The old man had almost forgotten his age as well as his real mission here. Hannah's radicalism had fixed all that. This was no casual flirtation between equals, and Hannah was no sweet young thing whose only danger was to middle-aged men she might turn on and then disappoint.

Quite possibly Hannah could be lethal.

In the seconds I was thinking this way, however, she recovered her sunny side. Grasping my arm, she tried to turn me back in the direction of the dancing. "Come! You have me hot! For more dancing."

Reminded of things, I resisted. "Is your family here?"

"Them? I suppose so. Come, darling!"

"Let's find your family. I'd like to meet them."

Her eyes flared again just for a second. "And switch me for Danisa?"

I slipped my arm around her waist. "There will *never* be anyone else for me, for the rest of my life."

She laughed and wriggled out of my grasp. "Hey, watch your fresh! Maybe I can get *you* in the army, too!"

Maybe you could at that, babe.

The rest of the Lechova family was at a table well back from the major hubbub: Danisa between her parents at the table, wearing a simple white dress with her hair tied back and no makeup, so she looked about fifteen; her father in a black suit and tie, his gray-speckled hair shiny with water and slicked down flat against his skull; her mother a surprisingly youthful redhead with freckles and green eyes and a guarded, austere expression.

"Momma! Poppa!" Hannah gushed. "Here is the man of my dreams for you to approve!"

"Hannah," Leon Lechova growled disapprovingly. He stood and held out his hand with all the welcome of a border guard. "I recognize you, Mr. Smith, from photographs. Welcome to Yugoslavia."

So they didn't know of his earlier intervention at the hotel. I went along. "It's a pleasure, Mr. Lechova."

"You have met Danni at the arena. Allow me to present my wife."

Geneta Lechova studied me coolly. She seemed drawn by tension despite the fact that she looked younger than I had expected, pretty, tan, athlete-slim. "Welcome to our country."

Lechova pulled up an extra chair and I sat down with them. Hannah sat close to me and made it a point to stroke my shoulder and make some silly remark. I exchanged looks with Danisa; there was a wary quality to her gaze, worried. Lechova said I would play with Danisa in the celebrity doubles. I said I would like that.

"Danisa understands she is not to exert herself in the celebrity playing," he added.

"We'll just have some fun," I said.

"Hannah and Danisa must be rested for the singles play. They have been placed in opposite brackets for the championships. They must be at their best. They must meet in the finals."

It was a shocking thing to say. Danisa, except for a slight, pained narrowing of her pretty eyes, showed no reaction to the pressure. I saw a deeper flicker of anguish in Hannah's expression, there and then gone instantly. No wonder Hannah acted a little crazy, I thought. Dear old dad. You *would* be the greatest. If it killed you. I wondered how long—forever?—he had played them against each other.

Geneta Lechova spoke into the widening silence. "Mr. Smith, you are to write an article about our daughters?"

"Yes," I said.

Lechova cut in. "About Danisa. But when Hannah meets Danni in the finals, the plan will have to be changed. The article will celebrate *both* our daughters."

Mrs. Lechova stiffened almost imperceptibly, and the look she gave her husband lasted microseconds. It was a look I had seen once in the eyes of a small boy some of us had visited during a celebrity tour of a hospital. It had been a ward for abused children, and the youngster had had a father who locked him in a dark closet for several hours every time he got less than 100 on his work in first grade.

She told her husband, "Both Hannah and Danisa will try."

Lechova stiffened. "Try? Try means fail. They will succeed!"

No one responded.

"And," Lechova went on, "Mr. Smith's articles will celebrate our family triumph."

"Leon," Mrs. Lechova said softly. "We have no guarantees—"

"We have waited. We have groomed both of them carefully. The time for greatness has finally come."

Mrs. Lechova stared at her husband for a moment with eyes that looked filled with disappointment. Then she turned back to me. "Your articles will make the girls celebrities, then?"

I pretended I didn't detect the hostility. "I'll write an honest piece, Mrs. Lechova."

"Win or lose?" She was challenging me because she couldn't challenge him.

"Win or lose," I echoed. "But to do a good job, I need considerable time with all of you in the next two or three days."

Her eyes, which had almost softened, showed new wariness. "I am not sure there will be a great amount of time—"

"We will make the time," Lechova cut in.

Their eyes locked.

The tension was getting as thick as butter. I turned to Danisa and asked how she was feeling on the eve of the tourney. It was a dumb journalistic question designed to cut some of the hostility, and she seemed to recognize that. While she was giving me a stock answer, a lanky boy with a sunburned nose came to the table and asked Hannah to dance. She hesitated, then hopped to her feet and they went off together.

Lechova watched them go. He seemed to cock his ear toward the music. The orchestra had come back: an old-time Glenn Miller song. His ascetic face actually warmed in a smile as he turned to his wife. "Geneta. Come." He stood and held her chair, and with a little flush of nervous pleasure she left the table to dance with him.

I studied Danisa briefly. She looked so pretty and vulnerable it made me ache for her. When her eyes met mine, the sadness in them was palpable.

"That leaves us," I told her. "Will you dance with me?"

She stood. "Of course."

I had enjoyed dancing with Paula Bansky, but Danisa was different, a dream. She responded to the slightest lead, and was so airy and graceful that it took a few turns for me to lighten up and really begin to enjoy her.

"You aren't abandoning your companion?" she asked.

So she had spotted me with Paula. "No problem. She's an official escort and she ran into friends."

"I see."

We danced in silence for a while.

I said, "Your father is excited about the tournament."

"You must not hold it against him that he pushes us so hard. You see, he was an Olympic athlete but then he injured his leg and could no longer compete."

"So you have to be a champion for him?"

"He and Mother have given us everything. We owe it to them to be as good as we can be."

She was so serene. I sensed that in earlier times the pressure must have been agony for her. She had come to terms with it all on her own. Whatever demons still drove her, she had befriended them. I had the first inkling of the extraordinary personality that lay behind the marvelous tennis machinery.

"Will there really be an article?" she asked.

"Yes. Whatever else happens, I'm really going to do a lot of interviewing with you and your family, and do the article."

She stiffened in my arms although she kept moving. "I know this is necessary. There is no other way for me to leave my country now, and I understand time is everything. I'm scared. I wish—" She stopped dancing and looked at me with eyes that were on the brink of tears.

I took her by the arm and hustled her unobtrusively off the dance floor. We came out on the edge of the second big room. I led her that way. Tall french doors led onto terraces and gardens. I took her outside and we stood on a brick

101

terrace looking down at a dimly lit fountain and rose garden. There were other couples outside too, mostly smokers. But no one close.

"I'm sorry," she said huskily. She was crying now.

Feeling awkward, I gave her my handkerchief. "No need to apologize. Christ. I know this is hard."

"I wanted to come to the West. I love your country. But I would never have abandoned my family and Yugoslavia like this, abruptly, with trickery. My poor mother. It will kill my father."

"It will hurt. But your father is tough as a boot."

"Why," she demanded in a soft burst of pain, "did they *do* this? All these years? Why didn't they tell me? Why did they hide it from him? My own brother! What kind of beasts are the Russians? And my own people? To do things like this to us!"

I had no idea what she was talking about. "I guess we'll get answers later."

"I hoped," she told me, "to be free. To travel the world, play in all the tournaments, live part of the year in the United States, but visit Yugoslavia often. Was that so bad?"

I was baffled because she was talking out of a background I didn't know anything about. "It doesn't sound bad at all."

"But when I learned about my brother, it changed everything. I can never have good feelings about my country again, that they could do this!"

The passion and pain in her voice hit hard. Not knowing what she was talking about, I couldn't answer.

She shook her head impatiently. "I'm sorry. I'm better now." She wiped her eyes and handed back my handkerchief, now moist with her tears. The face she raised to me was strong again, toughened by that resolve that must run in the family. "What are my instructions? What do we do next?"

"We wait," I told her. "We do the interviews, spend the time together. When they tell me what's coming down, I tell you and help with the arrangements. It happens next week. You're ready?"

She shuddered slightly, but jutted her chin. "Yes."

"Good. I know how hard this must be."

"Do you do this work a lot?" she asked.

"No."

She was watching me in the half-light. Her voice changed. "You are a funny man, I think, Brad Smith."

"Hilarious."

Her eyes suddenly became almost roguish, and she looked her age. "I understand why my sister is already in love with you."

"I get the impression Hannah falls in love about every fifteen minutes."

"But of course, and so do I!"

"Lucky guys."

"Shall I fall in love with you?"

I studied her incredible face. "Maybe you'd better not."

"Would you break my heart?"

"No. But you might break mine."

She smiled and moved away a few inches. "You're a gentle man. You're very nice."

"Sounds like the kind of thing people used to tell me after beating me in tournaments."

"I've seen films of your play at Wimbledon and Forest Hills. My father has films of all the greats. You were a wonderful competitor."

I didn't know what to say to that, so I just looked at her. In this light she was older, mysterious, wonderful-looking. My heart flip-flopped.

She said, "Is this very dangerous for you? It must be."

"Well, your country wouldn't like it a lot if they knew what was up. But I don't think I'm personally in such great danger. You're the one with more to lose. I'm sure that's been explained to you. These things don't always work out. If you try, and fail, you'll have hell *ever* getting out again."

"But I have no choice."

"Do you want to tell me more about that?"

"I think I've seen gradually, over a long time, that you can't fulfill yourself as an athlete if you retain citizenship in a country like Yugoslavia. There are always barriers . . . controls."

"Like when they kept you from playing at Wimbledon?"

Her jaw tightened and I got a glimpse of the iron inside her. "You know about that, then."

"Yes," I said.

"It was the last revelation," she said grimly.

I didn't say anything.

"Actually," she corrected herself, "it was the last revelation to me only about freedom in my country. It made me face the facts. But it was only after our passports had been picked up that your people came to me and told me the entire truth about the lies that had been told to me ever since I was born."

"I don't know about all the lies, Danisa."

Her eyes glistened with tears again. The shock and pain had broken through her strength and she was just a beautiful young woman with a huge load of pain and sadness.

She said, "We can talk later about some of that . . . if you wish." Her effort to shake herself mentally was visible as a tremor. "Not now . . . okay? Now is a party, and joy. Is that okay with you, Brad Smith?"

"That's fine."

We stood there a while in silence. At first I wondered about the pain she had suffered, and how she had come finally to this decision to leave her family and country. Then I thought how strange it was for us to be here like this, when within a day or two we might be pawns in a power game between international giants. Then, watching her, I became more aware again of our surroundings.

The old-fashioned dance music sounded fine, coming out of the ballroom. Distant garden searchlights probed the undersides of swollen gray clouds. The gardens smelled of lilacs. It was really very nice and we turned to look at each other, sharing the moment, and then she turned her profile to me, looking away, and neither of us said anything and then we just stood there some more, she looking out at the gardens and I watching her.

I don't know how to explain it, but there are times like that, very rarely, between a man and a woman. And never mind that I was old enough to be her father, or any of the other obvious reasons why such things should never happen in a world that's supposed to make sense.

Because there was no rationality to it, and I for one didn't give a damn. She, standing there, quiet and vulnerable and young and lovely, said nothing aloud; but everything was being said to me without words. And I guess my own messages were going back, because after quite a while she turned to me and smiled.

"Oh, my, Brad Smith," she said wonderingly. And her breath caught in her throat.

"We'd better go in," I said. My voice sounded funny.

"Yes," she said softly, the wonder still in her eyes.

We did.

ten

Saturday morning I found no surprises in the published results of tournament qualifying rounds held Friday at the Pionir Sports Hall or on the new courts close by in the Tašmajdan sports center. The surprise came when Michael Nariv didn't show up at the crack of dawn.

Instead, after eight, I was confronted in the hotel lobby by a short, rotund, nervously sweaty little man with no hair on top. His suit looked like something Louie once wore on *Taxi*.

"Mr. Smith? I am Victor Lobanov. I am assigned to escort you and other players in your group to the stadium for the celebrity matches."

"Victor, where's Michael today?"

"I do not know, sir, Mr. Smith. He is reported ill. I have a limousine outside with a driver. Please tell me: what time do you and your associates wish to automobile to the stadium?"

He was so earnest and nervous that I couldn't doubt his authenticity as a tournament committee flunky. I wondered if Michael was really sick, or had been pulled off as a precaution of some kind. There was nothing for me to do but follow the program and see what developed next.

I told Lobanov, "I haven't seen Karyn Wechsting or Ted

Treacher yet. They're the others who will be playing in the doubles with Danisa Lechova and me. And it's early. Why don't you relax for an hour or so?"

Lobanov's jaw set with painful tension. "Yes, sir. I will relax here in the lobby." He walked across the gleaming tile floor to one of several dark contemporary chairs arranged against a wall of mirrors. He sat down and crossed one chubby leg over the other and looked thoroughly miserable.

After exchanging a few friendly words with Bud Collins, I went into the breakfast room. Floor-to-ceiling draperies had been opened to provide a view into a garden. I spied Karyn Wechsting just sitting at a table halfway back along the glass wall.

As I approached her from one end of the room, two unmistakably American tourists approached from a table they had just abandoned nearer the back. The man was tall, overweight, bald, and fiftyish, and he was wearing Bermuda shorts and a yellow T-shirt and a straw hat, and he had two cameras slung around his neck. His lady friend was a foot shorter and broader, with copper-wire hair. Her dress resembled what they used to call a muumuu, and on her feet were scuffs. She had a copy of the official tournament program in hand.

"Mr. Smith?" the man boomed, turning heads. "Brad Smith, aren't you? Yeah! Wow, great! Hey, Brad, we're fellow Americans." He started pumping my hand. "Henry Beamer, and this is my wife, Muriel. Hays, Kansas. That's our hometown. I'm in the agricultural tool business. But hey, Brad! Would you be so kind as to sign our tournament program for us? We would be deeply and sincerely grateful, Brad."

Muriel Beamer chimed in, "It isn't for us, actually. It's for our daughter—"

"We've got Lendl and Mecir already," Beamer said as I scrawled my signature on the program. "Hey, Brad, thanks a million, that's really great, I really do appreciate it a bunch—"

His wife slammed him with an elbow and pointed to the newly discovered Karyn Wechsting.

"Oh, wow!" Beamer cried, dragging his wife to the table that had been my destination. "Miss Wechsting? Hey, this is great! This could make our day!"

I took a detour past the breakfast bar, and by the time I got to Karyn's table, the Beamers were departing. "Gee, we sure wish you the best in the tournament, Karyn! I mean that sincerely. I hope you just flat beat the pants off everybody and win the whole shooting match. And thanks a million for the autograph!"

"Our daughter will be thrilled," Muriel Beamer added. "I guess I told you it isn't for us, it's for our daughter. She's such a sweet little thing."

"Yeah!" Beamer chimed in. "When we tell her we actually met *the* Karyn Wechsting in Belgrade, of all places, well, gosh! She'll first say, 'Oh, Daddy, that's another of your whoppers!' and then she'll say, 'Well, if you're telling the truth, did you get her autograph for me?' So that's why, you see."

Karyn was gracious, although she had probably heard the "not for me" line a thousand times. No one ever asks for an autograph for himself. Funny how that works.

"Thank you again," Muriel Beamer said, and the couple scurried off on some other mission outside the breakfast room. Poor Muriel had her purse clutched tightly under her elbow in order to avoid ending up like the tourists Karl Malden always shows you for American Express. They seemed like nice enough people, but I felt vaguely embarrassed for them.

"Join you?" I asked Karyn.

"Great." She gave me a kilowatt smile.

Karyn was young, slender, freckled, sandy-haired, a California girl in the best sense, and really a sweet young woman, something of a loner, one of the few bright young stars of an American tennis establishment that badly needed some. In recent years, most of the good young ones—the

Sabatinis, Beckers, and Grafs—had been coming out of other countries. Even our best, Martina, was of Czech extraction, a naturalized citizen. Like everyone else, I had given considerable thought to why America suddenly seemed to be producing fewer tennis greats, and the best I could come up with was that most of our kids were coddled and rewarded too easily and too early, with the result that they burned out short of true greatness.

Or maybe greatness was not the goal for enough of them. Maybe too many of them were shoved, goaded, and bullied into machinelike precision of play because their parents wanted the reflected glory and they grew up only wanting the money, not really caring about the game.

Or maybe kids just didn't learn enough in America anymore about willingness to pay the price. I remember once when I was warming up for a match at Hilton Head and a girl in the crowd exclaimed exuberantly, "It's so *easy* for you!" I didn't answer her, but her remark made me remember, with some sense of irony, the millions of practice shots, the two pairs of tennis shoes I wore out every week during high school, some of the physical pain that I won't bore you with. In sports or writing or business, onlookers see only the end result in maximum achievers who have paid the price; such people usually make it look easy, whatever it is, because that effortless backhand or smooth drive or seamless piece of prose stands on agony and endless repetition that made it look that way. Do a lot of kids today achieve only high mediocre because they don't know this about real excellence—have no concept of paying the price?

Sorry. End of sermon and off the soapbox.

Anyway, Karyn was different. At twenty-four, she had come along late as a big-time tennis player. She wasn't even number one on the UCLA women's team as a collegian. After graduation she went into dentistry and played only a few tournaments until last year, when she finished her degree. She decided at that time to give it a whirl for a year on the pro tour before hanging out her shingle, or warming up her drills, or whatever dentists do, and promptly beat Chrissie in a Virginia Slims event in Florida. Made more money than she would have made in a year of capping teeth, but, more important from her standpoint, realized for the first time that she could be *really very good* at this.

She had told me once in a lengthy interview that she knew she would always be a good, but not outstanding, dentist. It came as a shock to realize she might truly excel on the courts.

So here she was, America's number two, looking tanned and whip-slender and vibrant, a tall girl with pale blue eyes and a face and figure that writers might call wholesome, because she didn't have classic features, she was just . . . *neat.*

"So it's Ted Treacher and me against you and Danisa Lechova later this morning," she said. "Do you want to surrender now, or play it out?"

Treacher was like me, an old party now mostly doing something more honest for a living. In his case it was shuttling around the world, putting in appearances and making publicity for the Snauwaert racket company and Pumas. He still played enough to be ranked about 160th in the world on some computers. I had seen him play six months earlier, and knew he still had his hard, flat serve and ability to scurry around and make impossible gets. He and the elegant Karyn made a good team. Despite the difference in their ages, they were an item offcourt, too.

I told her, "I guess we ought to play it out. Maybe Danisa can carry me."

"Isn't she great?" Karyn asked with her customary sunny enthusiasm. "God, I just love to watch her play! Martina and Steffi better watch out."

"She'll have to get by Sabatini and Evert first."

"Yeah, I expect some great matches. But I think Danni is just coming into her game. I saw her against Lisa Bonder in the French. My God, she just blew poor Lisa away. And she's such a nice person. We had a long visit yesterday and she's just as sweet and unassuming as she can be."

The waiter finally brought my *djezva* in the traditional way, on a tray, with sugar and a glass of lukewarm water. Sometimes I ordered a *djezva* of Turkish coffee to get the water.

"Maybe," I suggested to Karyn, "*you* want to surrender."

Karyn's crooked grin broadened. "Bullshit, cowboy. You'd better protect yourself up at that net today. I intend to make you eat those words."

It occurred to me to tell Karyn that *she* was one of the nicest people on the tour, but I didn't. We talked about other personalities in Belgrade for the tournament, and what was likely to happen at Flushing Meadows in the Open in September. We agreed that it would have to go a lot to match the drama of Wimbledon this year. After a while, as I put away my third cup of great, creamy coffee, so strong you could almost chew it, Karyn said she would go find Treacher and be ready to head for the indoor stadium in fifteen minutes. I dawdled, then went out into the lobby.

There I found a grim—as usual—Leon Lechova looking for me.

"Good morning," I said, mustering some cheer despite his dour attitude.

"I wish a few words with you," he told me.

"Shoot."

"I am seek reassurance that what you write about Hannah and Danisa will not criticize them, our family, or our country."

"That's not what I'm here for, Mr. Lechova."

He gritted his teeth. "Yes. Surely. But you must understand it is *totally important* that my daughters receive favorable publicity only."

"I've already told you I'm not here to do a hatchet job on anyone. What's the problem?"

"It is important."

"I understand that."

"Maybe you do not." He grimaced, plunged on. "What do you think my daughters' chances of having a good life—ease and riches—might be without their tennis?"

"Not very good?"

"Zero, Mr. Smith. Zero!"

Practicality of this kind was not one of the things I had expected from him. "I see."

He persisted grimly. "Do you know how much money they made last year in tennis?"

"I have a rough idea."

His jaw set. "Hannah—eighty thousand dollars. Danisa—one hundred, fifty-two thousand, eight eighty-eight."

"Impressive."

"There will be more. Much more."

"I'm sure." I made a note. "Why are you telling me this, Mr. Lechova?"

"I love my country. My poor Yugoslavia! Raped, pillaged, overrun, occupied, torn to pieces, for a thousand years. But today this country has great problems, Mr. Smith. I want everything for my daughters. If they are to have what we do not, it must be through their tennis. There is no other escape for them."

I stopped making my note. His use of the word "escape" had betrayed him. If I put that in my story, he would have visitors from the UDBA or plainclothes militia, sooner or later. *And why, Mr. Lechova, if you are a patriot, would you speak of escaping our country, as if it were a bad place—a prison? Explain yourself.*

"I see," I said.

"They will be good citizens," he added. "They will live in our beloved country. They will bring fame to Yugoslavia. They will be rich. When they can travel again to other countries—"

"Why can't they travel to other countries now?" I cut in.

He stopped, blinking, remembering himself. "A minor

technicality only. Because they travel so much, another investigation before issuing of new passports."

"That strikes me as very strange, if Yugoslavia wants them to bring glory to the country."

"It is a minor problem."

"But this 'minor problem' caused them to miss Wimbledon."

A vein pulsed in his neck. "Just remember what I have tell you. Your writings of them will be *favorable*." And with that he turned and plunged out of the hotel, a grim and wiry man with a fire inside.

I was still standing there thinking about it when Karyn came back with Ted Treacher in tow and we went to our limousine for the ride to the stadium.

On the way, they talked tennis and tourism, and I thought about some words I had had with Danisa last night quite late in the evening. They linked with the visit I had just had from her father.

"What will our interviews be about?" she had asked. "Will they be real?"

"Oh, yes. There will really be an article, too."

"And you will ask me what kinds of things?"

"About tennis. About your career."

"Like . . . ?"

"Like are you happy, making big money on the tour? Do you feel excited, knowing your future?"

"I was happy when we had no money. I am happy now."

"So winning makes no difference?"

"It makes *all* the difference. My parents sacrificed much for Hannah and me. I owe it to them to be just as good as I can be."

I studied her, thinking she was really one of the most beautiful women I had ever met, with a strength that few equaled. "Do you want to win, then, for them or for yourself?"

She frowned a moment, then shrugged and changed

the subject: "We're going to have fun tomorrow. I look forward to partnering with you. You were a wonderful player in your time and I bet you're still awfully good."

"I'll try not to fall down or something."

"You Americans! You either boast or you show this false modesty. I saw you on television at Wimbledon, the year you won and the time you played Borg in the finals. You almost had him."

I nodded, remembering, too. I didn't have to tell her that "almost" in tennis is nowhere at all. She was a pro. She understood that . . .

Now, approaching the stadium, I gave myself a small lecture about my age, hers, my station in life, hers, my real mission in Belgrade, middle-aged fantasies and their futility.

I just about had myself convinced to cool it by the time I had dressed for the doubles and walked through the tunnel to the brilliant lights of the floor, and saw her already on center court, warming up with Fjbk. She was gliding from one side of the court to the other, her blond, braided ponytail flapping, golden legs always in position for the next hit. I told myself to calm down.

"There you are!" she called sunnily. She waved toward her dour coach across the net. "Milo! Brad will warm up with me now!"

Fjbk turned his side of the court over to me with sour bad grace, and I took a couple of balls from the nearest ballboy and patted one over the net to her, sort of like poor Mecir did in the 1985 French Open, when he was so strung out he had to serve underhanded. Danisa popped it back gently to my backhand, and I stroked a return.

Two warmup shots, and I was slightly out of breath. That was from adrenaline. I felt like a teenager on his first date.

As we warmed up, other courts on both sides of us began to be occupied, and spectators filtered in. The sections of seats flanking our court began to fill up, with another notable clustering off to our right, where, three courts away, Hannah was oncourt. There was some cheering when Lendl and Becker showed up at the other end of the arena, but the Lechova women obviously were the big draw.

Seeing Danisa on television, and in warmups from the stands, had not prepared me for the experience of being on the same court with her. After a while we began to rally a little more intensely. Testing her, I hit one hard and deep to her backhand with some angle on it, and she glided over and slid three feet into the shot, conserving energy, then hit it back down the line, and when I went crosscourt on her she went over after it like a beautiful, soaring bird, and, God, it was like there should have been sound effects—a howitzer blast—when she hit the huge forehand behind me for a winner as I hustled toward midcourt.

"Nice shot!" she called happily. "Hard to get!"

It's hard to keep the ball down on clay, but she had no trouble at all.

Soon Karyn Wechsting and Ted Treacher strolled out to join us. We had some fun even with the warmups. The crowd continued to come in, more than half filling the place even this early in the afternoon, and the public address system came on, the officials came out, a small band played the Yugoslav national anthem, and we were ready to get down to business.

Danisa and I won the toss and said we would serve. Ted Treacher went back to receive first for them, with Karyn at net. Danisa walked back into our court with me. "You serve first," she said. "Get us off to a good start."

It was a nice compliment. I put my first serve down the middle and Ted sent a low, spinning backhand short over the net. I had taken exactly two steps forward when Danisa crossed like a bandit and put away a forehand volley that almost took one of Karyn's shoes off. Karyn yelped and the crowd laughed and applauded. This was really, really fun.

The best-two-of-three match went more than two

hours, much to Miloslav Fjbk's glowering displeasure from his front-row seat. He wanted it over more quickly to conserve Danisa's energy, but Karyn and Ted were great to play with, and our competitive juices got flowing. After winning my serve, Danisa and I promptly went down 1–3, mainly due to some flubbed net play on my part and some neat tricks by Karyn, who would have played tiddledywinks with total concentration and will to win. Then, however, I hit a lucky lob that saved us another game point, and we rallied, and took five in a row to win the first set.

Danisa, I learned, had more than a fine serve and the big forehand. The rest of her game was subtle but lethal: balanced, swift, patient, with pinpoint accuracy. She always managed to take the ball early on groundstrokes, with short preparation that no one could read. She hit acute-angle shots and could overspin or underslice the ball from either side. When she poached, it was for a putaway.

They won the second set, 6–3, and then we won the third, 6–2. The crowd was having a great time, applauding every good shot, but on the last point of the match the whole thing got spoiled.

I hit a deep return to Ted on break point, and he scooped it back short. Danisa poached and hit a wicked little drop shot crosscourt. Going for it all out, as she went after everything, Karyn slipped and took a nasty fall, her left ankle twisting under her.

By the time I got around the net to her, Ted was helping her up.

"Are you okay?" I demanded.

"Think so," Karyn said. But her face was white with pain.

"We'd better get you to the locker room right now," Ted said, and Karyn, limping badly, didn't argue with him, heading off to concerned applause from the stands.

Danisa got held up momentarily by the local press. I hung back, gathering my own equipment along with

Karyn's. Fjbk came over. Bent over my gear, I looked up at him and saw nothing but sour anger on his face.

"What?" I asked.

"You should not have extended the match."

"Tell Danisa."

"I tell *you*."

I stood to face him.

He put a thick hand on my shoulder and pushed me.

"Fjbk, you asshole—"

"Don't think you will turn her head," he said. He was breathing hard and sweating with his anger. "*I* am in charge of Danisa's career. You are a journalist, nothing more."

"Thank you very much for the advice."

"You will not ask impertinent questions in your interview. You will not—"

"Fjbk, I don't see me interviewing her at all. Now excuse me. I'm cooling off and I need to check on Karyn's injury."

"It could have been Danisa who was injured, playing this silly match too long!"

Oh, all right, I got it. It had scared him badly. "The Lechova women are that important to you?" I asked, testing.

"They are my career!"

"You had *your* career when you were a player."

That seemed to set him off again. "When I start to play tennis, they say I am too old, no talent. So I practice, practice, run, run, run, and then they say, 'Oh, this Fjbk, he can play a little, but he is dull, he only stays in backcourt, run everything down, get everything back, he is as exciting to watch as a backboard, ho-hum.' So I want to make money in tennis, I go back, practice more, eight hours a day, every day, sometimes more, serve and volley. Six months. Get pretty good at it. But *then* they watch me play and say, 'Oh, this Fjbk, he can serve and volley some, but he got no grace, he got no class, he can't win the big ones.' . . . You know what they call me?"

I said I had no idea.

He thumped his thumb on his own chest. " 'Ugly Gnome.' "

I just managed to keep from laughing. If I had laughed, I might have begun to experience a sudden loss of teeth.

Fjbk continued to glare. " 'Ugly Gnome,' right? Me! So I grow this magnificent beard, I lose some weight, win Davis Cup zone matches, they say I am colorless, no fun to watch. So I wear a hat, sweatband, hit moonballs sometimes like Harold Solomon, yell, cry, make faces, and they say, 'This Fjbk, he is crazy! No good!' "

Fjbk sighed.

"I coach players. Each one I make better than before. But they say I am not forgiving enough. Forgiving! You ever see a ball down the line *forgive* you when it goes in for winner against you, hanh? They say I am wet blanket. They get better, then they fire me.

"All my life it has been like that in tennis. But with Danisa I can show the world—the people that yawn when I play, the guys who fired me because I wasn't funny ha-ha coach, the press—everybody. I can show everybody I am the best—*all*."

He took a breath. *"All,"* he repeated.

He thumped his chest again. "Now I am more a star than any time when I played. I got my car, I got my boat, I got my bike, I got my apartment on Riviera. I got *everything*."

Yeah, you've got the sun in the morning and the moon at night. "And Danisa is the key to how long you keep it all," is what I said.

"You treat her right, see? You tire her out, you make her play any more celebrity crap with you, she could lose this tournament. And then *you* would answer to *me*."

He had talked some of the jealous rage out of himself. I nodded and got away from him, heading for the tunnel to the lockers.

"What was that all about with Milo?" she asked, toweling.

"Oh, just some friendly discussion of old times."

"What about Karyn? Is she all right?"

"I hope so. You can hurt an ankle awfully bad, falling that way."

Ted Treacher hurried back out to report Karyn thought she would be okay. Danisa and I exchanged looks of relief.

She said, "I think I will not play any more today."

"Good idea. About starting our interviews—"

"You will come to our house tomorrow and we will start there. After church. Two o'clock? And my mother says you will stay for dinner."

I nodded. She walked into the tunnel that led to the women's dressing rooms. I watched her go.

Ted Treacher put a sweaty hand on my shoulder. "Hey, my friend, be careful. There are photographers around here."

I looked sharply at him, a pulse of paranoia thumping.

He chuckled. "If they caught that expression on your puss, there's only one caption they could put under the picture: *'Old Gent Gets Hit by Cupid's Forehand.'*"

"Is it that obvious?"

"Hey. Is *vinjak* subtle?"

I started for the lockers. "I think you're full of *govno*, Treacher."

"Sure I am," he chortled, patting me on the back again. "Sure I am!"

In the shower I wondered when I was going to learn details of the plan to get Danisa out. I was starting to feel more anxious. But Karyn was on my mind. I hurried through the shower and change of clothes, and went outside to get a report from an attendant that Miss Wechsting had been in pain, and had been driven back to the hotel.

Ordinarily I would have taken to the stands and watched some of the other fun. But, concerned about Karyn, I hitched a ride on one of the special buses and went straight

119

back to the hotel myself, arriving far earlier than anyone could have anticipated.

At the desk they said Miss Wechsting had changed her mind, and someone had taken her to the medics. As I turned away, I was confronted by the tourist couple from Kansas who had been with Karyn in the coffee shop earlier. The Beamers, I remembered: Henry and Muriel.

"My gosh!" Henry groaned. "We just heard about poor Karyn! Do you think she's going to be all right?"

"Too early to say," I told them, fighting my impatience. "I suppose we'll know—"

"Do you think there's anything we should do?" Muriel demanded anxiously. "Should we send flowers? Henry, I think we should order flowers—"

He frowned. "Well, we're on a tight budget here, honey. No sense going overboard or anything."

I left them there, debating flowers, and went back to the desk long enough to leave instructions that I should be notified when Karyn returned.

Went up to my room.

Found the door standing slightly ajar.

Never suspecting—thinking it was the maid—I rapped lightly and swung the door open and took a step inside.

Whoever it was, he was frighteningly quick. I got only a surprised glimpse of a dark suit—a very large dark suit—before he finished crossing the room and hit me in the breadbasket. I doubled over in pain and he hit me with something behind the left ear and that was all I knew.

eleven

Elsewhere

New Belgrade

Michael Nariv swam up out of the ocean of pain and felt his heart lurch with a great thud as it resumed its beat.

Michael did not know his name anymore. He did not know anything but the pain and a red glare and what he must not tell.

The voice came from a great and icy distance: *"Do you hear me now?"*

"I hurt," Michael whined.

"Where do you hurt?"

"I don't know."

"Who do you work for at the American Embassy?"

Panic blew through Michael's pain. "No. No."

"You work for the CIA."

"No."

"Tell me the name of your CIA officer."

Blind and almost beyond cognition and feeling the great engine of his heart shuddering, Michael only knew he must fight on. "No!"

There was silence. Waves of new pain washed onto his consciousness. *I am doing so well,* he thought. And then at some time later the thought came, *I will not tell. You will be proud of me, Mother.* Then he saw the beautiful blond American girl in his mind, the one he would meet after he got to America . . .

The voice came again: *"Give him more."*

Another voice said something.

"I don't care! Give him more. Now!"

The pain increased and increased and increased.

Missoula, Montana

On the theory that no one would predict such a move, Dominic Partek had doubled back.

In Missoula he rented a room on Beckwith Avenue near the University of Montana campus. He used the name John Todd and told the landlady that he was a visiting professor. The woman gave him the address of a friend not far away on Mansfield who had a garage for rent. She seemed to buy his story without suspicion.

Partek knew, however, that his new cover was tissue-thin. He did not have a single scrap of documentation for the new name he had chosen—no driver's license, Social Security card, or insurance papers. The registration papers for his truck listed him as John Solasko. If he got stopped by police for even the most petty traffic violation, the questions would start coming fast and furious, and he would be in the deepest trouble.

He could not continue using the Solasko name, or the other one for which he had fake ID. The CIA had those names by now, which meant that the KGB probably had them, too.

After moving into his rented room, Partek took a little over $500 out of his double-locked toolbox and drove partway across the city to a small neighborhood bank open until 2 P.M. on Saturdays. Using his new address and latest adopted name, he opened a checking account. The bank's account-number card with his new name on it provided him with a thin claim to his latest identity.

Ordering a late breakfast in a quick-food restaurant, he

drank coffee that hit his stomach like battery acid. The Players cigarettes had started to give him a cough. He thought for an instant about quitting smoking, but it was reflex only; a man who might be killed at any moment was hardly in a position to worry about lung cancer.

His breakfast came and looked good, but he couldn't get much of it down. The waitress noticed and asked if there was something wrong and he said he thought he must be catching a cold. She said there was a lot of that going around.

He had more stomach-burning coffee and looked out at the cars parked in the lot, and the traffic streaming by. A young couple drove up and walked into the restaurant, the man heavyset and bearded, the girl willowy, blond, and leggy in pink shorts. The pang of loneliness and regret that hit Partek was devastating.

Since his earliest days at the Military Diplomatic Academy he had been a loner. The occasional woman only intensified his awareness that he had no family, no roots, and was entering a life in which he could scarcely afford close ties. During all the years past, he had told himself that one day he would find someone . . . that someday he would learn what had happened to his mother and the baby she had been carrying . . . that there would come a time when he would no longer have the vacuum hidden deep and cold in the center of his being.

He had told himself that his isolation was necessary for his work.

Since the profound shock of learning the true story of his mother's death—and the fact that he had a sister he had never known—his perceptions of himself had changed. It was an ongoing process. But he thought he saw now that he had spent his life alone because the only thing he had ever been able to trust was his belief in Communism—his work—and it had always provided a place where he could escape the self-hatred planted by his father. *You are alone,* he had thought with a flash of insight one night after the revelations, *because you are worthless—your father always proved that with his beatings and drunkenness—and without your patriotism you are a cipher.*

But the years in the KGB—life in America—had begun to erode his blind, true-believer faith in the political creed that had sustained him. His temptation to defect to the West had represented a letting go of the fanatic single-mindedness which had given him shelter from his real sense of personal worthlessness. He had been just so sick of all the secrecy, politics, and suspicion.

It was clear, however, that his associates suspected something. Otherwise the personnel file—his personnel file—would never have been left out "accidentally" for him to study.

The facts about his family leaped out at him. In shock, he confronted his superior.

Mikynian had been calm, icily controlled. "Yes, Dominic. All true."

"Why was I never *told?*"

"What good would have been served? The past is past."

"But to hide from a man that *he has a sister!*"

"She did not know, either. Why rake over ashes?"

"My God! What else do old files show that I have never known?"

Partek's father, Mikynian said dispassionately through a cloud of cigar smoke, had not died of natural causes in Moscow. He had been shot while attempting a burglary. Partek had never been told of this "because it was not deemed useful information for you."

Partek's mother, however, had been told the truth.

Nearly to term with her child, deserted and now in her eyes totally disgraced by her dead husband's fate, Martina Partek had packed her few things and gone to one of the poorest sections of Belgrade, assuming her maiden name of Naracic. She planned to write her son when she was resettled. She told the Housing Committee her husband had abandoned her; they ordered her housed in one room of a dilapidated structure that had once been an office building, sharing a hall bathroom with a family of five living in two adjacent rooms and a glowering, half-mad Bosnian welder who pounded on her wall at night and screamed obscenities at God.

Partek's mother—Partek's KGB chief calmly told him after all these years of silence—had had her baby prematurely in the ward of a state hospital. She took her daughter home after a few days, but carried an infection. When she returned to the clinic a week later for treatment, it was bungled, she developed more serious sepsis, and died, never having written her son.

No one knew where she had come from. No one knew of a living relative or friend. Her infant was placed in a state orphanage, later adopted.

Somewhere in the course of all this, Partek was told, an investigative officer found papers giving the real married name of the dead Martina "Naracic." But the report was routinely filed somewhere and never followed up, until it was discovered years later during a routine KGB rescreening of Partek's past.

At that time the KGB had decided "no benefit would come" from telling Partek about the family tragedy, or the fact that he had a living sister still in Belgrade. The sister, of course, also knew nothing. But the information had slept in the KGB personnel files like a little time bomb, and when doubts about Partek's emotional state surfaced recently, the complete dossier had been forwarded to New York, his place of assignment, for review.

Mikynian insisted Partek's discovery of the file was an accident.

"I do not believe you," Partek bit off.

Mikynian's eyes tightened at the unusual breach of courtesy, but he quickly became bland again. "It is of no consequence. Perhaps, in the new spirit of openness, you would have been informed soon anyway. You are of great value, Comrade Partek. If you desire, on your next trip

home, we can arrange that you will meet your sister at last,
and have the reunion you have earned."

"Then she knows also now?"

"She can be told if that is your wish."

"I . . . don't know. Her life would be disrupted. . . ."

The Resident added as if by afterthought, "Your loyalty
and devotion assure that she will always have safety and the
friendship of all the Soviet people."

Remembering now, Partek relived the scalding bitterness and entrapment he had felt then. They had betrayed
him and betrayed him again. His sister was an unknowing
hostage. If he defected, the reprisals would be taken against
her and whoever her adopted family was.

It was intolerable. Without a feeling of loyalty and love,
Partek could no longer serve his KGB masters. But if he left
them, the tragedy would befall his lost sister sooner than it
might catch him. He felt damned.

The persons from the CIA with whom he had been in
contact about "coming over," as they put it, were puzzled
by his sudden remoteness. They applied pressure, asked
questions. Partek told them part of it.

"Maybe we can help," one of them told him.

"How?"

"What if we could get her out?"

"What," Partek cried, "if she doesn't *want* out?"

"Hang loose. We'll be back in touch."

But it was too much. Partek felt he belonged with
neither faction. He had to think. He had to have some time.
He had to get away.

So he had prepared quickly but with some care, and
then he had run away.

And was still running.

He had thought time by himself away from the pressures from both sides would help him determine what his
course of action should be. The time alone had become time
of flight as he perceived that *both* sides were looking for him.
He was more confused and bitter than ever. Was he just a

piece of meat? Did his years of service mean nothing? Did the Americans really care so little about humans crunched between the jaws of the vise?

He knew far better than anyone how valuable he could be to the Americans. If he chose to give them the information he carried in his mind, the Soviet espionage apparatus inside the United States military would be set back ten years. But even knowing what he knew now, could he so betray the system that had reared him?

He was torn by old loyalties, new hates . . .

Sitting in the coffee shop, his hand cupped around a cooling empty cup, he knew he could not continue the charade much longer. Someone would find him, or he would lose his mind.

If he went back now, no one could say he had betrayed anything. His career was a shambles and he would never again be trusted. But in the new Soviet climate it would not be completely bad, he told himself: he would have the job of a minor functionary somewhere near Moscow. He could shuffle papers and try to forget, and someday he might still meet his sister, who would be safe.

But he longed for real freedom. He asked himself if he could go back after what they had done to him. Now he knew his sister was not free to leave Yugoslavia on her own. Did that mean the pressures created by his flight had already begun to wreck her life?

If she wanted to flee, could the CIA really help her?

The questions pounded. He finished his meal and drove to the address given him by his landlady. The woman rented him the garage. He hid the pickup truck in it and walked back to his latest temporary home. It was hot, and the mountains looked bare and inhospitable.

He wondered how much longer he could keep this up.

Belgrade
Thin rainfall streaked the windows of the American Embassy in Belgrade. In the office of the attaché for cultural

affairs, two technicians had just completed their routine daily sweep for electronic bugs, and the small scrambling-signal console in the corner was alight with LEDs which showed it fully functional.

Hiking his feet onto the corner of his desk, David Booth stared across the clutter of daily paperwork at his chief aide, Joe Mitchell.

"Then they've got him," Booth, a thin, graying man, concluded.

Mitchell, younger, with close-cropped curly black hair, wearing the immaculate uniform of a Marine major, nodded grimly. "Nariv wouldn't just vanish like this otherwise."

"Christ, I didn't think they would go that far."

"Poor Michael. The little fucker really enjoyed the work."

"Maybe he'll fool them. Maybe he'll walk in here yet."

Mitchell looked at his superior. "You think so?"

"No."

"Poor Michael."

"I've sent a report," Booth said. "But I assume we press on."

"Who maintains contact with Brad Smith?"

"The easy part is over. They may be watching him around the clock now. Pull Paula. Let him cool until we get back some new instructions."

"But surely the basic plan stays in place."

"Oh, I think so. This has the highest priority. The fuckers at Langley haven't left any doubt of that, with all their messages and duplicate instructions."

"Do you think we'll ever know the whole story?"

"Do you?"

"No."

"Neither do I."

Mitchell stood. "We'll need to contact him soon. Damn! I didn't think they would pull poor Michael in this way."

"Yes." Booth's eyes were autumnal. "I suppose it couldn't have been foreseen. But in terms of the operational plan, their nabbing Nariv may not be a bad thing at all. Adds to the verisimilitude."

"Tell that to poor Michael."

"He knew the risk."

"I still feel bad. He was a nice little guy. And Brad Smith is going to be really, really pissed."

Booth removed his feet from the desktop and reached for his pipe and tobacco. "It can't be helped. What's done is done. There's nothing we can do now for Nariv. As for Smith, nobody promised him a rose garden when he took the assignment. He won't even begin to tumble to what's really going on until the day after tomorrow, earliest, and by then it will be too late."

"Wechsting is out of the tournament!" Miloslav Fjbk said. "And it could have been Danisa."

"Or Hannah," Geneta Lechova added quickly.

"Oh, Mother." Hannah winced. "Everyone knows it is Danisa who is the star. I am so much extra baggage."

"No!" Fjbk growled, stricken by his error. "You are important also, Hannah! You can win many matches. The people love you—"

"*Govno,*" Hannah said without rancor.

"Hannah," Leon Lechova said reprovingly.

Hannah's eyes sparked. "I am no longer a child, Father. It is Danisa who is the shining star. I am a dismal little satellite, an orbiting cinder. I know this. Mother does not have to pretend otherwise. If I had hurt my ankle, as Karyn did today, it would be a sadness, but nothing serious. But for Danisa—a catastrophe!"

They were in the tiny kitchen of the Lechova apartment, high in a six-story building facing a tiny park in New Belgrade. It was stuffy, and no breeze entered through the narrow steel casement windows. Fjbk was sweating profusely, torn between his angry worry about an injury to Danisa and regret over his gaffe.

"The point," he said heavily, "is that *both* of you must

be careful. Danisa tried too hard in the stupid celebrity doubles. You, Hannah, extended yourself too much in your match also. Anything could happen. Karyn Wechsting is *finished.* I have it on the best authority. She has already said she will leave Belgrade early in the week to return to the United States." He scowled at Hannah. "What if you or your sister hurt yourself that way, and had to retire from this tournament?"

"Then I would go to America on a holiday, too!" Hannah shot back.

"You could not," the literal-minded Serb replied. "Your passport is being reviewed, as is Danisa's—"

"And we will miss the U.S. Open," Hannah cut in. "Why is that, Milo? I am as loyal as any Yugoslav citizen alive. I have never criticized the state in any way. Danisa does not belong to patriotic organizations, as I do, but she also is totally loyal. Why have our passports been taken from us?"

"*I* should know?" Fjbk asked, at a loss.

"Is it possible that you have had this done to keep us in this country, away from the bright lights of New York, in order to make us slave even harder on the practice court?"

"The idea is crazy!"

"Hannah," her father said warningly again.

"I have a right to an answer!" Hannah yelled back.

"I know nothing, I swear it!" Fjbk yelled in return.

"You are a cruel, mean, torturing man!" Hannah screamed.

"I only want what is best for you!"

"You only want my sister's body, you old liar!"

"*Hannah!*" Geneta Lechova cried.

"You will apologize at once!" Leon Lechova ordered angrily.

"No!"

"You will apologize, or you will not play in this tournament!"

Hannah went pale. The anger drained out of her. Her

shoulders slumped. She looked at the floor. "I'm sorry, Milo."

The squat Serb was impassive. "It is nothing."

Leon Lechova ordered, "Leave the apartment for a while. We will talk."

Hannah turned and rushed out of the kitchen. In seconds, the hall door slammed and she was gone.

Leon Lechova sighed. "I am sorry, my friend. She acts like she did when she was sixteen!"

"It is good," Fjbk told him.

"What?"

"It is the competitive fire burning bright. I have pushed them both very hard. Hannah is on edge. So is Danisa. They will go through the women's field like wildfire, and meet in the finals."

"But for her to say something vile like she did! To say you . . . desire . . . Danisa. My God, what kind of a man does she think you are? You are older than I am! Even to suggest such a thing is obscene!"

Geneta Lechova was watching Fjbk intensely when her husband said this. She saw the hairline flicker of deep pain before Fjbk made his dark face impassive again. *So it's true.* She felt icy foreboding in her veins. She had denied this possibility for what seemed forever. She could not deny it any longer. *My poor Danisa.*

My poor Hannah.

Fjbk gathered his practice notes and schedules and prepared to leave. "It will be as I explained. We have center court for one hour at seven hundred hours tomorrow. We will meet thirty minutes prior. Each girl will warm up lightly for no more than forty-five minutes. They will be brought directly back here in time for church. Even Hannah will attend *this* Sunday, to ask God for victories."

"It will be as you say," Lechova said.

The two men, so different in appearance and stature, stared at one another, then spontaneously shook hands.

You are alike, Geneta Lechova thought with a pang. *You*

would both destroy either of the girls to win your dream of number one ranking in the world.

But you are worse, she thought, again studying Fjbk's black expression as he lumbered toward the door. *You would inflict that gross, hairy, muscle-knotted body on my Danisa—fill her with your slime.*

For an instant, Geneta Lechova almost retched. My God, what was she to do? How could she ever extract her daughters from this insane carousel these two men had them on? What could she do to save them?

When he left the apartment, Fjbk strode outside to the curb, where his big Harley-Davidson motorcycle gleamed redly in the sun. Several children clustered around. Fjbk treated them to his darkest glower, and unlocked one of the luggage compartments in the bullet-shaped sidecar to remove his helmet, a crimson Bell that matched the color of the cycle. Taking a red scarf and gauntlet gloves from inside the helmet, he put them on, tossing the long end of the silk scarf over his shoulder with a flourish. Then, straddling the machine, he started the engine and backed it away from the curb. When he dropped the gear selector into first forward and blipped the throttle, the children took an involuntary step back.

Fjbk pulled away sedately, his heart warmed by knowledge of the wonderful spectacle he was making.

Twenty minutes later he was entering the apartment of Terinka.

"Terinka!" he called, striding into the living room, with its gypsy rugs and paintings. "Are you home, my dove?"

The bedroom door slammed back against the wall and a tall, reed-slender, dramatically dark-haired woman flew from the other room and into his arms, black blouse and red skirt billowing, milky arms ajangle with a great collection of ornate brass bracelets and chains.

"Oh, Milo!" she moaned, pressing passionately against him. "I thought you would never come to see your Terinka during this tournament! I am so happy!" And she hungrily shoved her tongue into his mouth.

Fjbk unceremoniously dumped her backward onto the floor, flipped up her skirts and petticoats, and shoved himself into her. She hiked her legs and began wildly humping with him.

If it was only Danisa, he thought, and in his mind pretended that it was.

Hannah found Danisa just where she had expected, in the little cafe across from the park. Alone at a corner table, Danisa was having a Serbian salad—tomato and leaves—with Turkish coffee in a demitasse.

"You won't tell," Danisa said when her sister sat down.

"Never," Hannah snapped. "Waiter! *Šljivovica!* And a chocolate torte!"

Danisa bent double with the giggles. "Plum brandy and a torte?"

"Do not worry." Hannah leered. "It is just like oral sex: it does not make you break out."

"You're awful!"

"No! I am wonderful!"

"If Milo saw us now, he would kill us both."

"Forget Milo! Hey! Are you looking forward to seeing this Brad Smith tomorrow?"

Danisa's face turned pink.

"Ha!" Hannah cried. "Maybe *this* will be the time when you stop being a virgin, huh?"

"Hannah!"

"Maybe, after you walk in the park, go talk someplace nice . . . alone . . . you get him to take you to his hotel room, huh? Then"—Hannah leered—"maybe some kiss, kiss, push, push."

"I couldn't do that!"

"Then how about turning him over to your big sister, eh? Oh, my! He can push, push with *me* anytime!"

"Oh, Hannah," Danisa gasped, fighting to control her

laughter. "How do you suppose we ever learned to love each other the way we do, with the way Poppa and Milo try to make us compete all the time?"

"Because we are sisters," Hannah said staunchly. "Because *nobody* comes between us!"

Danisa put down her fork and looked at Hannah and started to cry.

"Hey! *Now* what?"

"Nothing," Danisa lied, wiping her eyes on her napkin. "I'm just . . . tired. And the tournament—"

"Nobody is ever going to spoil our sisterhood," Hannah told her. "Nobody! You hear me? Hey, listen to me. We have always been special. Nobody changes that. I get mad at you, sure. Sometimes on the court I would like to tear your hair out."

Danisa started laughing again through the tears.

"How do you like that?" Hannah grinned, pleased. "But listen! Let us enjoy this tournament, right? Let us defeat everybody. Then let us *both* get this Brad Smith to do some kiss, kiss, push, push. How would that be, fine? But I am older, you must wait and go second."

Sometimes, Danisa thought, she felt they were almost Siamese twins. And yet Hannah knew nothing—suspected nothing—of the planned escape. Danisa wondered how any of this could ever work out well for any of them, leaving her parents, leaving this woman who was so unlike her, yet her emotional double in other ways, and so bound up in her spirit and soul. She was filled with sadness.

Not to be able to trust your own sister! It was almost the worst thing of this whole plan.

But all of it was bad, all of it had pain as a component. Danisa knew she was misleading her mother . . . her father. They had never done her any harm. They had always done their best for her. Even her father's terrible slave-driving was meant for her own good . . . more or less. He was not a bad man. He was only an obsessed one.

Danisa wondered if she would ever have considered

renouncing her citizenship and her homeland if she had not learned about her brother. That had come on top of all the other disillusionments and restless yearnings to make the decision possible.

Disgust with the excesses and cruelties of the government would never have motivated her to leave permanently. Even watching her father shrivel under the frustrations of bureaucratic travel limitations would not ever have made her go. Hate for the bureaucrats and bunglers who kept them in their tiny apartment while sycophants moved to better quarters—not even rage at that kind of unfairness would have done it.

Not even the fire inside herself—the drive to travel the world and face the best—to *be* clearly the best in women's tennis—might not have made her ready to slip away.

All together they had been enough. She was ready and committed, despite the sadness.

Hannah saw her expression. "Oh, all right," she said, sighing. "I'll go second. You can go first. But you've got to let me watch, okay? Fine? Good! Hey, where is my damned *Šljivovica?* Don't these people know they have two world champions here? Waiter? Hey!"

In the basement lab, Michael Nariv lay stripped naked on the bare metal table. IV tubing coiled down from a standard, feeding silvery fluid into a vein in the crook of his left arm. Thin rivulets of blood drained from both his nostrils, and his pain-shocked eyes stared unblinking into the brilliant light in the ceiling overhead.

"He is dead," the lab technician said, stepping back from the table.

Major Ladislav Maleeva wiped sweat from his forehead. He hated work like this. He had never liked working with old-fashioned drugs like sulfazin. Why couldn't they provide him with the new and better drugs, which were faster acting and less likely to kill the subject before you were through with him?

The technician looked stricken. "I am sorry," she said.

Maleeva forced himself to be charitable. "It is of little consequence. He told us what we had to know." He walked out of the lab.

And now, he thought, riding the lift out of the bowels of the building, he faced the distasteful task of reporting everything he had learned to M.Y. Altunyan. The idea of reporting the disloyalty of one of his own countrymen to the sneering Chekist revolted him. He detested all Chekists. They were all alike: vulgar, cynical, arrogant, contemptuous, overbearing. He wished he could tell Altunyan to take his orders and cram them.

That, however, was impossible. In this strange case, the KGB was calling the shots. The usually fiercely independent government of Yugoslavia had been subjected to such pressure that it had caved in, pledged complete cooperation and technical support.

Maleeva again wondered why, and had no theory.

The stench of death in his nostrils, he walked into an office where there was a secure telephone, and dialed the number Altunyan had given him.

twelve

"Brad, let me call for a doctor!"

"Damn it, Karyn, I said no!"

"There's probably one right here in the hotel."

"I don't care if there's one next door. I said *no*."

An upset Karyn Wechsting, leaning on the frame of the bathroom door to take weight off her twisted ankle, surveyed me with an uncomprehending look. "That lump over your ear is as big as an egg."

I looked in the mirror and used a cool cloth to touch the spot where somebody had slugged me. "I noticed."

"You winced when you even *grazed* it! You're hurt!"

Struggling against my dizziness, I turned from the mirror and gently but firmly took Karyn's arm, leading her back into the hotel bedroom. Hearing that I was looking for her, she had come directly to my room when she returned from having her ankle looked after. My door had been ajar and she had found me on the floor. Thank the lord for a professional athlete's nerves: she hadn't screamed and she hadn't run to the lobby to make a scene. First she had knelt to examine me, and when she touched me I had staggered back to consciousness.

That had been—I checked my watch and had trouble getting it into focus—ten minutes ago. Which made it an hour since I had barged into the room like an idiot and let him whack me.

I sat Karyn on the couch and took the chair facing her. I hung on to her hands, which were like ice cubes, to make sure she didn't run. "So what's the verdict on the ankle?" I asked.

"You dumb *shit!*" she moaned. "Here I find you almost killed by somebody, and you ask about my ankle."

I managed a dishonest grin. "I'm feeling fine, and I don't have to play in the tournament."

"Well, I'm not playing either . . . now."

"It's that bad?"

"There might be a hairline compression fracture. Probably not, but not to take chances, they said. Stay off it all I can for a week, and absolutely no tennis. Then new X-rays back home."

"You're out of the tournament? That's terrible!"

"Oh, hell, Brad, I had Martina in the second round anyhow and she's getting her game back together and would have probably waxed me." But then Karyn's vivid eyes showed her competitiveness. "I sure wanted a shot at her, though."

"When will you notify the tournament officials?"

"I already have. I'm officially withdrawn as of now."

"When do you go home?"

"I'm updating my tickets to next Thursday. Ted is going to change his flights and fly back with me in case I need some help."

"You can't get out any sooner?"

She shrugged. "I might be able to, standby. But I'm here. I might as well see some of the sights and watch part of the tournament. Assuming Danisa Lechova gets by Sabatini on Tuesday, she'll almost certainly meet Chrissie on Wednesday. I'd like to see that. Two great clay court players, head to head."

"Why not stay for all of it?"

"My agent is setting up an appointment for me with a sports orthopod next Friday. Earliest I can get in."

"Karyn," I said, "I'm truly sorry about your injury. Maybe Ted and I should have been acting the fool and not making it competitive out there."

"Don't be silly," she shot back. "Also, you're a jerk."

"What a quaint term. Whatever do you mean by it?"

"You're trying to talk my question into the ground, avoid discussing this attack on you."

I studied her. She was indignant about me, not about her own injury. "No problem," I told her.

She made a face. "What *happened?*"

"I must have walked in on a thief."

"Then we'll call the authorities."

"No."

"Why?"

"Look. I told you already. I'm a journalist. I don't want any trouble . . . any notoriety. The chance to spend a lot of interview time with Danisa Lechova is the biggest break I've ever gotten as a tennis writer. I'm not doing anything that might mess it up."

"How could reporting a robbery mess anything up?"

"I don't know. The militia might nag me with questions, cut into my time with the Lechovas."

"That's farfetched, Brad."

"Well, maybe, but I'm not taking a chance. Besides, I feel fine now."

Karyn's eyes narrowed. "Brad. What in the living hell is really going on here?"

"Nothing."

"Brad!"

"Karyn." I took her by the shoulders. "Listen. Trust me. We'll talk later, okay?"

It took some doing. She didn't want to leave and she was afraid I would lapse into a coma or something if left alone. I finally sweet-talked her into giving me time to clean up and change clothes, promising to meet her in the bar downstairs in one hour. On that basis she finally let me push her out of the room, locking the door behind her.

The dizziness was still with me, but I was tracking mentally. I searched the room with the knowledge that electronic eavesdropping devices these days are so tiny they can be hidden literally anywhere. I didn't find any, but that didn't mean they weren't there.

The tapes for my miniature cassette recorder were still sealed in their original cellophane wrappers, and the sealing wax hidden in the battery and tape compartments on the recorder popped reassuringly when I opened those tiny doors, so I felt reasonably sure that part of my equipment hadn't been compromised. A bug could have been placed in a lot of places inside the mysterious innards of the lap computer, so I would have to be careful about that. As to finding bugs that might have been placed in my clothing or tennis gear, forget it; I knew all about buttons that transmitted several hundred yards, and cloth tape devices stuck inside coat linings. I had to assume some of that had been done and I was now wired for sound.

The fact that someone had searched my room was in itself sufficient proof that I was—at best—under general suspicion. My feeling grew that I had about as much chance as a germ under a microscope. My superiors had to be notified about this at once, and I had to take whatever steps were possible to reduce the chances that I had become a walking radio station.

I washed my face, examined my bump again, took three Tylenol tablets, and rode downstairs to the lobby. My head felt slightly clearer, and I examined my options. The boys needed to know about the break-in right away. I didn't feel quite spry enough to do the walk-past at the old cathedral as a signal, and there wasn't time to wait for Paula Bansky or somebody to contact me. The first backup scheduled meeting wasn't until Sunday evening, if necessary. So that put me back to the third alternate.

Using a public telephone in the hotel lobby, I dialed the embassy. The girl who answered sounded Midwestern, which was reassuring, but she also sounded about eighteen, which wasn't.

I told her, "This is Bob Green calling for Mr. Booth."

"Sir, Mr. Booth is in conference. May I take a message?"

I gritted my teeth. If the little twit didn't get this right, I had called for nothing. "Yes. Please tell him I called. My name is Bob Green. *Green.* And the bridge game is at six o'clock tonight. Let me repeat that. The *bridge game* is at *six o'clock* tonight. Did you get that?"

"I'll give Mr. Booth your message, sir."

I hoped I wasn't panicking, giving them the green signal indicating a serious problem that I had to let them know about right away. "Bridge game" was certainly true enough: almost certainly I was under some form of surveillance now, and the meeting would have to be brief, in motion, and to all outward appearances not a meeting at all. The primary meeting site was obvious, since I hadn't specified, and we were operating on the rule of minus two, which meant we would meet at 4.

Which left me plenty of time.

It was a short walk to a nice little clothing store. I had intended to buy some Yugoslav slacks and shirts anyway, just for the hell of it. When I went back to the hotel, my shopping bag wasn't too conspicuous under my arm even though I now was also the proud owner of locally produced underwear, socks, and canvas shoes.

Karyn met me in the bar. We had spritzers. She tried again to wrestle information out of me, but I played dumb. Her ankle started hurting a little worse, and she limped out of the place feeling out of sorts with me. I stayed on a while and reflected on how much I liked her. I thought of June and wished I hadn't. Then I drifted mentally for a while, not quite tracking again, and then I mentally beat up on myself, telling myself how really ridiculous it was for a man of my age and background to be entertaining these vague erotic fantasies about someone like Danisa Lechova. Then I went up to the room, changed into my nice new casual clothes that I knew didn't have any listening devices in them, and strolled out again, avoiding my friends from Kansas, who seemed to live in the lobby. The cheap canvas shoes hurt my feet.

It was a steamy afternoon. My new clothes were moist by the time I approached Republic Square. People and cars were everywhere. It was exactly 4 o'clock.

Before I was halfway around the plaza, gawking up at the equestrian statue of Duke Mihajlo, I spotted my man.

It was Mitchell, dressed like a tourist, with sunglasses to complicate identification by observers. He saw me about the same time I saw him, and paused to open his Nikon and snap a couple of shots of the statue.

I walked near him, not making eye contact, and studied my guide book. "Somebody broke into my room, bashed me on the head. I'm okay but I think I must be blown."

He nodded, pulled out a cigarette, and lit it. "Means you're bugged. Those new clothes?"

"Yes. Just bought them from the skin out. So I think I'm clean for the moment."

"Michael Nariv got pulled in."

"Jesus, on what charge?"

"Don't know. We'll get somebody in your room to sweep it. Wait for our next contact. Keep on with what you're doing. Rent a car. For a week. Leave it at the rental agency. More instructions to follow." He turned and walked off.

I walked around the statue in the opposite direction, then sat on a bench for a few minutes before heading back to the hotel. Mitchell had vanished immediately.

When I got up to start back, I noticed the man standing on the far side, leaning against a lamp post. It was a long distance over there, but one thing Father Time has left intact for me is my eyesight. The guy was thin and nondescript and unremarkable, but he had been watching me with the keenest interest. When he looked away, he looked away too fast.

I could only hope my contact with Mitchell had not been recognized.

I went back to the hotel. New effects of the blow to the head: I felt slightly nauseated and totally worn out. I read a magazine and sat in the cafe with Jimmy Connors for a while and wished I could see Danisa before tomorrow. The headache got worse again. I went to my room, where I found a candy store business card on the end table, but no candy. There was no candy store. It was one of our contact numbers. So my room had been swept electronically for bugs. And presumably it was now clean.

I gave up and went to bed, but didn't sleep. I worried about poor Michael Nariv, and about tomorrow. I hoped I was doing things right. I hoped my feelings of impending disaster were inaccurate. If we failed Danisa Lechova after setting her up, every important aspect of her life could be wrecked.

thirteen

Sunday morning, the gentlemen of the press were all over poor Karyn, each trying to get a unique quote about her disappointment over her injury and withdrawal from the tournament. She was holding forth in a little courtyard adjacent to the hotel, and being very patient with them. Nursing my headache, I listened for a few minutes. The fifth time somebody asked her how she felt about getting hurt, I went elsewhere.

Out front, Bryant Gumbel and Jane Pauley were doing a satellite feed to be taped in New York and used as plug in case of transmission trouble during the live telecast on Monday. Bryant asked me to do two minutes with him and I did.

That done, I hung around, expecting a contact. Nothing. I fretted.

The time finally rolled around for my appointment at the Lechova home. I toted my Nikon and Sony microcassette machine across the Sava into New Belgrade and the apartment building where the family lived. They had just gotten back from church.

Hannah, wearing what I had learned was her trademark hot pink, descended on me like a lost lover. "Oh, here he is! I am so excited! Oh, Brad Smith! I thought you were

144

never coming! We are having coffee and cake. You will join us. Then do you *have to* interview my sister? Wouldn't you rather have an assignation with me in the woods?"

"Hannah." Geneta Lechova, pretty in an ivory summer suit, was quietly disapproving. "Someday a man will take you seriously. Then the trouble will be serious, too."

"Oh, I *hope* so!"

Leon Lechova, unknotting his tie, walked into the tiny living room from the room next door. He didn't act glad to see me. He looked half mad at the world, as usual. He coolly shook hands and offered me a seat. Danisa came out of another room. Her church dress and heels were *her* trademark color, the pale blue that so accented her eyes and complexion. Unlike Hannah, who always wore her hair flowing loosely down her back, Danisa's was tied in her customary braided ponytail.

"Ah-ha!" Hannah cried. "You have kept on your church clothes to impress our guest!"

Church clothes had nothing to do with how impressed I was. Hannah was pretty, and fun. But when Danisa walked in, she seemed glad to see me and that made things go flip-flop in my chest. It was, I lectured myself, ridiculous.

We talked about Karyn's injury, and Mrs. Lechova went into the closet-sized kitchen, and soon the aroma of brewing coffee filled the apartment. She came back with coffee cake and *baklava* on a tray, and then with the coffee, cups on little saucers, utensils, napkins, water, sugar, fresh cream.

We ate around the coffee table. Faint breezes stirred the blinds at the windows, but it was already hot in the room. Hannah prattled and flirted outrageously. I tried to respond good-naturedly, but could not keep my eyes off Danisa. Hannah noticed, and began to get irritated.

I tried to take control, telling Lechova, "You have a nice place here. Convenient to a sports hall, too."

He nodded stiffly. "We are comfortable."

"Yes," Hannah burst in. "But after Danisa and I are

world champions and we are even more rich, the Housing Committee will move us to Dedinje!"

"Hannah," Lechova growled.

"What is Dedinje?" I asked.

"It is where the very rich once lived."

Hannah put in, "Before the revolution did away with classes in our society."

"Now, high party officials and other very important people live there," Danisa added.

I smiled before I could catch myself.

"What?" Danisa asked softly.

"The old privileged go, the new privileged move in," I said.

And instantly knew my mistake.

Hannah's coffee cup rattled on its saucer. The eyes she turned to me blazed with sudden anger. "There is no comparison," she snapped.

"Sorry."

"The people who live in Dedinje now have *earned* their privileges through service to the state. And loyalty. The people who used to live there had done nothing—only inherited wealth from corrupt ancestors who stole from the peasants."

I tried to recoup. "I don't know your country very well. I'm sure you're right."

But she didn't take criticism of Yugoslavia well—obviously—and she had already been teed off at my obvious preference for Danisa. Being the older sister—and number two—had to chafe.

She threw down her napkin, got up abruptly, and left the room, closing the bedroom door behind her none too gently.

"I apologize," Geneta Lechova said quickly. "We seldom attend Mass, and we required Hannah to join us today. It made her irritable."

"I should be the one to apologize."

"Why?" Danisa asked softly. "Because you spoke the truth?"

Lechova said quickly, "There will be none of that talk here."

"But Hannah will be the first to wallow in the luxury of the rich if we are successful enough, and the committee assigns us housing in Dedinje," Danisa insisted.

"If we have earned such an honor—"

"Yes. We all will accept it, take it as our due. But Poppa, will we really have *earned* a great house with gardens because we can strike a ball across a net? Is that so praiseworthy, and deserving of high honor, when compared with a man who has worked forty years in a steel mill or a mine, so that his eyes are seared nearly blind and his lungs are filled with tar?"

"That," Lechova snapped, "will be enough."

Danisa flushed angrily, shot me a rebellious look, but lowered her gaze to her plate. In the deep silence, Mrs. Lechova extended a dish. "Another cake, Mr. Smith?"

I took one. I felt a little like Alice at the tea party.

After more coffee, Geneta Lechova cleared the table with Danisa's help, and Leon Lechova went off to another room, perhaps to lecture Hannah. She came back after a while and acted as if nothing had happened, then sailed out of the apartment to go watch some of the qualifying matches on the outdoor courts. Danisa was off changing clothes, and her mother was in the kitchen. Lechova faced me in the living room.

"The slight disagreements in our family are of no importance," he told me with his grim bulldog look.

"Understood."

"They will not be included in your story."

"I see your point of view."

"My daughters are devoted and loyal. They compete in tennis but they stand together as a family."

"They're remarkable," I agreed. "You have a fine family."

But he would not let go of it, this stern, unhappy, driven man. "Hannah may never be the tennis player that Danisa has become. She accepts this, and takes joy in her own excellent talents. Competition between the girls does not alter their love. Minor differences in political opinion are of no consequence. Nothing will ever divide our family."

"Mr. Lechova, I have no desire to drive a wedge between your daughters. If time allows, I hope to do a piece on Hannah, too. It wasn't part of the assignment, but I can place it somewhere."

He nodded, just as unhappy. "They are as devoted and loving as any real blood sisters could be."

The implication of that startled me. I showed it.

He said, "Hannah and Danisa are adopted, Mr. Smith. Hannah in 1965, Danisa a year later."

"They look enough alike to be real sisters."

"The state matches children to the physical characteristics of the parents when possible."

"I see."

"My family is excellent," he went on. "Nothing will ever separate us. We are loyal to each other and nothing can change that."

It was heartfelt. I didn't reply. If my mission succeeded, I thought, he would never get over the pain.

Danisa came back, wearing white slacks and canvas shoes and a sleeveless shell in her trademark pale blue. She had gotten over the tense scene with her sister, and had that serene and beautiful grace about her again.

She perched on the edge of a chair, crossing long legs. "You said we would . . . conduct the interview in another location?"

"I thought it might be easier in the park," I said.

"I'm ready."

We left the apartment, me toting the camera and recording gear again, and rode the elevator to street level. A lot of people were out, apartment dwellers, strolling or visiting. There was an old-fashioned neighborhood feel about it that I liked. In the park across the street, parents with children were everywhere, and the yelps and laughter of the little ones would have trashed any recording. Danisa said there was a quieter adult park nearby, and we walked down a concrete canyon of sterile apartment buildings in search of it.

"Once we get to the park and are settled," I told her, "nothing gets said that might compromise our real business together in any way."

She looked puzzled. "But if we find an isolated spot in the trees, who could overhear?"

I gave her the Reader's Digest Condensed version of finding someone in my room, getting creamed, and suspecting electronic surveillance. "Walking like this is the best we can do," I concluded. "Once we're settled, somebody could have a listening bazooka trained on us from a couple of hundred yards."

"And that's why you wear these Belgrade clothes?" she asked in dismay.

"I'm afraid so, yes."

"But what if they have put a listening device in *my* clothing?"

"I don't think it's likely. They don't really have any reason to suspect you of anything . . . do they?"

"Not that I know of. But—"

"It's a chance we have to take. There are a few things we have to talk about before we start the interview. After the cassette is running, even if they're not pointing a sound gun at us, they might get at the tapes. So they have to be clean."

She was pale now, but she nodded gamely. "We will take this turn and walk an extra two blocks to reach the park."

"Danisa. Are you sure you want to defect?"

She didn't hesitate. "Yes."

"It's going to hurt your father. A lot."

"And my mother," she added. "And Hannah." The set of her jaw reminded me faintly of her father's grimness.

"It might get very dangerous."

"I know."

"Aren't you happy enough here? Why do this?"

"I have always been happy," she said in a tone that didn't sound like it. "I love my parents . . . Hannah. But now there is no choice. No choice at all. You know that."

"Because they've pulled your passport? Restricted your travel to play tennis?"

She stopped on the crowded sidewalk and stared at me in disbelief. "They send you here to help me and you don't know the true story?"

"I'm a contact man. A scut. What I don't need to know—"

"I had thought much about the West, as I told you before. But I think—probably—I would never have left my family this way, permanently. But my *real* family—my real brother—is in America!"

Surprised, I stared at her. It began to make sense. "You have a brother?"

"I knew none of it. Oh, my parents—my parents *here*—told Hannah and me we were adopted. We were both orphans, they said, and had no living kin. I know my mother and father—*this* mother and father—believed that. But someone knew otherwise."

People were looking at us. I started walking again and she fell in beside me.

"You'd better tell me all you know," I said.

"I know now that my mother had a son, many years older than I. She died here soon after I was born. I was placed in the state home. That was where the Lechovas adopted me when I was very, very young, still an infant. They had adopted Hannah a year earlier."

"Your father just told me that. It isn't generally known."

"It is of no consequence. We are a real family. In love."

Her voice cracked. "But that was before I learned of my blood brother."

I kept walking, taking it in, and said nothing. She would tell it now because she was driven to do so, get it out as much for her own hearing as mine. I had to strain to hear her voice, which was faint with emotion.

"My brother was already in the army when I was born. My father died. There was some . . . great disgrace. My mother came here, went back to her maiden name. I was born and she died. No one knew who I was for a long time and I was adopted. My brother, far away, lost me.

"But someone, searching my real mother's things, found some paper that said her real name. Partek."

I chilled. *"Partek?"*

She cut into my racing thoughts: "Whoever it was, he filed a report . . . somewhere. And I think it must have lain buried and forgotten for a long, long time. But my brother became . . . important. He was a member of the Yugoslav military, and then he was recruited by the Soviet KGB. He went to Paris and London and later to the United Nations, and I think he did much work for Russia as a spy."

"Dominic Partek," I said. "Jesus Christ."

"Lately he wanted to defect to the West," Danisa went on. "It was then that the KGB, knowing of my existence, let him learn about me for the first time. They hinted, I think, that if he showed disloyalty . . . I would never get to leave this country again, and my adoptive family would be in disgrace."

It all made sense now: why a lone Yugoslav tennis player, practically still a girl, rated all our attention.

I said, "But Partek still wanted to come over to our side?"

"Yes. But unless I can get to safety in the West, they can control him forever by using me as a hostage."

"But is that enough to make you ready to leave your family—abandon your citizenship here?"

"Would you stay in a country that used its people like this? This is just one example! Look at my father! A wonderful man, once a fine athlete, paid almost nothing for the good work he does every day in the *gymnazia*. My mother is given even less—because she is a woman. I *hate* Yugoslavia for what it does to people!"

The depth of her bitterness took me off guard. We went on to the street corner in silence.

We paused there, waiting for a city bus to cross with other traffic. The sprawling park, trees and sidewalks and statuary, was just ahead.

"So," I said, "if we get you out, it makes it safe for Partek to come over to our side."

"It will save his life!"

We started across the street and I had to ask one more question even though I knew the answer and didn't want to hear it from her. "Who told you all this?"

"A man from your embassy."

Ah, we were such wonderful guys.

Danisa was a pawn for us as much as for them. They would use her to keep Dominic Partek in line. We would use her to make it safe for him to come over to our side, so his treasure of KGB information could be ours.

But it wasn't quite that simple, despite my feelings of angry dismay. June's ambiguity again—and wasn't *I* the one who was supposed to be able to deal with that?

If Partek wanted to defect, I told myself, he had the right, and would be better off for it. If Danisa had learned of a long-lost brother decades after she should have been told, that was not our fault. If she wanted to go to the U.S. and see him at last, what was wrong with that?

On balance (always on balance!), we were in the right.

And then it occurred to me that right or wrong didn't make any difference. Danisa wanted out. I was here to help her. And I would have helped her right now regardless.

We reached the far curb, skirted a heroic statue of a soldier carrying a rifle, passed a flower seller and children eating ice cream, and moved under the shade of a maple, following a cobblestone path. Children ran and played far away, and just ahead was a park bench with no one near it, and squirrels and pigeons on the opulent grass.

Danisa asked, "What else must we talk about before we sit down?"

God, she was a great lady: back on track ahead of me, the supposed professional. I forced my aching head into the proper track. "I don't know what procedure we'll use to get you out. I don't have those instructions yet. But I need an accurate and detailed timetable from you: practice times, likely match times, other engagements, everything. For planning purposes."

She nodded. "I will write it tonight."

"I'm going to conduct a very long interview here. Remember we may be overheard, or the tapes monitored later."

"Yes."

I brushed some peanut hulls and leaf fragments off the bench for her to sit down. "That's it, then."

She faced me, her eyes narrowed with determination. "One more thing, Brad Smith."

"Yes?"

"It is my decision. It has been made. I trust you. I will do what you order. You are never to feel that I am being used, because I am not. I am a free woman." Her eyes shone with sudden tears.

Before I quite knew what I was doing, I reached for her and pulled her close in a hug that ached because it felt so right. Her breath caught and for a second she responded, electric in my arms.

I just held her for a moment.

We pulled apart awkwardly. I sat down, started my recorder, and took my notepad from my shirt pocket. "We'll begin at the beginning," I said, brisk and businesslike. But my voice, even to me, sounded hoarse.

* * *

I used all of one ninety-minute microcassette and most of another. At one point a vendor strolled through, pushing his cart, and we stopped the tape long enough to buy lemonade and peanuts from him. But except for a couple of comments about the need to take a break, we continued the interview.

Assuming I wrote the story one day, I saw how it would go. Danisa was a wonderful interview subject: candid, verbal, bright, informed. She gave me some quotes about her father and her early tennis training that would have curled any Svengali's hair. It was a complicated family, Leon Lechova driving the girls and accepting nothing less than his version of perfection, Geneta Lechova quietly trying to protect them and nurture them so they would not be destroyed emotionally by a parent who could never be satisfied.

Leon Lechova was not a happy man, but he didn't know that. Teaching physical culture in the *gymnazia* was a high calling for a man of his peasant background. He was proud of his status as a professor. But he had old scripts of his own: he would always be angry with himself for not being an Olympic champion, and he would always carry the vague and uneasy feeling that something in his life was *not . . . quite . . . right.*

Danisa's mother was simpler, in her way more sad. She was loyal to her family. Danisa had never heard her complain about the sometimes harsh discipline of their home, or Leon Lechova's seeming inability to be tender. She had spent her life protecting her daughters and would do anything for them.

Danisa was frighteningly bright. She understood tennis theory and technique at a conscious level as well as in her gut. But she knew the world, and history. The names of leaders, minor events, and trends came off her tongue with the ease of serious thought. She was unfailingly generous and forgiving.

We talked about Hannah, and the relationship between the two of them. She thought Hannah was funny. She also saw how Hannah had gone a different ideological way. The young military man I had seen at the ball was not the only one who had been turned in by Hannah for suspected deviationism. Hannah was warm, volatile, emotional, loving, supportive, generous, unselfish, suspicious, watchful, vengeful, cold. Take your pick.

We filled almost an entire tape with observations about tennis, other world-class players, Danisa's experiences and hopes for the future, and the Belgrade tournament.

After we had gotten well into it, I caught her asking *me* questions, turning my interview technique back on myself. It became an exchange, a mutual learning. She was one of the most caring and understanding people I had ever met. And through all of it there was the physical side: the pale glow of sunlight through the trees on wisps of her hair that had escaped the ponytail; the way she tossed her bare-ankled shoe, moving her long leg; her hands and the way she used them when she got excited about what she was saying; her eyes and mouth.

Finally we stopped talking and looked at one another. Her smile came, dawning. I reached over and turned the recorder off.

"Thank you," I told her.

We stood and walked out of the park. She turned and smiled at me and impulsively reached for my hand. We walked partway through the shade holding hands like kids. Then I let her go.

I had no clear idea of how she felt. But the hours with her today, and then the way she reached out to me, without artifice, changed me. Once before I had felt something like this. With Elizabeth. But I had been a kid then and hadn't understood about pain. This time I could stand back just a little and gauge the depth and quality of the feeling, and know the likely outcome.

No matter about the likely final outcome. Being physically close to her was driving me crazy. It was too late to question the feelings, or control them. I would do anything for her.

We crossed the street at the same intersection and started back toward her home.

I forgot to check for surveillance.

fourteen

Elsewhere

New Belgrade

Colonel V. N. Ubezhko, chief of the UDBA for the Belgrade-Surčin district, folded beefy hands over his desk blotter. "We can assume Nariv was in the employ of the CIA. Beyond that, we know nothing."

Facing his superior, Major Ladislav Maleeva felt deeper foreboding. First the pressure to cooperate with Altunyan of the KGB. Now this attack on his investigation. "Who could have known someone like Nariv would fight the drug so tenaciously?"

Ubezhko's fist hammered the desk. "*You* should have known it!"

Maleeva fought for calm. "I believe there was nothing more to be gotten from him."

"I have read your report. If Nariv knew no more than he told you, he had to have been brain-dead before you arrested him!"

Maleeva bit his lip and remained silent.

"Well"—Ubezhko sighed heavily—"it is done. What is your recommendation—if any—to maintain control of the situation?"

"We are maintaining surveillance—"

"I know that! Speak to me of new measures!"

"We do not know what, if anything, may actually be planned—"

"Maleeva! Kindly stop reviewing our state of ignorance and make recommendations!"

"Altunyan says this Brad Smith should be expelled from our country at once."

Ubezhko's liverish lips curled in a sneer. "Altunyan does not operate this office or our government."

"But our orders to cooperate—"

"Those orders do not mean we let the KGB issue us orders!"

Maleeva fell silent. He saw that his superior was as angry at the situation—at the forced cooperation with the KGB—as he was with their abysmal ignorance of what, if anything, the Americans were planning. This was interesting. It also meant his job was in less jeopardy than he had momentarily feared.

"This tennis tournament," Ubezhko said, "is a major event designed at the highest levels of government to encourage tourist visits, place the healthy, open nature of our society on display for the world to see, and set the stage for next year's international games. We will *not* smear ourselves in the eyes of the world by harrassing or interrogating or expelling Western journalists."

"But," Maleeva pointed out cautiously, "if Nariv was CIA, and his assignment was as contact with this man Smith, then Smith—"

"Obviously is CIA, also. Yes."

"And Smith has established continuing close contact with the Lechova family."

"Yes." Ubezhko sighed. "It appears he is in Yugoslavia to assist in the flight and defection of Danisa Lechova. But we have no proof."

"But if we can't expel Smith, Danisa Lechova must be placed in protective custody, immediately!"

"We can't do that, you fool."

"But if she plans to try to defect—"

"We *fear* she plans to defect. Why else do you think her passport, and that of her sister, were withdrawn for 'routine review'? But we cannot arrest her. She is in this tournament. The eyes of the world are on her . . . and us. She is a national heroine."

"Then . . . what?"

"There is a chance that their operation will be abandoned, now that they know of Nariv's disappearance and likely arrest. If that happens, our goal of keeping Danisa Lechova in our country has already been met. If they persist, round-the-clock vigilance pertaining to this Brad Smith, and to anyone he contacts, will prevent any successful attempt to spirit her across our national borders."

"Then we intensify our watch on Smith."

"Yes."

"And wait."

"For now—yes."

"What of Altunyan? He is persistent—"

"I," Ubezhko said, "will deal with Altunyan. He will not interfere in our jurisdiction. There will be no problem.

When M. Y. Altunyan concluded his own meeting with Ubezhko less than two hours later, however, his view was quite different.

Altunyan was in a towering rage.

The goddamn Yugoslavs, he thought, simply did not—or would not—understand the scope and seriousness of the problem facing the Soviet Union. Even the extreme pressure brought to bear by Moscow for cooperation in this case had not convinced the Yugoslav government of the severity of the situation.

Very well, then. Additional steps had to be taken.

Altunyan went directly from Ubezhko's headquarters to the Soviet Embassy. There he drafted and encoded his report and recommendations.

As he watched the computer equipment packetize the

159

message and send it in a single brief radio burst to Moscow, he knew his plan of action was so drastic as to call for review at the highest levels in the First Chief Directorate, and almost certainly beyond. The case officers of civilized nations had an unspoken agreement that was seldom breached. One did not simply exterminate officers of a rival service, however extreme the provocation, unless one was North Korean, or Albanian, or a maniac from somewhere in the Middle East.

But this situation, Altunyan felt sure, was an exception.

It would take time for a decision—approval—to come back to him. In the meantime, he had plenty to do. Leaving orders that he should be notified immediately when Moscow's message came back, he left the building.

In the United States Embassy, David Booth spread the materials on the worktable for Joe Mitchell to examine. Mitchell did so, with great care.

The most interesting were the new passports, issued to David and Helen Spalding, husband and wife, from Philadelphia. The passports were dated as having been issued in 1985, and contained visa stamps from France and Great Britain in that year, West Germany, Italy, and Austria last summer, and a Yugoslav visa stamp dated one week ago.

The picture of David Spalding was a good likeness of Brad Smith. Danisa Lechova's photo, taken from a slight distance with a long lens and then blown up, was grainy but passable. The signatures were forged.

Other items on the table were a road map of Yugoslavia that showed the border crossing into Italy at Trieste; an envelope containing 20,000 dinars; and a collection of souvenirs: picture postcards from Sarajevo, Belgrade, Dubrovnik, and Zadar, matchbook covers from restaurants in these and other cities, and a small Croatian silver bracelet.

"Elaborate," Mitchell concluded. "This stuff ought to fool anybody."

"Let's get it to Smith," Booth said, "and hope it fools him."

That night, Hannah and Danisa went to bed at 10 o'clock, leaving their parents in front of a television set displaying an episode of *Dallas*. It was routine on the night before tournament play: a light supper, early to bed. As was also routine, neither sister could sleep.

"Was he wonderful?" Hannah whispered across the narrow gap separating the twin beds.

Danisa smiled in the dark. "He is a very nice man."

"Did he ask if he could put it in you?"

"He is a gentleman."

Hannah chuckled throatily. "He is a *man*."

Danisa didn't answer. She thought of how she had felt in his arms today. She felt warm and hectic and excited, just remembering it. The excitement mixed with her sadness and apprehension.

"You must win the tournament for him," Hannah told her now.

"Hannah?"

"Yes?"

Danisa felt driven. "If you knew of someone who . . . was thinking about some disloyal act . . . what would you do?"

"Inform the authorities, of course," Hannah said at once. Then, more sharply: "Do you know of someone?"

"No. I was just thinking. During a tournament like this, there must be so many temptations for our younger players, the ones hypnotized by Western music, styles, culture."

Hannah's voice still sounded hard in the dark: "If you have any suspicion, it is your duty to turn them in."

"There isn't anyone," Danisa told her. "It was just . . . idle speculation."

Hannah was silent for a while. Then she said: "If you have suspicions, and lack the will to contact the UDBA, you will tell me. I know of a person to speak to."

"Good," Danisa said, her throat dry.

"I am not afraid, Danisa. I will report anyone. You will remember that?"

"I'll remember."

"Good." Hannah sounded comfy again. "Now tell me everything that was said today of a personal nature. Tell me if he tried to kiss you or feel you up. I must know! Oh, that man *excites* me! If I have an opportunity like you had today, I will throw myself all over him!"

Alexandria, Virginia

Kinkaid was at his home in Alexandria when the telephone rang and he answered it, immediately recognizing Dwight's voice.

"We think he's in Missoula, Montana," Dwight said. "Get up there. Contact Lannigan. He'll explain."

"On my way," Kinkaid said at once.

"We're telling Belgrade to move everything up. So get cracking."

"Roger."

fifteen

The first Belgrade International got into high gear early Monday morning, and I had no inkling that it was also to be the day when everything started to go really, seriously wrong.

Danisa and Hannah teamed in the women's doubles at 10 A.M. About 4,000 people were already in the stands, sunlight filtering through the great translucent plastic dome of the stadium, to watch the Lechovas take on an Italian pair.

The Lechovas started fast, going up 4–0 in the first set. They looked good, and Miloslav Fjbk, sitting next to me in the first row, put on his own show for the reporters around us.

"How do they look to you today?" someone asked him.

Uncoiling bare, hairy arms from the pipe railing in front of our row of seats, Fjbk made two fists. "Hey, rush and crush, right? The officials ought to call out—what do you call it in your country?—the Humane Society, right? Is cruelty, put ordinary players in with my rush-and-crush girls."

Pencils scribbled. Fjbk saw he was making a hit.

"My coaching genius is pay off," he went on. "Sometimes I think how tennis would be if the game had not had

163

me, Miloslav Fjbk. Look at that shot down the line! You see that shot? I gave her that shot. I taught them everything they know. No wonder I am now a celebrity, eh? People recognize me. I am the best at what I do, which is make players be the best at what they do. Rush and crush. No mercy."

Someone asked, "Will the Lechovas meet in the women's finals?"

"Sure! No problem! I said all along they ought to have two brackets, my girls in one and everybody else in the other. Let me tell you something—Look at that volley! We have closed the gates of mercy! If anyone wants to be great, they should contact me. Even if Ivan want to come back, he can contact my agent. Maybe I will give him a break, help him become a really good player. I have the secret. Rush and crush. Today we start a new era in history of the world. I am unleash my rush-and-crush girls. Get that down."

Danisa and Hannah won the first set, 6–1, and Fjbk's repartee sharpened and became more outrageous. The guys around us were laughing as they got down what he said. In the second set, however, Hannah started hitting some shots long, and Danisa's serve faltered. The Italians, with nothing to lose, began hitting harder. Possibly there was a letdown on the Lechova side. It went to a long tiebreaker before Danisa hit a winning crosscourt volley between her opponents for a 10–8 edge.

The players headed for the locker-room tunnel. Fjbk, whose good humor had faltered late in the match, waved to the press and hustled up the stairs to meet his players at the tunnel. I went with him.

We found Danisa and Hannah had already gone inside the locker room. We waited outside with a few press people and a cadre of security guards. I went to the water fountain against the far wall and Fjbk followed me.

"Goddamn you," he rumbled, blocking me as I turned from the water. His eyes were smoky and he looked a different man than the one who had clowned for the press upstairs.

"What's the problem?" I demanded.

"You saw how they played in the second set! They lost concentration."

"What's that got to do with me?"

"Maybe they would not have done it if you had not been with them all day yesterday, distracting them, filling them full of nonsense."

I found it interesting, how his English improved when he was not performing for someone. "Fjbk, don't try to lay off their poor play on me. I'm just doing a job here."

He punched a finger into my chest. "Stay away from them for rest of tournament."

"You're crazy."

"They played bad in second set. I must refocus their attention. We will find a place to hit after lunch. One hour. You will *not* distract them no more."

"They look great to me. Loose. Confident."

"Danisa's timing is bad. She must improve before tonight."

"You don't expect her to have much trouble with Tauziat, do you?"

"Perhaps," he said glaring, "I would not—if you had not spent all day with her yesterday, distracting her mind from this tournament."

"Fjbk, you can't keep her in a bottle all her life."

"I have waited all my life for this one. You will not ruin her for me. She is my *chance*."

I studied him, trying to fathom the complex depths of his passion. There was more here than ambition, more than his obvious adoration of Danisa. I didn't understand what was driving him.

He seemed to read my mind. He punched my chest with his finger again. "You know how long I waited for this chance?"

"Maybe I don't."

"I was born in Kragujevac. When I was a little boy, the Germans came in with their trucks, their machine guns.

They killed seven thousand—*seven thousand!*—in our city in a single day. Reprisals. I joined partisans and began fighting when I was nine years old. One day I killed a German soldier with my rifle, long shot. Once I got shrapnel in my leg . . . here . . . from a plane, strafing.''

Fjbk paused, breathed. His teeth clicked like the jaws of a steel trap. "After war, sweep garbage here in Beograd. Army. Learn tennis. Tennis is my life. You think I want to go back sweeping garbage? You think I don't have it coming to me after Kragujevac, all the rest, to be rich? She is my chance! *Nobody* is going to take her from me. *This* time I have my champion, who will stay with me always, and show the world Miloslav Fjbk coaches champions!''

"What happens," I asked, "when she meets a man and falls in love?"

"Goddamn you! Don't talk about that! I will always have her. I control her. She is mine. You hear me?"

His eyes were crazy. I thought I would be glad when we were out of here.

I left the arena and rode the press van back to the hotel. From there I walked a few blocks to a car rental agency.

I rented a dark blue Fiat and told the sullen clerk behind the wicket that I would leave the car parked with him for the time being. He didn't act happy about that, but he would not have been happy, judging from the available evidence, if Debra Winger had thrown herself into his arms and pledged undying passion.

Back at the hotel, a small potted plant had been delivered to my room. I opened the window and put the pot out on the ledge. Then I left the hotel and walked via a circuitous route to the Kalemegdan. It was a steamy day, the bridges and old fortress hazy through dense humidity, adding to the sweep and grandeur of the huge park.

Despite the bad news about Michael Nariv, I didn't see any signs of being followed. Knowing I could be wrong, I did my thing. My avoidance tactics, however, were simple and probably inadequate.

In thrillers, the prey always walks a few blocks, doubles back, goes through a crowded department store, takes a cab, hops out in a busy district, gets on a streetcar, hops back off just as it departs, takes one subway a mile in one direction and a bus a mile in another, changes cabs twice more, and—*voila!*—has eluded his shadow. There are a couple of problems with this: first, if you're being followed routinely, such behavior tips off your guilt and makes your shadow a lot more interested; and second, if they really want you, none of it will work anyway because they can put an army of shadows on the street with you: the guy behind you, the guy doubling ahead, the telephone repair van, the girl selling flowers on the corner, the young couple holding hands across the street, the three cars that mill around in the traffic, staying on all sides of you, the skinny kid in a dirty T-shirt.

Nevertheless, I worked hard enough to be sweaty by the time I reached and entered the museum.

It was blessedly cool and quiet in the great building, and not very crowded. I took a turn of a couple of rooms, watching the central foyer, and recognized one of Booth's men at once when he came in. Our eyes met through a wide, tall connecting doorway and he walked on. I waited for a count of a hundred and followed. He was leaving the restroom when I turned the corner. He went west and I walked into the restroom he had just vacated.

In the first stall inside, the newspaper was stuck behind the flush handle, and the thin nine-by-twelve envelope was inside the newspaper. I stuck the envelope in my belt inside my shirt and folded the newspaper under my arm. After washing my hands, I went back out into the corridor. Booth's man and I passed in adjacent rooms a minute later so he could see that the drop had gone okay.

Back at the hotel I examined the contents of the envelope. I felt like Alice: things were getting stranger and stranger. I was supposed to be a middleman, a contact between Danisa and the people who were getting her out. But here were phony IDs and all the evidence of a tourist trip through southern Yugoslavia.

Was *I* supposed to drive her out of Belgrade? And why in hell had they had me rent a car under my own name if I was going to be this other joker in a day or so?

I didn't like it.

Danisa was getting edgy, too.

She sat with me in the stands while Hannah played Bettina Fulco of Argentina on center court indoors that afternoon. In the first set Hannah struggled a little, making several unforced errors and double-faulting four times. But in the tiebreaker she got herself together, saved one match point, and won it 9–7. She started the second set with a service break and love game, and Danisa leaned back to talk.

"You have given them the paper with my schedule?" she asked.

"It was passed to my contact person an hour ago."

"When will it happen?"

"That isn't certain yet."

"Why are we waiting? Why do we just *wait?*" The tension made her voice crack slightly.

"As soon as I know something, you'll know something," I told her.

"And you will be with me?"

"I don't know that. Maybe at first. Someone else will actually take you out."

"I wish you were going to be with me. I am very frightened."

"Danisa, they're going slowly because these things have to be orchestrated very, very carefully. Everything is being arranged. That takes time. It's going to be all right."

She sighed, said nothing.

I wished I felt half as confident as I had just sounded.

I was still brooding about the fake papers and souvenirs in the envelope in my briefcase beside me. Was I going to be driving to Trieste? I had about as much business really trying to take Danisa across as I had of playing Lendl in this tournament. I didn't know procedures. I had no experience. I had never been more than a messenger boy, a go-between, and that was what I had been told I would be here.

Michael Nariv's disappearance had to be viewed in the worst possible light. It meant arrest. Which meant interrogation. I harbored no illusions about the UDBA's preoccupation with humane treatment of prisoners in interrogation. If they had him they would break him. Then they would know—at least—that I was here under false colors.

That likelihood, combined with Paula Bansky's stupid phone call the first night, all but took me out of the operation. One had to assume I had been blown. And whoever was calling the shots at the embassy must know that. Yet they seemed intent on pressing on. It was almost as if they wanted the operation to go down the tubes.

I needed something to happen.

It was about to.

sixteen

That night, Danisa and Hannah had opening singles matches.

Danisa went on first, at 7 P.M. The stadium was packed to the rafters with Belgrade sports nuts anxious to see their heroine take her first step toward the championship.

I sat in the stands with Ted Treacher and Karyn Wechsting.

On the third point of the first game, Zrubakova, serving, hit a fine driving shot to Danisa's backhand corner. Danisa made an incredible get and, with Zrubakova coming to net, flipped up a humming topspin lob that the Czech player couldn't have reached with a broomhandle before it made chalk fly where it hit the back line crosscourt.

The crowd erupted. The shot unsettled Zrubakova, and Danisa cruised to a 6–0 victory in the first set.

Danisa served to open the second. In a vast hush, she tossed the ball high and brought her entire long and powerful body through the motion. The ball was a curving blur over the net and Zrubakova lunged wide right, barely nicking it with the tip of her racket. An opening ace.

It was simply no contest.

Poor Zrubakova was a fine player, and she worked hellaciously hard, scurrying from side to side, making some incredible gets, hitting lines, playing angles, changing tactics and coming to net after it became apparent that she simply couldn't win many points in backcourt dueling. She won game 2, but Danisa took the third at love and broke her again in game 4.

"My God," Karyn murmured, "when she's on like this, I wouldn't want to play her."

"Nobody should have to play her," Treacher added.

The rest of the set was a slaughter. Some players might have extended things a bit by trying impossible angle shots, but Danisa was kinder. There is nothing "decent" or "kind" about extending a match when you are vastly superior. Dropping a game or two by trying the impossible is only insulting, really, and she knew that. Stony-faced, beautiful, her pigtail almost black with sweat, she was relentless.

Danisa had no weaknesses, and her game was so fluid, graceful, and powerful, with impeccable court tactics, that I sat entranced as I watched her. I don't mean she was invincible; Martina could have stayed with her, and possibly even won. Steffi Graf can beat anyone on a given day, and Chrissie with her perfect emotional control and courageous spirit might have rallied endlessly with her, fighting for every microscopic advantage. I knew that an able-bodied Karyn too might be able to take Danisa to the outer limits of her strength.

But this was Danisa's night, no question about that.

There is a beauty in tennis that comes to you sometimes when you're playing. Every movement and countermovement becomes part of an unfolding dance that can even envelop the knowing spectator. Serve becomes the opening lead in the duet. Return—counterpoint. And the ball comes back, and your body and spirit are one with it, and even with the movement of your opponent, seen vaguely across the net. There is no striking of the ball per se; the ball simply gets struck. And body, mind, ball, racket, court, opponent, angles, sweat, lights, tactics, reflexes, all become part of something very difficult to define. You can hate your opponent and want to whip his ass, yet love him at the same time for *being part of this* with you, making it possible.

Danisa's concentration was so total, her movements so harmonious and clever and powerful and *right*, that she wove that kind of spell. I think even her opponent— frustrated, fighting herself as well as Danisa, seeing it all slip away with every point—felt it.

I was bowled over. She was one in a million. And maybe, feeling about her as I did, I would have sat there in a trance of admiration if she *hadn't* been such a great player. But she was, and my admiration for her skills and temperament just kept going higher.

There was no limit to how far she could go in tennis.

If we got her out of here and into the part of the world where government bureaucracy couldn't hold her back.

The match was over in fifty-five minutes. Danisa walked off with her arm over her opponent's shoulders. She looked up toward us in the stands—her parents were just behind us—and sent a joyous smile that would have melted an iceberg.

There was time to move a few sections and see all of Hannah's match. Ted and Karyn left me at that point because they wanted to watch Sabatini's match on an outside court.

I found a single chair behind the railing in the first row, right behind where Hannah was finishing her warmups. She spotted me and walked back after her final practice serves, getting a towel off the chair against the wall.

"Hi, lover." She grinned, toweling her face.

"You look sharp," I told her.

"For you I will show off, baby. Hey, if I win in straight sets, we will have time to go park in your car, hah?"

I nodded my head toward the far tunnel entrance, where Fjbk was reemerging after walking Danisa to the showers. "Not with Dick Tracy around."

She looked that way and grimaced. "He is a dick, all

right. And now here come Momma and Poppa down the stairs behind you. Oh, boy, our romance has not got a chance!'' With that, she turned and strode toward the sidelines, where the referee was waiting to give the contestants a final word before they started play.

The Lechovas came down the stairs and slid into two seats across the aisle that had been saved for them. Fjbk came across the arena backfloor and climbed over the pipe to join them. He gave me another look that I couldn't read.

Right here, I thought, were my two biggest problems relating to Danisa's possible escape: her sister and her coach. One or the other was with her almost all the time. And either would do just about anything to thwart what we had in mind. I wondered how my pals at the embassy were going to get around these two.

The match started with Hannah winning the toss and electing to serve. She was not as smooth, not as overpowering, as Danisa. But the Fjbk style was there, and despite some stutters she worked really hard and got into the flow of the match.

She won in straight sets in less than an hour.

I expected Danisa to come out and join the family in watching her sister. I think the Lechovas did too, because I saw both of them turn around and look expectantly up the steps a number of times. But Danisa didn't show. Even Hannah glanced up hopefully after the match, as if looking for her sister, and her face fell a little when she saw Danisa wasn't there.

When Hannah headed for the lockers after her match, her parents and Fjbk trailed. I went along too, stopping to stand in line in a crowded men's room. That still left me plenty of time to loiter in the concrete tunnel with friends and relatives of several women players.

Hannah finally came out. She hadn't showered or changed yet. She walked over to her waiting parents, who had been talking with Fjbk. I joined them.

"She is not inside," Hannah told us, speaking English for my benefit.

"But she is not out here!" Leon Lechova said blankly.

"I know," Hannah said. "Danisa told an attendant that she had a bad headache, and was going to walk home to get the fresh air."

"Home without us?" Lechova repeated, his face darkening with worry. "But she has never done such a thing!"

That was when I started to worry.

"It is not like Danisa!" Mrs. Lechova added.

"But," Hannah said worriedly, "the attendant walked with her to the players' gate, Gate sixty-four, downstairs. He saw her leave."

Both parents looked stunned. Fjbk muttered something about questioning the guard, and pushed into the crowd in front of the locker-room doors.

Leon Lechova said, "Geneta. You will start home. At once. I will wait here for Hannah. We will join you as soon as possible."

I left them there, and headed for the players' gate.

Something serious had happened. I was starting to feel badly scared. Maybe somebody at Gate 64 had seen where Danisa headed when she left . . . whether someone intercepted her, or picked her up.

Unfortunately, Gate 64 was not normally manned, and was blocked to the public from outside. It was at the end of a long, narrow, poorly lighted concrete tunnel, and evidently had been picked for player use because it was well off the beaten path. When I got there, the tunnel and gate alike were deserted.

I looked around, thinking that by some wild chance I might find a clue or something. Just inside the steel doors were two cabinets, one containing a house police telephone, the other a fire alarm box and fire axe. Except for a poster advertising the tournament, there was nothing else around, the walls were bare.

I cracked the gate doors and peered outside. The doors

opened onto a subterranean ramp leading up to a black corner of a parking lot. *What had happened?*

I was upset. I even propped the gate door a crack with my copy of the tournament program and climbed the dark outside ramp to look around. Naturally I saw nothing helpful: cars gleaming under sodium vapor lot lights, some screening trees, sporadic traffic on the boulevard beyond the fencing, city lights.

Danisa had not planned a getaway. She would have told me if anything was afoot. She could not have played so flawlessly if she had known anything out of the ordinary was imminent.

Then somebody had nabbed her. And there was no way that could be good.

Deep in worried thought, I descended the concrete ramp and swung the gate door open to reenter the tunnel.

Standing there waiting for me, breathing fire, was Fjbk.

"What have you done to her?" he rasped.

"Oh, swell," I muttered.

"You must know about this! Tell me!"

I thought I had seen him looking crazy before, but at this moment he looked like a total maniac. His eyes were wild, without clear focus. He crossed the small distance between us with a squat, powerful grace that said bad things to me at the instinctive level. I tried to back away from him but the tunnel wall stopped me. Up close he seemed a lot bigger, and he reeked of physical power.

"What have you done with her?"

"Fjbk, I don't know anything about this!"

"She never did such a thing before. You must be responsible. Tell me!"

"Fjbk—!"

He swung at me. I half blocked the blow with my left arm, which went numb under the impact. Even with the major force of the blow deflected, his fist crashed into my throat with a force that knocked me sideways, seeing stars.

I did not go all the way down. The wall propped me up.

He charged right after me. I ducked, but not fast enough. His fist hammered into my midsection, doubling me over, and he simply grabbed me by the shoulders and *threw* me about six feet up the tunnel, where I hit the floor with shocking impact.

Scrambling, I managed to get to my knees when he hit me again. Things broke in my face and red stuff sprayed in all directions. I was half blinded.

He bear-hugged me and, muttering hoarse Serbian obscenities, started hammering my skull against the concrete wall. He was completely out of his head and he was going to destroy me.

Panic gave me added strength. I got a knee into his groin and twisted free. He was terrifyingly quick to react. I got one step away from him when he slammed his right arm down onto my shoulder, buckling me again. As I started to go down he hit me in the face again, and on the side of my skull.

"You will die," he said, panting.

I managed to get in a weak left hand. It surprised him and made him crazier. He knocked me back against the wall and went to my body, hammering me with both hands. Christ, he was *strong*. And for the first time I began to feel primitive fear. There was nobody around. And he meant it when he said I was going to die. He was out of his mind and he was going to beat me to death unless I could get away from him somehow.

"Fjbk," I managed through a mouthful of blood, "I don't know anything about this—"

A paralyzing right hand crashed into my head, knocking me to my knees. I tried to shake the pink confusion out of my brain. I felt him pick me up bodily. He threw me again.

This time I hit the wall near the doorway.

Right beside the security phone and fire emergency station.

And there in my blood-blurred line of sight was the panel with the fire axe behind it.

I jerked it open and broke the axe out of its bracket. Almost dropped it because my hands were slippery from my own blood. Fjbk, in the act of charging me again, saw the axe and skidded to a stop, his eyes going suddenly wide with fear.

That look in his eyes gave me a jolt of strength I didn't know I had in me.

And I went a little crazy myself.

"Son of a bitch!" I said, and swung the axe at him.

I missed by a mile. The axe powdered the concrete wall, sending chunks and dust everywhere. But I was trying. So help me, I would have taken his head off. Everything inside me that hadn't been beaten to a pulp was yelling for revenge. Every once in a while something happens to us to let us know we aren't all that far out of the cave. Part of me was insanely exultant, seeing the damned idiot back off another step.

I went after him. The next swing of the axe turned me completely around and I almost winged him on the second swing. I was yelling something but didn't know what. My next swing took out one of the low tunnel roof lights, and shards of glass bit hotly simultaneous with the loud pop of the exploding bulb.

"Fjbk," I blubbered, "you're a dead man." And swung again.

It was all he could take. He danced back another step, wide-eyed with alarm. Then, as I kept coming, he *turned and ran.*

I couldn't believe it.

I stood there, axe over my shoulder, leaking from my nose and mouth, staring at the suddenly empty tunnel after he had fled around its curve.

What do you know? I thought. Amazing.

Which was when my burst of adrenaline began to run low.

The agony from all the punishment I had absorbed began to break through the body's defenses.

It dropped me to my knees, where I knelt with my head down, bleeding all over everything.

A minute or two passed.

I heard running footsteps approaching.

The maniac was coming back.

Oh shit.

I managed to get to my feet.

seventeen

Elsewhere

Belgrade

In the dark back seat of the dirty Volkswagen sedan, Danisa Lechova tried breathing slowly and deeply, but her heart was crashing about in her chest as it had never done in any match. She wriggled around, trying to get more comfortable in the clutter back here with her, including the leather case containing her rackets and a small blue duffel bag along with suitcases and clothing that didn't belong to her.

This was the moment she had dreamed of and dreaded, and she would leave her country with nothing but her rackets and duffel.

In the front seat, the heads of Henry and Muriel Beamer were palely outlined against the lights of an oncoming car. The other car passed with an instant's brightness that made Danisa flinch involuntarily. Then, under the dimness of the streetlights in this ancient section of the city, the Beamers were indistinct again.

Danisa's shocked feeling of unreadiness had been intensified by the fact that it was these two—the silly little American tourists who had been bothering everybody for autographs for their daughter in America—who were to take her out.

But there wasn't any doubt.

She had thought they wanted another autograph when they met her at the door of the dressing room. Beamer had chattered about that for a minute or two, so that even the bored security guard drifted down the hall and out of hearing.

Then Beamer had said softly and distinctly, in quite a different tone, "Your best effort was a star-spangled success."

For an instant Danisa stared at him in mute surprise.

Muriel Beamer's smile was soft and seemingly brainless, as usual, but her eyes were flint. "We're the ones, Danisa. This is the all-American sweepstakes. Now."

The statements contained both of what the man from the embassy had called . . . what? . . . verbal bona fides. Danisa had thought the term silly and quaint. She didn't see anything silly or quaint about it now. The Beamers had just repeated both of them to perfection.

"I thought—Brad Smith—" Danisa fumbled.

Beamer took her by the arm in what looked like a casual gesture. His fingers bit painfully into her arm. "The folks with the camera are right outside," he said loudly enough for the guard to hear. "We'll just go out there and get the picture took, by golly, and you can get right back inside!"

The guards ignored them. Danisa went down the tunnel and out into the black edge of the parking lot with the American couple. She was still in a daze.

There was no one else there.

"Where is the car?" she asked, confused.

Beamer said briskly, "You're to go back inside, be seen again by the guards, use the back security tunnel, walk two blocks east, to the corner where the lighted statue of the partisan fighter is." He studied her keenly. "You know where that is?"

His voice and demeanor were so different—so chill and efficient. Danisa stared.

"You know where that is?" he repeated sharply.

"Yes. Yes!"

"Get inside. Be seen again. The security tunnel. Walk. We'll be in a dirty yellow Volkswagen."

Danisa started to turn back toward the door.

"Nothing more than you usually take home after a match," Muriel Beamer said.

Danisa stared at her, and saw a personality in her eyes that hadn't been there before.

"Yes," she mumbled, and hurried back into the arena.

It had taken only minutes to leave the complex as they had instructed. First she walked to Gate 64, as if leaving routinely. Then, after the guard had gone back, leaving her inside the door, she had doubled back in the direction she really wanted to go.

The security tunnel was for use by militia in case of demonstrations or other trouble, and was not guarded during times like this, when it was presumably sealed off and not in use. But somebody had neatly broken the lockbars at both ends of the tunnel; Danisa went through without trouble.

Once on the street she had hurried, and the Beamers, as in a dream, had been there.

Now they had been driving a while—she was too wrought up to know how long, and she had forgotten her watch in the locker room—and they were out beyond the ancient renovation area, the Skadarlija, on a bumpy side street, passing by a warehouse and a small factory of some kind, with the yellowish lights of the airport highway, the road to Surčin, just ahead.

Henry Beamer pulled the Volkswagen onto the highway, falling in behind a Mercedes truck heavy with cargo, and headed south. He shifted neatly and well, and Danisa sensed an enormous competence in him.

Muriel Beamer looked over the seatback at her. "Are you all right?"

"Yes. I'm just so confused. I didn't expect it so soon."

The older woman nodded. "If you need something for your nerves, I have something."

"No!" The idea scared Danisa. *They might give me anything.* "I'm fine."

They drove past a large electric substation, its security lights making the squat transformers and spiderwebs of wiring look unearthly behind high safety fencing. Henry Beamer told her, "We've got a long drive tonight. I hope there's enough room back there with all our luggage and everything."

"It's—fine."

"If you're hungry, there are sandwiches and some pastries in a plastic bag on the floor behind my seat. There's a thermos with water."

"No. Nothing." Danisa was still struggling to get oriented. "I thought Brad Smith was here to contact me—make the arrangements—"

"That's what you were supposed to think," Beamer said cheerfully.

"He deceived me? It was all a trick?"

"Don't worry about him."

Danisa reeled inwardly. Brad had lied to her from the beginning, she thought. She had trusted him. She had thought he was so honest. So wonderful. But now everything had changed. She was shocked and disillusioned. *It was just a trick to him—a job, deluding the stupid little peasant girl. And I thought he really, really liked me.*

She asked, "Are we going to try to get onto an airplane? My clothes will—"

"We'll be turning straight west in a few more miles," Beamer told her. He was driving at a steady, sedate speed, meeting few cars and trucks coming from the opposite direction. "We cross the border at Trieste."

"They'll have missed me long before we can reach Trieste," Danisa said, worried. "You're Americans, and maybe the UDBA will have missed you, too."

Beamer chuckled. "We entered at Trieste, and managed a flat tire right at the border station. We established ourselves in every guard's memory as inept nerds."

"But if they search this car—"

"Jane and I cross in the car. You don't."

"I don't understand."

"There's a farmer near the border who has a dairy. He sells his milk in the city, across the border. Every morning he takes his cartload of big milk cans through the checkpoint on the way to sale. *Big* cans. It will be a tight squeeze, but you'll fit inside one of them very nicely."

Danisa felt her panic try to rise. "How will I breathe?"

Muriel Beamer—or Jane—said, "There are air holes. You won't be in the can very long. We'll give you a pill to make you drowsy and help you relax."

"And we'll be raising all kinds of hell with the guards at the same time," Beamer added cheerfully. "They don't let you take dinars back out and we've got a pile of them." He changed magically to his nasal, whining voice: " 'How is that *fair*? How was we supposed to know about not taking this funny money back out? Are you guys trying to cheat us, or what? I demand to see your boss!' "

Muriel Beamer studied Danisa's expression in the lights of an oncoming truck. "Not very elegant, dear. But it will work."

"And then?" Danisa asked, dismayed.

"No problem, dear. We'll be met and you'll be on your way."

They had neared the outskirts of the city. Up ahead were flashing yellow lights. Beamer slowed abruptly, peering through the windshield. "Shit," he muttered, braking.

"What is it?" the woman asked tautly.

"Some kind of roadblock, I don't know."

"They must be checking licenses, permits," Danisa said. "They do that a lot around the city. There have been many fatal accidents, and trucks are running overloaded—"

Beamer got the VW onto the shoulder and cranked the wheel sharply, making a U-turn and heading back the way they had come.

"Might be routine," Muriel Beamer said.

"Can't risk it."

"What now, then?"

"I'm thinking."

"We could go north, into Zagreb."

"It's longer that way. Let me think."

They drove a mile or two in silence. Headlights of a car behind them shone faintly into the passenger compartment. They passed the electric substation again.

"We'll try the other highway," Beamer said. He sounded grim. "Once in the country we'll just have to risk driving faster." He glanced back at Danisa. "No sweat. It's just an added irritation."

"Have you done this often?" Danisa demanded. "Are you vastly experienced?"

Both the Beamers chuckled at that. Muriel said, "Bless your heart, honey, we've done something like, yes. Look at us. We're old folks. You don't get these wrinkles and bags without a few memories."

"That's what we call it," Beamer added. "Building memories. Lots of fun."

Then, before Danisa could react, he added: "We're being followed."

Muriel twisted in the seat to look back. "Damn! That light truck back there?"

"He isn't gaining and he isn't falling back." Beamer's voice had a cutting edge now. "Let's just see." He removed his foot from the accelerator and the VW slowed by what felt like fifteen kilometers per hour. Danisa, peering through the back window, saw the following headlights get a little nearer for a moment, then fall back again.

Beamer increased speed steadily until the engine began to whine and a slightly out-of-round rear wheel started thumping. The lights behind them remained at the same distance.

"That tears it," Beamer said. His face in the rearview mirror was heavily lined by disgust and worry. "Danisa. Listen. I'm taking the highway straight back into the city. Once we get there, I'll drive around some city streets. I'll take a couple of corners, and when I stop, you have to hop out, fast. You understand?"

"What do I do?" Danisa demanded. "Do you pick me up later?"

"Not tonight. This thing is rapidly turning to shit. I take a couple of corners, I stop abruptly, you jump out, and take your stuff. That other car will be pretty close behind, so I'll try to pick a spot where you can duck into a doorway or something. Which you do the *instant* you're out of this car. Got it?"

"Yes—I think so—"

"You'll be contacted. We've got to go again. Once you're clear of this Jug on our tail, you get yourself home, say you were strung out and wanted a nice long walk to relax. Okay?"

"Okay," Danisa echoed. She felt dazed.

"You got money for a cab or bus most of the way home?"

"No. Hardly any—"

Muriel dug a wad of dinars out of her purse and handed them back. Danisa clutched them.

"Honey," the woman said softly, "I'm sure sorry we didn't get this dance after all. But you be ready. We'll get reorganized and be back in touch." She smiled brightly. "Right?"

"Yes," Danisa managed. Her mouth was desert-dry. Brad Smith would not have let things get mixed up, she thought. But she remembered that he had known some of this all along. He had lied all the time. And to set up this flimsy plan, so easily thwarted.

She was pitched forward suddenly as Beamer braked sharply.

"What?" Muriel demanded.

"Look."

Danisa looked forward between them. Up ahead on the highway were flashing red lights.

"God! Another checkpoint?"

"Might be. Might be a wreck."

"Either way—"

"We can't risk it." Beamer peered around through the side windows. "Hang on, guys." He spun the wheel.

The Volkswagen left the highway and hit the grass on the side. The road was elevated here, limited access, and off to the side, well below, was a parallel roadway running along past warehouses and small factory buildings. Beamer guided the Volkswagen down the embankment at a terrifying angle, knocking Danisa against the side of the back seat.

They bounded over a curve, losing a hubcap that clattered and careened away at an angle, and Beamer got things righted again on the parallel street. An approaching car bleated its horn, the driver scolding them for their tactic. Beamer spun the wheel again and sent the VW down a black side alley.

Nothing had gone right, Danisa thought with despair. None of this had been adequately planned. Her chance for freedom was gone.

At the next corner, Beamer turned left again. It was a major street, some other traffic on it, and he pressed the accelerator, driving as fast as he dared. Ahead was the Sava, with city sprawl growing brighter around them.

"Don't see any sign of pursuit now."

Danisa was watching out the back. As they passed under intersection lights, she saw something that made her stomach twist. "There!"

Beamer turned. "Where?" He spied the panel truck in the intersection behind them. "Shit!"

They sped across the bridge and into the old city. A light was changing as they approached an intersection, and people moved out into the pedestrian crossing as cross-traffic began to flow. Beamer didn't hesitate. He slapped the horn, downshifted, and scooted through a right turn. People scattered, yelling angrily, and horns blared. They made it.

"Okay, now we get serious," he muttered.

At the next corner they turned left, and at the next right again. Danisa was getting dizzy. She saw they had moved into a decrepit neighborhood, old thrift stores and deserted office buildings and several taverns, with shadowy figures on the dark sidewalks.

"Get ready, Danisa," Beamer said tightly.

He turned again. There were warehouses, an old church, a vacant lot, what looked like stores converted to living quarters. At the next corner he turned left, flashing past lighted storefronts, a cafe, a movie theater, a drugstore, a bistro, a pastry shop. At the corner was a tiny old hotel, next door to it another cafe.

Beamer glanced in the rearview mirror and sawed the Volkswagen around another corner. He pulled up sharply at the curb in front of a small rooming house of some kind, with a drinking club next door.

"Out," he clipped.

Danisa grabbed her rackets and duffel and climbed past the seatback to get out the front door. She stepped out onto gritty sidewalk. Muriel Beamer hauled the door shut behind her and the VW leaped from the curb. Danisa scurried for the doorway of the club. As she reached it, the VW went around a corner a half block distant, turning right, and a gray panel truck bounced around the corner to Danisa's left, the way she and the Beamers had just come.

The panel shot past, and she got a glimpse of blue uniforms inside.

She leaned back against the rough stone wall of the building, hearing her heartbeat in her ears. The sidewalk here was virtually deserted, and she didn't think anyone had even seen her exit. A young couple walked by hand in hand, love conspirators, and the boy said something and the girl's laugh trailed behind her. For an instant, Danisa hated and envied them.

But she didn't have time for that. Everything had failed. There might not even be another chance. She was shaken, scared, and filled with rage at Brad Smith. He had tricked her. Then he had abandoned her. How he must have laughed at her! She hated him.

She didn't want to walk far, lugging her tennis gear. She would be recognized, and then there would be a lot more hard questions to answer. But, looking across the street, she saw she wouldn't have to walk far, risking recognition. There was a cab stand, and a cab parked at it.

She crossed the street briskly. If the cab driver recognized her, he gave no evidence of it. She told him an address three blocks from her parents' apartment, and sank back into the dark rear seat as he started off. Then, with the letdown and aftermath of her scare, the silent tears came.

Browning, Montana

In the motel room, the telephone rang for the first time in days.

"Yes?"

"*Sylvester?*"

"Yes."

"*Instructions.*"

"Yes."

"*Missoula. Call on arrival.*"

"Yes," the man called Sylvester said, and hung up.

Twenty minutes later, he had checked out of the motel and was on the road, driving fast.

So, my poor old friend, he thought dispassionately, *it was a good trick, turning back west. But we have you.*

Missoula, Montana

Dominic Partek had made a mistake. It was a very slight mistake, one involving his truck. But bad luck magnified the error.

He knew there was every chance that his pursuers had had time to observe his lifestyle in Browning, including the description and license of his pickup truck. He had replaced the plates with an extra set prepared earlier for such an emergency. But he did not know whether they would get out a general description of the truck so law enforcement officers could watch for it, and he did not want to take any more chances than he had to. That was why he had rented a garage in Missoula to help keep the truck out of sight.

Unfortunately for Partek, the divorcée who rented the garage to him was dating a Missoula policeman.

"Yeah, I rented it, finally," she told her boyfriend the same night. "I didn't really have any hope of renting it again before winter. But this weird guy wanted it, paid a month in advance in cash, and then all he had to put in it was this beat-up Chevy pickup."

"Why do you say he's weird?" the police officer asked casually.

"His accent. It's just the slightest shade *off,* somehow. Of course that's not much. But he told me he's a visiting professor at the university, and I *know* that's a lie."

Boyfriend sat up a little straighter, interested. "How do you know, babe?"

"His fingernails."

"His fingernails?"

"Yeah! You could tell he'd been scrubbing at them like mad, but they were black. All around the cuticle, too: black. Grease. Like you get when you're a car mechanic or something like that, and you just can't get it all scrubbed out

189

no matter what you do. I mean, if that guy is a professor, I'm a credenza."

"That is kind of interesting, Meg. You still got an extra key to the garage?"

"Sure. Why?"

"Oh, I just thought I'd go have a look at that truck."

"You don't think it's stolen, do you?"

Boyfriend shrugged and yawned. "Probably not. But it never hurts to check."

"Damn! Just when I get a renter! I should keep my big mouth shut!"

The garage was later opened, and the license plate number of the truck, along with serial number and description, was run through the computer. The truck did not check stolen, but the computer cross-checked against other information and gave the duty captain a number to call.

When Washington responded, it was noted with great interest by a close department observer who reported regularly to a friend who in turn reported to a telephone number in Detroit. This was how the man called Sylvester was notified within twelve hours of the original police computer check.

The lady who rented the garage, however, was a great talker. When Partek visited the garage later to check the water in his battery and add a quart of oil in case of a need for quick use, she sailed out of the house and chatted with him all the while he worked.

"Pretty nice truck," she told him, rubbing a finger through the grime on the rear quarterpanel. "Dirty, though. My boyfriend said you ought to run it through the car wash. You could still have salt up under there from last winter, as dirty as it is, he said. And that salt can rust right through a fender faster than you can say Jack Robinson."

"When did your boyfriend see the truck?" Partek asked casually.

The lady looked blank, but tried to cover up. "Gosh! I

don't know! I guess I just *mentioned* to him that it was real dirty."

Good try, but no cigar. Partek knew better. She had already boasted about her boyfriend being a cop. So one bit of luck was counterbalanced by another. Partek felt a chill on his spine, and heeded it.

Several hours before the Continental flight with Kinkaid on board landed at Missoula's airport, Partek got on a bus and left town.

Belgrade

In the room at the Metropol adjacent to the one occupied by Brad Smith, Major Ladislav Maleeva chain-smoked cigarettes and awaited reports. The two technicians manning the eavesdropping equipment sat silent, bored, nothing to do. The tape machines, receivers, and vibration-modulation detector units were idle, their panel lights amber for standby. In the room next door it was silent, nobody home.

Except for the heavy smoking, Maleeva showed no sign of his inner turmoil.

He had no idea what had happened. Danisa Lechova was missing. Did this mean her defection scheme was in motion? If it was, then Maleeva's career was finished because he had guessed wrong on everything, and his lavish attention to the American, Brad Smith, had been a costly— disastrous—waste of time.

Maleeva could not believe he had been so wrong, even if all the evidence at this moment pointed toward that conclusion. Feverishly he reviewed in his mind the things he knew: authorities were certain the Lechova girl would defect at once if given a chance. Brad Smith had been contacted— clumsily—on arrival by not one but two agents of the CIA. Michael Nariv had confirmed that he was one such contact. Altunyan, using information probably from the highest echelons of the KGB, felt certain Smith constituted the major threat of Danisa Lechova's escape.

So it had to be Smith. Maleeva could not be wrong.

But Danisa Lechova was missing, and Smith had been seen since her disappearance.

It made no sense. Maleeva's stomach sent out stabbing pains, reminding him that he had not eaten since breakfast, despite the doctors' statements that many small meals a day should help calm the ulcer, and prevent a surgery that might make him unfit for duty. He needed to eat.

And this hotel-room waiting was intolerable anyway.

Maleeva called a number and told the duty officer of his intentions. Then, after a few words with the stolid electronics technicians, he left the hotel and proceeded directly to his home.

Home for Maleeva was atop a luxury apartment building across the river from the Kalemegdan. But it was no penthouse. A metal structure with two wooden windows added as an afterthought, it had once been a guardhouse. Maleeva had been assigned it as a dwelling place after his divorce. He knew he should be grateful.

Riding the building elevator to the top, or seventh, floor, he walked down the tiled hallway, heels clicking softly, to the fire escape door at the south end. The steel staircase beyond the fire door went both up and down. Maleeva climbed up one floor and used his key to open that door, which took him out onto the flat gravel roof under a panoply of stars. Walking around a cylindrical ventilation stack, he came to his house. He unlocked the windowless metal door and stepped inside, breathing the hot, trapped air redolent of stale cigarette smoke and mildew.

He turned on a light. The overhead fixture—three bulbs at the end of what looked like a three-headed snake—cast a gloomy amber light over his living room: thin yellowish-green rug, faded and nearly colorless floral couch with overstuffed cushions that sagged against one another in exhaustion, a brown cloth chair with ragged holes worn through to the grayish stuffing on both arms, an end table bearing his twelve-inch television set, a bookcase made of cinderblocks and planks holding magazines and his books about his craft and a biography of Tito.

The window on the far wall looked out onto the ventilation stack.

Maleeva sighed.

Going into the efficiency kitchen, he turned on another light. Roaches scampered for hiding in the dirty dishes and food packages piled on the sinkboard. Maleeva opened the refrigerator and got out a beer and opened it. The room was too stuffy. He was sweating. His professional predicament gnawed at his gut. He got back into the refrigerator and removed a chunk of stale black bread and the last of a small wheel of pale white cheese. Using his penknife, he peeled some mold off one end of the cheese and then carried the bread and cheese and beer outside onto the roof.

The lights of other buildings stared at him from all sides—pale windows without features, vacant roofs with odd protuberances like his ventilation stack. From his roof he could look past one adjacent, and see through a little chasm to the river, with its glints of reflected light and sometimes a boat on some mysterious mission, and, beyond, the dark sprawl of the Kalemegdan, with the scattered little lights of the old city beyond that on all sides, stretching out to the horizon.

Maleeva bit off some cheese and managed to rip a chunk off the stale bread. The crust was so hard and dry that he slightly cut his lip on it. The blood tasted bright with the bread and cheese.

Maleeva was very tired.

He knew this case was immensely important although he had no idea why. He hated working with Chekists, but felt driven to prove to Altunyan how efficient he and the UDBA really were. So he had been working night and day, and now perhaps he had been entirely wrong and proven a fool.

He still felt a little depressed about Michael Nariv. He wished the pressure had not forced him to conduct the interrogations in such a crude and violent manner. His country was making such strides. Shouldn't they be beyond such barbarisms? And how dismaying it was to learn this way that Yugoslavia was not entirely free of pressure from Moscow.

The thought recurred: *Where is she?*

She had to be found. This had to be a mistake—a romantic tryst, perhaps, or the temperamental erraticism of a high-strung and gifted athlete. Danisa Lechova had never been known for such flights—her files made no mention of same, and they were very complete—but the Belgrade tournament and the adulation of the Yugoslav people had put more pressure on both Lechova women than they had ever known.

So there was still hope.

There had to be hope. Maleeva could not have failed. He had nothing except his career. Blazena (the slut, the whore, the pig!) had taken their daughter away. Blazena (the bitch, the castrating piece of shit!) had taken their furniture, their car, even some of his clothes and books. She had said he was cold. Stupid. Inept. Dull. Doomed to mediocrity or failure. She was wrong. He had often proved her wrong. The girls he saw sometimes told him he was wonderful as a lover, and they didn't have to say such things just because he paid them to be with him. His record in his work was perfect: no mistakes, no failures of loyalty or devotion. And this case, given the importance obviously assigned to it by the highest authority, was to climax his career and mark him as a man ready for even greater responsibility, perhaps work as a supervisor in headquarters.

Assuming he succeeded . . .

The telephone rang in his house. Stuffing the last of the cheese in his mouth, he hurried to answer it.

It was Lieutenant Rodor, in charge of the detail which

had arrived to watch the Lechova apartment. What were his orders?

Maleeva issued instructions. Then he hung up the telephone, tossed the last of the abominable bread at the wastebasket, missing, and locked up his house again before hurrying below.

eighteen

Luckily for me, the person I heard pounding down the corridor of Gate 64 was not Fjbk coming back for round 2.

Instead it was Ted Treacher, who had heard what was going on and guessed that I might have headed for the gate where Danisa had last been seen. Partway down he had encountered Fjbk, boiling up the tunnel in the opposite direction with blood on his shirt and hands. From that point Ted had come running.

When I recognized him, I dropped the axe and let nature take its course. Which in this case meant sinking back to my knees.

"Holy shit!" he said, squatting beside me. "What the hell happened to you?"

"A truck?" I muttered through my handkerchief as I tried to slow down some of the bleeding.

He didn't get the joke. "I'm getting help!"

I grabbed him. "No!"

"No? *No?* You look like you need a doctor, man!"

"Help me to the nearest men's room."

"I'll call the security people—"

"Ted, just give me a hand, okay? Do what I ask!"

Thoroughly confused and upset, he obeyed. I collected my briefcase where it had fallen earlier. Then, leaning on him, I limped into the major tunnel and spotted a restroom. This was under the far end of the stadium, the least desirable seats, and except for two teenagers who watched wide-eyed, no one saw Ted help me into the can.

He stood by in mute concern while I did what fixing-up I could do at a basin in front of the mirrors.

Once I got the bleeding stopped from my nose and mouth, and some mopping done, the evidence was not as bad as it should have been. I was missing one tooth on the left side and some others felt loose. My tongue had been bitten almost through. My nose made an unhappy crunching sound when I moved it side to side with my fingers. I was going to have a black eye, and a lot of swelling around my mouth was already getting started. But I was reasonably intact.

Fjbk had done a nice and brutal job on the body. A rib or two gave me stabbing pains whenever I breathed deeply. Judging by the feel around my kidneys, I would have some technicolor urine. But overall, by the time I got done washing and checking systems out, I knew I had been very lucky. My bloody clothes looked worse than I did.

"Do you want me to call the security guards now?" Ted demanded as I turned from the basin.

"No, thanks. What I want is a ride back to the hotel in your courtesy car, if you have time."

"Have time! You dumb shit, you've been beaten up! Why not call the cops? At least let me take you to a hospital!"

"Ted, if you want to help me, just get me back to the hotel."

"Did Fjbk do this?"

"I fell down."

"You're a lying bastard."

His concern was touching, but I just didn't have time. "Ted, will you help me in the way I want, or not?"

"Fuckhead," he growled. But he capitulated.

Some people saw us on the way out and gave me curious stares, but we didn't get stopped. Ted drove efficiently back into the downtown area toward the Metropol. He still wanted to notify the militia or get a doctor.

"Fjbk did this to you, and I don't know why the hell you want to protect him," he argued.

"I'll handle it in my own way, Ted. Right now the Lechovas don't need their coach arrested, and a big brouhaha."

"You're being awfully civilized for a man that just got the hell beaten out of him."

I didn't answer that.

He persisted. "Do you want to tell me what it's all about?"

"No."

"Dammit, Brad, I don't like this!"

"Ted, if you want to help me right now, just cool it. One of these days—maybe pretty quick—I'll explain. But if you want to help me right now, just drop me at the hotel's back door and forget this happened."

He gave me a hard sideways look, almost protested again, and then thought better of it. We drove on to the hotel in silence.

"Anything else?" he asked with a trace of sarcasm as I got out of the car at the rear entrance.

"We'll talk later, Ted. Thanks."

I left him looking deeply puzzled and frustrated.

Inside the hotel I did some further patch work on my face, washed down, and changed into fresh clothes. Some aftershave talcum masked the darkening facial bruises. Nothing short of a false face would hide the swelling. I hid my briefcase inside the Lark and locked it.

Feeling like something that had been shot out of a cannon, I found a taxi and rode to the Lechova family's New Belgrade address.

There were two UDBA operatives—one man and one woman—stationed at the doorway to the Lechova apartment building when I arrived. The UDBA looked as worried as I was.

If the UDBA had been responsible for Danisa's disappearing act, they would have been conspicuous now by their absence. They were not subtle, and the fact that they were here, looking nervous, was good indication to me that they really had no more idea of Danisa's whereabouts than the rest of us.

Which, I thought, probably meant that the most likely explanation for Danisa's disappearance was *us*.

Right now, I thought, she was almost certainly on her way out of the country.

The boys had swung into action without bothering to tell me about it.

Which shouldn't have surprised me, really. I had already begun to suspect that I had been set up to act as an attention-getter, a diversion. The stupid telephone call and Michael Nariv's clumsiness had not been accidental at all. They had *wanted* the UDBA to notice and suspect me. While the real work was done by someone else.

If that was true, why should I have imagined that they would do me the courtesy of warning me when Danisa was going out?

At least she was getting out, I lectured myself. And I had done my part, even if it was to act stupid and get myself watched. Nobody had ever promised me I would be let in on everything. Hadn't I been downright fluent in explaining such stuff to June only a few weeks ago?

Anyway, the UDBA folk let me go up to the apartment. Leon Lechova responded to my knock. His wife and Hannah were in the small living room, along with Fjbk. The tension was thick enough to slice, and the Lechovas didn't even seem to notice my face. Fjbk stiffened visibly but kept under control as I joined them in the living room.

"What happened to you?" Lechova demanded.

"I fell," I said. "What of Danisa?"

Lechova shook his head and resumed pacing in front of

the window looking onto the street. "Geneta came home and there was no sign Danisa had been here. The authorities have been notified. We know nothing."

I glanced at Fjbk. "I wish I knew something."

"You don't?" he rumbled.

"No more than you," I told him.

His sullen eyes showed his disbelief. But there were both uncertainty and worry there, too. He was smart enough to see that I probably wouldn't have been here if I knew anything about Danisa's disappearance. He also had to be wondering why I hadn't turned him in to the militia for assault.

Fine, I thought. Let the bastard stew.

No one spoke for a while. Outside traffic sounds and voices from an adjacent apartment came in. My ears began to ring. My body hurt all over. I figured my only remaining job on the mission was to stay with the family and act dumb—make no waves—until Danisa was out safe. After the way I had been tricked into being a decoy, I felt well qualified to act dumb. As to making waves, I would have dearly loved to file a complaint against Fjbk, and might still do so tomorrow or the next day. But doing that right now would only create more of a sensation, and possibly jeopardize Danisa in ways I had no method of predicting. So I sat there.

Hannah left the room and came back with a cup of tea. The depth of her worry was proved by the fact that she forgot to ask if anyone else wanted anything. She sat down and stared and put the teacup on the end table with a small clatter.

"Where *is* she?" she cried. "What has happened to her?"

Geneta Lechova patted her daughter's arm. "We must try to stay calm, Hannah."

"Calm! How can we stay calm when—"

"They said Danisa left the stadium alone, of her own free will. There may be some explanation for all of this."

"But she never—"

"I know. But we must not start thinking the worst. We have to be calm. It may be well."

It was a nice speech, and a brave one. But the haunted look in Geneta Lechova's eyes said it was a lie.

Conversation lapsed again. The situation seemed unreal. Part of that came from my ear-ringing headache, all the other discomforts, and my proximity to Fjbk. I picked up an English-language magazine and tried to read it, and time ticked away.

God, I hope I'm right that she's on the way out, I thought. It didn't feel good to think I had been had by my superiors, but any other explanation meant Danisa was not missing of her own free will.

I fretted about *that* possibility for a while.

An hour passed.

Then there was a commotion downstairs. We heard voices. Lechova leaned far out the living room window and turned back to us with fierce elation. "It is Danisa!"

Fjbk sprang to his feet. Hannah whooped and clapped her hands. Geneta Lechova hugged herself, wet-eyed. Lechova rushed out of the apartment and in a moment was back.

Danisa behind him.

She had her racket bag and duffel as if nothing had happened and she had just strolled out of the locker room. But her shocking pallor told a different story.

Whatever had happened, she was trying to hide it.

My relief was so intense my knees got weak. Whatever had happened, she was *safe*.

"*Danisa!*" Hannah screeched the moment she saw her sister, and then did her hysterical number, swooping across the small living room like a gymnast, grabbing Danisa in her arms, twirling her around and making her drop her duffel and racket bag, eyes spurting dramatic tears. "Where have you been? We have all been insane with our worry! Oh, Danisa! If something had happened to you, I would have killed myself! I would have thrown myself in the Sava and sunk to the bottom and never drawn another breath!"

Danisa gave her father and mother a half-frightened, contrite look, and me a glance I couldn't read. "I'm sorry. I was so upset with my play tonight, I decided to take a little walk to calm my nerves. And then I walked much too far. I had no money for a cab and had to walk all the way home. I'm fine. There is no problem."

"But why didn't you tell someone?" Hannah demanded, flipping her hand through her long, loose-flowing hair. "My God! I thought *everything!* I thought, 'Some terrible mugger, with yellow teeth and bad breath and a knife, has taken her into a park and slashed her body!' I thought, 'She has fallen and hurt herself, and now she does not know who she is, and she will become a street girl in the Skadarlija, and we will never see her again because she will be stolen by gypsies.' I thought, 'A car, driven by a crazy man, has run over her in the street and crushed her body and he has taken her to the river and he will throw her in and she will float down the Sava and fishes will eat her, and—' "

"You just . . . walked?" Danisa's mother cut in, staring at her with teary eyes in a face that was still the color of flour. "But you never do things like this to us, Danisa."

"I was—overwrought," Danisa said. She seemed deeply contrite. "If I had just thought. But the pressure just made me . . . break."

"You're all right?" her father demanded. His face was a cold mask but his eyes burned with bleak, bewildered anger. "There is nothing more that happened?"

Danisa dropped into a rocker near the kitchen entry. She stretched out her legs, long and shapely even in her trademark blue sweatpants. "What can I say but how sorry I am?"

All of this had been in English—quick, fluent, virtually unaccented except for the words spoken by the parents. They were all proud of their bilingualism and had made it a

202

stern point of etiquette never to speak Yugoslavian when I was in the room. Now, however, Leon Lechova said something long, strained, and angry in his native tongue. His wife and the two sisters listened, and Danisa reacted by flushing with mortification.

"I know," she said, and then said something in her own language which I couldn't begin to follow.

He snapped back, bitter. An artery pulsed in his neck.

They stared at each other. It was thickly silent in the room.

Fjbk, who had been standing by like a hairy statue, rumbled a few words that sounded like an attempt to calm things. Lechova turned fiery eyes on him and let loose a string of language that could only be an angry order to mind his own blankety business. Fjbk flinched as if he had been slapped, replied in monosyllables, and headed for the front door.

"Milo!" Danisa called huskily. Then she asked him a question.

Already in the doorway, Fjbk glowered back at her, obviously fighting to get a hold of himself. Then he said something with numbers in it.

"Yes," Danisa said breathlessly, solemn. "Ten. I understand.—I am sorry, Milo, to have worried you, too."

Fjbk locked glances with Lechova for an instant, then was gone. The door closed firmly behind him.

Danisa said, "I wish you had not attacked him, Poppa. He was afraid for me."

"We were all afraid for you!"

"I know . . ."

"You must *never* do anything like this to us again!"

Her words were almost inaudible. "I won't."

She had given me only the briefest glance.

Her mother hugged her, and so did Hannah. There were some tears.

Lechova sighed. "It is very late. Both of you will play two matches tomorrow. We will leave for the arena at nine hundred hours, and loosen up on an outdoor court for forty-five minutes, as planned. First matches are about eleven hundred."

Danisa lowered her head. "Yes, Poppa."

Her mother asked quietly, "Do you want food? Milk?"

"No, Momma. Nothing. Thank you."

"You have worried us almost beyond endurance," Lechova said.

"I'm sorry. It was silly and thoughtless and it will never happen again."

He got to his feet, still glaring daggers at her. Her stricken expression got to him. With a little groan he crossed the room and took her in his arms, hugging her convulsively. "You girls!" he groaned. "You two girls!"

Hannah started crying with relief. Danisa, her face wet, disengaged from her father and put an arm around Hannah. The two of them trooped out of the room and through the doorway I had come to think of as their shared bedroom. The door closed behind them.

Mrs. Lechova looked at me. "You have been kind to stay with us through our worry."

"I thank you for letting me be with the family at a time like this," I told her.

"Will this . . . be in your story?"

"This is private. I wasn't here for any story."

She studied me, and I had the uncomfortable feeling that, motherlike, she had read every emotion I had been through in the past three hours.

She said quietly, "I did not think you were here as a journalist tonight, Mr. Smith." She got up and went into the kitchen.

I hesitated. Surely Danisa was going to come back out and say something to me?

Lechova walked to the door and stood by it, obviously waiting for my departure.

At that moment, the bedroom door opened and Danisa came out again. Without looking at either of us, she snatched up her gear where she had dropped it and started back toward the bedroom.

"Danisa—?" I said.

She turned on me with eyes that brimmed with rage. "I have no quotations for you!" she snapped, and went out of sight.

I went down alone in the elevator. I still had no idea what the hell had happened. I had to contact my pals at the embassy as soon as possible without arousing undue attention in the wrong quarters.

Was it possible that I had been wrong in guessing that there had been an attempt to get Danisa out? Obviously, if a try had been made, it had failed. What did that mean?

And why was Danisa blaming me?

In the lobby downstairs I met the UDBA man, Maleeva, coming the other direction. He spoke stiffly and went into the elevator I had just vacated. I stayed long enough to see the indicator show that he had gotten off on the Lechovas' floor. So now his interest was active and overt. And everything was getting harder and harder . . . unless tonight's unknown events had already moved things into the realm of the manifestly impossible.

I caught a taxi and headed back to the Metropol. I hurt all over, and nothing was going according to Hoyle. I wondered what else could go wrong.

We never guess bad enough.

nineteen

Elsewhere

The Soviet Embassy, Belgrade

The man who flew into Belgrade from Moscow early Tuesday morning was named Sislinsky. He was tall and gaunt, with a perpetual shadow of stubble on his cheeks and chin, and eyes like a corpse. He was, M. Y. Altunyan knew, thoroughly reliable as a courier. The two men had done business before.

They conferred in the quiet room on the second floor, the one with lead screening in the walls and windows, white-noise generator, and other devices to thwart electronic eavesdropping.

"Your request for authorization to take extreme measures in the matter of Mr. Brad Smith is denied," Sislinsky said immediately, with absolutely no emotion.

Altunyan was disappointed but not surprised. "You will please note that I understand my request for authorization is denied, but I respectfully dissent from the decision."

Sislinsky's dead eyes showed nothing. "Noted."

"I have every reason to believe that a defection attempt was aborted for unknown reasons last night," Altunyan went on. He was aware that his face was hot and his voice sounded tight with suppressed anger. "The subject vanished for more than three hours. I believe Smith arranged a rendezvous for departure with other case officers presently unknown to us, but bad luck or timing intervened. I believe he will make another and more direct attempt within the next twenty-four hours."

"I note your concerns. However, as I was about to say, I have brought additional case information in the form of an oral report which is nowhere committed to paper or computer memory. This information may alter your perceptions in this case."

"What is your new information?" Altunyan demanded.

Sislinsky told him.

"If this is true, it changes everything," Altunyan said.

"The turning-back of the couple being identified as Beamer is additional proof," Sislinsky told him.

Altunyan leaned back in his chair, taken aback by the new data. It was simple, elegant, and wholly logical. He was struck by grudging admiration for his American counterparts.

"I withdraw my exception to denial of my request concerning Smith," he said.

"Noted."

"And my instructions?"

"The subject must remain in Belgrade, pending satisfactory conclusion of business elsewhere. Your orders are to assure that she does not—cannot—elude the UDBA and make good on her defection schemes."

Altunyan thought about it. "By whatever means I find appropriate?"

"She is to remain alive."

"Of course. But beyond that proviso, my instructions are . . . ?"

"To use your best judgment. And do whatever is necessary."

Altunyan nodded understanding. The men talked another few minutes, but of nothing consequential, merely details. Then they shook hands and Sislinsky left the room, and the KGB Resident was left to ponder how best he could make sure that Danisa Lechova was kept under absolute control and in no danger of going anywhere.

A decision was not long in coming. If Altunyan had learned one thing in his years of espionage and countermeasures, it was that the simplest, most direct approach often yielded the most satisfactory results.

Langley, Virginia

It was before 6 A.M. when Dwight and Exerblein reported to Simon Bixby's office, and found they had walked into a buzz saw.

Bixby was a fleshy man of fifty whose car had been blown up by a terrorist in Beirut a few years earlier. The attack was not a random one, and proved that Bixby's cover had been blown before his car was. He had almost lost his life in the explosion, and did lose his left hand. As a result, after lengthy hospitalization, he had been returned to administration at Langley, and was now a close adviser and aide to Director Jeremy Malcomber.

Bixby was known as a quiet, controlled man who worked behind the scenes. But when Dwight and Exerblein walked into his office in response to his emergency telephone summonses, Bixby was clearly in a towering rage. His eyes were bloodshot. Sitting behind his desk in rumpled shirtsleeves, unshaven, his collar open, stump of his left arm resting on a thin stack of classified messages, he didn't smile and he didn't bother with preambles.

"What the *fuck* is going on?" he rasped.

"About what?" Dwight asked. He figured he knew, but it never hurt to ask.

"In Belgrade! In Montana! Jesus Christ! Last night I get a call: Partek has vanished again; this time in Missoula. So I come into the office to try to assess the damage. In the Partek file I notice a cross-reference number. I dig it out. I find it's a Belgrade embassy file. I see a message in it saying one of our agents there"—fuming, Bixby stirred his TWXs with his stump—"Nariv . . . Michael Nariv—young guy, perfect health—got picked up by the UDBA and then showed up cold at the state morgue with a rigged-up official death certificate that says he died of a heart attack. *Then* comes in another message from over there, saying Speer and Beckman had to abort their operation last night, and are there any further instructions or do they press on as before."

Bixby paused, an angry facial tic leaping under his eye. He seemed to be waiting for Dwight to say something. Dwight stood still, expressionless, and said nothing. This was bad enough already.

Bixby resumed. "And *I* don't know what's been coming down. *I* haven't been informed. We've got a most serious operation in motion over there against an ostensibly friendly government, the Russians are messed up in it, and a couple of trusted supervisors here are playing Cowboys and Indians and not bothering to tell me or anybody else what's going on."

"Every decision and action has been memoed," Dwight said.

"Yes," Bixby exploded, "and buried in a goddamn file and put into this fucking ocean of paperwork that goes through here every day, and you could report the second coming on a routine Top Secret and nobody would probably pick up on it for six weeks!"

Dwight kept quiet. Beside him, Exerblein was like a statue. *There goes your perfect record, asshole,* Dwight thought.

"Jesus *Christ!*" Bixby went on. "What were you guys thinking of? You can't just mount an operation like this practically in a closet! You should have kept all of us informed! You should have asked for staff consultation! The days of this kind of freelance shit are *gone!* Hasn't that been made clear enough for you people?"

"I thought you knew," Dwight said with absolute honesty. He was amazed. He had forgotten—again—what a labyrinth this place could be. He felt something bordering on panic. He had really fouled up.

"And what's this report from Collie Davis?" Bixby asked, his voice rising again. "What's all this about Brad Smith? What the hell was in your mind? You can't just set up a trusted former employee—a U.S. citizen—this way!"

Exerblein stirred. In his colorless voice he said, "Smith volunteered to work on contract."

"I don't care how he came on board! You're fixing to get him killed or imprisoned for about thirty years and you're liable to have an international incident here at a time when we're trying to improve trade relations with those people and set up new channels of information into Albania. With our other people probably blown, the fucking plan won't work anyway. It's ridiculous!"

"What do you want us to do?" Dwight asked.

"Stop playing Wyatt Earp. Get Kinkaid back from Missoula. Cancel your little adventure in Belgrade."

"What happens to Danisa Lechova?"

"As far as we're concerned right now, she's had it. She stays put. If that changes, I'll let you know."

Dwight had a bad taste in his mouth. "And Partek?"

"Unlike you, Dwight, I think I'll go higher up with what I know and let my superiors make that decision. Of course at the moment we've lost him again anyhow. Maybe the KGB hasn't, and he's feeding the fish in Lake Ontario by now. We'll see."

"And Smith?"

Bixby's eyes became opaque. "Smith? I don't think I know anybody named Smith. I don't think you do, either."

twenty

Thanks to Fjbk's brutal artistry I didn't get much sleep Monday night. The application of a lot of ice kept the facial swelling within manageable limits. A rib definitely was cracked but otherwise I didn't think any serious body damage had been done.

Worry kept me awake as much as the pain did. I badly needed to know exactly what had happened. And why Danisa was angry with me.

Good boy that I was, however, I did not use any of the emergency telephone numbers during the night. I couldn't justify calling the situation a life-threatening crisis.

Tuesday morning, however, I was awake and pacing at dawn. I put the flowerpot out on my ledge and waited. Nobody showed up across the street and no one called my room with a wrong number. So I would have to fume a while longer before they were going to acknowledge my request for a contact.

At 8:05, Karyn Wechsting knocked on my door, took one look at my face, and came in like an avenging angel.

"You look like hell!" she told me.

"Hey, thanks."

"Goddamn it, Brad, don't make corny jokes! Ted told me about it this morning. Have you called the police?"

"No."

"It has to be reported!"

"No, nobody is going to report anything."

"He could have killed you!"

"Well, he didn't intend to do that, and he didn't."

"*Why* not call the police?"

"Having Fjbk arrested would just create nasty publicity, bring me notoriety I don't need, and ruin the Lechovas' concentration for the tournament. It wouldn't gain anybody a thing."

Karyn flounced into a chair, relieving pressure on her bad leg. "Have you seen a doctor?"

"No. I'm okay."

Her eyes narrowed. "All right."

"All right what?"

"All right, what's really going on here?"

"Nothing. Forget it."

"You mean he attacked you for no reason?"

"No. Of course not. He's jealous."

"Of *you?*"

I felt my face flush. "Silly, right?"

"I didn't mean—" she began quickly.

"Right."

"Brad—"

"Look," I cut in, getting tired of it. "Fjbk considers the Lechova women his meal ticket for the indefinite future. I've spent some time with both Hannah and Danisa, and then Danisa pulled an uncharacteristic vanishing act last night."

"I heard about that—"

"She was upset with her play, and took a long walk alone. But Fjbk was upset as hell when no one knew where she was, and somehow his anxiety spilled over on me—he blamed me for getting Danisa off stride and maybe doing something a lot more uncharacteristic and dangerous than taking a walk. So he lost his cool and had at me."

Karyn climbed to her feet again and gave me a disgusted, probing look.

"So," I said lamely, "that's all there is to it. It won't happen again."

"Long speech for you," she said.

"What?"

"I said, you just made a very long speech. The only other time I ever heard you make a long speech like that, you were lying through your teeth."

"Karyn, I never lie, and that's the truth."

She sighed bitterly and headed for the door. "I'm not through with you yet."

"Come back often," I replied cheerfully.

She left. I fretted. I hoped she wasn't going to create new problems for me.

Thirty minutes later, still no signal in response to my flowerpot. I reverted to plan 2.

In the breakfast room I encountered Martina, Paul Annacone, and Aaron Krickstein, plus some of their entourages, at two adjacent corner tables. I squeezed in and had coffee. The rolls looked good, but my mouth couldn't handle the hard crust this morning.

Everybody was in a good humor, although Martina was a little tight and subdued; assuming she got past Bettina Fulco of Argentina in her noon match, she would be coming back tonight against Steffi Graf. Playing two singles matches was unusual and bad enough for someone of her stature, but everyone had accepted the killing density of the Belgrade brackets when they accepted the invitation. What really was on her mind, I guessed, was recent memory of what had happened against Graf in the French. She wanted to maintain her Wimbledon form and not backslide on the black clay courts here. I told her I hoped she would knock both girls' teats off, and she giggled.

We talked about the brackets, how smoothly the officials were keeping things on schedule, and some of the erratic line calls. Jimmy Arias and a couple of other Americans came in, but sat at another table after exchanging pleasantries. Danisa's vanishing act last night was mentioned casually. Tennis pros were used to behavior a lot more eccentric than that.

When I left and walked to the Church of the Assumption, there was no one to meet me. I waited an hour. I told myself the signal had been late in being noticed, or the boys had bigger fish to fry. I went back to my hotel room, where I walked in to a ringing telephone.

"Brad Smith speaking."

"Brad? Is that you, Brad?" It was a voice I had never heard before. I thought it must be somebody at the magazine.

"Yes," I said. "Who's calling, please?"

"Brad. This is your uncle Carl."

My pulse rose enough that I felt it. "Uncle Carl," I said. "How are you? How are Aunt Margaret and the rest of the family in the old neighborhood?"

"Brad, I have bad news. Aunt Margaret is very, very sick."

"I'm sorry to hear that. How bad is it?"

"Very bad. As a matter of fact, the doctors have abandoned all hope for her recovery. They have abandoned all hope. They say there is nothing more to be done." The voice repeated that, too: "There is nothing more to be done." There was hissing and a momentary fade on the satellite relay. Then the voice asked clearly, "Did you hear what I said, Brad?"

"I heard you, yes," I said. "Aunt Margaret is really that sick? They have really abandoned all hope?"

"Yes, Brad. I'm sorry to say that is correct."

I stayed on the line another minute or two, inanely ad-libbing sad remarks about my nonexistent aunt Margaret to my equally nonexistent uncle Carl. I told him I would be home soon and he said he thought that would be a good idea, and then I hung up.

And stood there, looking out the window at the hazy noon, absolutely stunned by surprise and disappointment.

* * *

TIEBREAKER

There was no opportunity to speak with Danisa before her early match with Gabriela Sabatini. I sat in the stands with Karyn Wechsting rather than in the press row and pretended to jot a few notes, but that was primarily to keep myself from having to maintain a running conversation.

I didn't expect Danisa to play very well after whatever had happened to her last night. Right.

The match started with Danisa's double-faulting. That set the tone for the early going. With a little frown creasing her forehead, she moved around the court like a pretty blue robot, ponytail bobbing as she continually got just a little out of position or failed to anticipate. The only thing that kept her in the first set at all was that Sabatini, for some reason, was also having a bad day: she made more unforced errors than I had ever seen her make, and her serve was off a mile. She broke Danisa in the fifth game to win the first set, 6–4, but Danisa seemed to be concentrating a bit better toward the end and it was anybody's match as they started set 2.

"She isn't playing well," Karyn observed.

"She hasn't gotten into it yet."

"You're not much into it, either."

"Thinking about the story," I told her.

Karyn studied me, and her questions were clear in her pretty, vivid eyes. "You absolutely refuse to talk about it?"

"Talk about what?"

"Okay, Brad, fine. You get mysteriously mugged in your hotel room and won't call the police or a doctor. Then you get mugged by Fjbk under the stadium, and you won't report that, either. You come in here looking like the walking wounded, and there's obviously something weird going on, but you play dumb. *Okay.* Fine, Brad! I'd like to be your friend. But if you say no, then it's no."

I liked her a lot. I felt uncomfortable, wishing I could open up with her. But it was out of the question. "Karyn, I appreciate it. Better we just let things stand where they are."

She studied me. "Sure?"

"Sure."

"Okay." She didn't like it a bit.

We returned our attention to the match, more or less. But my thoughts were miles away.

There were always prearranged signals to order an abort. For a meeting at a cafe, for example, you might find your intended contact fiddling with an unlit cigarette, which could mean *keep going, don't approach*. A magazine, or lack of one, could initiate or abort a drop. A letter from home, a chalked mark on the side of a certain utility pole, or a spilled drink in a crowded bar might signal possible surveillance. Once in Frankfurt I had been supposed to leave my watch at a certain shop for adjustment and pick it—and something else—up the following day. When my watch was brought to my hotel that night by a commercial deliveryman, along with a bill for a few DM and nothing else, I correctly read it as a signal to forget the whole thing.

In the case of Belgrade, the Uncle Carl signal had been set up before I headed for Chicago and the JAT flight connection. But I had never expected to hear it.

It meant simply that whatever I had been doing, forget it: my part in the operation was scrubbed. Which in this case meant that as of now, presumably, I really was nothing more than a working magazine journalist. I could finish up whatever I needed to do for the writing assignment, forget about Danisa Lechova in any other connection, and head home.

In some circumstances I would have accepted the orders and thought little more about it.

This time it hit me hard.

First—let's be honest—was the way I now felt about the lady in blue out there on the court in front of me. I have not done a good job of defining the feelings that seemed to flow between us every time we were close. Maybe those things can't be defined. I knew the gulf in our backgrounds, and the age difference, logically made my feelings absurd. But there they were. Her strength and intelligence were part of it. She responded to me with a quickness and sensitivity that I had experienced only once before, in the earliest times with Elizabeth, before everything changed. But Danisa was deeper, more genuine, than Elizabeth had ever been. And there was a sense of reliability—of straightforward openness—that was unique to her. I felt crazy every time I looked at her, too: her hair, her eyes, the sweet and liquid movements of her body. The old gent was crazy about her, against all logic and sanity, and there just wasn't a lot more to be said about it.

I didn't hold out hope that the personal thing would ever get much beyond its present stage. That was all right. I had intended to help in the operation to get her out, and enjoy the good feelings that left me. As for the rest of my feelings, disappointment was something I had learned to handle. But helping her had become very important to me, and I hated to be robbed of that satisfaction.

Another reason my abort order rankled was that I had the unpleasant feeling that it meant the whole operation had been canceled. If this was the case, then Danisa might face a long time before she ever played tennis again in the free world. And that, quite aside from my personal involvement, was simply a damned shame and a gross injustice.

I still intended to talk to the boys. Maybe I could get some explanations. At least they might tell me what had happened last night, and if it—whatever it was—had affected the decision to cancel me out of the operation.

The idea of abandoning Danisa made me sick. But I didn't know what I could do by myself.

Karyn's squeal of pleasure brought my mind back to the match, where Danisa had just hit a rifle shot down the line to complete a service break.

"She's paying attention now," Karyn told me. "Damn!" she added with grudging admiration. "She's really something!"

I started paying attention, too.

Sabatini was continuing to have a serious off day. But

Danisa had that frown of concentration now, and her movements oncourt had become smooth and purposeful. Whatever had been bothering her was out of her mind and she was in the zone, playing the match, not knowing much else. She held serve at love and won another three points in a row to have Sabatini down 0–40 before yielding one breaker to a great backhand, and then came in behind a driving return of serve to complete another break. She won the second set, 6–1.

There are people who show some aspects of their character in their play. Connors used to be like that when he was down in a match and suddenly began playing with a wild, controlled ferocity: his eyes would get a curious glaze, and against all odds and ideas of safety he would blast a two-handed backhand deep to a corner and charge the net, knowing that a wrong guess would result in a passing shot to end the match in his opponent's favor. It was as if he were saying, *Win or die, this is my game and I can't play any other way, so to hell with it, here I come at you.* You see character in Lendl, too: ice and relentless pressure, the flawlessness of a machine. And did anyone ever watch Chrissie prepare to serve late in an exhausting match—see that total emotional control and determination—and fail to realize that this was a lady to contend with in *any* situation?

Danisa's character was overwhelming in the third and deciding set. She was everywhere. Every forehand smoked. There was absolutely no wasted motion, no error, and she was relentless. Sabatini did not go quietly. But she went, in less than fifty minutes.

I told Karyn, "I'm going to go belowdecks and see if I can get a few words with her."

Karyn eyed me. "For the story."

"Of course for the story."

"Tell me something, Smith," she said bluntly. "Have you got something going with that girl?"

"You must be out of your mind," I said. "I'm old enough to be her father."

"Oh, sure."

"I'm a tennis news hack, Karyn. That's all."

"I wish you trusted me, Brad. I really do."

"Karyn, I don't know what you're talking about."

"There are *all kinds* of shit going on here that I don't understand. You get beat up and won't call the police. Danisa vanishes for half the night. You watch her play with an expression like a mortician. Hey. I'm trustworthy, buddy. Why not tell me some of the real facts, here, whatever they are?"

I stood. "Karyn, I certainly wish half your suspicions were accurate. Nothing has happened between Danisa and me, although I'm not above trying to seduce beautiful young women—which is something you'd better keep in mind, incidentally, for your own protection."

She colored just a little, around all her freckles, and the gambit shunted her attention from being quite so close to fact-based suspicions. "Promises, promises," she said wryly, and I grinned at her and left the stands.

Down below, the usual collection of onlookers, press people, and security guards jammed the tunnel. Danisa, sweat-soaked, with a towel over her head, came down from the arena floor with Sabatini, a couple more guards, and Fjbk carrying her rackets and gear bag. There was confusion and I managed to get onto the edge of the mess enough to catch her eye. In the crowded shoving, with people calling questions and a few fans applauding in the background of the melee, she started past me.

"Danisa," I said. "When can we talk?"

The look she gave me was quick, spiteful, bitter. "You are a liar."

"What?"

"I know now," she bit off. "You were never to help me. It was a lie. All a lie." Then, before I could respond, she whirled away, her long-legged stride carrying her through the doors of the locker room and out of my reach.

I took an involuntary step after her. Fjbk was right there. He shoved me back. A security guard grabbed my arm and made sure I didn't go any farther. Fjbk hadn't missed the bitterness of our exchange, although he could not have heard the actual words. His expression was fiercely triumphant. I didn't know what the hell had happened. I felt like I had been shot.

twenty-one

Björn Borg, having first surprised everybody by accepting the invitation to Belgrade, surprised Pat Cash on court 3 early Tuesday, burying him under an avalanche of drop shots, looping topspin passes down the lines, and unerring lobs. I saw part of it between trips to the Church of St. Mark. Nobody showed up to meet me there, either.

I was getting desperate. Finally, a few minutes before five o'clock, I called the embassy from a pay telephone, identified myself as Jim Fever, and gave the woman a seemingly innocuous message that told Booth I needed to see him *now* in the designated pastry shop off Slavija Square: emergency.

Again: nobody.

They had dropped me. Period.

What I was supposed to do was forget it; go home.

I couldn't do it.

One of the endless press/celebrity parties was on for 6 P.M., this one thrown by Reebok at the Hotel Jugoslavija. I went.

My theory was that I might see Hannah there. Her second match of the day was already over, and tourney officials were putting pressure on the athletes to grace as many of the social functions as possible, consistent with

221

conditioning. I hoped she just might be able to shed some light on why Danisa suddenly seemed to think I had rabies or something.

There were doubles matches going on at the stadium, but a lot of the press had abandoned the arena in favor of free food and drinks. A number of Yugoslav dignitaries were on hand, and everybody attacked the huge platters of *ražnjići, ćevapčići,* and *burek* like it was a last meal. The sponsor had supplied a spicy apple punch along with coffee and tea, champagne, spritzers, and *šljivovica.* Everybody seemed pretty happy but me. I visited some with Tony Trabert, and was on the outskirts of a boring cocktail filibuster by Belgrade's director of people's recreation when Hannah came in, her mother at her side.

I detached myself from the recreation director's group and made my way through the crowd toward them. Hannah looked bright, freshly scrubbed, and gorgeous, wearing a hot-pink pantsuit that would have drawn attention in any crowd, with her silver-blond hair flowing onto her shoulders in cascades of dramatic, pencil-thin braids. I approached her and Mrs. Lechova confidently, expecting, I guess, Hannah's usual effusive flirtatiousness.

Both women spied me just as I neared them.

"Hello," I said. "Hannah, congratulations on a fine match—"

"Swine!" she spat, her eyes ablaze and her entire body coiling as if she were about to strike. "Never try to speak to me again!"

A few people nearby heard her outburst, and turned in surprise. I didn't know what the hell was going on. "Hannah, whatever you're—"

"My sister was happy, just fine, until you came along," Hannah cut in bitterly. "I don't know what you do, Mr. so-called journalism man, but Danisa is now sad. She won't tell me nothing. You have taken advantage of her and broken her heart and I think you are nothing but a pig, and I hope you die, I would like to see you stuck in some building on fire, with no way to get out, and I would laugh!"

"Hannah—"

I got no further. She had already turned to flounce away through the crowd, elegant hips swaying in angry rhythm. I looked at Mrs. Lechova. My face was hot. I half expected her to strike me.

Geneta Lechova was very pale and very solemn, but the eyes with which she studied me were neither angry nor hateful. In her simple gray dress and medium white heels she looked almost as young as her daughters, and austerely handsome. "I am sorry for Hannah's outburst," she said quietly.

"I don't understand," I told her.

"We must talk."

"Yes."

She looked past me into the crowded room. "If we walk to the tables, we can get punch, do you think? Then perhaps outside someplace we can find a quiet place to talk."

"Yes," I repeated. Maybe she could shed some light. At least she didn't seem ready to kill me, like everybody else in the family.

She linked her arm with mine and we worked our way to the punch. Then we got back out of the party room and into the hotel corridor. Walking partway toward the lobby stairs, we found a small, abandoned alcove with two high-backed red velvet chairs arranged under a tall old painting of a mountain scene, with a horseman on the path at its foot.

We sat down. Geneta Lechova put her punch cup on the small table and I did the same. She surprised me by producing a pack of cigarettes from her purse and offered me one. I took it gratefully and she lit up for both of us with a tiny gold lighter.

She crossed her legs and smiled grimly at me through the smoke. "This is my little secret. To my husband, I quit smoking years ago."

"I've quit often myself," I told her.

"My husband admits no weaknesses. I humor his illusions."

I nodded and said nothing. The smoke hit me almost at once and it felt good. I was strung guywire tight.

"Please forgive Hannah's outburst," she said with grave formality. "She is very emotional."

"I noticed."

She smiled at that. "She and Danisa are very close. Closer than most true sisters."

"Mrs. Lechova, I know Danisa is outraged at me, and so now is Hannah. I need you to know that I didn't do anything."

She nodded and inhaled again. As the smoke curled around her, she said calmly, "I understand. However—I am guessing—Danisa must be very disappointed and shocked. Does her disappearance and return last night mean you will not be able at all to help her leave our country?"

My surprise must have been clear on my face. Before I could think of something to say, she added: "Mr. Smith. At first I did not guess. But I know my daughter. She likes you very . . . very much. You know that?"

I stared at her. "I can't read her."

"Her feeling is deep. Her behavior has given her away. To me, at least. Because I know her best. My husband thinks he knows her best. Of course Milo imagines he knows her best, and understands her, when in fact he understands nothing at all. I know my daughters. I know Danisa has been unhappy. The government kept her from playing in the French, and at Wimbledon. Tennis is her life and she has not been allowed a passport to travel out of our country since New South Wales, last February. Now . . . this matter out of the past."

I didn't reply. I instinctively liked this woman. Trust was another matter.

She said, "You must get her out, Mr. Smith."

"What?"

"Do not pretend. I am not a fool. You must get her out!"

"Mrs. Lechova, even if there was a chance—"

"You are here not only as a writer. You are to arrange it so my daughter can escape."

I gave up on pretense. Hell, maybe she could help. "My role was very small. I didn't know any of the details."

"'Was'?" she repeated. "You are no longer involved?"

"I don't know what I am. I don't know what happened last night, but it changed everything. My instructions seem to be to go home and forget it."

She remained eerily calm, in control. I began to see that all the strength had not flowed from Danisa's natural parents, whoever they had been. Geneta Lechova, quiet and behind the scenes, was perhaps a greater force than anyone else.

She said, "My heart breaks to think of her leaving. I think it may be a very great mistake. But we talked. She told me how she has been watched . . . followed. She told me *everything*."

"Everything," I echoed.

"About her real brother, yes. Which neither my husband nor I knew anything about. Everything."

Again I didn't know how to respond. Danisa really had told her all of it. Instead of panicking, this amazing woman had seen—and accepted—her daughter's point of view.

As much as it would hurt, she was ready to help Danisa go.

I owed her as much honesty in return. "Mrs. Lechova, it may be that the idea of helping her escape at this time has been abandoned."

"She must go. She will never be free here. Knowing what she knows now, her heart will break. And there is the added problem of Milo."

I misunderstood. "He can be kept in the dark."

"No, no. I mean that he is a problem for Danisa now."

I touched my sore jaw before I could stop myself. "Yes."

"He wants her. My husband does not see this. He does not want to see it because Milo is a great coach. I see it and my blood runs cold."

"Your husband thinks a lot of him."

Her face became stone. "Leon is a good man. Strong. He loves us very much."

Jack M. Bickham

It was one of those statements that didn't seem finished. I said nothing, waiting.

She looked back at me, and her jaw set. "He does not understand about Milo. He does not understand that a young woman must live her own life—must grow up and leave, and her parents must do the hardest thing they ever did out of love for her: let her go."

"If he gets wind of any of this—"

"He will stop you, of course. Lock Danisa in her room. Notify the militia, even. And as much as she loves her sister, so might Hannah. She is hard, my Hannah. Like her father in some ways. Very patriotic. And that is good. But is the state supposed to stand in the way of a citizen's happiness? I think not."

"I wish I could promise to do something."

"You must."

"I can't even see her. She won't see me."

"She will. I have convinced her. Tonight."

"She plays Zina Garrison in less than two hours. The Sabatini match was tough. Win or lose, she'll be exhausted."

"You think that will matter when her whole life—that of her lost brother—may be at stake?"

"Where, then?"

"In the park near our home. One to two hours after the match."

"I'll be there."

She nodded. She was close to tears. "I must find my headstrong Hannah now, and start for the stadium." She dabbed at her eyes with a small handkerchief, stood, and walked briskly back toward the ballroom, heels clicking.

I went to the men's room and then started back to the party for another drink before heading to the arena. As I approached the room, I saw Paula Bansky, dressed to the nines, starting in ahead of me. She looked gorgeous in a wine-colored cocktail dress and full makeup, very high heels and dark hose. Her eyes met mine for just an instant. I signaled her. She turned and headed back the way she had come, retreating for the elevator.

226

Startled and angry, I hurried after her. The elevator door closed in my face. I ran to the stairs and plunged down, getting to the lobby a floor below just as the elevator opened its doors and disgorged several people, including Paula. She saw me again and half ran for the lobby, swaying on her heels.

"Paula!" She kept going.

I caught her by the arm just as she was about to rush out through the revolving doors. The force of my capture swung her around off balance and she half fell against me.

"Release me!" she hissed.

"I need to talk to somebody," I told her. "I need to know what's going on."

She pulled free. She looked angry, and badly scared. "I know nothing! Get away from me! I'm to have nothing to do with you!"

"Tell them I have to see them. Tell them to react to my signals for a meeting."

"Do you want to have me *arrested?*" she demanded, and turned and bolted out through the glass doors, which revolved wildly in her wake.

I went to the stadium. It was impossible to keep my mind on my alleged job as a journalist. Paula Bansky's reactions left no doubt that my instructions in the call from New York had been accurate: I had been canceled out.

The sensible thing was to accept it and go home like a good little boy.

I knew I wasn't going to do that.

After some of the things the tennis establishment had done to Zina Garrison, I really wanted her to do well in this tournament, even against Danisa. But Zina's morning match had been a three-set killer with endless rallies and leg-numbing movement from side to side on the worst of the outdoor courts. She came out looking stiff and tired. Danisa, on the other hand, came out wearing a new pale blue minidress, her braided ponytail fixed by a little bow with sparkles on it. She looked grim but fresh as a daisy. I sat by myself and watched her put Zina away, 6–3, 6–1, in a match that required only fifty-four minutes.

There was a lot more good tennis to come later in the evening, but I left the arena and took a cab to an address several blocks from the Lechova apartments. Then I went through my walkabout routine and even rode a trolley bus a few blocks before doubling back. I felt pretty futile and very much alone when I finally walked into the park and sat on a bench in the deep shadows of an oak.

After wishing for a cigarette for about an hour and being startled twice by strolling lovers, I spotted a familiar figure hurrying along the path in my direction, slender, graceful, wearing close-fitting sweats and tennis shoes.

"I am sorry," Geneta Lechova said, sitting down beside me.

"Where is she?"

She gestured in the air, and I noticed a bandage around her wrist. "When we reached home, we made an excuse for coming here. But Leon would not hear of it. He ordered her straight to bed. She argued. I took her side. There was a very big argument. We could not convince him to let Danisa take the briefest walk to cool down."

"How did you hurt your wrist?" I asked.

"Leon broke some glassware."

I got a glimpse of it in my mind. A "very big argument," indeed. Leon Lechova would have been tighter than a racket string in any case during this tournament, where his daughters must shine for the home crowds. Danisa's disappearance last night and erratic play in the morning must have driven him up the wall. I wondered that he let his wife out.

She seemed to read my mind. "It was necessary that I go to buy additional bandage material. He also cut himself —his hand—when he smashed the pitcher on the table."

"It sounds like you've been having a wonderful evening."

"My husband has very strong feelings about right and wrong. About training."

"Well, if you're allegedly at the drugstore now, I know you don't have much time."

I saw her nod in the darkness. "Tomorrow is only the one quarterfinal match, against your Chris Evert, at about seven o'clock in the evening. I will say I am taking Danisa to look at a dress, to take her mind away from worry over tennis. Leon will like that."

"And we can meet?"

"Yes."

"Where and when?" I felt a scintilla of hope stirring around in me somewhere.

"Your hotel. Between ten o'clock and eleven."

"I'll make it a point to be in the coffee shop during that time."

"Done," she said, and stood.

"You're sure you're all right," I said, asking her.

"Of course," she said as if the structure of her life weren't caving in.

I reached for her and, despite her little gasp of surprise, briefly hugged her. Then I let her go and she hurried away.

Finding a cab at the hour was difficult, but I was beginning to catch on to the bus system. The trolley I caught was not the right one, but at least it got me over the Sava and into the general vicinity of the hotel. From where I disembarked, I walked. There was little traffic, and blue-uniformed police on most corners. I didn't know whether to be glad for the protection from potential muggers or worried about how I could help Danisa when every street seemed to be crawling with fuzz.

When I got to the hotel I went straight upstairs, headed for my room. As my elevator doors opened and I turned down the corridor, I saw the briefest flash of a blue police uniform at the end of the hall, just beyond my room door. It was a militiaman, slender and young, carrying a tray loaded with sandwiches and cakes and containers that looked like coffee. He was just going into the room next to mine, and I got only the briefest look at his back.

It didn't take a stroke of genius to draw the obvious

229

conclusion. I was still being bugged, and the electronics boys had moved into the room right next to mine to make their work as easy as possible. It almost struck me as funny. I wondered if they would be burning up all those kilowatt hours of electricity if they could know my case officer had declared me persona non grata. Spying on me at this point was about like placing a bet on a horse right after it had dropped dead at the far turn.

On the other hand, I decided, that wasn't a very apt simile. I wasn't dead yet, even if the boys were acting like it.

I went right to bed but slept badly again. I was glad when daylight came so I could get up. I showered and dressed, forgot my damaged ribs, and rehurt them a little. My mouth still hurt.

Downstairs at 10:20 they arrived, Geneta Lechova, in her coffee-colored afternoon dress, and Danisa in her trademark blue, this time a brief sundress. She looked tired and tense but marvelous, all suntanned arms and legs.

They came over and sat down. I signaled for more coffee and rolls. Danisa gave me a wan, cautious smile. "My mother says you do not know anything of what happened the other night with the American couple."

"I don't even know what couple you're talking about."

"They have been everywhere, asking autographs, mingling with everyone. The man slightly loud, foolish. The woman with frilly dresses, or sometimes garish shorts, and he has two cameras—"

I tumbled. "Christ. *The Beamers?*"

"Yes. The Beamers, that is their name. They met me in the tunnel. They knew the code words. I left the arena, met them. They were in a Volkswagen. They said we were heading for the border. They had food and drink. But there was a roadblock, a license check, I think, and they turned back, and then we were followed and we ran fast and Mr. Beamer stopped the car, I jumped out fast, they went on, a police car went by, I made my way home."

The Beamers! But hell, it made sense. They had been

too touristy to be true in the first place.

I said, "No wonder you were scared."

"It was a chase. I think we were lucky to escape arrest."

"Did anyone see you?"

"No. I am sure of that."

I reached across the table and took her hand. *Bad thing to do. Might be observed.* Too late, and to hell with it. "Danisa, I didn't know an attempt was going to be made. I've been completely in the dark."

She frowned. "In the dark?"

"Uninformed."

"But I thought you were here to help me. The interviews—everything—to cover it up for you to be of assistance."

"I was to be a contact man, as I told you. Nothing more."

"But then they didn't use you!"

I didn't have the heart to tell her I had been a dupe. "Plans change."

Her lip trembled. "But what is to happen now?"

"I don't know that, either. I'm trying to find out."

"I thought you had...what is it called?...set me up."

"You weren't the one who was set up, Danisa. My people haven't been straight with me."

Her eyes were alive and beautiful again. "I am glad you did not betray me—abandon me."

"I would never do that."

"What, then, are your instructions for me now?"

"You had reason to feel tricked," I told her. "So did I. But we're going to get it straightened out yet. Hang in there. Just give me a little more time."

Her expression changed in a way that cut to my heart. She said, "I will do as you say."

So she trusted me again. I had to help her.

The boys at the embassy would not be pleased. I had served my decoy function, the Beamers had failed, and that was the end of it, in their way of thinking.

I had news for them.

twenty-two

Elsewhere

New York

Dominic Partek's flight from Denver landed at La-Guardia shortly after dawn.

He felt crushed by fatigue.

The bus had taken him from Missoula to Helena. After waiting five hours he had caught a flight to Denver, where the connection was delayed. But now at last he was back in the city where he knew the territory . . . where they would never expect him to try to hide.

Partek took a taxi to Park Avenue South. He had breakfast at a cafeteria not far from where the taxi let him out. Fighting sleep, he stalled over his coffee until the banks were open. He walked east and south to his bank. He had to risk cashing a check; he was getting low on funds.

Skin prickling with the sense that someone was watching, he completed his transaction and walked out of the bank with $2,000 in cash in his pocket. He started south again on foot.

A block or two later, the feeling of surveillance became so intense that sweat bolted out of his pores.

It cannot be.

Partek waited at a pedestrian signal. Jaywalkers pushed

past him and brazenly slipped between gridlocked cars. Partek looked up the street in the direction he had come. In a second he burned everyone into his memory.

The light changed. He crossed the intersection, walked the next block, turned right, went through a wood tunnel built around a construction project, skirted a street crew blasting into the pavement with air hammers, and turned left at the next corner with his ears ringing from the racket.

At the next corner he looked back again.

And felt his blood chill.

There were two of them.

A thickset man his own age, wearing a dark suit and carrying a pale tan leather attaché case, a quarter of the way down the block behind him.

On the other side of the street and almost opposite him near the far corner, a younger man, blond, dressed in the uniform of a delivery service and carrying a small parcel.

So despite all Partek's expectations they had indulged in the luxury of maintaining constant surveillance of the banks.

There were five branches of his bank in Manhattan. The branch he had used was not his usual one. So they had gone so far as to watch all of them.

He had underestimated his importance to them. Or their desperation.

Too late now to castigate himself about the miscalculation.

The light changed. Partek crossed, walking faster, weaving in and out of the thick pedestrian traffic. *What can I do? How can I escape?*

He had to assume the worst, that they were KGB. Certainly the person watching the bank had recognized him and called for backup. The two behind Partek were only the first to reach the scene. There would have been calls by radio or cellular phone. More would be arriving. If he had any chance whatsoever to shake them, he had to do it now before they had people all over the street on all sides of him.

The area around him was composed of business buildings, none too new, with lobby entrances into office por-
tions and small shops along the streetfronts. Partek turned
into a shabby-looking store whose windows were filled
with junky souvenirs, cameras, watches, and small electronic gear.

A half-dozen customers lined the counters in the long,
narrow store. Partek saw a back partition and a doorway. He
walked toward the back.

A swarthy man behind the counter said to him, "Can I
help you?"

His fear dancing, Partek ignored the question and kept
walking toward the back door.

"Hey, buddy!" the man called sharply.

Partek pulled the door open. It led to a dirty, narrow
hallway. Another doorway on the right revealed a toilet.
Boxes, some empty, littered the hallway.

"Hey!" the voice called. "You can't go back there!"

Partek rushed down the hallway. There was a storage
room, packed to the ceiling with boxes and crates, and in the
bare brick wall at the back a steel rear door.

Partek pulled the security bar out of its cradle on the
door and pushed, hard. The door swung out onto a trash-
littered alley.

"Hey!"

Partek stepped into the alley. He looked up and down.
Other doorways, closed. Trash dumpsters. Halfway down to
the right, a UPS truck with its back open and the driver
carrying a box inside another building.

Partek ran.

The delivery driver was just coming back out as Partek
went in. Another store—clothing on racks, high shelving, a
man and two female clerks looking up wide-eyed from their
inventory of the delivery.

The man said, "You can't come in this way—"

Partek pushed past him into a front corridor where the

234

brighter lights of the front portion shone. He came out into the shop—women's clothing on bare racks, a couple of customers. He ran for the front. Somebody yelled at him. He pushed through the front door and out onto the street.

Poorer shops. Sidewalk vendors with scarves and watches. Lighter one-way traffic southbound, moving fast, vacant spaces in the lanes. Partek stepped off the curb between parked cars, looking for a break in the traffic that would let him cross.

The quick movement at the next corner, north, caught his eyes at once: the blond man, running around the corner, skidding on the sidewalk as he looked up and down—his head coming up as he instantly spied Partek.

A brief break in the fast traffic. Partek took a step into the street. Then he realized that three of the lanes coming at him were yellow cabs.

He raised his hand and waved frantically.

The center-lane taxi braked, swerved right behind one of the others, and lurched to a halt just past where Partek stood. He ran forward, jerked open the back door, got in. A car behind them honked angrily. The driver pulled away. Partek looked back. The blond man was standing on the curb, angry hands on his hips.

Partek told the driver, "St. Patrick's."

That made the driver turn right at the next street. Partek waited half a block and then said, "No, no. I was mistaken. Please take me to Battery Park."

"Make up your mind, man," the driver said gruffly over the sound of his rock-music cassette.

Partek leaned back against the grimy seat. His heart lurched in his chest like a wild thing.

Belgrade

M. Y. Altunyan felt good to be taking decisive action.

Activities by the American Brad Smith in recent hours had further convinced him of two things: the plot was in motion to slip Danisa Lechova out of Yugoslavia, and Smith intended to make his final moves within forty-eight hours.

Altunyan had been surprised and admiring earlier, when Sislinsky brought Moscow's analysis that Smith was a decoy to divert attention from some other hidden plan to get Danisa Lechova out of Yugoslavia. At that time, Altunyan had been ready to take Smith out.

Since Sislinsky's report, however, Altunyan had been ready to dismiss Smith entirely. Fortunately, his colleagues in the UDBA had maintained a routine watch on Smith. The American's recent actions—trips about the city and telephone calls that had to be in code—had now caused Altunyan to reevaluate once more.

Clearly now, he thought, the decoy plan had been dropped, but Smith could be the major player in a new and complex American scheme.

Unable to perceive the outlines of the new American plan, Altunyan could not be sure of blocking it at the Smith end. This meant Altunyan was now compelled to carry out his contingency plan directly affecting Danisa Lechova as approved earlier in principle.

For the next few days, the only certain safety lay in making sure Danisa could not travel anywhere. But she could not simply be abducted. Strong-arm tactics might be revealed, poisoning Soviet-Yugoslav relations.

Subtlety, then.

Altunyan's first stop of the day was on the eastern outskirts of the city, where he had previously visited a junkyard and farm-equipment store which also sold seed, fertilizers, and farm and garden chemical products. He had spoken to the operator the day before, posing as a city dweller with a keen interest in his home vegetable garden.

Entering the store, Altunyan waited patiently while the operator dealt with several area farmers. When it was his turn, he purchased a small plastic container of an organic phosphate insecticide that the owner had assured him

would control pests in the shrubbery and brush surrounding his garden.

The owner also sold him a hand-pumped pressure
sprayer to apply the chemical, pointed out the instructions
for mixing the powder to the proper strength, and sternly
reminded him of the dangers of applying the material too
close to food products near their harvest time.

"Please always to remember, sir: phosphate products of
this kind are very, very powerful and dangerous."

"Yes. Thank you. I will remember. Goodbye."

Altunyan drove back into the city.

His next stop was at the large hospital nearest the sports
arena where the tennis tournament was under way. He had
to wait a while before the young doctor was able to meet
him in the cafeteria.

"You will be on emergency duty this evening,"
Altunyan verified.

"Yes," the doctor, whose name was Bulganik, said. He
was pale and very frightened. He had many relatives in
Romania and the Soviet Union. "I can arrange the schedule
to be in charge."

"Good." Altunyan nodded. "And you understand exactly what is to happen, and what you are to do."

The doctor nodded and started to speak, but the word
caught in his throat and he coughed wetly. Then he said,
"Yes."

"There must be no slipups of any kind."

"There will be none. I will be ready."

"And you remember what you are to say, also."

"Yes. Yes. I remember everything."

The doctor was pitiful in his frightened eagerness to
please. It made Altunyan feel good to have people so in his
power. He gave the wretch a somber, calculating look
designed to intimidate him further, got up from the cafeteria
table without another word, and left the hospital sure there
would be no problem here.

Once in his Mercedes, Altunyan permitted himself to hum a tune.

Queens, New York

In his new rented room in a shabby residential section of Queens, Dominic Partek read an Associated Press story in the *Times* about the first annual Belgrade International. The story led with Danisa Lechova, "headed for a showdown with America's Chris Evert in the round of sixteen" this Wednesday night. It said Danisa—the sister Partek had never known he had—was sluggish against Argentina's Gabriela Sabatini in her Tuesday morning match, but was sharp and relentless in ousting America's Zina Garrison in the evening.

There was a blurred LaserPhoto of Danisa serving in the Sabatini match.

Partek studied the photo. His sister was so young! And despite the grainy quality of the photo, he could tell she was blond and beautiful. His heart ached, seeing her like this.

He wanted more than anything in the world to see her in person—to have his arms around her. She was a gift from the God he had always pretended he did not believe in. He had lived his adult life thinking he had no family anywhere. But now here she was, in his beloved Belgrade, a wonderful athlete, powerful, agile, destined for greatness according to all accounts.

Would he ever see her?

The question tore at his heart.

He was shockingly tired after the long flights, the horror of this morning, the finding of this room. But the near thing this morning, coupled with this story and picture of Danisa, made sleep impossible.

He had to know if the Americans were any closer to getting her out. He could not run much longer. Someone would spot him again.

Perhaps, he told himself, he could think more clearly after some rest.

But how could he rest? *Everyone* was after him: the CIA, the police, the FBI, surely the KGB. If the KGB located him now, he thought, he would at best be taken prisoner and flown to Russia at once, where he would stand trial for treason. At worst they would simplify matters—make absolutely sure his information never reached the West, and that he stood as an example for any other KGB Residents who might be wavering in their loyalty: they would simply have him murdered.

If he sought CIA protection, the KGB would know. And it would be Danisa—this beautiful young athlete in the grainy LaserPhoto—who would suffer.

He seemed damned either way: trapped beyond help.

Partek did not delude himself about the lengths the KGB and UDBA would go to pressure his return or force his silence through Danisa. First would come the news that she had decided to "retire" from competition. Next, a state agency would announce that she had accepted an appointment as director of physical culture at some remote gymnazia in a corner of Istria or Macedonia. Although it would never be admitted, her passport would be permanently revoked. And she would simply never be heard of again.

Partek tried to tell himself that such a fate was not so bad. The life of a professional athlete was very short anyway. She would not miss so much. She would probably do good work in some little town a universe from civilization, meet a nice young man, settle down, come to accept her lot in life, have babies . . .

Coward! another voice screamed inside Partek's head. *Lying bastard!*

He was astonished by his own weakness, disgusted by it to the bottom of his soul. Was he really so terrified of the KGB? Had he actually sunk so low that he would sacrifice the life of his beautiful young sister for a few years of "freedom"—in hiding, under an assumed identity—for his own putrid self?

He told himself there was more than his own life involved. His work in organizing and overseeing the network that had penetrated missile defense secrets of the United States was among the most powerful espionage operations of the century. He knew the network was still fully functioning, gathering new intelligence about the MX, modifications to the B1-B, Stealth, and the Strategic Defense Initiative with an efficiency and breadth that would shock American counterintelligence. If he defected and told all he knew to the CIA and FBI, more than forty crucially placed spies would instantly be rounded up and jailed or even executed. A hole in American security as serious as the Rosenberg case would stand revealed.

After seeing in recent years what had happened to some of his friends at the hands of the supposedly "new" Soviet regime, knowing better than most the cynical dishonesty of Soviet foreign policy, Partek knew in his heart that his decision to defect was the correct moral choice. His disillusionment had been growing for years, and was now ripe. The KGB's cruelty in exploiting his totally innocent, long-lost sister was just the final blow that made it impossible for him ever again to feel loyalty to such a system.

But he could *not* simply throw himself on the CIA and FBI, and let Danisa twist in the wind.

It seemed to him now that whatever he did, he was doomed.

He reverted again to the American promises. Could they deliver?

He had to know.

He thought about it for another hour or so, pacing his room, chain-smoking. He ran out of cigarettes, which meant a trip to the corner. The need to get out anyway was what decided him.

He simply had to take a chance in order to find out where things stood.

Leaving the rooming house, he walked down the street past other dilapidated old frame-and-brick houses, and at the corner he bought a carton of Marlboros and made sure he had plenty of quarters in the change. There was a public telephone on the same corner. Puffing furiously, Partek dialed the Manhattan number that was still stark in his memory.

"Yes?" a woman's voice answered after the first ring. She gave the number. "May I know who is calling, please?"

"This is Mr. East. I must speak to Mr. Martin at once."

There was only the slightest pause, during which the woman might have held back her gasp of surprise. "Please hold."

The line clicked to music for perhaps fifteen seconds, an eternity to Partek. Then Martin's familiar voice came on the line. "Hello? Can I help you?"

"This is East. And every hound must have its day."

Martin's voice changed remarkably. "Where the hell are you? Are you all right?"

"I am nearby. We must meet. I must know what has happened about my . . . acquaintance across the ocean."

"I understand. Let me think. Christ. Let me think. Are you in New York?"

"I can meet at a place of your choosing in the area."

"Okay . . . hang on . . . I'm thinking . . ." Martin seemed to fade out for a few seconds. "Okay, fine. You want to meet here in Manhattan?"

"No, no!"

"Okay, then. Uh . . . all right, how about this? Listen. There is an inn in Chappaqua. You know where that is? Upstate, on the rail line?"

"That sounds better. I can find it."

"Great. The inn there is called Darlington House. Easy walking distance from the train station. You know how to get to Grand Central and take the train north, up through Pleasantville, right?"

"Yes—"

Go there. The Darlington Inn, Chappaqua. We'll meet you there tonight."

"Not tonight," Partek corrected. As desperately as he wanted to have the meeting at once, he had to find a second-hand store and get some clothes no one could recognize from his previous use. He had to rent a car. And his brain was dying for lack of sleep. "Tomorrow night," he said.

"Okay, friend. That's just fine . . . You're all right?"

"Yes. For now I am fine. But I *must* know about . . . the things we have discussed relative to overseas. Perhaps then I can . . . come over."

"I understand. We will have an update for you."

"Yes. Please." Partek hung up.

In the Beekman Place offices, Charles Martin placed an immediate, high-security telephone call to Langley. He spoke to Dwight. Dwight said he would make an oral report and be on the afternoon shuttle. This, he said, might change a lot of recent decisions.

Dwight was excited.

So was Constance Hazeltine, the thirty-seven-year-old divorced mother of two who answered all the incoming calls. But she waited until after work that evening to call her friend.

His name was Bill Adwan. He was a member of the permanent United States diplomatic staff at the U.N., a translator and expert on Middle Eastern culture. He had been Constance's lover for almost two years and she worshiped him. She would not have allowed herself to doubt his word even if it had occurred to her to question his story about his "other duties" involving investigation of security risks.

She told Adwan about the telephone call from "Mr. East." She also told him what she had heard—at hair-raising personal risk—about the meeting to be held in Chappaqua.

Adwan could scarcely contain himself. He told her she was the most wonderful person in the world, and this information would be of great interest to his supervisors at the highest levels of U.S. government.

He said there would be another bonus in it for her.

Constance Hazeltine was thrilled. She was a good American, and she loved being of help. She could use the bonus, too. The last one had been for $2,000.

Adwan immediately made a call of his own to set up an emergency meeting with his contact person. But that person was about as far away from *any* branch of the U.S. government as it was possible to go.

twenty-three

"I suppose," Karyn Wechsting said Wednesday afternoon, "you still haven't reported Fjbk's attack on you."

"That's over with," I told her.

She gave me a disgusted look. "When do you go back home?"

"My flight is Sunday night."

"Well, we're reconfirmed for tomorrow. I think I'm more than ready. It's a beautiful city and the people are great—the crowds have been marvelous. But this ankle isn't getting any better, and if you're going to hang around until Fjbk has another go at you, I'd just as soon not be around to see the results."

"Karyn, there's no problem."

But of course there was a problem.

Already it had been a bastard of a day.

They ignored another meeting signal in the morning, and my "Jack Black" telephone call to the embassy was not answered, either. Of the five fictitious names on my memorized signal list, Jack Black was the ultimate escalation: *It has all hit the fan and we must meet at the designated place just as soon as you can get there.*

In this case, the final emergency place was in a park

near the Gazela Bridge. I stood there for almost three hours, pretending to take pictures, and nobody showed up.

So after the visit with Karyn I took the most circuitous route imaginable to the embassy. The bull by the horns, et cetera.

The Marine guard viewed me suspiciously, the receptionist was cold, the attaché for traveler assistance was baffled, and when I finally got into David Booth's office, he was livid.

"Can't you understand the message?" he asked hotly. "You have been pulled out. You're out of it. It's over."

"Fine work," I told him. "You meant all along to blow my cover and set me up, and you finally managed it."

"Nobody set you up. Just get out of here."

"Drop dead. I wasn't smart enough earlier, but even slow learners finally see the pattern: the stupid phone call on a bugged line, tipping the bona fides; Michael Nariv being so obvious; Paula Bansky, about as subtle as a Sherman tank. You intended for me to be picked up by the UDBA security system from the time I got off the plane."

"Not true," Booth said stiffly, without much conviction.

"The idea," I went on heatedly, "was for the militia to be watching me while you got the Beamer couple—or whatever their real names are—set up to do the deed while I had everybody looking the wrong way."

Booth sat back down behind his big, fancy walnut desk. His eyes sagged with something between contempt and fatigue. "Let's assume that's true. I'm not admitting it. But let's assume for argument's sake that it's true. The Beamers' attempt failed because of a fluke, and that can't be tried again. You're blown—and if you weren't before, you probably dragged half the UDBA down the street behind you just now. We're out of bullets, friend. When the bullets run out, you quit."

"Does that mean Danisa Lechova is being abandoned?"

Booth just stared at me.

"You can't abandon her," I said.

"Forget it."

"She'll never get out again after this, not while her brother is out of their control somewhere."

Booth's eyes narrowed. "You know about that part, do you?"

"I may be a little slow, but I'm not brain-dead. You told her about Partek. She made a tough decision. You got her hopes up. Now you just drop her? Say, 'Hey, forget it, we changed our mind'?"

Booth's mouth tightened. "Was there anything further? If it's sermon time, you might find an audience down the street at the Church of the—"

"Goddamn it!"

"I'm sorry this worked out badly from your viewpoint, Smith. You took the assignment in good faith and things didn't mesh. I regret that. But these things happen. The best course now is to prevent further losses. The girl is safe enough. The matter will be reviewed. Maybe something will be done at a later time."

"And that's that?" I said bitterly.

"That," he said, "is that."

I felt like hell when I walked into the stadium for the Evert match. Nobody was going to help, and after tonight's match I was going to have to tell Danisa that I was powerless.

It didn't make me feel any better, sitting in the stands with Karyn and Ted Treacher, when Danisa came out for the warmups, obviously searched for me with her eyes, and lit up when she saw me. Her wave—despite all the pressures —was pure joy.

"Oh, my," Karyn murmured ironically.

In the warmups Danisa looked cool and smooth, although the capacity crowd tonight, after the hot, sunny day, had already made the domed interior stifling hot, and both she and Evert began to perspire heavily. Chris lobbed up a few for Danisa and she blasted well-timed overheads. Imperturbable as always, Chris dumped some of them back into the net for the ballboys. Most of them went past her for winners.

I expected a hard and taxing match. It had not been a good year for Evert up until her fine losing effort at Wimbledon, and there was still speculation in the press about her possible retirement from the tour grind. She looked lean and concentrated tonight, however, and had played well in earlier matches. The soft, dark clay brought into the arena for this tournament at enormous cost was ideal for her patient, backcourt game. And I, like everybody else in the press corps, knew how much she wanted another crack at Martina or Steffi.

The linespeople were already in their chairs, and the referee came out and climbed up into the center-court chair as the women finished warmups with serves to opposite courts. Evert walked to her bench and Danisa to hers. They both toweled down, unusual after warmups but not in this oppressive heat. I noticed Danisa slip pale blue sweatbands over both wrists, something not normal for her. With these conditions, added to natural tenseness, the hands could sweat profusely, making the racket handle wet and slippery. It would be interesting to see how Danisa responded, having played so much of her career in cooler conditions.

While the woman in the chair summoned both players over for a few final words, my mind shunted to what I was now defining as The Problem.

How was I going to live with myself after abandoning her?

They couldn't keep her in the country forever, I told myself. Something would happen to her brother, Partek, wherever he was. Either he would vanish for good and the KGB and UDBA would have to make decisions on retaliation against the Lechovas when nothing was to be gained by it, or the KGB in America would locate Partek and make a dead man out of him.

That would free Danisa, as she would no longer have value as a bargaining chip. She might travel then . . . might even become a U.S. citizen one day. But she would never get to see or talk to her brother. And as for me, I would be seen as one of those who had failed her and contributed to her loss.

Letting her down was what rankled. Thinking I would never be with her again after the next day or two was what hurt.

Karyn Wechsting nudged me, gave me an inquiring look. "Are you paying attention?"

"Absolutely," I lied.

The players had gone back onto the court, Evert to serve. Playing a match with other contests going on simultaneously in this kind of proximity was still a new experience for Chris, too. She got the balls from the ballboy behind her and paused at the service line, waiting for the crowd to quiet. Only the people in the nearest sections did so. Others were caught up in the other matches going on so close by.

Evert looked across the net at Danisa, in her crouch, tiny blue skirt swaying slightly as she shifted her weight from foot to foot in anticipation. Then Evert tossed the ball and served, and the match was on.

From the outset it was close. Evert held serve at love, and Danisa returned the favor. In the third game Danisa worked the score to deuce with a howitzer forehand down the line, but Evert held through two long, seesaw rallies.

Danisa held in game 4, hitting her first ace. Both women traded hard, flat returns with underspin and occasional moon shots to break the pace. Evert toweled off again during the court change. As Danisa went to her bench and did likewise, she stumbled ever so slightly. I tensed, noticing it, and below me Fjbk sat up like he had been stabbed.

Danisa seemed to think nothing of it. She wiped her hands and racket handle again and returned to the court.

Evert spun in her serves and retreated a step deeper behind the baseline, setting up a prospective backcourt duel of attrition. I thought she might be making a mistake, as Danisa was so much younger and in superb condition. Twice in this game, however, Danisa seemed to start a fraction of a second late in moving crosscourt. She failed to get to either ball, although neither was particularly hard hit or severely angled.

"She looks leg-weary," Ted Treacher observed.

"These two-a-days have been a grind," Karyn said.

"Chrissie has been on the same schedule. She looks fresh enough."

Karyn frowned. "That's true. What think, Brad? Does Danisa look badly off form to you?"

"She looks loggy," I admitted. Even as we talked about it, I saw more signs of fatigue and even disorientation. I was worried. "She's missed some shots."

"Maybe she'll get going," Karyn said, ever the optimist.

For a few minutes it looked like she might be right. In the sixth game Danisa held again after being at deuce five times. The rallies had lengthened. Once I counted, and the ball crossed the net thirty-one times before Danisa made an unforced error off her forehand.

In the seventh game Danisa staggered slightly again on a change to the add court. She rubbed her hand across her forehead as if she were dazed. People around us noticed this time, and we could sense the little ripple of concerned speculation.

Danisa's color seemed to have gone in a twinkling. Her face glowed ghostlike under the brilliant overhead lights. All at once the concern hit me deep. *Was she really sick?*

Game 8. The second point. I leaned forward worriedly, watching with everything in me. Danisa's left knee seemed to buckle as she started forward to hit a short ball. She stopped and the shot passed her. She turned and looked after it, and then tilted her head to look up in the stands. And then she simply went down in a heap.

People cried out in alarm. One of the linesmen ran forward to help her, and Evert stared in disbelief, then hurried around the net to see what was going on. A couple of security people rushed out of the tunnel at the far end. Below us, the Lechovas were on their feet and Fjbk jumped the railing, knocking a security man down, to run onto the court.

"What the hell?" Karyn gasped. We were standing, too. Everyone was, and it was hard to see anything.

"Heat prostration?" Ted Treacher asked.

"It's not *that* hot, and it's early in the first set."

I peered down between people. Danisa lay sprawled on the clay. Her pale blue dress was stained black on one side where she had hit and rolled. She had gagged up a thin stream of colorless vomitus, and now stared up at Fjbk and the others with eyes that looked vacant and on the edge of shock.

There was a hurried consultation. A couple of locker room assistants, along with a man who must have been a doctor, came out. They had a stretcher and Danisa was gently placed on it. They carried her into the exit tunnel. The applause was scattered, shocked.

I turned to my companions. "I've got to go see."

They nodded and didn't try to go with me. I climbed to the top row and then fought the milling crowds in getting to the far end. There was a hassle with a security guard who didn't know whether to honor press credentials. When I finally got into the bleacher tunnel and made my way to the locker rooms, it was pandemonium.

Blue and white lights rotated, flashing blindingly, at an opened outside door. Medical technicians were just loading a gurney inside. Danisa, apparently unconscious, was on it. I tried to work my way through, but didn't make it in time. The attendants jumped into the ambulance behind the gurney and closed the doors. The ambulance pulled away, lights still flashing, siren beginning to wail.

twenty-four

The hospital was an ugly concrete monolith surrounded by parking lots and squalid apartments. It looked its origins: the hasty, haphazard construction that had come in the early years after World War II, when no one had time for good planning or design, and everything had to be "proletarian"—for which read "big and tasteless"—anyway.

The interior of the main building looked like something that had been built cheaply on designs for 1920: bare plaster walls, yellow tile floors, high wood windows, and doors with transoms, ceilings with exposed pipes and ventilators. I found the emergency area, and there, standing in a waiting room with shabby plastic furniture and faded cardboard pictures of mountains, were the rest of the Lechova family, a couple of uniformed militia, and of course Fjbk.

Just down a narrow hallway, through an open divider, I spotted a flurry of activity in an emergency treatment room. I could see two nurses and a pharmacist or lab technician and a doctor. They were all working over somebody—Danisa?—on a gurney.

The Lechovas turned anxiously to me as I entered. Fjbk, standing slightly apart at a window, was so worried he forgot to glower.

"You are here, Mr. Smith," Mrs. Lechova said with great solemnity. "Good." She was pale and her eyes looked haunted.

Before I could respond, Hannah ran to me and seized both my arms. Tears bolted from her vivid eyes. "Oh, Brad Smith! Did you see what happened? Of course you did! Poor Danisa! What can be wrong with her? My God! What if she is dying? I will find poison for myself! I could not live a day with such tragedy!"

"It might be something a lot simpler, Hannah. The heat—"

"Or food poisoning," Leon Lechova said. He fixed me with eyes that were at pinpoints of shock. "She said she started having a headache in the third game. And then—she felt weak, and some of the balls seemed blurred in her vision. You saw how she began sweating."

"It was awfully hot."

"But not that hot. She was sweating far more than Evert. We noticed that, commented on it. And then she was dizzy—she stumbled—"

"I saw that."

"And she vomited."

"What does the doctor say?"

Lechova shook his head. "The doctor says he knows nothing yet. They will test."

"Is that what they're doing back there now?"

"I watched until they put me out. They said I was in the way. They washed her hands and arms, repeatedly. They put a needle in her arm, gave her some kind of injection."

I looked at Mrs. Lechova. "That sounds to me like they've got some kind of idea what's wrong."

"She is very weak. The doctor told us she will be fine. But how can he know?"

Hannah cried, "She must be fine! She must recover from this and be as good as new again!"

There was an interruption. Chris Evert, with two

companions, hurried in. She was still sweat-soaked, in the dress she had worn on court.

I was nearest the corridor, so she saw me first. "Hi, Brad. How is she?"

"Holding her own," I told her.

"What happened to her? One minute she was going along fine, and the next she started looking really bad!"

"We don't know yet, Chris."

"She's going to be okay, right?"

"Well, she's no worse."

"It was a wonderful match. She's great. I really like her. Damn." She went on into the room to speak to the others.

After a few minutes she said she was going back to the stadium to shower and change, but would call in an hour to check Danisa's condition at that time. She told the Lechovas how sorry she was, and what a wonderful competitor Danisa was. Lechova was stiff, proud. Geneta Lechova let a tear escape and slide down her face, and Hannah impulsively gave Chrissie a hug as she started out. Through all of it, Fjbk remained at the window, black eyes missing nothing, but taking no part; he acted like a man in a trance.

During the visit I managed to slip closer to the hallway leading to the treatment rooms. I needed a clue about what had happened, if I could get it. From the head of the hall I could see Danisa's sock feet sticking out from the end of the white cloth that covered her. The doctor was gaunt, black-bearded, and intent. As I watched, he injected a tiny amount of a clear fluid into the IV connector attached to Danisa's left arm. One of the nurses sponged and dried her hands.

Danisa appeared to be conscious. Unlike her appearance on court, when her pallor had been scary, she looked flushed, and I could tell she was breathing hard. I saw one of the nurses give her a drink of water.

Evert and her friends left the emergency area. I turned back.

"She is wonderful!" Hannah said. "It was wonderful for her to come. She is great lady and I like her a lot."

"Danisa would have beaten her," Lechova said hollowly. He looked hard at Hannah. "Now you will play her."

"I can't think about that now! I am so worried!"

"But you *must* think about it!" Lechova snapped.

"What?"

His face worked angrily. "Danisa is now out of the tournament she would have won. It is all up to you now, Hannah."

Hannah's gasp was audible.

Lechova waggled a finger at her. "You carry the family name. You have a responsibility to your sister—to us—to Yugoslavia."

"Poppa—"

"You must be great now, and win!"

Hannah looked stricken, like a child given an impossible school task. Her mother was standing just beyond her. For an instant, Geneta Lechova's expression twisted in transparent disappointment and pain.

Lechova seemed to sense he had gone too far. "Danisa will want you to win for her," he added lamely.

"I will do my best, Poppa."

"It is, furthermore, your chance for greatness. Such a personal challenge can be the making—"

"Leon," Mrs. Lechova said, putting a hand on his arm. "Not now."

He flushed, looked at the floor, and then walked across the waiting area to say something to Fjbk.

Hannah stared at her mother, then at me. I felt sorry for her. In this unguarded moment, all the breezy flamboyance was gone and she stood there for what she was: a pretty, uncertain kid who was scared half out of her wits.

She left the waiting room.

I went closer to Geneta Lechova. "It's going to be fine," I told her with more confidence than I felt.

"You see how it is with us," she said dully.

"He's upset. He wasn't thinking."

"Danisa must get away. If not now, then when she can. He would have her destroy herself for"—she trembled violently with revulsion—"pride. *His* pride."

I kept quiet. There were no words that could undo two decades of Lechova's corrosive, unyielding ambition.

But this, I saw, was one of the two reasons why Danisa's mother could be my ally. Geneta Lechova might never escape her husband's vise of unhappy perfectionism. But she could help me try to give Danisa the liberation her mother would never know.

The other reason? Love.

We were interrupted by one of the male attendants coming out of the treatment area. He glanced around and spied Danisa's clothes bag and rackets, which had been tossed into the ambulance with her and brought to the waiting room. They were stacked against the wall beside a yellow plastic chair.

The attendant picked up the gear and carried it back down the narrow treatment corridor. I could see him enter a doorway at the far end.

A suspicion dawned in me. "What was that all about?" I asked.

"They wish to examine those things," Lechova said. He was matter-of-fact, preoccupied.

We stood around a minute or two.

"I must go see if Hannah is all right," Mrs. Lechova said, and walked out of the waiting area, going in the direction Hannah had gone.

I shifted my weight from foot to foot. The two police stood just outside in the hall, smoking. Lechova and Fjbk were in deep, quiet conversation, Lechova's arm over Fjbk's brawny shoulders in brotherly fashion. No one was paying any attention to me, and this was my chance.

I went through the doorway into the treatment corridor. They were still busy with Danisa in the second room. I went past that door and to the end of the corridor.

It was a utility washroom and the door stood open.

Inside, the male attendant was bent over a deep sink half
filled with sudsy water. Danisa's rackets were out of their
case and on the cabinet beside him—all but the one he had
in his hands. He was scrubbing hell out of the handle and
grip with a soapy towel.

That told me enough to make an educated guess.

I turned and went back the way I had come. Nobody
noticed me. I was so angry I began to shake in the waiting
room. But nobody noticed that, either.

We waited interminably, more than two additional
hours. The doctor, whose name was Bulganik, came out
several times to say Danisa was doing fine. He said he had
no idea yet what had caused her collapse, but her tempera-
ture was getting back to normal and her other symptoms
were abating. He was not a good liar, but no one else
seemed to notice the evasive shifting of his eyes.

Maleeva, the UDBA man, appeared. He asked a lot of
questions and seemed genuinely upset. I thought he was a
good actor. I wanted very, very badly to punch him out. He
conferred with the militia in the outside hallway, gave me a
long and suspicious stare, and said he would be back later.

More time passed. The wall clock passed ten. Finally
there was more activity visible in the treatment corridor:
attendants wheeling Danisa out and in our direction.

She was conscious. We surrounded her gurney for a few
seconds. She still looked flushed, and her pupils were
widely dilated.

"Oh, Danisa! We were so worried!" Hannah exploded.

"I'm fine now," Danisa said weakly.

"We love you," her mother said, squeezing her hand.

Danisa's dazed eyes found me. "Brad . . .?" Tears
came.

I bent over her and soothed my hand through her
moist, wonderful hair. I kissed her forehead. "You're okay,
babe. It's okay."

She clutched my hand for an instant, then let go as the attendants moved her gurney on.

Her father and Fjbk stood mute, at a loss for a reaction.

The attendants wheeled her on out of the area. Dr. Bulganik came out of the treatment rooms and faced us. Out of deference to me or because he was proud of the ability, he spoke heavily accented English.

"We wish to keep her here through the night to assure ourselves there is no more trouble," he told us. "But I think for sure she can be released in morning, go home."

"What caused the sickness?" Leon Lechova demanded.

"More studies must be done before any final answer can be given. But we think food poisoning."

"I knew it!"

"But she is okay. That is biggest thing, eh?"

He hurried away. The family conferred. Respecting their privacy, I drifted into the hall.

Who the hell . . . ? I thought.

Which was when I saw him.

Standing at the far end of the hall, smoking a cigarette.

The KGB man, Altunyan.

Good God!

I took a step in his direction, but got no farther because Fjbk came out of the emergency room behind me and caught my arm.

"She will be of no more use to you now," he said blackly. "You will leave her alone so she can get well."

"You idiot," I said hotly. "Are you so hung up on your jealousy you still haven't figured out what probably happened to her?"

He went blank and let go of my arm. "You know?"

"Not for sure." I pointed. "You see shitface down there? Our friendly neighborhood KGB man? Ask *him* what happened. Or ask Maleeva."

"What would they know? Danisa had heatstroke!"

"You poor, dumb bastard."

"What do you know?" He seized my arm again, hurting me. "You tell me!"

"Ask him," I said, angling my head in Altunyan's direction.

Fjbk stared. "He is gone."

I glanced down there. He was right. Altunyan was nowhere to be seen.

"You tell me," Fjbk rumbled threateningly.

"No. Have one of *them* tell you. Ask yourself why they scrubbed her racket handles."

"You think the Chekist made my Danisa sick?"

"Ask him, Fjbk." I walked away from him and left the hospital and found a cab.

On the way back across the Sava to the hotel, I reviewed what had happened. I was no longer of a mind to be a good soldier. This time they had gone too far. This time they had *hurt* her, might have ended her life. Was there any way—the slimmest chance—that I could get her out of this madhouse country without help from the boys downtown or anybody else?

One idea was forming in my mind. I examined it. It was a long shot, but if Danisa was released in the morning as the doctor had promised—and if she could possibly walk a few hundred yards—it might just be crazy enough to work.

And after what had just happened, I was ready to try anything.

twenty-five

Elsewhere

New York

The flight with the man named Sylvester on board landed at LaGuardia shortly after 6 o'clock Wednesday evening. Sylvester retrieved his check-through suitcase and went directly to the Hertz counter. By 7:30 P.M. he was off airport property and driving his rented car through hectic freeway traffic.

Sylvester had not eaten for many hours, but food was the last thing on his mind. When he stopped outside a convenience store in White Plains, it was to unlock his suitcase and feel through the clothing inside to assure himself that his foil- and towel-wrapped Makarov pistol had not been disturbed. Both the automatic and its paper-wrapped package of 9 mm ammunition were just as he had packed them. The syringe and puff device were fine, too.

As an afterthought, he went into the convenience store and bought a plastic cup of coffee and a package of Hostess cupcakes. He downed his meager supper on the road.

He drove sedately. There was no hurry now. He knew his quarry would be in Chappaqua soon. This time there would be no slips.

259

* * *

Virginia

At almost the same time Sylvester began his drive north, Kinkaid and Exerblein met Dwight at his home. He had a pot of coffee ready, and they took their cups into the paneled office he had built into his basement. It was quiet there, and virtually soundproof, a good-sized room with closed-in ceiling, shag carpet, fishing pictures and a map of Southeast Asia on the walls, a desk, two occasional chairs, and a sleeper sofa.

Kinkaid sat on the couch, the waxen Exerblein on one of the chairs. Both were still in their suit pants and dress shirts open at the collar. Dwight, wearing shapeless golf slacks and a Lands' End cotton T-shirt, stood behind his desk.

"This time everything has been cleared and recleared," he told them. He grimaced. "You take the shuttle in the morning. You'll be met by a man with your car. He doesn't go along; it's just the two of you. You drive on up there. You check into this motel"—he held up a match folder with advertising on it—"under your traveling names. Your contact from the FBI is Joe Darby. He'll call you no later than six o'clock."

Dwight paused, looking at both men. The slight curl of his lip betrayed his displeasure. "You will tell him his sister is safe. We are still working on getting her out. We urgently request him to surrender himself now and seek immediate political asylum.

"We are now playing by all the rules. The surrender itself—assuming he agrees—will be an FBI operation. Since Partek knows you, Kinkaid, you have to be in on the meeting to make sure he sees he's being approached by the right people. The FBI will take him into protective custody. I am informed that the FBI guys will then take him straight back to New York in an armored limousine, and our interviews will be started either in a safe house there or back in this area."

"How many people will they have there?" Kinkaid asked.

"Not more than three, under cover."

"Is that enough? If the other side gets wind of this—"

"No, I agree with this part of the plan, anyway. The fewer people we put on the deal, the less attention we draw. Partek will be checked in at the inn and you and the FBI man will make a simple, direct contact. Once he has been reassured, we think he'll go for our offer. Assuming so, you then walk him outside and into the limo. Exerblein, you're outside the building in your separate car. You'll be armed for this one."

Exerblein nodded. He looked almost sleepy. "And the extra FBI agents will know to stay out of sight—be discreet?"

"We can devoutly hope so."

Kinkaid said, "I would prefer that we did this by ourselves."

"That's been overruled, so forget it."

"Is there any reason to believe the other side has any inkling of this?"

"None. But we had no warning the other time, either."

"So we assume there just might be trouble."

"Of course. But we don't expect it."

"Why do we wait until tomorrow evening?"

"Our trace showed he was calling from Queens. He has to get to Chappaqua and we know he left his truck in Montana. He seemed to think he needed the time. We had no choice in the matter."

"I don't like the extra waiting. It just gives the other side more time to catch on."

"Not if we keep the operation small and quiet. Which we're doing."

"Okay."

The three men looked at each other.

Kinkaid asked, "What time do we plan actually to make the contact?"

"Darby will decide on the scene. But the tentative schedule says ten o'clock tomorrow night, after the dinner hour, with things nice and quiet in the inn."

Nobody said anything.

"Other questions?" Dwight asked.

It was Kinkaid who broached the matter: "What's the truth about his sister in Belgrade?"

Dwight's eyes turned more bleak. "It is the judgment at this time that no opportunities exist for a viable attempt to remove Danisa Lechova from Belgrade. The matter will be reviewed on a regular basis."

"In other words, she's fucked."

"Let's just not mess up the Partek defection. Convince him to come over now. Once we have him safe and starting interrogation, maybe the Danisa Lechova matter will look different to higher-ups."

Exerblein stirred. "Yes," he said with absolutely no emotion. "After all, once we have Partek, the Lechova woman doesn't really matter much, does she?"

Dwight's distaste was obvious, but he said nothing in response. Instead he picked up a map case off the floor behind his desk, opened it atop the flat surface, and took out a city map and some faded blueprints. "Let's look at the street layout in Chappaqua, and the design of the building. Then we can run it all through in detail."

Kinkaid and Exerblein got up and joined Dwight in bending over the desk.

New Belgrade

The hour was now far past midnight. Miloslav Fjbk still stood in the deepest shadows of the hospital's emergency parking lot.

The others had departed. Upstairs, his beloved Danisa slept, a pale statue. The doctor had said she would recover totally, and be discharged in the morning, perhaps as little as ten hours from now. But Fjbk's shocked senses still reeled under the knowledge that she had seemed so very sick, so on the brink of death itself.

Fjbk was not sure whether to believe Brad Smith. But he had surreptitiously examined Danisa's racket case after it was placed in the small metal locker in her ward. Smith had not lied about that part: the handles of all five rackets were soaked from washing.

Smith had pointed to Altunyan, who, Fjbk knew, was a secret operative, almost surely KGB. Altunyan had vanished. But Fjbk had to have an answer to this. He had to know if Altunyan knew what had happened to his Danisa, and who had done whatever had been done to her.

Altunyan, Fjbk thought, would be back yet this night if he was suspicious that Danisa had been purposely harmed.

And if Altunyan returned, Fjbk would ask him directly.

The shocking collapse during the match with Chris Evert had been a vast disappointment to Fjbk. He had known—felt in his bones—that at last she was ready, and would prevail. And that was to be the start of a march to world dominance in women's tennis . . . her glory as well as his vindication and revenge on the Lendls and Beckers, all who had dismissed him. This tourney was to have been the first step on the final road to fame and fortune for both of them.

The disappointment about the tournament, however, was nothing compared to Fjbk's pain for Danisa herself. The thought that someone would purposely harm this beautiful, graceful, compelling woman filled him with miserable rage. He had vowed that no one would ever harm her, and it had happened right under his nose!

He would wait all night, if necessary, to see if Altunyan came back, could shed any light. He intended to make this crime his personal crusade. He owed it to Danisa. He would never rest until the mystery had been solved and she had been avenged.

Fjbk did not have to wait all night.

His wrist chronometer showed a few minutes past 1:30
A.M. when a dark Mercedes pulled into the lot and parked
near the emergency room doors. In the feeble light from the
entranceway, Fjbk's adjusted eyes clearly saw Altunyan get
out of the car and hurry inside.

Fjbk waited, blood thumping turgidly in his ears. His
worry and anger made him feel not himself, almost sick at
his stomach.

Twenty minutes passed.

Then Altunyan came back out, walking briskly for his
car.

Fjbk left the deepest shadows and hurried across the
pavement, intercepting the Russian beside his car. "Comrade. A word, please," he said in his best Russian.

Altunyan spun, recognized him, and relaxed slightly.
"You startled me, my friend."

"What of Danisa?"

"I have just inquired of the doctors. She is recovering.
She will be released in the morning, but will be very weak
for several days. All is well."

"What was done to her?"

"I have no idea," Altunyan said innocently. "My concern is that of a sports enthusiast—"

"No lies!" Fjbk rasped. "I know you are security. I think
you are of the KGB. That is of no consequence. Danisa is my
ward, my pupil. Her safety is my overriding concern. I must
know what happened to her!" In his fervor he grabbed the
lapels of Altunyan's jacket.

The Russian, though considerably taller, was pushed
off balance against the car. "Release me!"

"Tell me the truth! I know they washed the handles of
the rackets! She was poisoned!"

The Russian's face twisted with surprise and alarm.
"Who told you such a thing?"

"Tell me what you know! I will find the people who did
this!"

Now it was Altunyan who grabbed Fjbk, clutching his

thick bare arms in his hands. "Fjbk. I know your background. You have worked for the KGB. Your loyalty has never been in question."

Fjbk felt shock trickle through him. "How do you know this?" Then he saw. "It is true, then. You *are* KGB."

Altunyan nodded, admitting it. "Now you must listen, Fjbk. There are factors here beyond your knowledge. What I did to the Lechova girl was for her own safety, for her country as well as mine."

Fjbk staggered back a half-step. It felt like he had been hit in the chest with a sledgehammer. *"You did this?"*

"Silence! Lower your voice! Listen to me! The organic phosphate insecticide, with a penetrating agent, could not seriously harm her. Painted on her rackets, it penetrated when she sweated. But the treatment with atropine sulfate is reliable, and all was in readiness for treatment."

"She could have died!"

"Lower your voice, I say! No. She was never in danger."

Fjbk reeled mentally. Altunyan and everything else had gotten blurry, red-tinged and indistinct. The horror and anger were out of all bounds, like nothing Fjbk had ever experienced, even as a terrified youth in the war.

"You swine!" he said. "You *govno!*"

"Control yourself, Fjbk. You—"

"You just hurt my Danisa! You will pay for it!"

Altunyan moved, and a small automatic appeared in his hand. "Get back, you fool."

Fjbk's rage burst out of control.

With a guttural obscenity and speed far faster than the Russian anticipated, he knocked the gun out of his hand. Fjbk then went for Altunyan's throat with both hands— closed powerful fists around the Russian's windpipe.

Altunyan lurched sideways, trying to fight. But he was too late and the Serb was far too strong in his crazy rage. Altunyan's very movement in self-defense twisted his body too far, wrenching his neck just as Fjbk squeezed convulsively.

There was a crunching sound.

Altunyan gasped and went limp.

His collapse to the pavement almost pulled Fjbk down on top of him.

Sobbing for air, Fjbk looked down at what he had done. He dropped to one knee and probed with his fingertips for the carotid artery, easily detected in the lolling, grotesquely shattered neck.

There was no pulse.

Fjbk panicked. He looked around.

Only a few feet from the parked car stood a large trash container, heavy steel, with a canted lid, of the type that was picked up whole by a collection truck and carried away for dumping. With strength born of his desperation, Fjbk picked up Altunyan's body and heaved it over the high lip of the container and out of sight. Looking around again, he saw no one. It had all been unobserved. He turned and ran.

twenty-six

I was in the shower at 6:15 Thursday morning when the hotel telephone started ringing. *The hospital? Danisa?*

Insides shriveling at the thought of a turn for the worse, I padded out of the bathroom and picked up the receiver.

"Yes?"

"Your car is ready." The connection broke.

I stood there for a few seconds, dripping and listening to dial tone. Then I remembered to hang up. It had been a man's voice I had never heard before. But there was no mistaking the message. I toweled off and pulled clothes on fast.

Less than ten minutes later I walked through the Metropol lobby and out into the humid gray of dawn. A slight breeze tossed the trees in the Tašmajdan. A sleepy porter stood against the wall, hands in his pockets. A Fiat with a tournament official sticker on its side pulled out of the parking and up to the curb in front of me. The driver—young, male, a stranger—leaned across the front seat to pop the door open for me. I got in.

We drove onto Bulevar Revolucije. It was almost devoid of traffic. My driver, sandy-haired, freckled, with the arms of a weight lifter, promptly turned right, went a block, and turned left again. He had one eye on the rearview mirror.

"What's happened?" I asked.

"I don't know, sir," he said with the faintest New England accent.

"Where are we going?"

"Please just wait, sir."

Fine, I thought. *Ignore me for a week and then drag me out with the emergency signal and start this cloak-and-dagger shit.*

I watched unfamiliar parts of the city stream past the car windows, and tried to still the scared voice of panic inside, the one yammering that Danisa had taken a turn for the worse at the hospital . . . *oh my God* . . . might be dead.

It was not yet 7 A.M. when the driver nosed our Fiat into a cobblestone alley running behind medieval houses and small business buildings in what felt like an area far from the city center. He pulled up behind a home with a crumbling rock wall and unkempt small trees and tangled vines in the garden beyond. There was a broken wrought-iron archway and gate.

"Through there, sir."

"Through the garden, here?"

"Right."

I got out of the car and slammed the door. He pulled away smartly, leaving me standing there. Feeling suddenly very small and very vulnerable, I hustled through the broken iron gate, along a narrow brick walk almost hidden by creepers, and to the back wooden door of the house. The door was standing open. I went in. Booth himself stood waiting for me in the dusty kitchen.

"You made good time," he told me.

"What's happened?" I demanded.

He signaled to a door into a hallway. "In here."

I followed him. The hall ran the depth of the old house with high-ceilinged rooms opening off either side. There was a heavyset man in a summer suit standing partway up the hall, the kind of man one senses he does not want to irritate. Up toward the front door another man stood; he was rumpled, soft-faced, evidently half-asleep, with eyes that just for an instant gave me an examination of X-ray intensity. Sometimes the lazy-looking country boys are the most dangerous.

Booth led me into a parlor—old overstuffed couch and chairs, end tables with peeling mahogany veneer, fringed lampshades, an antique coffee table holding white Styrofoam cups of steaming coffee, some file folders, three Motorola walkie-talkies. Mitchell was there, on his feet, by a lace-curtained window.

Booth signaled me to one of the fat old chairs. "Do you know anything about Altunyan?" he demanded.

"He's KGB. I think he doped Danisa Lechova's racket handles to make—"

"Fuck that. He's dead."

"What?"

Booth's eyes looked like rocks. "Altunyan is dead. His body was found in a trash dumpster behind the hospital about two hours ago. The hospital where they took Lechova last night, and you were last seen before you turned up at the hotel."

I was stunned. "What happened to him?"

"Somebody broke his neck for him."

"Great. But I didn't do it."

Both Booth and Mitchell were watching me the way an experimental psychologist watches her rats. "You don't know anything about it?"

"Hell no! Did you think I would? Is that why you had me hauled over here? You thought I killed Altunyan?"

"More likely, you know who did."

"I don't know anything. Listen. I'm beginning to feel pissed off here. I don't know anything about anything. I've begged you guys for a contact for days. You've ignored me. *Now* you drag me out to give me the third degree about a murder. Did you ever read my folder? I'm a scut. I deliver papers and pass messages. I'm chickenshit. I had to take the hand-weapons course twice to pass it. I'm a devout coward. I walk around bugs on the sidewalk to avoid bloodshed. If somebody killed Altunyan, great. I'm happy. But I don't know anything about it."

Booth studied me intently during my effusion. His shoulders slumped a bit as he seemed to relax. "Good," he said finally. "Do you want some coffee?"

I accepted one of the white plastic cups. "What does this do to the Lechova operation?"

"There is no Lechova operation."

"She's been abandoned?"

"It's been put on hold."

"Because?"

Booth sat down on the couch facing me and crossed his legs. "Because those are our orders from home. So let's not have any discussion."

"I want to tell you something."

"Tell."

I told them about seeing the orderly scrubbing the racket handles in the treatment room, and what I thought had happened.

"Interesting," Booth said when I finished. "You figure Altunyan did it?"

"Who else?"

"Why not Maleeva or some other UDBA scut?"

"It doesn't figure. Yugoslavia has too much invested in making Danisa a world star. The poisoning took her out of the tournament."

Booth nodded. "Let's just surmise something. Let's surmise that you've gotten involved with this Lechova girl."

"I—!"

"Be calm, Smith. Nobody would blame you too much. I've seen her. Beautiful girl. Great legs. So let's surmise you've gotten involved—all right, *mildly* involved—with her. Then we abort the mission. You're upset. Then somebody damned near kills her and you figure out it almost has to be Altunyan. You confront him. He tells you to blow it out your barracks bag. You struggle and you manage somehow to break his neck."

"There are only two things wrong with that, Booth. I'm incapable of beating up a trained agent like Altunyan, number one, and number two, I didn't do it."

"Who, then?"

I had already been coming to a conclusion while we talked about the rest of it. "Fjbk."

"Why?"

"I told him I thought the Russian had doped the handles."

Booth exchanged glances with the silent Mitchell. "All right. That makes sense."

"Why does it matter, as long as it wasn't me?" I demanded.

"First, we had to feel fairly confident it wasn't you, so we'll know how to proceed if they arrest you."

"They wouldn't—"

"The hell they wouldn't, if they strongly suspect you. Second, this changes things pertaining to Danisa Lechova. The UDBA is going to be in a shitstorm over this murder. Up until now, they couldn't touch Danisa because, like you said, she's an emerging national heroine and she was in this tournament. Now she's out of the tournament and not exempt from arrest anymore."

"Why would they arrest her?"

"Why wouldn't they arrest anybody they thought might shed some light on the Altunyan murder? They'll surely see some kind of a cause-and-effect relationship between her sudden illness and the finding of Altunyan's body behind her hospital less than twelve hours later."

So Danisa was in more peril than before. My stomach hurt.

Booth suddenly asked, "When do you go home?"

"Sunday."

"Good. In the meantime, keep your nose clean."

"What about Danisa?"

"I told you: it's not our problem anymore."

"And if she gets arrested or hassled?"

Booth patiently repeated, "It's not our problem any-more." He picked up one of the walkie-talkies and pressed the transmit button for about two seconds. A moment later, its speaker hissed with the carrier of a return signal carrying no audio.

"The car will be back for you in a couple of minutes," he told me. He stood and offered his hand. "Thanks for the information. My advice to you is to stay clear of Danisa Lechova until you leave Yugoslavia. She may be in some trouble and there's no reason for you to get involved."

"Thank you," I said.

Fuck you, I thought.

I had decided last night that I was going to go into the kind of Wyatt Earp configuration I had always despised in others. Danisa deserved a chance, and I thought I saw a way to offer it to her. It was risky and it would take luck, but okay: I already had the plan tentatively in motion.

And nothing these guys had said to me changed that a bit. On the contrary. Now I was sure I had to get her out, or—

I almost said, "die trying."

I didn't expect to die if I failed.

Twenty years in a Yugoslav prison, maybe. Along with the knowledge that I had wrecked her life with my bungling. Enough.

The driver dumped me off close to the hotel. I shaved and changed clothes and took a taxi to the hospital. It was after 9 A.M. when the doctor signed authorization for Danisa to be discharged.

Geneta Lechova waited with me. She had a small bag with Danisa's going-home clothes.

"My husband has taken Hannah for a light workout," she told me. Her expression was that flinty kind people sometimes get when they are hiding everything. "They will meet us at home later."

"Fjbk is with them?"

She countered, "Are you going to help her?"

"I'm going to try."

"When—"

"Maybe the less you know, the better. Besides," I added lamely, "nothing definite has been decided anyway."

She accepted that with grave silence.

In a little while we were allowed upstairs. We found Danisa in a medium-sized ward, pale sunlight spilling across the barren room from high, soot-streaked windows. Several other women lay in their beds or plodded about in hospital robes and slippers. Danisa got up from the side of her thin bed when we walked in. Wearing a faded green robe and shapeless canvas slippers, she looked totally wrung out and colorless. But her smile beamed, lighting her face, when she saw us. We hurried over, her mother embraced her. I did, too.

"How do you feel?" her mother asked.

Danisa brushed a wisp of hair out of her eyes. The gesture emphasized her feminine vulnerability. "Weak. A little fuzzy. I don't remember a lot after the match started, Momma."

"Have you eaten this morning?"

"Horse food."

"What?"

Danisa made a funny child's face of revulsion. "Oat cereal! I left it."

Mrs. Lechova laughed. "Once you are dressed, we can go home. There is no horse food there, but fresh rolls and cakes."

Danisa moved closer to look at the contents of the suitcase. She moved slowly and cautiously, as if aware she might lose her balance and fall. That didn't bode well for my plan.

I said I would wait for them outside the ward. I located a visitors' waiting area not far from the nursing station and

273

stood at the dirty window, burning one of my newly acquired Yugoslav cigarettes. They were harsh and not very pleasant, but any nicotine in a storm.

There had been no problem last night in tracking down Ted Treacher, deep in a poker game at the hotel. Karyn Wechsting had been out on the town with a couple of reporters and several other tournament players, but had come back not long after midnight with a sad face and questions about why Communists didn't dance. I asked the two of them to go for a stroll with me, and both read my expression and agreed, puzzled.

The Belgrade streets were vast and vacant, streetlights shining on empty pavement and black storefronts. I didn't see any signs of being followed. After they had asked about Danisa's condition and expressed their puzzlement, I told them I could explain a lot of things.

Except for the part about Danisa's brother in America, I gave it to them fairly straight. I left out some things.

"I *knew* that business about a burglar in your room was bullshit," Karyn said triumphantly. "And that's why you wouldn't notify the police."

"So what happens now?" Treacher demanded. "Hell! You really think somebody *poisoned* her to try to keep her home?"

"I think so," I said. "But there still may be a chance to get her out. It's a long shot but it might be tried."

"Can we help?" Karyn asked.

"As a matter of fact, yes."

"Tell us."

I did.

"Great!" Karyn said when I finished.

"Ted? What think?"

Treacher's face filled with laugh lines. "I'll do my part. So will Karyn. So go for it."

Maybe it was crazy. But I intended to. Right now, working on my third cigarette, I was aware of the pressure starting to build.

We didn't have a lot of time.

Danisa and her mother walked out of the ward. Mrs. Lechova carried the bag and everything else. Danisa looked pale, and walked slowly. They joined me.

"I will sign the papers at the desk," Danisa's mother said.

Danisa looked toward the elevators. "Brad and I will go on downstairs—wait for you out in the fresh air."

I took part of the gear from Mrs. Lechova and we separated, Danisa and I heading for the first floor. She sighed a couple of times in the elevator and I saw the close quarters were bothering her. Once out in front of the great concrete monolith, however, under a thin sun and with a humid breeze stirring her hair, she seemed better.

"I think I'm hungry," she said with a smile.

"Danisa, we don't have much time. If we're going, it's right away."

"There is some chance?" she asked, surprised.

"There's one possible way. It isn't authorized. It doesn't have backing. The chances of its working may be less than fifty-fifty, and we'll need some luck. But if you want to try it, we will."

She continued to study my face, and her expression made butterflies in my midsection. Finally she said, "Will you take me?"

"Yes."

"Then I am ready."

twenty-seven

Elsewhere

Militia Headquarters

At 10:10 A.M., Major Ladislav Maleeva's emergency meeting was interrupted by the insistent chirping of his beeper.

"Continue," he told the other investigators in the room. He went to a private office nearby and called the operator.

Lieutenant Rodor, in charge of surveillance on the street, had left a number. Maleeva called it.

Rodor told him, "The Smith man appeared at the hospital. He met Mrs. Lechova. Danisa Lechova was released from the hospital. Smith went with the two women to the Lechova apartment. He then returned to the Metropol. The electronic equipment proves he is still in his room."

"How did Danisa Lechova look to you?" Maleeva asked.

"Not good. Very weak, like someone after a long illness."

"And she is . . . ?"

"At the family apartment. We believe, however, she will leave shortly to meet Smith at the hotel."

"On what basis?"

"Our telephone tap intercepted a message from Smith to Danisa. He said he wishes one more interview before his Sunday departure. He asked when she might feel well enough to talk. Danisa Lechova stated that she could meet him at his hotel room to assure no interruption of their final talk. When asked when the meeting might be held, she told Smith she would prefer to meet him as soon as possible. She said she and her mother may take a few days' recuperation on the Adriatic coast."

"All right," Maleeva said after a moment's thought. "You will continue surveillance of Danisa Lechova. If she goes into Smith's room, use the monitors next door and make sure every word is recorded for analysis."

"Do we also post a man in the hall and lobby?"

"No. We need our manpower on the Altunyan investigation. You stay in the electronic surveillance room. The listening equipment will warn us in time when the interview is concluded and one or both are about to leave. I will join you within the hour."

Lieutenant Rodor rang off. Maleeva headed back for the meeting room.

Maleeva was irritated, puzzled, and worried. He did not know what, if anything, Smith was now planning.

The Altunyan disaster, meanwhile, had complicated everything a thousandfold.

The body of the KGB Resident, his neck broken, had been found by a hospital orderly in the predawn hours. Shock waves had already rippled all the way to Moscow, and everybody higher up was screaming. Maleeva had no idea how or why the murder had occurred, or even precisely when.

Maleeva was hardly heartbroken about it. He hadn't liked Altunyan. He had never liked or trusted any Chekist. But having a trusted senior operative of the KGB murdered in your jurisdiction was not the kind of thing that looked good on your record. Maleeva had to pull out all the stops in trying to solve this one.

The earlier mystery—Danisa Lechova's collapse during tournament play Wednesday night—was now partly explained. Maleeva's man inside the hospital had reported promptly and well. Lechova had been treated with repeated 2-milligram doses of atropine sulfate. Her collapse had been caused by skin absorption of a powerful insecticide. The doctor's instructions to an aide for cleansing of the handles of her tennis rackets pointed incontrovertibly to the fact that the poison had been painted on the handles, probably with an added agent such as PCP to facilitate absorption. When Lechova began perspiring freely during her match, her pores had opened and the poison had entered her system to begin its work.

The doctor was being questioned now. So far, although obviously frightened, he was pretending ignorance. He would be broken eventually; his diagnosis at the hospital emergency room had been too swift for guesswork, and his instructions to wash the racket handles made a mockery of his pretense of innocence.

Maleeva suspected Brad Smith of involvement in the attack on Lechova, although the logic of such an escapade eluded him. Perhaps a plan to make her sick, and spirit her away in a bogus ambulance? Whatever the scheme, it had backfired. Smith had appeared truly concerned at the hospital.

Despite this evident failure of a CIA scheme, however, Smith now had Maleeva's total attention.

There was the matter of the American's surprise early departure from the hotel this morning. Preoccupied with the shocking news about Altunyan, Maleeva had been lucky that a hotel informer noticed the trip by Smith at all. But no one had followed the American, no one could guess where he had gone. Maleeva was forced to conclude that he had been gone on a contact . . . which deepened suspicion that the Americans were still scheming, with Smith the focus of their effort.

The American couple identified as Henry and Muriel Beamer had first come to Maleeva's serious attention earlier in the week when they were routinely stopped late at night by a security patrol and had a flimsy story about their destination. Since that time they had been watched closely. This morning had come confirmation that the Beamers had departed Yugoslavia through a checkpoint on the Austrian border and were now in Vienna. This proved that they were no longer involved in any plan to take Lechova out. Which further sharpened the focus on Smith.

Despite these conclusions, the fearful pressure resulting from the Chekist's murder some time last night had forced Maleeva to accommodate to political realities. He had to mount a major investigation, or face professional ruin. Three of the officers who had been maintaining surveillance on Smith had been recalled. The team watching the Lechova family had been reduced from four to two. The manpower thus freed up was being transferred immediately to the Altunyan investigation.

The information that Lechova was going to meet Smith once more in his hotel room for a final interview did nothing to change Maleeva's perceptions or plans. The electronic equipment would keep an eye on them. And in the meantime, Maleeva had other business of a more pressing nature. The murder of a Soviet Resident was just about as serious as one could get.

He went back into the police meeting discussing Altunyan's death and the investigation now getting into high gear.

New Belgrade
"Momma! Where is Danisa?"

Back from her morning warm-ups, Hannah Lechova had left her father at the sports center and returned home buoyant with expectation of seeing her sister safe and recovering. But when she breezed into their shared bedroom, she found the bed unrumpled, Danisa nowhere in view.

Now Hannah rushed into the kitchen where her mother was cleaning fruit for a salad. "Momma! I said: Danisa is not here!"

"I know," Geneta Lechova said, calm and stoic.

Hannah noticed her mother's pallor. "But what happened? Was she not released from the hospital? Oh, my God! Has there been a setback? This is horrible! Tell me! What has happened?"

Her mother left the berries and melons in the sink, carefully dried her hands on her pink apron, and came to the tiny dining table, where she sat down. "There's no need for alarm, Hannah. She has gone out."

"But she just got out of the hospital! She should be in bed."

"She needed to go for a final interview with Mr. Smith."

Hannah could scarcely believe her ears. "How could you let her go to be interviewed again in her condition? It is madness!"

"The doctor said she should go slowly, but could do as much as she felt able to do."

"Why the sudden rush to meet Brad Smith, then? And why did he not come here?"

"He is leaving Sunday. It was Danisa's idea to meet at once, to have the talk behind her. And she suggested the meeting place. She wanted privacy, no interruptions, so it could be done as quickly as possible."

"Where are they meeting?" Hannah demanded, aghast.

"At Mr. Smith's hotel."

Hannah's vivid imagination saw X-rated pictures. "In his hotel? *In his room,* Momma?"

"I believe so, yes."

"Oh! How could you let her do such a thing? Don't you know all men are alike? Momma! Where was your sanity? You would never have let *me* do such a thing!"

280

"Well, you have both become grown women. Isn't it time I—and your father, too—recognized that fact?"

Hannah started out of the dining area. "I will go there at once! She must have a chaperon. She is not well, and I do not trust that man!"

"Hannah!" her mother called very sharply.

Surprised at the tone of voice, Hannah stopped and looked back. Her mother was still at the table, her hands folded in front of her.

"No," Geneta Lechova said.

"But Momma—"

"No."

"I do not understand! I am going! You cannot stop me! When Poppa hears of this, he will—"

"Hannah," her mother said very firmly. "Sit down."

"But—!"

"Sit. Down."

"If you will not protect your own daughter, then I shall! At the least I will notify the militia, so they can be near."

"Hannah." Geneta Lechova's voice had quiet steel in it. "Come here, as I told you."

Baffled, Hannah came back and obeyed, facing her mother across the table where the family had had a thousand meals.

"Hannah, you will not interfere in this."

Hannah had never seen her mother like this. There was a control, a strength of purpose, that was new. Hannah detected the sadness too, a nearness to tears that the older woman simply would not allow at this time.

"What is it?" Hannah asked hoarsely. "What has happened?"

"I know of your patriotism, your loyalty to Yugoslavia. But I know also how much you love Danisa, and us. I could lie to you, Hannah, but I will not. I will trust your love for your family above all things."

Hannah waited, silent for once, holding her breath.

"Danisa is fleeing from this country," her mother

began somberly. "No, no, you may not interrupt. For once you are going to listen, Hannah."

Geneta Lechova stared at her hands, twisted on the tabletop. "It is Danisa's wish to leave Yugoslavia. She has asked the United States to help her, since the state chose to withdraw your passports and keep you in Belgrade. Brad Smith has some work with the United States. At this hour he is trying to get her out of the country."

"But that's—that's mad! That is treason to our nation! Oh! This is even worse than I had imagined! My poor sister, her head and heart turned by an imperialist—"

"Hannah. Danisa asked the Americans. They did not ask her. *Look* at what has been done to her! They knew she wished freedom in the West; that is why your passports were withdrawn . . . why you could not play at Paris, or at Wimbledon. She has been watched, Hannah. And your father has known nothing, because he would side with the state, keep both of you here forever. Milo may even have been in the conspiracy. Are you fully aware of Milo's unhealthy fascination with your sister, Hannah?"

It was too much too fast. Hannah reeled. But the part about Fjbk hit home. She thought, *Danisa can be safe from him now!* And then was shocked at herself.

She tried to think straight. "It is my duty to report this at once. They cannot yet be out of the country."

"If you report them," her mother said, "you will live with the knowledge the rest of your life."

"But it is my sacred duty, I tell you!"

"What of your duty to your sister?"

"She is wrong! Misguided!"

"And you know better than Danisa what is best for Danisa? Who does that kind of statement sound like, Hannah?"

Hannah saw. She hung her head. "Poppa."

"Yes, Poppa. Will you try to run lives the way he has always tried to run yours?"

"But I have my duty . . . to report deviationism," Hannah said miserably, wavering.

"If you betray Danisa, Hannah, never again imagine that I will consider you my daughter."

"Momma!"

"I love you more than you know. You will do the right thing because you are a good person, filled with love, and your family is more important to you than the state. I know this. I trust you. God bless you."

Geneta Lechova stood and went back to the sink.

Hannah stared at her back. Her emotions swirled in total confusion: shock, rage, disappointment, fear, even jealousy.

Yes: jealousy. She realized that one aspect of her feelings was about Danisa . . . with Brad Smith.

Danisa could love Brad Smith. Hannah had been almost in love with him herself. *And I must report them, have them arrested.*

But she would be happy in the West . . . I know some of her misery here . . . and she would never have to fear Milo again.

Or Poppa.

Dazed, Hannah left the dining area. She went back to the bedroom, and stared at the unrumpled bed, the pictures on the walls. She remembered all the times they had giggled in the night, and told each other outrageous lies and even more astounding shared truths.

Weeping without sound, she sat on her bed.

After a while she tried to get herself together. Where were they going? How in the world could they hope to get out? She prowled the room, trying to see what Danisa had taken. She had taken little, but some things could be identified by their absence: her rackets, the little doll from Sarajevo . . .

Hannah thought feverishly. Of course it had to be the airport.

But Danisa was so well known. She would be recognized in an instant merely by her trademark blue, and her pigtail. They were sure to catch her. The plan surely was doomed.

Unless Danisa went in disguise.

But even then she might be noticed.

Hannah imagined her sister in the airport, sick and frightened, trying to slip past sharp-eyed passport inspectors. Fear wrenched Hannah's gut.

Which was when her wonderful imagination made another leap. She realized that she was no longer thinking at all about supposed duty to the state, or about her own dilemma.

Danisa was in peril. Hannah knew nothing else.

And if she really wanted to leave, *why should she not leave?*

The pain welled up in Hannah's throat again. It was going to be so hard . . . so lonely.

But if it was what Danisa wanted . . .

Hannah thought, *She has the right.*

Then she thought, *Is there any way I can help my sister?*

With the Altunyan murder investigation meeting concluded, Major Maleeva left the militia headquarters and drove directly to the Metropol Hotel. He went straight to the floor of Brad Smith's room, and into the room next door.

Lieutenant Rodor was there, along with a lone technician operating the banks of equipment which monitored every sound in the adjacent room.

"Anything . . . ?" Maleeva asked.

Lieutenant Rodor removed his set of headphones and put them on the table. "They are conducting the interview."

"You are dismissed. Meet Lieutenant Fyodor at headquarters."

Lieutenant Rodor silently left the room. Maleeva watched the reels on a tape recorder turn lazily, diodes blinking in time with the voices being picked up by microphones hidden next door. He crossed the room and put on the other set of headphones. The voices from the next room were sharp and distinct, and unmistakable: Smith's baritone, Danisa Lechova's soft alto:

"Danisa, do you consider your win in the New South Wales your best performance to date?"

"Grass is not my best surface, and I was pleased to do so well there. I only wish I had gone to Wimbledon to try on grass again."

"You consider clay your best surface."

"I think so at this time, yes. But I am working hard on pavement, and I think that will speed my game on all kinds of courts."

There was a slight flaw in the equipment, a high and mildly irritating hiss in the headphones. Maleeva removed them, satisfied that everything was being recorded accurately.

He crossed the room and sat down at a telephone table to call his office and confirm his plan to stay here until the interview was over. Then, he had decided, he would ask Danisa to answer some questions on a voluntary basis. He would mask his probing of the Smith mission with questions about the attempt last night to make her ill.

In her weakened condition, Maleeva thought, she might give something away. And then he could arrest her. He disliked the prospect, but duty was duty.

Maleeva lit a cigarette and sat back to wait until the interview was over.

twenty-eight

The car I had rented earlier in the week, blindly following instructions, paid off after all.

Danisa, wearing shapeless coveralls, a shawl that hid her hair, and big sunglasses, got out of a taxi to meet me at the rental agency. She had her racket bag and a cosmetic case hidden in paper shopping bags. She looked pale and shaky.

"You okay?" I asked as we waited for the car to be brought around.

"A little hazy, but yes, fine," she said. She didn't look at all fine, but she was dead game. We were going to need that.

The car came. Except for the garage driver who brought it, and the sour woman behind the wicket, no one was around. Neither employee gave us a second look. I tossed Danisa's things in the back seat with my borrowed satchel, closed the door behind her, got behind the wheel, and drove off immediately.

"How much time do we have?" she asked nervously, looking at everyone on the street like they might be UDBA.

"Plenty." I turned left.

"You're going in the wrong direction!" Her sharp tone betrayed how tight she was. Her pallor was shocking.

"No. We have time, and I want to try to make sure no

one is routinely following us." I turned right, went a block, and turned left again. Then once more to the right, and across a wide boulevard just as the traffic signal was changing.

I did the cops-and-robbers thing through four more turns. There was no sign of a familiar car in the rearview mirror. Finally I headed for the highway.

"You understand how we're doing this," I said.

"Yes. You brought the other clothes?"

I pointed to the bag in the back.

"Where is your computer?" she asked with alarm. "Your camera and other clothing?"

"All that stuff says 'reporter,' and some of it even has my initials monogrammed on it. They can have it." I looked down at my Yugoslav slacks and shirt, and the new pair of crummy shoes I had bought only this morning on the way to the rental agency. "After all, I've got this wonderful, unbugged stuff to take with me."

"I hate to see you leave everything else behind!"

"No problem. There was an attaché case with some stuff in it, but I ditched that in the river. Ted is going to bring my credit cards and personal stuff out with him, and I've got everything else I want or need right here in this car with me."

It was almost an unconscious remark; I was referring—mostly—to our borrowed IDs and papers, a wad of money loose in my pants pocket, and my real passport stuffed in the bottom of my uncomfortable shoe. But her little intake of breath told me that she took it as meaning *her*.

I glanced at her. She had momentarily removed her sunglasses, and the look in her eyes was so open and so vulnerable that I almost forgot to turn back to watch where I was going. My heart began pounding faster.

"It's true," I said.

She didn't say anything.

I kept my eyes on the traffic. "But you needn't worry. I don't expect any kind of payback, Danisa."

"Oh, Brad." She sighed. "Sometimes you can be a little stuffy, you know."

I risked a startled glance her way and saw she was smiling at me. "What?"

"Stuffy," she said. "Prim. Don't you know how much I like you?"

"You don't know me!"

"Stuffy," she repeated. "Sometimes you remind me just a bit of Poppa."

"I'm old enough to be your poppa!"

"You didn't kiss me like Poppa. You didn't hold me like Poppa. You don't look at me like a poppa."

"Stop!"

She giggled nervously, managing to sound delighted and scared at the same time. I realized that fear and excitement had made her hyper.

"It'll be okay," I told her.

Her mood changed instantly. "I'm scared. I'm sad, too."

"We'll make it, babe."

"Will we?"

"Yes." I reached across the seat with my free hand to grasp hers. She squeezed my hand hard with fingers that were icy from nervousness. Then I had to free myself to shift as we entered the highway leading to the airport.

"I guess I'd better get ready," she said.

"Right."

She crawled into the back seat and rummaged around, changing clothes. I checked my watch and mentally recalculated our plans for the next hour. Talking over my shoulder, I repeated everything. Danisa said she understood. When she crawled back over into the front seat in her bright California clothes and began brushing out her hair, she looked like a different person.

When we reached the airport, we still had more than thirty minutes to kill. I parked in short-term parking and we got out under a hazy sky threatening drizzle. It was very hot and humid and I started to sweat more heavily as we unloaded our few things out of the car: my mostly empty satchel and racket bag, Danisa's rackets and cosmetic case. She put on the wide-brimmed straw sunhat, pulling it over her right eye at a rakish angle, and I put on Ted's cap. We both wore sunglasses. When we checked each other over, it was quite amazing. The girl who stood there with me, apprehensive eyes hidden, in those lime-colored slacks and a pink sleeveless shell with white loafers and the dramatic hat, didn't look at all like Danisa Lechova.

Whether she looked enough like who she was supposed to be—that would be learned in less than forty-five minutes.

"Well, Ted?" she asked tautly.

"Perfect, Karyn," I told her.

We walked into the airport to find it crowded, with militia everywhere as usual. I noticed a few people glancing our way, and decided we looked our parts: tennis celebrities headed home.

We walked to the departure area and checked schedules. Flight 608 for Frankfurt, with an intermediate stop in Munich, was still listed as on time, departing at 1 P.M.

"Do we go now to the gate area?" Danisa asked softly.

I looked over some of the militia standing about, knowing there were any number of UDBA plainclothesmen also in the crowd. "We'll get a snack," I replied.

"I couldn't eat anything!"

"I know that, Danisa. But we don't want to get to the customs area any sooner than we absolutely have to. The later we are, the faster they may look at these passports and shoo us through. But we shouldn't just stand here, inviting attention, for the next fifteen minutes."

"I can have tea," she said.

We went looking for a place. I noticed that she walked slowly, and not in a perfectly straight line. She was badly tired already, and all the hard part was still ahead of us.

Once we were in the tearoom, however, and sitting down, she seemed to perk up a little. She even reverted to a totally unfamiliar coquette role, touching her toe against my leg under the table.

"You're wonderful," she told me.

"Tell me again after we're out of here."

"I will."

We drank our tea. Strangers swirled around us. The PA system announced flights in different languages. I was tight as a tick. We were so close now, so far. The gamble that had looked good an hour ago now seemed wildly improbable and doomed to failure.

I told myself the tension came in part from my wanting so badly to help her get out. If we failed now, it could be years before she got another chance. In that time, Dominic Partek could be dead, all her best reasons for escape destroyed.

Four uniformed militia came in and sat at a nearby table. They were young, and approvingly eyed Danisa's long legs, their outlines revealed by the showy slacks.

Their attention made her tighten visibly. I took her hand again and squeezed it. *What the hell am I doing, making her take this risk?* I asked myself.

After a while I checked my watch. "It's time."

She heaved a deep breath. "I'm ready."

We left the tearoom and started toward the distant international gate area—and the people who would examine our passports. Danisa seemed physically rested a little, and stronger. But her mood changed again.

"Will I ever come back?" she asked softly.

"Hell yes, you will. Of course you will."

"I love them."

"I know."

"I'm really scared, Brad."

"It's going to be all right."

"Thank you for saying that. I need you to tell me that a lot."

"It's going to be just fine."

We neared the gate area for our flight. There was a hellacious line backed out of Passport Inspection. I could see, up at the front, that they had three clerks checking passports and visas, and four or five militia standing nearby, eyeballing every passenger.

I did not like the look of it. The militia's added eyes were a complication I hadn't anticipated. And the length of the line made it impossible to estimate just when we should approach in order to rush through at the last possible moment.

I slowed a bit.

"Are we too early?" Danisa asked, alarmed.

Suddenly I got a little tired of feeling like a mouse. "Shit, no. Let's go."

We went through the metal detectors in fine shape, then filed in at the end of the line of passengers waiting to have their exit papers stamped. There was a pair of militiamen at this end of the line, too. One of them had a small plastic folder in his hands, and although he was not looking at it at the moment, I could see it contained several small photographs glued to a card. I got a good look at the pictures as we moved by, and my guts went icy.

One of the pictures leaped out at me because it was Danisa.

Couldn't be anyone else.

So they were pictures of people the cops were supposed to be especially watchful for. *Dangerous. Do not allow to leave Yugoslavia.* My pulse speeded.

One of the militiamen looked us over with idle curiosity. The sleek, sweet lines of Danisa's legs, in Karyn Wechsting's sexy pants, drew a second look. He studied Danisa's face behind the sunglasses, and I tightened, not sure what the hell I was going to do when he pulled us out of the line.

He did no such thing. Like the boys in the tearoom, he was young; he simply liked what he saw. His eyes moved hungrily over Danisa's breasts, subtly outlined under the pale shell, and then he caught himself and looked away.

I glanced at Danisa. She had missed the byplay entirely. My brief inspection of her was reassuring to me. Without her trademark blue, without her braid, wearing uncharacteristic clothes, she *wasn't* Danisa Lechova. Not to a casual glance.

Now if the passport checkers would just please be casual . . .

We did not speak to each other as the line edged forward. It went slowly. We still had about a dozen people between us and the checkpoints, with only a few latecomers in line behind us. The clock said departure time was only twenty minutes away. The airline people at the boarding-pass counter were looking harried and irritated, and I saw an elderly official repeatedly checking his watch.

Clearly the passport checkers were holding things up, and clearly they were aware of it. I saw the woman at the head of our branch of the line glare and very carefully . . . so very carefully . . . look at the next passenger's passport and face, comparing several times. No damned airline would hurry *her*, she was saying.

She was being careful. Too careful.

At that moment I became aware of some kind of commotion in the wide corridor just beyond our departure lounge. People were turning to stare. Two of the militia at the head of our line detached themselves and hurried out to join whatever was going on.

My first thought was dismay and the certainty that somebody was coming after us. But whatever was happening out there was *staying* out there. With Danisa craning her neck beside me, I located the commotion.

Beyond the gate area glass in the broad concourse, several uniformed militia. Some travelers who had slowed to watch.

A young woman surrounded by the uniforms.

Shock traveled through me:

Danisa.

Danisa, in every way except that the woman out there *couldn't* be Danisa, because Danisa was still close beside me.

But the woman out there was wearing Danisa's exact shade of blue. She had the pigtail down her back. She even had a tennis racket under her arm, just to make sure you noticed. She was gesturing—arguing heatedly with a militia lieutenant and his men who had her practically surrounded. I saw that at least two of them had photos in their hands.

As our line moved up a clump, and we were almost next, I tried to figure out what was going on. The woman out there had plainly been mistaken for Danisa. She was drawing the attention of everybody within a hundred yards. Even the checkers ahead of us looked a little distracted.

Then Danisa stiffened convulsively beside me.

"What?" I demanded softly.

She turned to me. Her face was slack with shock. "Hannah!"

Christ, it *was* Hannah.

Couldn't be anyone else.

In her blue dress and the pigtail—the trademarks Danisa had adopted for individuality—she could have fooled anyone who didn't know both women. She was surrounded by the security guards, arguing with them. She gestured angrily and started to walk away from them. One moved, blocking her way. She tried to push indignantly past him. Another officer moved to restrain her on the other side.

Danisa took a half step out of line. I caught her arm, twisting it.

She winced and tried to pull free. "I have to help her!" she whispered.

"No! Don't you get it? She's doing this on purpose to help you!"

"But she's in trouble!"

"We don't have time to argue. Look."

Danisa looked. The people in line ahead of us were moving through, and the airline people gestured at us to move faster to have our passports checked.

A couple of the people in line behind us moved past us with irritated glances.

"Come *on*, Danisa," I hissed. "And don't forget your ankle."

"But Hannah—!"

"Now!"

She hesitated, agonizing. Out beyond the departure-gate glass, Hannah argued more heatedly, waving her arms and drawing even more attention. Everyone—out there and in here—was watching.

"Now!" I repeated.

Danisa gave a last, despairing glance, then moved forward. She remembered to limp.

Heart in my throat, I stayed close to her. She was really pale now, and shaking visibly. I didn't know how much strength she had left.

The woman at the counter tore her eyes away from the confusion outside the gate area long enough to take Danisa's passport and glance at the picture inside, then at Danisa.

She said with a smile, "We were sorry to hear of your injury, Miss Wechsting."

"Thank you," Danisa murmured.

"We hope you will visit us again." The rubber exit stamp came down on the visa page of the passport. She took my passport. "Mr. Treacher. I hope you enjoyed your visit to our country."

"Very much," I told her.

The rubber stamp came down again. The woman was already looking past the last passengers in line, trying to make out what was happening with Hannah.

We went to the ticket counter. They checked our boarding passes.

"The flight is boarding, sir. Please move ahead into the jetway."

We went down the ersatz tunnel and into the plane. It was packed. I managed to cram our gear into an overhead and we slid into our seats. Danisa leaned against me, shaking.

"Hang on," I soothed. I found her hand and held it.

The last handful of passengers came on board. The flight crew seemed intent, for once, on getting a plane out on time. The door closed at once and the lights flickered for an instant as engines were started. I sat tight, holding Danisa's hand, while the cabin attendants went through the safety rules.

Come on, come on!

The plane backed out, taxied, held short of the runway. It seemed like forever. A TWA 747 landed. We taxied into position. The pilot ran up the engines. We rolled.

Moments later we were airborne. I breathed.

twenty-nine

Elsewhere

Belgrade

Major Ladislav Maleeva was still in the electronic surveillance room at the hotel, watching recorder lights flicker to the rhythm of the Smith-Lechova interview in progress next door, when his beeper sounded. He returned the telephone call at once.

"Major Maleeva," Lieutenant Rodor said, sounding excited, "I knew you would want to be notified at once. Danisa Lechova has been apprehended at the airport. She is being held there by Security."

Maleeva couldn't believe his ears. "Lechova? It cannot be Lechova!"

"Sir, the officers have made positive identification. They recognized her at once, and the Lechova woman attempted to escape, which is why they are holding her pending your instructions."

Maleeva grabbed the extra headphones. He heard the ongoing murmur of voices next door. The lights on the equipment still flickered, showing recording in progress. He did not understand—!

And then he did.

"Hold," he snapped into the telephone.

Leaving the recording room, he rushed to the elevators and into the lobby. The startled desk clerk produced a duplicate key to Smith's room at once. Maleeva was breathing hard by the time he got back to the floor and ran to Smith's door.

He threw it open and went in to find what he had realized, only moments before, he must find.

On the coffee table in the middle of the room sat a cassette recorder, its pale green dial light showing *on*. From its speaker came the recorded voices of Smith and Lechova —and the telltale tape hiss Maleeva's mind had not identified through the wall.

With an angry motion he cut the machine off, swooped it under his arm, and ran back next door, where his technician was on his feet in confusion.

Maleeva grabbed the telephone. "Tell them to hold her. I am on the way there immediately."

Hudson River Valley, New York
Dominic Partek drove north toward Chappaqua.

He had begun the drive in despair. But now the beautiful valley had begun to restore him. He told himself that the news would be good in his meeting with the Americans. He was going to see his sister and both of them were going to have a new life.

Partek wondered if Danisa would want to share some of her new life with him. Then he realized with a pang of sadness that at best his meetings with her might always have to be clandestine. The KGB would not molest her; she had done nothing, and had been valuable to them only as a bargaining chip. But their desire for revenge on Partek, and their need to make an example of him, would be virtually never-ending. The rest of his life, he would live under an assumed name and in virtual hiding. And every precaution would have to be taken to prevent the KGB's following Danisa as a way of locating him.

Well, so be it. If the Americans had good news this

evening, it could be that Partek would see her soon. It would be joyous. And there would be other meetings, even if in secret.

As to his own future, Partek thought, he would never again be able to tap the checking account he had gotten into yesterday. But the cash he had hidden against the eventuality of defection, while not an enormous amount, might be enough to buy a small piece of property in the mountains somewhere, perhaps the part of western Colorado he had read about not long ago in *National Geographic*. He didn't need much to live. He had a dream about a small cabin, an A-frame, on perhaps an acre. If it was near a small town, he could find work as an auto mechanic or small appliance repairman. If a larger city was nearby, his knowledge of computers might bring in spending money. And conceivably he might write a book . . .

Driving up the Hudson River Valley, Partek removed his small recorder from his luggage and dictated an hour's notes. He would play the recording for the FBI when he was in a safe house somewhere. It would save time.

He concisely laid out most of the major operations he had taken part in, including names, dates, and places.

When he drove into the picturesque outskirts of Chappaqua, he slipped the recorder back into his bag and concentrated on his driving. He found the inn with no difficulty, and drove twice around its environs, the old habit of caution prompting search for suspicious persons and reconnaissance of quick escape routes. Then, satisfied, he pulled into the tree-shaded parking lot beside the old inn and went directly inside.

His reservation under the name of Archibald was in good order. He took the room key and climbed the staircase to the second floor, where he found his room at the back.

Before inspecting the room, he looked up and down the narrow, carpeted hallway. He saw that a back door had been cut in the building to provide a fire escape. Cracking the door a few inches, he examined the steel stairs leading down to the backyard. The security lock on the door was a good one, and the door closed again with a satisfying *chunk.*

His room was high-ceilinged, airy, with chintz curtains at the window, a big canopy bed, an old-fashioned maple dresser and mirror, a small, immaculate adjacent bath. Gentle summer breeze stirred the curtains, and beyond the window a cardinal made a song in the willow.

Partek went into the bathroom, used the toilet, and sponged off his face and arms with a cool, wet hand towel. He went back to the locked corridor door, heading for the parking lot so he could bring in his bag.

Humming softly, he swung the door open.

Somebody was standing there. Partek recognized him, and fear gusted. *Sylvester.*

In panic, Partek tried to slam the door.

He was much too late.

The man in the hallway had a small, cylindrical object in his hand, and before the door could be closed, the cylinder made a spiteful little puffing sound. A stinging cloud of gas shot into Partek's face and he felt a very strong, very sharp, very astonishing pain.

Belgrade

All morning, Miloslav Fjbk had expected the militia to arrest him.

He had not slept at all, but the dreaded pounding on the door of his apartment had not come. When he had gone to the arena for the early light workout with Hannah, he had been sure he would be arrested. But again no one had shown up.

Now he was home again, and he knew they must have found the body by now. But he was still unmolested.

With each passing hour, Fjbk had begun to feel a hope that he dared not harbor.

But now he began to see that hope might be realistic: he might get away with what he had done.

Nervously he reviewed for the hundredth time everything that had happened. No one had seen him waiting in the hospital lot. No one had seen him with Altunyan. He had been miles away, surely, before Altunyan's body could possibly be found. There was nothing he could think of to link him with the KGB Resident, except his own very old KGB connections. And he had been inactive for many years.

Unless he cracked, or gave away his nervousness, Fjbk simply was not likely to be suspected in any way. And with so many foreigners in Belgrade, the police and UDBA had many other problems to split the focus of their attention.

Fjbk would forever remember the ghastly sound of Altunyan's neck snapping in his hands. He would remember the sudden feel, too. It was the stuff of nightmares, and he knew he would have them forever.

But Fjbk had killed before, in the war. And he could not regret that Altunyan was dead. The Russian had been a pig. He had hurt Danisa.

Now Danisa was safe. And Fjbk could allow himself to dream. One day, he thought, he might even tell her how he had avenged her sickness on the pig who had caused it. Danisa would be so grateful, he thought . . . and proud of him. Her smile would come and she would put her arms around his neck . . .

It was too early to relax entirely, Fjbk reminded himself. But he had begun to feel much better. He decided to shower, touch up his beard, and visit the Lechova home at once. He was eager to see Danisa and learn how she was this morning.

And after visiting the Lechovas, perhaps Terinka would be home, and receptive.

Oh, yes: Fjbk was beginning to feel fine again.

He hummed an old Serbian folk tune in his shower.

Forty-five minutes after leaving the hotel, Major Maleeva parked illegally at the main entrance to the air terminal and hurried inside, going directly to the airport security office. Several militiamen lounging outside the glazed glass doors snapped to attention, recognizing him as he bolted past them and went inside.

A uniformed sergeant and a plainclothes security guard stood in the reception room.

"Where is she?" Maleeva demanded harshly.

"Here, sir," the sergeant said, springing to open a door into the adjacent room.

Maleeva went inside. Three more officers were in the office, and she was sitting on a couch against a side wall. Her large, frightened eyes swept up to meet his, and Maleeva experienced a shock greater than any he had had previously on this blighted day.

"*You?*" He appeared stunned.

"Major Maleeva!" Hannah Lechova cried, jumping to her feet. "Thank God! Someone who can straighten out this thing! Tell them who I am, please! Why have I been held? What is going on?"

"You cretins," Maleeva snarled. "This is not Danisa Lechova. This is her sister, Hannah!" He grabbed Hannah's arm, twisting it painfully. "Where is your sister?"

"At home! You're hurting me! Please! Why are you treating me like this? I only came to the airport to see off my friends Karyn Wechsting and Ted Treacher, and these swine accosted me—I tried to argue with them—"

"Major," one of the officers said hoarsely, "she said nothing to indicate she was not Danisa Lechova! Her clothing—the way of her hair—all match the description—"

"You mean you thought I was Danisa?" Hannah cried in a very good semblance of surprise. "But all you had to do was *ask* my name! Oh, you fools, you swine—!"

"Take her to headquarters," Maleeva snapped. "There will be an investigation."

"But I have done nothing! I am a loyal—"

"We will sort this out later, Hannah. Right now I have other things to do."

Maleeva rushed to the telephone in the adjacent office

and called in to order an immediate visit to the Lechova apartment. Danisa Lechova was missing, and had to be located at once. Then, fuming, he hurried back to his car and drove back into the city at maniac speed.

He was almost there when he got back-to-back calls on his radio.

Danisa Lechova was nowhere to be found.

And two American visitors, tennis players staying at the Metropol, had reported burglary of their rooms and theft of travel documents.

Maleeva nearly ran a bread truck and a Fiat taxi off the road as he cut to the exit and increased his speed, changing course from the Lechova apartment to the hotel.

When he reached the hotel, Maleeva hurried to the manager's office. He found Karyn Wechsting and Ted Treacher apparently in a state of high excitement and outrage.

"Someone broke into our rooms," Treacher told him. "Our passports have been stolen, and some of our other papers!"

"When did you discover this?" Maleeva demanded. He was beginning to see the pattern, and feel sick.

"Just a while ago!" Karyn Wechsting told him. "We were getting ready to go to the airport, and now we've looked so long, we've missed our flight!"

"What are you going to do?" Treacher demanded.

"What flight?" Maleeva asked.

"Our money was taken, too, and—"

"What flight?" Maleeva's voice thundered.

"The one leaving for Frankfurt—the—"

Maleeva rushed to the telephone. He went straight through to state security headquarters, his commander. In stunned tones, his commander asked two key questions, then said he would ring right back.

Maleeva turned to the two Americans. "It is possible," he said with acid sarcasm, "that a Yugoslav national and a renegade of the American CIA have used your credentials to flee our country. But you would not know anything about that, would you?"

"I don't know, old man," Treacher said, "and I don't care. I demand to see someone from the United States Embassy."

"And," Karyn Wechsting said, "I demand to know what you intend to do about this abominable theft. What kind of security do you have in this country?"

Maleeva lit a cigarette. His hands were unsteady. *Govno.* It had all been going so well, and suddenly it was all turned to *govno.* And his career, too.

The telephone rang. He picked it up. His commander started talking excitedly. Maleeva listened to the sound of his future going down the sewer.

The flight could not be called back. It had already landed in Munich, and disgorged some of its passengers.

Chappaqua, New York

Very late, Kinkaid and his associate from the FBI parked in the inn lot and went inside. The other security people were on station and all seemed well. It was a beautiful warm night.

Kinkaid led the way to the head of the stairs, then down the hallway to "Mr. Archibald's" room.

When the door swung open at his knock, he started to feel sick.

He groped for a light switch, started in, and looked down. He stopped so abruptly that the FBI agent bumped into him from behind.

"Oh, hell," Kinkaid said. "Oh, damn."

The FBI man pushed past him to stare. Then, after bending over to make the briefest and really unnecessary examination, he pulled his walkie-talkie out from under his jacket and started talking into it very quietly, with no tone in his voice whatsoever.

Kinkaid went to the window and looked out. When the others started arriving, he just stayed at the window, staring into the dark, as if something out there were very interesting. But there was nothing out there at all.

thirty

It was a beautiful Sunday morning in Westchester County, and in Belgrade, half a world away, they were probably staging the ceremonies that closed Yugoslavia's first big venture into international tennis. Pam Shriver had shocked everyone to win the women's title, beating Martina in three sets. Martina had beaten Hannah in straight sets in the semis. Lendl was the men's champion.

But none of that seemed to matter much.

"Are you okay?" I asked Danisa as I pulled into the parking lot of the colonial-style brick building where her brother's body was being held.

"Yes," she said tonelessly. "Okay." She was wearing a pale tan sundress and heels she had bought, without much sense of pleasure, at Bloomies the previous day. She had gotten most of her color back and was regaining strength after the poisoning in Belgrade. But the death of Dominic Partek had hit her very hard.

"I must see him," she told me for the fifth or sixth time.

I parked beside a nondescript Plymouth that had to belong to some government agency. Collie Davis, who had shown up at Kennedy and stayed with us ever since, popped his rear door and got out of the back seat to open Danisa's side for her. I walked around to join them and the three of us went inside.

Except for a security policeman at a desk, the tile-floored front lobby was vastly empty. We crossed it, after getting directions, and went through double glass doors to another part of the building. At the end of this hallway we found another office, and in it were a couple more guys from Langley named Kinkaid and Dwight, and a slab-faced, yuppie-style FBI agent who said his name was Darby. I introduced Danisa, and they all seemed genuinely sorry about what had happened.

Kinkaid told her, "If there had been any way to prevent what happened, Miss Lechova, we would have done it."

Danisa studied him with solemn dignity. "But it was all for nothing."

"No," Dwight said. "Not for nothing."

"He's *dead.*"

"Miss Lechova, maybe it's small consolation. But he wanted to come over to our side if you could be made safe. He wanted to *be* on our side. We found a tape among the things in his car. You mustn't mention this to anyone. It's very top secret. But that tape contained information that's extremely valuable to us. It's going to help the free world."

Danisa digested this. Her throat worked. "Where is he? I want to see him."

Dwight nodded with a frown. He turned to Darby. "Joe, if you could take Miss Lechova into the other office for a cup of coffee, we'll take just a couple of minutes with Brad, here, before the viewing."

Darby, slow-moving and gentle out of all proportion to his bulk, took Danisa's arm. She looked questioningly at me, then went with him.

The door into the next room closed behind them.

Collie Davis said, "The girl thinks a lot of you, buddy."

"I think a lot of her."

Dwight said, "You ought to know. That tape Partek left us is dynamite. The FBI will be rounding up a dozen people right now, today, and putting surveillance on ten or fifteen more. The sonsofbitches might have gotten him, but he got *them*, too."

"What's happened to her family back home? And to Karyn and Ted?"

"Karyn and Ted flew out of there a couple of hours ago. The Jugs couldn't make anything stick. I mean, Wechsting and Treacher were victims of a burglary, right?"

"How about Danisa's family?"

"It's too early to say. But Hannah played well in that tournament. She's got the world press watching her. The government can't afford to make an object lesson of her. With Danisa gone, the Yugoslav policy already seems to be to make Hannah the new national heroine. So we think she's safe, protected by her new role."

"They know she tricked them to help us get out."

"Yes." Dwight smiled ironically. "Are they going to prosecute her for that, and admit they were fooled by a girl?"

"Or," Kinkaid added, "even admit that they were trying to keep Danisa a prisoner?"

The answer to the latter was obvious. There had been no brouhaha about Danisa's departure. The Yugoslav government hadn't made a peep. As far as the world knew, she had routinely left Belgrade for a vacation. They were saving face by pretending nothing had happened.

"How about the rest of the family?" I asked.

"It's too early for us to know much. Her father is torn up, from what we hear."

"He would be. He invested a lot of his life's hopes in Danisa."

"It's sad," Collie Davis said. "But that's life."

"You're all heart, Collie."

"There's something else you have to know," Kinkaid said. "The Russians are raising hell, alleging we murdered Partek, et cetera, et cetera."

"Plus," Dwight told me, "they're sending some embassy goons up here this morning to try to claim his body."

"Fuck that," I said instantly.

Dwight shrugged. "We're on uncertain ground. He is a Russian national. They have a right."

"You can't let them murder him and then take the body! That's crazy!"

"We've got calls in. It's being checked out."

I lit a cigarette. "What other wonderful news do you have for me?"

"That's all." Dwight studied me. "You did a hell of a job, Brad. You disobeyed orders and got half the staff severely bent out of shape. But you did it."

Collie said, "They'll probably never want to use you again."

"I weep," I told him.

Nobody answered that.

"So can she see her brother's body now?" I asked.

Dwight signaled Kinkaid, who went out and came back with the FBI man and Danisa. She looked ashen.

"Are you ready, Miss Partek?"

"Yes." Almost inaudibly.

Kinkaid led us to another door. He held it for us and we went into a chill, barren room that might have had lab equipment and chemicals behind locked plywood doors. There was a gurney in the middle of the gleaming dark green tile floor, and the body on it was covered completely by a long white cloth drape.

"Death was caused by inhalation of a swift-acting chemical substance which caused heart failure," Kinkaid said. His voice echoed flatly around the room. "The specific chemical composition has not been fully determined." He paused and looked at Danisa, "There wasn't any pain," he added softly. "We know that. And it was quick—instant."

Danisa started across the room. I stayed close to her. Kinkaid moved ahead, studied Danisa's face for an instant, glanced at me, and then slowly—almost tenderly—drew the sheet down to reveal Dominic Partek's head and shoulders.

Partek lay peacefully under the bright lights, as if asleep. As is often the case with death, the first shock was of his pallor, a porcelain whiteness, almost a transparency to his skin. His dark hair seemed blue-black against his skin. His face was calm, thank God—no sign of the agony of sudden death. He looked younger than I would have imagined, very calm, ruggedly handsome.

Danisa began to cry silently. She moved out of my grasp and leaned over the gurney, intensely studying her dead brother's face. It was as if she wanted to memorize—take in and burn into her mind—every detail.

Tenderly she raised one hand to his face. She touched fingertips to his hair, his eyebrows, the side of his head. She was caressing him in death as she never had in life.

It was tomb-silent in the lab.

She moved nearer the body, bent over, and kissed his forehead and then his cold lips.

"I love you, my brother," she said. Then her grief broke through and she started to sob.

I let her get some of it out and then I couldn't stand it anymore. I put my arms around her. "Come on, Danisa," I said. "Come on, babe."

"I never saw him except this way, dead."

"I know. Come on, now."

"He was my brother. I loved him."

"I know, I know. Come on."

I led her away from the gurney. Kinkaid again covered the body. She stumbled slightly as we reached the doors and I went into the next room with her, somewhat supporting her weight.

We got her some fresh coffee. Nobody knew what to say because there wasn't anything. She sat on a straight chair. After a few minutes she began to get hold of herself, and that was when the Russians arrived.

There were five of them, probably because they always

look for a way to intimidate you, and thought numbers might do it: five bulky, wool-suited diplomat-types with briefcases and cloddy black shoes and Rolexes. The boss was perhaps sixty, steel-gray, with a face that belonged on a Soviet Mount Rushmore.

"I," he announced, "am Anatoli Gulgradnik, first officer for cultural affairs of the embassy of the Soviet Union, New York. We have come to claim the body of a Yugoslav national, an employee of our delegation at the United Nations, one Dominic Partek. Where is he, please?"

Danisa looked up at them, the tears fading into something else.

Dwight told them formally, "The question of custody of the body is being discussed at the highest levels. You will be informed of the decision of the United States government."

They bristled. Gulgradnik drew himself up to his full height, probably five inches over six feet. "The Union of Soviet Socialist Republics will not tolerate delay! We demand *now* that the body of Dominic Partek be turned over to our rightful jurisdiction! We have an ambulance. We are prepared to take him to New York City at once."

Dwight started to reply, but Danisa sprang to her feet. "No!"

Surprised, the Russian turned to her. So did everyone else.

"What right do you have to interfere?" Gulgradnik asked loftily. "You will be silent." He looked at Dwight. "Who is this—"

"I am Danisa Lechova!" Danisa shot back. "His *sister*."

Gulgradnik must have anticipated it. He was not flustered. "Partek had no living relatives. As a citizen of Yugoslavia and employee of the Soviet Union, he must be returned to us."

"Never!"

Gulgradnik towered over her. "You have no rights here. You are a criminal in your own country, and have no status in the United States. You are an illegal alien."

Danisa stood toe to toe with him, glaring up. "And you," she bit off, "are a son of a bitch."

The Russian turned angrily toward Dwight. "The government of the Soviet Union—"

"You'll never have him!" Danisa cut in. Her eyes were alight with combat. She looked wonderful. "I am his sister—his only living relative—and I will say where his body stays, where it is buried."

"You have no basis under law."

"I have the law of blood. And I say he will be buried here, in America!"

Gulgradnik's hairy ears turned the color of old beef. "You do not know what you are dealing with, here."

Danisa put her fists on her hips and glared up at the phalanx of them. "No. You are the one who does not know what he is dealing with."

The Russian's face kept darkening with frustrated anger. He swung around to Dwight. "Are you going to allow this kind of affront to the delegation of the Union of Soviet—"

"I think so, yes," Dwight cut in.

The Russian turned back to Danisa. He stabbed the air with his index finger. "You will regret this. We will seek legal orders. We have the right." He looked back at Dwight, who was now grinning fiendishly. "Your job will be had! This woman has—what do you call it?—no leg to stand on!"

"I doubt it, sir." Dwight was grinning now. "There was a legal question. However, Miss Lechova is the next of kin. I have already been informed that the question of custody would be difficult only if next-of-kin did not step forward with a request. As I understand it, Miss Lechova, you are making such a request for custody?"

"Yes," Danisa shot back.

"Then," Dwight told Gulgradnik, "I suspect Miss Lechova has every leg to stand on, and you don't have doodley."

"Your government will hear of this!"

"Yes, sir. Thank you, sir. Was there anything else you gentlemen wished to discuss before you leave?"

The Russian turned back to Danisa. "Traitor!"

She glared up at him, her eyes shooting sparks. "Bastard!"

His eyes bulged and his lips worked. A dribble of saliva appeared on his liverish lips. With a muffled Russian oath, he turned to his entourage. "Come! We are getting nowhere here!"

They filed out. Danisa, hands defiantly on her hips, watched them go.

The door slammed behind them.

Danisa turned and looked at me like she didn't know if I would approve. I held out my arms and she fled into them.

"Oh, Brad, I was scared! But they made me so mad—!"

"You, lady," I told her, "are so wonderful."

She rolled her eyes. "I have to go to the bathroom!"

Still smiling, Kinkaid led her out. Darby went to a telephone to make a report. A building security man came in to see what was happening, and Dwight took him over into a corner for a confab.

Which left Collie and me.

I lit a cigarette and exhaled an explosion of smoke. "Collie," I said, "is she the world's greatest, or what?"

"You, sir, have a serious problem," he replied.

"Meaning what?"

He came across the room and put an arm over my shoulder. "I got you into this operation. I feel slightly responsible. So let me ask you. What are you going to do about this girl?"

"What do you mean, 'do about' her?"

"Brad, hell. I admit she's dynamite. Great-looking, courageous, loyal. She's *great*. And any idiot could watch her with you for five minutes and know she's crazy about you."

"Any idiot would know that?"

"Of course. But what are you going to do about her, Brad?"

"Do?"

"Do. Yes. About her. You can't just"—he gestured aimlessly—"take advantage of her."

"What do you think I should do, Collie?"

"Brad." He squeezed my shoulder big-brother-fashion, always a bad sign with someone like Collie. "She's far too young for you."

"Is she?"

"Hell yes! Brad. Take this from me as a friend. You're too old. She's infatuated with you right now, sure. But later that will wear off. Then where would you be? You've got a real problem here. She might be crazy about you now, but it won't last, and you'll end up getting dumped." He paused. "Everybody will end up getting hurt."

I was still chewing on the delightful morsel of information that she was obviously crazy about me. I had been afraid to believe the evidence until now. "So your advice is . . . ?"

"Cut your losses, man. Don't set yourself up for disappointment. No one is worth that risk. Be nice, be friendly. But you'll be finished with debriefing in a few days. End it right away before things get messy."

Through the glass doors I could see Danisa coming back in our direction. She looked shattered. She also looked young, beautiful, strong, full of fight and the rage to live.

She saw me watching her. Her whole demeanor changed by magic. Her smile came, filled with love.

"So?" Collie goaded, with another brotherly squeeze.

I breathed. "Well, Collie, you are undoubtedly right. But I'll tell you what. Right now she does love me. And I'm just going to go with that, as long as it lasts, and to hell with later on down the road."

"Brad, you'll be sorry."

Danisa came into the room, ponytail swishing.

"Collie," I said, "you've got to be insane."

313

* * *

When Danisa and I returned to the car an hour or so later, she sat in the front seat and wept again, softly, from fatigue and hurt and relief.

"He will be buried here," she told me again. "In America."

"Yes," I said. "He will."

"Here," she insisted. "In America."

"Yes, Danisa. And what about you, now that he's dead?"

She thought about it a minute or two, and it was very quiet in the car. Then her chin came up. "I will not go back. I will bury my brother here. I will stay in America. I will play tennis and make my new country proud of me."

My own eyes felt hot. "I'll help you all I can, if you want."

"Yes," she said softly.

"I have to go back to Texas in a few days. I've got a job there and all."

She watched me with those great, vulnerable, trusting eyes.

It was dragged out of me. "Would you think about going to Texas with me?"

"I will go anywhere in the world with you."

I took her face between my palms. "You know what you're saying, babe?"

Now even my idiot eyes could see her love. "Oh, yes," she said. "I know what I am saying. Now hold me, Brad. Please hold me."

I did.